A Siren's Call

A Siren's Call

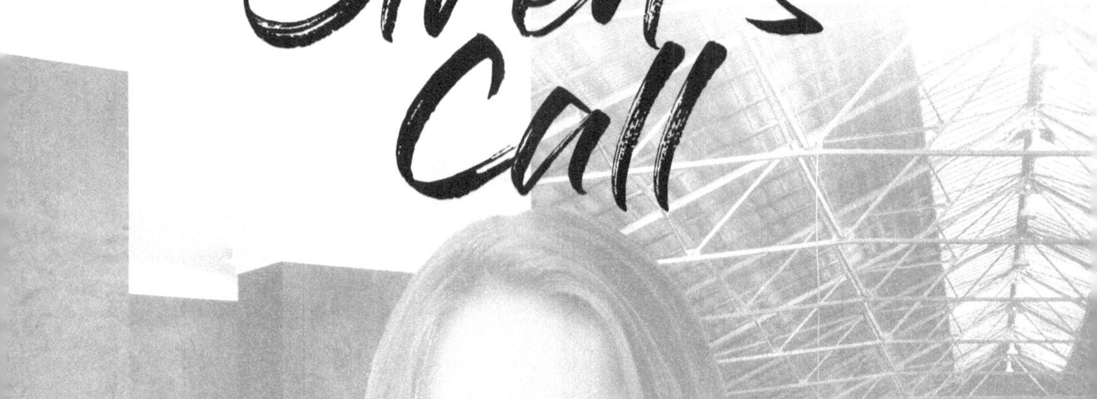

TIM B. WOLFE

ARPress
45 Dan Road Suite 5
Canton MA 02021

Hotline: 1(888) 821-0229
Fax: 1(508) 545-7580

Ordering Information:

Quantity sales. Special discounts are available on quantity purchases by corporations, associations, and others. For details, contact the publisher at the address above.

Printed in the United States of America.

ISBN-13:   Paperback   979-8-89356-856-1
                eBook   979-8-89356-857-8
                Hardback   979-8-89356-862-2

Library of Congress Control Number: 2024909005

TABLE OF CONTENTS

1-HENRY HUNTER

A city is where people gather. It is where each person strives to find their own special skill and businesses look for these individuals for their companies to thrive. The cities remain small or continue to grow outwards and upwards. Some people find good jobs while others scavenge the lower echelons of society looking for a meaning to their own self-worth.

The city of Mizu Huki was a huge city, with roaring towers hundreds of feet tall and covered in mirrored glass, showing the tops of other buildings, and made to give the owners and visitors a sense of superiority, a sense that they were figuratively and literally above the rest. Above all others, Hunterik Industries was far above the rest, with its one hundred and one floors of immense steel and glass, and the entirety of the building was for the one company and its CEO and Founder Henry Hunter.

German born, blue cobalt eyes saw everything that could be his and he made it so. He was a firm believer in survival of the fittest and his company had seen failed takeovers many times, until he became the one taking over, and he was good at it. Now, at 60 years of age, he was at the pinnacle of his height, and he'd be damned if one of his fledgling competitors tried to increase market share or try to cut into his profits.

He was a hard man; firm and vicious. His late wife however, was an angel by comparison. She was the only one who could calm him down and the companies that had worked with her charities had earned much more of his business than others who competed against him. He thought himself a wise and careful man, and with his wife's passing, he felt a need in this last year to find a way to give back to the world. It was not a way to forgive his sins; he cared not for that. This was to make his wife's memory immortal, so that no one could say anything but good things about her.

That was why the woman before him was here, in his office on the 96th floor of Hunterik Tower. He sat upright on his burgundy couch looking over the papers before him and smiled. His wife would be happy with these people he would be sponsoring. Of course, he could not have pulled this off if not again for the older woman before him.

"Does everything seem to be in order on your end, Mr. Hunter?" The woman asked and he looked at her. He loved his late wife, and doubted he'd be with another woman, but if he would, he'd ask the older woman before him. Blonde hair as if silk blew down her hair to her chest, of which was truly impressive itself, pushed together with a nice green blazer, and suit pants with six-inch heels to give her the height needed to match Mr. Hunter himself.

"They do indeed, Ms. Hana." He smiled and began to sign the papers. After his wife's death, he had been at a loss for what to do. After all, his company was at the top of the business world. He didn't need to do anything and not continue to make a profit. Every day was bland and gray; wake up in his Victorian house, take his private chopper to the Tower, endure numerous meetings of numbers that were always in the green, and head home…. alone.

But eight months ago, at a private auction, he'd been impressed by Ms. Hana, the way she held herself and conducted her business was admirable. She had sold artwork left and right while maintaining such a deep smile of pure bliss, and yet when he had asked her to lunch, that smile turned into determination to get his wallet.

Most women went for his wallet. She was no exception. She knew who he was from the start, after he stepped into her charity event that evening. She had spent three hours that day with him talking about the work that they were doing at Slug LLC. He had laughed with her at the name, but she had shown a sad smile, mentioning her late husband calling her a Slug Princess growing up, and he her Toad Sage. He had started a small information gathering company and she supported him in that endeavor. When he passed away, she sold the company and started her own, supporting multiple charities in their projects and getting funding for them as well.

Before Mr. Hunter had known it, he took her to dinner the next night and the following week inside his own home, where she smiled at his staff and his children who got along with her young daughter who was around their age. Henry looked up after the last signature and slid the papers over to his attorney who signed the check after him.

"Here you are, Ms. Hana." He leaned forward, his hand enveloping her own as he did so, and saw her blush. He still had a way with women, it seemed. She smiled down at the check and sent the smile back at him.

"I can't believe you would agree to this, Mr. Hunter. It is the greatest thing my company could have hoped for."

"Nonsense. With this, you can fund those sixteen charities who you represent for the future. Of course, this check is purely for your records and isn't more than a show of faith. I assure you that the money is being transferred as we speak." Mr. Hunter emphasized his strength; his word was good anywhere, and no one could take it without his say so.

"I... I can't express my gratitude enough." Mr. Hunter stood up then and sat down beside her, his hand staying on her thigh for comfort.

"When you admitted to me how that bad press pulled out so much money last month, I knew I had to do something. Your charities depend on donations from others, and my wife loved children and those at risk of losing their homes." He paused when she reached over and held his hand.

"I'm sorry for your loss. As one to another who shares your pain, may I say that this gesture will not go unrewarded."

"Thank you." He nodded his head and they both stood up, Ms. Hana grabbing the papers and folders and bringing them to her chest.

Mr. Hunter walked out of his office with her, and as he entered the reception area, he smiled at the woman who had helped him in more ways than one. Before him was a young 23-year-old woman with blonde hair the same shade as her mother, but with glasses over her eyes. Whereas her mother wore it up, the girl left her hair back in a soft ponytail. Whereas her mother's cobalt eyes were bright, her daughter's were dark as if a mysterious storm, but that storm was filled with intelligence and a need to prove oneself in life.

"Anita, I'm sorry if we kept you." Her mother moved forward, and Anita stood up, her red pencil skirt and white blouse still pristine and with no signs of wrinkles. Mr. Hunter was still impressed as he knew that she had been working the entire time that the meeting had taken place. Even now, an earpiece lay inside her left ear, waiting for another call. On her shoulder were two bags full of documents and in her arms were not one or two, but in fact three tablets, each with their own operating systems and purposes. Mr. Hunter had visited their office many times in the last few months, and while on a simple floor in one of many towers, he could attribute most of their success to this girl in particular.

Anita Mariam Hana, age 23, a very gifted student at a middle placed high school when she was younger. Attended a single year of college before she withdrew and began to work for her mother's company after her father's passing. Currently single, but two boyfriends in the past, one of which was rough with her, and had a restraining order currently.

All of this he had dug up through his resources, and if she were to know, Mr. Hunter was confident that she would stay alert and reply back without embarrassment, though inside she would be mortified that others knew her young secrets.

She was always on those devices, entering different equations and systems where her hands moved between laser keyboards and running different jobs at once. He knew that without her, her mother's business would be hampered immensely, but he still tried to poach her for himself a few times, to her smile and refusal. She was a strong woman in the making and was one of a few people outside his inner circle that he had grown to trust.

It was two months ago that his company was under attack from a mysterious hacker group, trying to steal their information when Anita was delivering papers to him from her mother. The confidence she had shown that day, calmly linking with their systems and cutting off the hacker's way in was masterful and had shown him the inert talent of one so self-taught.

"Did we come to an arrangement, Mother?" Anita asked in a rare form of worry.

"We did, my dear. Mr. Hunter granted us six hundred to support our charities. This will help them recover their losses and ensure our bright future." Mr. Hunter listened and saw Anita smile brightly at that.

"Mr. Hunter, thank you very much. I can't believe you helped us in our plight."

"I couldn't help myself, Anita." Mr. Hunter smiled. He hadn't first heard of the plight from Ms. Hana. No, she had too much pride for that. But Anita was young and more open. It had occurred when she was returning a list from her company to Mr. Hunter of possible charities he may support. He had seen her tears at the surface and had comforted the young girl.

Apparently, that boyfriend she had a restraining order on had powerful connections and had brought up false accusations on her mother's company. None of it was true and yet none of it needed to be. His research on it later that day proved the facts and he had seen his wife's smile in the one Anita gave him when he offered to help. The meeting today had accomplished both helping the company and more importantly, helping his wife's legacy be born.

"If that is all Mr. Hunter, we will take our leave." Ms. Hana mentioned and pressed the button for the elevator, but Mr. Hunter stepped forward.

"Ms. Hana, now that this matter is resolved, would you be so kind as to accompany me to dinner?" Mr. Hunter leaned in, smiling slightly.

"Why, Mr. Hunter." Ms. Hana blushed but smiled back at him. "I am sorry, but I must look over many files with my daughter.

"It is fine, Mother. I can do that on my own." Mr. Hunter smiled at the eagerness of the young beauty to help him in his romantic endeavors. "You may spend time with Mr. Hunter. He has done us a great service today, after all."

"Anita, you are such a darling! May I impose you with all those documents yourself?" Ms. Hana looked over at her daughter and Mr. Hunter sent an amused smirk between them. Her daughter again had three tablets to hold, one shoulder bag, and another bag over it. Surely, she'd drop them after no time if Ms. Hana added her own documents to her daughters.

Mr. Hunter couldn't impose on Anita any longer. "Ms. Hana, perhaps another time. I do not wish to impose all those papers on your poor daughter who has already amazed me with her intelligence and hardworking demeanor."

"Y-You honor me, Mr. Hunter." Anita bowed low to him, to almost her waist, and the top tablet leaned precariously over the edge of the others, only held there by the buttons of her blouse with some cleavage of her young chest to hold it in place. Still, the tablet tilted forward, clipping off her button and Anita rushed to push it back in place, before righting herself and smiling gratefully with a heavy blush.

"You honor my family, Mr. Hunter. I thank you. I'm sure my mother has some free time next week for more...social greetings." Anita offered.

"And I hope I have time with you, Anita." Mr. Hunter stepped forward and grabbed her free hand, kissing the knuckles fondly. "I wish to extend once again my offer to you. If you need any reference, please do not hesitate to call me, and whatever job will be yours."

The girl's blue eyes shined brightly as well as her blonde hair. "I will, sir. Thank you."

Both women bowed and stepped into the awaiting elevator and nodded their heads before the door closed. Mr. Hunter turned back but stopped to smile at the sound of utter joy emerging through the metal doors. He chuckled to himself as he moved back into his office. If her mother would allow it, her daughter could be a very successful person in this world. Ah! But she was grooming her for taking over the company of course.

Mr. Hunter's gaze looked down at his reception desk on the other side of the room where young Anita had sat and picked up the origami of the slug that was their company's logo. He smiled. 600 million dollars well spent to ensure his wife's legacy.

In the elevator that made its way downwards, two women stood there, chests out, backs straight, and shoulders set: rigid with proper etiquette and poise.

"...He really seemed like a nice guy to date, Mom."

"Now, dear, he is a wall street crook. His company steals billions and crushes dreams. Whatever makes you believe that I would want to date a man such as that?"

Anita was quiet for a second, the elevator the only sound as it dropped them lower. "He sounds a lot like Dad." She looked over and smiled darkly.

Ms. Hana looked back at her daughter and grinned. "Oh, stop it, you. Stay in character until we get to the car."

"Yes *Mom.*" Anita grinned toothily.

The pair walked out soon after, moving through the underground garage and paid the valet to bring the car around. As the sedan came up, each got in, with the mother driving. They smiled at the guard at the ramp and turned onto the main road, heading out of town.

"...We're clear, Mother." Anita called out as voices sounded in her ear.

"I must say that you were fabulous, my hard-working daughter." Ms. Hana praised her daughter as she pushed her fingers into her eyes, pulling out her contacts with a bright blue dye on the irises, showing instead a chocolate brown set of eyes.

"Yes, Mother. I believe I was pretty great." Anita smiled brightly out the window, ruffing out her ponytail before dragging it up and over her head, the entire blonde wig falling into her hands as long cascades of lighter strawberry blonde locks flowed down to below her shoulders.

"Tess......" The older woman sounded, turning to see the girl beside her taking out her own pair of contacts "…. We did it."

Tess smiled, her eyes opening to show the deep emerald that she was born with, and her eyes watered in both irritation and joy. "Damn, Mom. Then these eight months were worth it." Tess reached up and wiped at her eyes.

"You alright, dear?"

"Damn these long-lasting contacts." Tess sniffled and rubbed them. "They hurt my eyes."

"I'm sure they do." The older woman smiled.

"Amelia," Tess smiled back, "This is our biggest con yet."

Amelia pulled over the car to the side of the road, and Tess and she moved from the Sedan to an older car, old and clunky, while Tess grabbed their disguises and laid them in a trash bin, before opening a lighter and lit them up. Tess smiled and stepped back into the car, with Tess driving this time, where Amelia looked at her across from the console. "Tess...This was my last con. I'm done."

"...Sure, you want to retire, Mom?"

Amelia looked over at Tess and sighed through her mouth, her shoulders sagging in resignation. "I am sure, Tess." She spoke as she watched Tess start up the car and move along the backroads. "You know Tess, when I picked you up ten years ago, you were such a brat."

Tess smiled in agreement, nodding her head as she giggled. "I really was."

"But you've grown into a wonderful and beautiful con artist."

"I learned from the best after all."

"Perhaps, but you have a talent for so much, I've always wondered if it was really my teaching or just you."

They travelled for another twenty minutes before they reached their destination; a large warehouse that had seen better days. Tess smiled as she turned off the engine and prepared to get out.

"Tess," Amelia spoke up. "Please, a moment."

"What is it, Mother?" She asked, leaning back towards her, giving her undivided attention.

"Tess, this life is wonderful. It is fun and exciting, and the faces of those who realize what you've done to them makes you feel such a rush."

"I know, Mom. It's the best feeling, isn't it?" Tess smiled, and Amelia watched her eyes glimmer in the memory of past cons.

"Yes, but Tess...there is more to life than this."

"What?"

"Tess, you know my one regret in my youth. Not accepting that pervert's affection and marrying him. Having children of my own to raise. I'll always wonder if I could have raised children as smart as you and your sisters."

"Amelia," Tess smiled at her in confusion. "What are you trying to say?"

Amelia sighed. Her best child had interrupted her great speech. "What I mean is that you should find someone to spend your time with, Tess. Someone other than fellow thieves. Someone who knows the deepest parts of you that even they don't know about. I want you to make memories with someone you love more than money."

Tess half smiled with sarcasm dripping from her mouth. "Of course, I will, Mother." Tess grinned wider, "Just maybe after I train up my own crew and major score."

Amelia smiled sourly at that. Her prodigal child never took romance seriously. She had seduced many a man, finding their delight in her figure, but in the con, she was a queen. Outside of that, she didn't really mind being single. "The time of youth, Tess." Amelia warned. "Don't regret it." Tess nodded as Amelia hugged Tess tightly. "Six hundred million dollars, Tess. Six hundred. This is the biggest score in years, and you planned it all. Everything went perfectly."

Tess blushed as her mentor and adoptive mother praised her. "Stop that, mom. I could only pull this off with your help." Tess looked at her mother's saddened eyes and sighs. "Okay Mom…. I'll look around for boys, alright?"

Amelia ruffled her daughter's hair and smiled happily. "Come on. Let's give the rest of the crew the good news."

Meanwhile, outside the warehouse, a radio squawked into the air of the van. "Subjects on site. Permission to enter?"

"Negative. Stay and observe. Prep for entry."

Tess and Amelia entered together inside the warehouse; its bleak interior only lit by the sunlight shining through the grimy windows. Inside, in a small half-circle ten feet apart from each person with a large crate in the middle, three women stood apart, while behind and around them were six motorcycles, all fueled and ready to head out. Tess and Amelia entered the circle and stood before their own bikes. Five women, six bikes.

"Where is Raven?" Tess asked.

"He's finishing up." A black-haired woman smiled, playing with her hair idly. "I can't wait to take this dye out of my hair. My baby hasn't seen me in months."

"Now, now Hawk. This was our biggest score yet. I'm sure your husband will agree." Tess smiled.

"SO! I'm here." Raven called out as he entered through another door. Tess saw him and scowled, her knuckles tightening at his appearance. He was a no-good pretty boy, and though he was on this team, Tess hated his morals and his ideas. They clashed with her own and honestly, she wanted to beat him up and kick him out. At least this was the last job she would ever take with him. She would make her own crew and leave him behind. Raven passed her by and joined the circle before Amelia nodded to him and stepped forward near the center.

"So, let me first thank each of you individually, and with codenames!" Amelia smiled as two of them groaned at the old school tradition.

Amelia turned to a girl with frizzy hair jutting everywhere. "First of all, Desert, you did an amazing job finding our new offices, designing our outfits, building our surveillance system from scratch, and created each of our tangible aliases."

"Thank you, Slug." Desert replied with a smile.

"And Hawk," Amelia smiled. "Princess could not have gained Mr. Hunter's trust if not for you."

"Hear that, Princess? You so owe me." The black-haired girl smirked at Princess who grinned back.

"Don't think too much about it, Hawk." Princess called over as she whipped her blonde hair back, looking at her own nails as if she was as fashion oriented as Hawk. "You may have hacked into Hunterik Industries, but you still needed me on the inside to let you in, and make it look like I was shutting you down."

Hawk smiled back, her mocking sister smiling back as she looked at her stylish outfit that she currently wore. "True enough Princess, and after Mom convinced him to let her into his home, we were able to see his every interaction thanks to my skills. After all, it was I who was able to filter his entire library internet searches and show him Alex's trumped-up charges on our company."

"And this was all Princess's idea." A pale-eyed girl piped up, shyer than the rest.

"And of course, Rabbit did a great job in the various roles she played."

"Yeah, great job Rabbit."

"Thanks guys." Rabbit spoke, though it was a whisper. "This was my first mission, so I'm grateful for the chance to have done this with you all. And-"

"Enough of this! Amelia, get on with it."

"Don't talk like that to her, Raven!" Princess yelled over hotly.

"Oh, Tess. Perhaps you didn't like the picture of me holding you against a wall, my lips joined with your own spread all over the internet, but I sure did."

Tess began to move when she saw her mom shake her head. She breathed out through her nose and calmed down. Raven was lucky that her mentor was here, otherwise...

"Anyways, this is our biggest score ever, and as I've told you all, it is my last. I am proud of each one of you. The story of this score will be shared among our kind for decades to come."

"What about the money?" Raven spoke up, and the rest of the team scowled at the mention of it. Now was their time of glory and boasting, not counting the money.

"Always the money with you Alex." Amelia sighed, dropping the codename. "You still need to learn to focus."

"It was my plan." He grinned confidently.

"Your plan called for kidnapping Mr. Hunter and transferring the money." Tess scowled.

"And?"

"You wanted to kill him. We don't murder, Alex." Amelia reminded as the sole male of the group looked at her with a scowl. "Don't worry Alex. Even the planner gets an equal share. There are six of us here, so each of us gets 100 million. As I said, the score of a lifetime."

"You know," Alex stepped forward. "You make a sound argument, Amelia. Equal shares keep everyone accountable, but that's so last generation."

"Alex, back off or I'll-" Tess took an angry step forward before Alex slid his hand out of his jacket and a colt .45 appearing in view stopped Tess in her tracks.

"I think that's enough out of you."

"W-where'd you get that?"

"Hawk doesn't check everywhere." Alex smirked as Hawk growled behind him. "One sixth sounds reasonable, 100 million, but 600 million sounds even better. Now then, shall we?"

"Here, Alex." Tess gritted her teeth and reached into her skirt to pull out the check that Mr. Hunter had handed to Amelia, who had handed it to Tess in the car. Alex smiled as his hand graced along her bare arm, making Tess shiver at the touch.

"Thank you, Tess. However," Alex tsked as he brought his gloved hands together and ripped the check in two. "I am not an idiot. You have by now transferred the money to a private account on the way over. Amelia, if you would please step forward." He nudged with his gun as he brought out a device with a single opening down onto the crate. "If you would be so kind."

Amelia stepped forward past Tess and to the crate. Alex smiled at her as she reached between her breasts and pulled out a black card. There were no numbers or anything to identify it, but as she inserted it, the machine started to whir, and a slot slid out as Amelia punched in the numbers.

Alex watched her every move, and as she typed in the 17th digit, he clicked his tongue. "That's a long account number, Amelia."

"Has to be."

"Now then, let's have the password." Amelia bent back down, but Alex clicked his tongue. "Ah ah ah! Nice try. But you would never let it be that easy." Alex smiled darkly and turned to his right. "Tess?" The girl did not move.

Bang and a bullet inserted itself at her feet, and she did not move, but out of another door emerged three more men, all with guns in their hands. "You'll have to forgive me, girls!" Alex spoke louder. "I decided to hire some spare muscle. Just in case." He spoke as they aimed their guns at the other girls. "Now Tess?"

Tess bristled with rage as she stayed where she stood. "Come on, Tess. I haven't got all day." Tess heard him mock her and bit the inside of her cheek. holding in her rage. But seeing no way around the situation, she complied as she looked around the room.

There was no way out of this. Alex for his part smiled lewdly as Tess bent down to her knees and began to slide her black stocking down her left leg until she reached her lower thigh.

Tess pulled out her own card, a silver one with no distinguishable emblems and inserted it in the machine. As she inserted her numbers, Alex stepped forward and breathed into her ear. "You know, Tess, I hope we can be in the same bed again. Those legs of yours are very erotic." Tess leaned away from him and pressed the last number into the machine as it whirred even faster.

"Now then," Alex grinned. "All of you line up." All the girls stepped together and got on their knees while Alex watched his machine whir away until finally it clicked, a green light shining on the screen, illuminating Alex's face as he looked up at his former team.

"And that concludes our business. Have a nice life, ladies."

Alex turned towards his exit and Tess seized with rage. *How dare he?!? That coward!!! His plan would have failed if they'd done it his way, and now after all I've done for this heist, he's just going to run away?!? That- That-!!!'*

"Bastard!" Amelia's voice yelled out, startling Tess out of her mental blood rage. That's right. It didn't matter. The score didn't matter. The code had been broken. They'd get their revenge.

"Ah Amelia." Alex stopped in place, looking back to shake his head at her.

"Bastard!! You won't get away with this, Alex! We'll find you and you can't hide forever!"

"You know? You're right." Alex smiled darkly, and sound failed Tess as she watched Alex's finger pull the trigger. She didn't hear anything as Amelia's chest suddenly seized as red blood spurted out, staining the ground as she fell backwards to the concrete floor.

"Mom!!!" Tess yelled as lights erupted all around them and doors crashed to the ground in metal clangs.

"Police! We have a search warrant!!!"

"Mom!!!" Tess screeched as she jumped forward to her mother's body. The girls and Alex scattered all around her, but she stayed where she lay, her mother's eyes shaking as she looked lovingly at her daughter.

"T-Tess…."

"Don't worry, Mom. I'll get you help."

"T-Tess…. I'm sorry."

"Don't say that!"

"I… I wanted to take care of your children…"

"You can! I swear I'll have children! I swear I'll find a man I can have a life with! Just please don't die!" Tess cried into her chest, her hands twisting over the wound as blood flooded over her hands, caking under her nails, polished by her mother just this morning, as she vainly tried to stem the blood.

"Tess!" Hawk appeared at her side and tried to desperately pull her arm. Tess's grip tightened on Amelia as Hawk struggled to pull her away. "Tess! We have to go! Come on!"

"Then go!" Tess yelled through her tears as Hawk's arms disappeared.

"Tess?..."

"I'm-.... I'm here, Mom."

"...Live a nice life…"

Tess felt herself go weightless as her body was tackled by an officer and she found herself on the ground on her stomach with her arms pulled behind her back. The officers were a little rough on her, but she felt no pain. All she could see were the open eyes on her mother's face, the way her blonde hair had started turning white despite her mother denying how old she was getting. Her chocolate eyes were greying out and turning white. But Tess's throat closed out and she gagged for air when she saw the life leave her, a smile gracing her face as she looked aimlessly in her direction.

II-HER NAME IS TESS

our old coffee and stale bagels are the usual smell that he walks past every day where he works. His department was just what people thought of when they thought of a state trooper. Underpaid, understaffed, and always sipping coffee and eating bagels. Man, how Simon had taken after his father too much.

His father had been a cop shot in the line of duty. Most would think of horror at their child taking after such a profession, but Simon didn't think about it one bit. He had been injured as well in the line of duty, and did that stop him? No; he surged ahead, showing his scarred eye with a line over it as a badge of honor. It helped to deter criminals from puffing up around him and made them think twice against fighting a cop with a knife wound. Simon smiled as he passed the break room. It had been a piece of glass and he had been walking when he tripped and fell into a pile of them. Pretty sad story really, but criminals didn't need to know that did they?

The saddest thing about being a state trooper was the lack of facilities. Even now with his current bust, he was using a precinct close by in Mizu Huki. He preferred his own Precinct 7, but Precinct 10 was alright too. Simon moved towards the end of the offices and turned into the corridors which held the interrogation rooms. He moved past the officer on duty and passed into the furthest corridor and proceeded to the second to last door and knocked lightly before heading inside.

What greeted him was the standard setup. Recording devices and computers lay along the far wall, documenting everything that was seen and heard in the room, but there was nothing to document, so for now, they just showed flat lines and little else. Three officers sat in the room and turned to nod to Simon as he raised his coffee up in acknowledgment.

Simon turned to look through the mirror and had to hold himself back from swearing that he was looking at an innocent young woman. She sat on the far side of the table, her arms drawn forward to be handcuffed to the bar in the middle, but besides that, she was ramrod straight against the back of the chair, as her eyes scanned around the room, the emerald eyes greyed and looking.... bored.

Simon watched this girl for ten minutes, taking in every detail of her figure and the way she carried herself. She seemed to want to be anywhere but here, and yet her posture showed that she was perfectly capable of resigning herself to stay here until they released her. "Here you are, sir." A man reached over and handed him a file and he nodded his thanks and read it over carefully. He would not go in without all the ammunition he could muster.

"How long has she been here, officer?"

"Just over 24 hours now, sir."

"Find anything on her?"

"Only her wallet and keys for the motorcycle we found in the warehouse. And a switchblade hidden in the seams of her jacket."

"I'm heading in." He murmured before he walked out and grabbed a soda before knocking on the door and headed inside to meet this woman of mystery.

"Hello there." Simon greeted as he entered. The woman turned to face him but said nothing. Her face did not even change, nor her muscles. She was in fact looking at him, but she was in no way scared of him. He smiled. This might be fun. "I am Detective Beckett. I'll be handling your case, Ms.?"

"........"

No Answer. He breathed through his nose and sat down. "I don't suppose you're thirsty, but just in case, I got you a Sprite." He placed it within her reach and backed away, before placing the file on the desk.

"I suppose I should get started, but we seem to have plenty of time. After all, you were carrying a weapon on you when you were arrested."

He smiled as she gripped the can but did not open it. He looked at her fingers, still bloody from the woman she had been grabbed from. It was also splattered up to her blouse and under her fingernails as well. She'd been slowly scraping it off to pass the time but seemed hesitant to do so quickly.

"I don't suppose you wish to wash your hands thoroughly, do you? It might do you good." Her eyes narrowed the smallest bit at that, but still nothing.

"Alright then. Let me go first." Simon pulled out a number of pictures, one of a blonde girl with blue eyes, another black haired girl with brown eyes, and yet another brown haired girl with green eyes following those.

"These are all you, are they not? Let's see...The first would be Anita Hana, a very smart technical assistant at her mother's company here in the city. Very bright for her age, but unfortunately a college drop out when her father passed away.

"Next is one Alice O'Connell...Ran away from home at 16, but found a nice simple job as a receptionist at Kyugen Technologies, was taught the basics, but after that, your coworkers said that you were... what was it? A natural at just about anything. Of course, when the business lost a very expensive patent to a competitor last year, she vanished, off the grid.

"But this last girl, now she has a full story to tell. She is Tess Miles, age 23, grew up in the foster system after her parents were murdered by a serial killer. She was 6 at the time, and yet by the age of 10, she ran away when she was abused by her foster brother, and finally left the system when an older boy at school assaulted her when she was 11.

"But then life turned around for her sometime after that. One Amelia Walter started to spread her wealth around and adopted a few daughters, one being little Tess at 13. She was homeschooled after that, and currently lives a quiet single life in a number of homes owned by Ms. Walter."

Simon closes the file and leans forward. ".... Nice to meet you, Tess."

And there it was. A simple, honest smile, but she didn't say anything yet again. Simon nodded to her and looked down. "May I try that?" A soft spoken, southern drawl escaped his subject's lips, and he was surprised he got her to speak. He expected to try for another hour.

"Try what?"

She smiled wider and Simon wondered what she would say.

"You're 35-no, 34 years of age, your scar seems creepy, but based on most scars, it was probably minor, but you use that to your advantage, especially in a place like this. If I look at your hands, they show old blisters that have calloused well over the years from a routine use of lotion in your younger years. You played with a variety of swords growing up I'm sure, well trained by your posture. I'm surprised you're not reaching for your phone every few minutes, but you must have spent time without it, so you're used to that. So then ex-military, but more on the side of the Agent Branch?"

Silence was apparent as the recording devices watched and heard them breathe between each other. Simon looked again at the girl's face as stoic as ever. It was as if she was just stating facts off in her head, and her emotions were hidden. It was as if she was a student in a class explaining their answer to the teacher.

Simon grinned and chuckled, leaning back to stroke at his hair. "Not bad. Most people think military, but it takes one with good eyes to notice the blisters from my agent training. Impressive."

"Oh, I'm just getting started."

"Then please." Simon smirked. Whatever she said could only help him to learn more about her.

"First off, that quip about a weapon is smoke in the wind. That blade of mine is 5 inches, perfectly legal in this state. Next, you need to train these guys around you better to not show their watches. I understand you trying to wear me down, but giving me 4 meals in 24 hours....36 mins? That's just cruel, and overbudget Simon. The standard 2 meals a day for those in holding is the set minimum. Of course, you may have expected me to know that, but as I said about watches, your officers shouldn't allow a suspect to see the time every moment they come inside."

Simon smiled. "I'm sure you would have kept count of time either way."

"My mother taught me to never be late, and to encourage me to stick to a strict timetable. Also," Tess replied as she pushed the pictures across the table. "None of these are me. I don't know why you think the last picture is me, but I'm pretty recognizable as a blonde, and that shade would look terrible on me. I'd never change my hair to that."

Simon had nodded along with her but smiled at that. "They say the best grifters can become anyone."

"And what is a grifter?" The girl asked, her face for the first time making a confused face.

"Now, now……. Tess." Simon smiled as Tess eyed him. "No need for you to act dumb now. All of your aliases call for a young, beautiful and intelligent street urchin who is making her way up in the world."

"I again, am saying that those girls aren't me. I am Tess, you got that part right, but why did you arrest me? I was just visiting some friends of my mother's when you stormed in." Tess's eyes turned downcast. "You didn't even let me say goodbye."

"I do apologize on behalf of my men, but we heard a gunshot. Can you tell us what happened?"

Tess just shrugged. "I don't know. My mother wanted us to get together for a picture with our bikes, and then Bang!....She didn't deserve to die."

"You really cared about her."

"Of course, I care." Tess spoke, Simon noting her slip of using the present tense. "She is my mother."

"Adoptive mother, and a con artist at that." Simon leaned back in. "A grifter, Ms. Miles, is someone who can become anyone and convince people of things that they would normally never believe or do. They get alarms lowered, or expensive pieces of art given over. It can be as simple as getting some money for your troubles or getting reparations for a car crash that never happened. Your mother was a thief, and she has made you the spitting image of her."

Simon moved to continue when he paused. Tess's muscles were pulled taut, her body jittering, and her eyes turning a haze of red. Clearly, he was pushing the right buttons, and she was beginning to crack. "Tess, what I am trying to say-"

He paused again as he watched it happen. The muscles slacked and loosened. Her body started quivering, and wet tears dropped down her eyes and joined her quivering lips. "My mother...was the strongest woman who ever lived…...and I miss her. You have no right to talk bad about someone who raised a pathetic child like myself from the street into the intelligent woman you see now. She is…. was everything I had, and I assure you Simon, you'd better find whoever did this to her, because as you said, my mother was rich, and with those resources, if I find the ones responsible, you won't find a spread of them on this earth."

Simon sighed back into his seat, defeated. Even if he pressed forward, there would be no point. Even if she was accused of a crime, a jury would never convict this girl after such an act, an act caught on video and audio that the police were required to hand over if asked for. He smiled though; he could still get more information. "What do you take yourselves as, Tess? You and your team of friends? Robin Hood?"

Tess smirked through her tears, just now ebbing away. "I would never say that. I just want to live my life in peace."

"And you don't know who it is that killed your mother? Tell us that, and you can go free."

Tess herself leaned back as the chains grew taut and extended in front of her. "You can never truly cage an innocent girl like me."

"But are you truly innocent?"

"No one in the world is completely innocent, Simon." Tess smiled. "You bring a plant across the border; that's illegal even if the state trooper doesn't arrest you for it. I mean, if a guy gives a girl a check full of money out of the goodness of his heart, with no contract and only goodness, is it a crime to accept it?" Tess hunched her shoulders and peaked her fingers together over her eyes and let out a sniffle. "Let me go... now. I need to bury my mother."

Simon stood up but slid a card across the table. "We'll get you processed out. But if you hear anything or if you commit a crime, please call me. Acting out in revenge is never the answer, but you can litigate for a lower sentence if you plead guilty."

"Thank you…. officer."

"...It's Detective…..."

Simon watched the girl sign some forms at the processing station and grabbed his best man for the job. "I want twenty-four-hour surveillance on her and undercover agents following her every move. Do not lose sight of her. She'll head back to her friends eventually. We'll get them then."

"Yes, Sir." His man nodded and moved off, as Simon watched Tess take back her wallet and knife.

They had been robbing the worst of people blind and this was the police's chance to catch them. The only problem was that none of them had the money and there was no proof they'd done it. Only a single name to go on, Tess Miles.

Three days later, Tess stood in front of a fresh grave, her outfit suited for the occasion. Black trench coat with a fashioned belt over her outfit with 6-inch heels. In her hands were a bouquet of black roses, as black and deadly as could be if a single petal cut into the skin, and Tess had no gloves on.

She looked around and saw no one there with her. No one to share with Tess their stories or their pain at her loss. Amelia had outlived all her old crew and was about to retire. Tess's grip tightened on the flowers. No one retired from this life but were transformed into the next generation. Tess was Amelia incarnate, her soul rested inside her heart and in those of her sisters.

Soft footsteps sounded behind her, but she just kept looking at the fresh earth before her. The body joined her with another trench coat and large hat. They both stared at the grave, neither making a sound.

"It was sunny this morning, with rainbows all over." The woman mentioned, making Tess smile.

"And yet now it is bleak and raining." She replied, though no rain poured around them. "It is good to see you, Sarah."

"I'm sorry I wasn't able to make it back in time."

"You had your own con to oversee."

"You know, I may have been adopted first, Tess, but she never stopped talking about how proud she was of you. Of how much she saw herself in you."

"I just wish I had more time with her, Sarah."

"Trust me, Tess. The pain feels the same for me, but time is not the only indicator of how much we feel for people. Your bond with mom is just as strong as mine."

"Sarah? I need a pass."

"Of course." Sarah smiled as the two women moved to a tree and leaned against it; they hugged together, cried together, and when all was over, the black-haired woman headed back down the hill, leaving her sister to mourn the loss of her mother.

Knees bent down to the ground and the black flowers leaned against the marble stone that held Amelia's real name and age, despite what she had told nearly ten thousand people during her life. Fresh tears flowed down the woman's face, and more cries erupted from atop the hill.

Down below, men watched the scene above with binoculars and a parabolic antenna attached to a part of their SUV. Behind them, two officers in plain clothes watched the one attendee for the funeral walk away before turning their gaze back to the hill.

Up on the hill, the tears didn't stop flowing, and frankly they were ruining her makeup. If it ran too much, then her complexion would not match that of her sister anymore. Already, the hair on her head pulled at her scalp. She had never liked to have long hair, but her sister sure did; Sarah would miss her.

At the gate to the cemetery, Tess turned back just once to look towards the hill and prayed that her mother was happy to be placed alongside the grave of her late love. Tess had gotten the story seven years ago when she gained her first real score. She'd never met John, but the smile on mom's face every time she spoke of him had shown her what true love looked like.

Tess pulled at her short black hair, freshly dyed, and hidden under the large hat that she now wore, the same length as Sarah's. She sniffled. Amelia had always loved to stroke her fingers through her long hair. Tess shook away the tears. Her hair would grow back, the wig she'd made from it now on Sarah's head.

"I promise you mom, I'll find Alex, get back our score, and I'll murder him." Tess's eyes mixed with a red hue. "...And if I can manage, find love." Tess laughed humorlessly at herself. Yeah right. Like she was cut out for love.

III-DANIEL THE GUARD

(6 Months Later)

Birds were his first sign that it was morning. The man groaned as his senses became active and a muscled arm crossed over his eyes to alleviate some sense of light from his cerulean eyes. Why did he place his bed in the direct path of the sun's morning rays? He sighed and sat up, moving sheets around as he moved his way over to the small bathroom in his one-bedroom apartment.

The guy leaned down and turned the handle as cold water dripped down the drain. He scooped it with his hands and washed his face to wipe away the cold sweat that had formed on his face. He sighed and turned to the shower and turned it on next. Turning back, he gripped at his blond hair before turning to trace a light scar that trailed down along his shoulder.

A large sword had sliced right through him like butter in training years ago, back when he was ambitious and wanting a thrill. He had turned eighteen and signed up for boot camp on his birthday. He still remembered it, signing Daniel Alias Thompson on the forms alongside his social security number. He had spent three months training, working his butt off when they had moved to real combat and that sword delved straight into him. After that, he couldn't stop thinking about it, his nightmares a weekly event, and he dropped out of the program soon after.

After his shower, Daniel moved back to his dresser and prepared himself for the day. He looked at himself in the mirror and smiled, approving his attire, and moving around his apartment for his remaining things. It had been four years since his failed time in the military and he had grown since then. His sense of thrill had dampened over the years, and he was now fine with the simple things in life. He didn't need the fast, adventurous life that he had grown up wanting. He was content with his current job and his current situation. He smiled. He liked his life just fine.

Daniel grabbed his grey jacket as well as his bookbag and moved to the hallway. He locked it up, all three locks, and moved down the stairs next to his room. As he made his way down to the first floor, he smiled. Most people would take the elevator, preferring not to expend energy, but he liked the more physical things of life.

Thinking on that, he smiled wider as he passed through the center of the apartment complex, through the community garden that the old lady who lived below him tended to every day. He moved to the shaded area and bent down to his bike to unlock it.

It was a nice Trek bike, with an option to use an electric motor if he so wished, but he didn't have to travel far. "Oi! Daniel!" An older man called out from his 2nd floor window, making Daniel turn his head. "Thanks for fixing the pipes last night Daniel! My wife was very happy to have warm water again."

"No problem, Steven. I hope your son does well on his test today."

"Oh! He'd better if he wants to go on that date with that girl he won't shut up about." Steven leaned over as both men smiled. "But Daniel, I really appreciate it. I mean, doing that last night after the late shift at your job, I can't imagine you sleeping well."

"Ah! No big deal. You and the Mrs. just enjoy yourselves." Daniel smiled and straddled his bike, before peddling out onto the road. Luckily for Daniel, he lived in a nice area of Kavala, a small city with only 60,000 residents within the city limits. He biked along main street for three miles, a light bike ride for most as it was relatively flat, before he turned to the right and headed up a small hill that held the shopping area of Kavala and his workplace of the last four years.

He approached the back of the building, turning between a night pub and another set of apartments to get into the alley behind a museum. He moved into a small alcove to stash his bike and casually locked it to the chain link gate it was next to before moving to the door of the museum. Daniel waved to the camera as he pulled out a magnetic card and held it to the door before it beeped and opened for him.

On the inside was the back area of the museum, and Daniel slid into the first door on the right to where the guards kept their equipment and spare uniforms. Daniel undid his padlock and placed his possessions inside, as well as his grey jacket, before he pulled out his spare uniform grey jacket, with the same style and design as the one he'd just put in, minus the sweat from his journey to work.

After adding his keys and mace to his belt, he reached in and grabbed his spare tie. He smiled. He hadn't had time last night to get a wash done, so having a spare was definite relief. After he laced up his boots all the way up, he slid back out the door, making sure he had his keys before he closed it, the door locking behind him. He moved to the end of the hall and knocked on the bullet proof glass.

A buzz sounded and Daniel opened the door to get inside quickly, and he smiled in greeting. "How was the night, Carter?"

The guard known as Carter turned in his chair, away from the camera screens, and smiled at his junior guard. "Are you really here already, Thompson?"

"It's almost 9am, Carter." Daniel smiled as he grabbed a fresh radio and earpiece, bringing it around his back until it clipped to his jacket pocket.

"I understand that Thompson, but you were here until 10 last night." Carter shook his head and rolled his eyes. "Why you always volunteer for those extra shifts, I don't know. You don't have to worry about money."

"Carter, they were renovating the east wing gallery and needed the extra guard. The boss requested it."

"Ah the boss, right." Carter chuckled. "You know this place better than anyone here, Thompson. In my opinion, you should be running this place already."

Daniel shrugged his shoulders. He really had no ambition anymore. "I like the physical work more than a laid-back office job.

I mean, put me in front of the cameras over an excel spreadsheet any day."

"Oh well…. that's right, the boss wanted to see you in the main atrium."

"Oh, now you tell me. Trying to make me look bad, Carter?" Daniel joked.

"Only you can make yourself look bad, Daniel." Carter smiled as Daniel entered the code on the inside of the security booth, unlocking the door as he moved out back into the hallway. Daniel made a last check of his uniform and froze.

"It had better not be another camera." He annoyingly muttered before he stepped out into the main atrium, just behind the reception area where people bought their tickets for the multiple galleries, the planetarium, and the IMAX center. The young 19-year-old receptionist sent a flirtatious smile his way and he smiled back, before he saw his boss opening the doors and went to help him.

"Thanks for the help, Daniel."

"Anytime, boss." Daniel nodded to a young couple heading inside thirty minutes later. "So then, Sir, Carter said that you needed to speak with me.

"Ah!" His boss scratched his beard for a few seconds, making Daniel nervous.

"Sir?"

"Sorry, Daniel but…...Another camera broke."

Daniel groaned and rubbed his eyes. "At least tell me it's the software again." Daniel pleaded. He'd spent fourteen hours of his shift last week going through system checks and code to find the decayed line and updating it with the current patch.

"Actually, I think it's the old wiring."

"Sir," Daniel sighed. He was already exhausted for his day. "I keep telling you that the whole system needs updating."

"Daniel, I believe I have told you this before as well. We get many visitors, but not that many. There are seven museums in this city, and of them, we have the best security our region has to offer. That will just have to do. Besides Daniel, as technology goes up, the old school tech becomes harder to hack."

"Only because people don't want to learn it, Sir."

"Hence why the museum still employs guards like us." The boss smiled. "Besides, we have the most prestigious work in the whole region." The boss saw Daniel nod in agreement and stroked his ego. "I really appreciate your skills, Daniel. We really can't afford a technical staff so having you is truly a godsend for us. You could always go into the tech sector Daniel. You really are too good to be a simple security guard."

"That's where you're wrong, Sir." Daniel shook his head. "I'm happy to work here, sir."

"Alright then sector 2 red wall."

"Red wall, got it." Daniel repeated before he made his way inside. He moved to head straight to the gallery when he stopped to see a little girl in the center of the room in pigtails looking around in circles. He smiled and made his way over to the girl. "Hey there."

The little girl turned to face him, her eyes bleary with tears and her bottom lip wobbling. she looked up at him and immediately started to whimper. "Hey there," Daniel bent down to her level, his knee on the ground as he leaned forward as the girl looked teary eyed at him.

"Are you lost?" He asked, and the little girl hid her head lower, her neck disappearing like a turtle. "I bet your mom told you not to talk to strangers, right?" At the little girl's tiny nod, he smiled brighter. "Smart. You see that symbol over there?" He pointed to the museum's picture on the wall. "You see this symbol here too." He pointed to his lapel on his shoulder.

The little girl looked over at his shoulder and nodded again. "That means I work here. So, we're not really strangers, are we?" The girl slowly shakes her head and her head raised out of her collar. Daniel leaned in again, whispering as he did so.

"You know, we can use the speakers to find your mom. Would you like that?" Daniel asked. The girl's smile became a beam that shined into his face. Daniel gently grabbed her hand and led her towards the booth.

"Thank you so much, sir!" The girl's mother cried so hard as she hugged her baby girl who instead of hugging her mother hugged Daniel's leg. Daniel ruffled the little girl's hair and bent down.

"You stay with your mom now, okay?" The little girl nodded and followed her mother who walked down to the Imax center. Daniel leaned over to the receptionist who was aweing the whole time at him and the little girl and smiled. "I'll be in S2."

'Finally,' Daniel thought as he leaned the ladder upon the wall below the defective camera in question and began his way up. As he got to the top, he leaned on one leg and looked behind the camera where the wire was and sighed. The wire was indeed busted. The cord looked as if an electrical current had surged through and melted the copper wires inside it. A simple fix he supposed, just changing the wire, but a total repair all the same.

Daniel sighed and looked down at the gallery below him and prepared to take a step back down. That was the moment he had a heart attack.

IV-FIRST MEETING

eart attacks are the heart not pumping regularly to the body's rhythm. It's what keeps the body aligned and on track to keep functioning. The heart is what keeps it steady. So, what causes a heart to change its rhythm? A number of reasons could be the answer, but for Daniel, it was just one.

Daniel was looking at the gallery down below him. It could have been the height, but it wasn't. It could be that he had a thought of death when falling off the ladder, but it wasn't. No; it was as his eyes turned to the entrance that his heart froze. His eyes opened wider to receive the information as a young woman, maybe around his age, stepped into the gallery. Her pace was steady enough that her hair flew back from her face, glowing like silk on a chocolate ground. The brunette's eyes were open, and even from up here, he couldn't help his eyes looking deeply into hers, how they were as bright as a blue cobalt sky with some grey clouds mixed inside. Maybe his heart was falling to its death, because he had never seen a girl with such a beautiful face before.

He was a guy; he couldn't help it. Daniel's eyes glanced down at her petite, lean frame. His eyes immediately dropped to her blue floor length skirt that was longer in the back and shorter in the front, making a rippling wind of motion that entranced the eyes. The brown leather boots came to her mid thighs, and yet were silent as she walked forward to the first painting.

Daniel by now had gained his heart back, but it was at the cost of his breath. He gulped, his tongue licking over his parched lips at the sight of the t-shirt covering her stomach, but it was a tight shirt, emphasizing the strong stomach and the swell of her breasts that pushed against the fabric. A dark colored flannel shirt covered her sides and arms, but Daniel watched as her smooth neck craned towards the other paintings around the room, imagining what it would be like to touch such smooth, unblemished skin.

Those bright eyes, the opposite of his own ocean blue ones, stunned him in place as they turned to look at the ladder and then followed it up to look at him. The girl cocked her head cutely to the side and smiled up at him, her eyes shining. Daniel couldn't stop his smile from forming.

"Damn!" Daniel cursed to himself as his foot slipped and he gripped the ladder to steady himself, the ladder banging on the wall loudly. Daniel heard an angelic giggle sound from below and blushed deeply in embarrassment. Same story with any girl he was around. He made a fool of himself. Daniel looked down to see the woman hiding her giggles with her manicured hand but giggled a little as she made her way over to the bottom of the ladder and looked up at him. Daniel tried to keep his eyes on her face, and not the swell of her chest, but with her under him, it was all too easy to drift his gaze back and forth.

"Excuse me, Sir." The woman's voice was just as angelic as her laugh. Smooth and silky. "Do you know anything about these beautiful paintings?"

"Um...yeah." Daniel replied nervously as he noticed her direct gaze upon him; solely on him. It made his heart flutter in his chest, like butterflies. Daniel felt drawn to get down this ladder and chat with this young lady, but as he began, he sighed as his hand touched the camera. "Unfortunately," Daniel sighed. "I'll be a few more minutes with this."

The girl shrugged nonchalantly. "I don't mind waiting."

Daniel nodded and turned back to the camera, his deft hands opening the back of the device before he carefully turned off the power and then slowly pulled the bad wire out from the back, taking out a clipper to snap off the bad wiring from the rest of the machine. Over the minutes this took, he couldn't help but see out of the corner of his eye how the girl leaned forward on the ladder, looking up at him with her foot swishing lightly behind her.

"Alright," Daniel said aloud and prepared to come down. "Now I just need the new-" He began before he turned to see the woman holding the exact wires he needed. He smiled gratefully and reached down, as the girl's soft hands made contact with his gloved ones, but slid across his skin, nonetheless, taking the bad wires while exchanging them for the new ones.

Daniel smiled as he stepped back up and inserted the wires, clamping them together with the machine before he tested the connectivity and smiled as the connection ran as if it was brand new. He swiftly closed the machine and turned it on before scaling down the ladder eagerly. Now he could talk to this beauty!

"That should do it. So then-" Daniel lost his voice.

He had twirled around to talk to the girl, but she had not moved back at all. Now, their bodies were within an inch of each other, his lips within two inches of her own, her small nose lightly touching his as her bright eyes widened at the sudden closeness as he'd invaded her personal space. Her eyes were so amazing, and he stared into her irises. They told him so much about her with words. The passion in her eyes showed her determination in what she did. The deep intelligence that lurked just under the surface, and her personality; it was so deep, and he wanted to learn just how far he could drown in those orbs.

"......You have beautiful eyes." Daniel uttered huskily before his filter could stop himself.

"Thank you." The woman giggled, smiling as he turned back blushing to grab the ladder.

Daniel bit his lip in frustration. He blew it! What a stupid utterly dumb thing to say! He was such a klutz around attractive women, but this girl was just something else!

"Are you updating the cameras with X-ray and such?" She asked curiously.

Daniel appreciated her willingness to ignore his blunder and continue on. He laughed as he pulled the ladder down, closing it up together. "No, just replacing the wires." He smiled back at her. "Don't worry ma'am, x-ray is not allowed in a public space. We want our visitors to feel safe at all times."

The woman smiled innocently. "But don't you work here? I feel safe with you watching me." Daniel saw the girl blush as she said that last part and smiled. "I mean," she continued. "Why would you need cameras if we have you?"

Daniel smiled. "Not everything has to be done externally, ma'am. It's more beneficial when we're not here, but also to help people in case they lose something here or there."

"I see." She smiled. "So, you're a tech guy then, keeping all this up to date?"

Daniel shrugged as he tied the ladder together. "Among other things."

She straightened up her body and moved to hold her purse in front of her as he turned to grab the ladder. "Just one little thing more." He mentioned as he took the ladder to an empty wall where no paintings were located. He lightly pressed against the wall until a soft click sounded and the wall opened into a secret hallway. Daniel leaned forward to place the ladder there against the wall and closed the secret door.

Daniel came back to see the young woman impressed with the secret door. "Is that in all art museums?" She asked as he led her to the first painting.

"Only the best." Daniel beamed as the girl smiled brighter. "So then, this painting here." Daniel began to tell her all about the paintings in the room. No one else came in to look at the paintings, it still being rather early in the museum's day.

Daniel kept talking though, telling her the little tidbits that others may not know. After four years here, he had done much research on the paintings as he had to stand in front of them for 4-7 hours a day after all. He may as well appreciate the art and help visitors to appreciate the art better. He smiled though. Usually, people just nodded their heads and moved on. This girl did not.

She asked him questions on what he said, what kind of life the painter led, the kind of paint used. She even argued with him over his research as she had read something different in another article. He would smile and point out that he was looking into newer research while she preferred the older documents that speculated less and knew more about their lives.

He tried to be professional, and help her out, but she stood so close to him, and more than once, her chest pressed into his arm after a funny joke or with the warmth of shared embarrassment on both their parts. Daniel's cheeks were surely permanently red as he turned to her and sighed.

"Y-you know," Daniel uttered. "You can go to the counter and get a guide for five bucks."

"That's good advice." The woman smiled gratefully, making him sad at losing her company. She leaned closer, surely innocently, but then he gulped harder as she slid her arm through his, making him freeze as she invaded his personal space. He definitely liked the invasion as her arm pressed his arm between her chest, as she leaned closer to his ear. "But I like your voice better. It's not a recording…"

Daniel grinned as he turned to face her and saw her smirk. "-And I can flirt with you."

"Flirt with me?" He blushed and felt blood rush down his body. She had seen him checking her out after all. "Um, listen, I-" He began before a soft, delicate finger touched his lips, crushing whatever defense he had been about to say.

"You stared at me fondly, and not at me lewdly or spoke anything offensive."

Daniel looked away in shame. "I thank you for the confidence, but I did look at you with desire."

The woman smiled back as she shrugged. "Maybe you looked a little, but eyes wander after all, and… y-you commented on my eyes." The girl spoke as she brought a hand up to her face, splaying her fingers on her cheek. "I've always liked my eyes best, so I appreciated the comment."

'This girl…she's so unpredictable.' Daniel thought as he smiled at her. He hadn't had a girl flirt with him since…. high school? Did girls ever flirt with him? He could not recall.

The silence grew and became awkward, but she helped him out as they stepped sideways to the direct middle of the room where a nice bench was situated in front of another painting. "And what's this one?"

Daniel turned and smiled brightly. "Oh! This is the best and most recent addition to the gallery, and" Daniel turned to smile at her, "My personal favorite. This...is a Walter."

He saw her look confusingly back at him. "A what?"

He apparently found something she hadn't known before, and pride filled his body as he delved into his wealth of knowledge. "She was a young female artist forty years ago who made brushstrokes, not with actual brushes but with her fingers as a twist to show her own style. The detail is so good that it fooled many experts for actual brushstrokes for ten years. A large group of these paintings were discovered around five years ago and became a major hit and sought after, especially here in Kavala where the mysterious painter grew up. You may not know this," Daniel whispered, "but this one is worth 500k."

He smiled as her eyes lit up. "No way. Then it must have the best security around it." She smiled coquettishly back at him. "But you can't tell me, can you?"

Daniel smiled back. "No, I can't, but I can tell you that it's very secure. This painting is not going anywhere without the owner's permission."

The pair turned away towards the following artwork and paused as the painting before them was the first painting he'd talked on. "Um, well that's all for this gallery." Daniel noted as they reached the other side where the exit door was.

"Oh…" The girl muttered as she looked at the door, but her feet did not move. Daniel saw her nod her head to herself before turning back to look up at him. "Can I get your number?"

Daniel smiled. "Well, I work here so if you have questions anyone can-"

The girl giggled at his response. "I very much enjoyed the gallery, don't get me wrong, but um…I was hoping to ask you out…" The girl smiled brightly as she turned her eyes towards his jacket where his name was…" Daniel."

"Oh?...Oh!" Daniel exclaimed as he realized what she was asking for. Not for a contact for questions, but...for him personally. "Wow um wow. This...has never happened to me before." Daniel blubbered as he scratched the back of his neck.

She leaned closer, her shining lip gloss tantalizing him even more now that he knew that she found him at least attractive. "Forgive me, Daniel but...I like to be forward, and while I love art, I was actually hoping you'd show me around town?" The girl's eyes showed a mirth that wished for more than just a tour of the town, and Daniel blushed as thoughts formed of both in a more indecent setting filled his head.

"I just moved here; you see." She clarified when he didn't respond. "So, I don't know any good spots to eat and check out."

"I really shouldn't." Daniel gulped back his wanton lust. He was an idiot for saying no to a girl his age who had the courage he didn't have to ask him out. He thought about the fear of rejection and failure that always stopped him. But he saw her smile did not change, or she was not deterred by his refusal. Did she know just how much he didn't want to reject her advances?

"If you'd like, it can just be coffee and a movie? Please?"

"Well...alright." Daniel sighed and smiled. He reached into his pocket and pulled out his phone. "We're really not supposed to do this." He said but passed his phone to the girl. She smiled in victory as she entered her number into the contact list. He looked up at the camera and gulped. No doubt Carter was going to use this to blackmail him into another shift coverage. He looked back confused as she entered something else into his phone, but the thought left him as she quickly leaned up and left a quick, searing kiss to his cheek.

"Thank you...Daniel." She breathed into his ear and turned towards the exit. Daniel beamed brightly as he smiled. Screw blackmail, this was worth it. "Oh Daniel!" He turned to look at her. "I never told you my name. I'm Paige."

Paige, Daniel thought happily as she walked away, the sway of her hips dragging his attention downwards to see a fine ass. Had he really missed how tight her skirt was? His eyes caught the mirror at the exit and Paige's smile towards him. He looked away and coughed. She'd caught him checking out her ass and she was fine with him looking. Daniel moved back to the corner of the room, and while standing there, sighed.

Paige. Surely it was the name of a most beautiful woman. He had a sudden urge to look at flowers.

V-HELLO, I'M PAIGE

"I never told you my name. I'm Paige." She smiled as she turned around and walked away, telling herself to sway her hips hypnotically and walk slowly to emphasize her long legs. Paige bit her lip seductively when she looked into the mirror near the end of the hall and saw Daniel's eyes staring directly at her ass. She almost drew blood from her lower lip when she saw the lustful look in his eyes. It was a look that Paige was tempted to elicit very soon.

Paige made her way to the exit of the museum and started down the stairs. The way that guard looked at her made her loins stir and her breathing more erratic as goosebumps covered her arms. It was a very pleasant feeling to know that a guy as innocent as him found her attractive.

She continued down the stairs and into the parking lot before sliding into her car. Paige looked down at her attire and smiled. It was a little tight, showing off her entire figure, but damn did it make her feel confident in herself. Paige started her car as smooth jazz started playing from her radio and immediately started screaming in joy!! She did it!!!

After a few seconds of elation, Paige casually drove down to the main street and started to drive towards her residence. And to think, she used to be so bad at flirting too!! The brunette turned off the road towards the warehouse district and remembered what her mother had taught her about flirting.

Touch their shoulder and hand, as she'd done when she pressed herself against Daniel's arm. Giggle at the right moments when the subject feels awkward such as when he nearly tripped off the ladder at the mere sight of her. That part made her blush at how cute it was. Lean in close to instill a sense of bond they share, like when she asked him out. Actually, listen to what they say, as she had about the paintings in the room. She'd pulled it off perfectly.

Paige smiled as she pulled up to the sidewalk and parked her car. Walking down the street, she turned right into the entryway of a front store business. Paige took out a key and unlocked the door before she stepped inside and made her way inside. She passed a staircase that led to the residential floor where she lived.

Paige paused as she stopped in front of a frosted door. When she thought about it, she didn't even think about the steps to seduce a mark. They came naturally to her, as if she was trying to get an actual date with the guy. Paige's smile became bigger as she stepped inside. Daniel really was an easy mark; she usually didn't deal with people who were so genuine and honest.

He wasn't like others she'd had to seduce and flirt with before. Usually, she had more…ambitious characters to tempt, with more hands and grabbing tendencies that had her annoyed and ready to leave as soon as the job was done. Apparently, Paige liked to be in charge it seemed. Having a guy who was less confident about themselves and nervous about flirting back with a girl was definitely a turn on for her. Paige decided that she was glad she had asked for his number. She had spent more than enough time flirting with him and learning about him than she needed to, but he was rather handsome to her. Paige licked her lips at the thought of kissing him. She may in fact call him up for that date. Paige smiled as she stopped in the center of the room. She had promised her mother after all to look around for a boy.

When Paige had first shown up a month ago, she had hated the look of this rundown place. Luckily after some simple comforts, this part of the commercial and residential building was up to her usual standards. The ceiling above them was steel beams and was an open floor plan of a warehouse with some small offices and a hallway and bathroom. Upstairs in the living area was a loft where she ate and slept. *'And a good thing I had frosted glass windows installed on the front of the shop to keep people from peeping inside.'* Paige thought as she looked forward to the sight of her sister.

For there was her blonde bombshell of a sister, her curvy proportions that of a model, and what was she wearing? Nothing but her underwear! Paige sighed. She should really, really be used to this by now. In front of a bank of computers, her sister moved casually between monitors as views from the museum appeared on one of the monitors. Paige admired her sister's confidence in attire as right now her purple bra was on simply to keep her chest tight and her lacy panties made Paige wonder if she had just gotten up for the day.

"Hey Julia. I'm back." Paige greeted as she plopped her purse down on the glass table and moved to the fridge by the wall.

Julia leaned back in the chair and swiveled to face her sister, her blonde hair framing her face as it moved down to the small of her back. "So? How was it over there?"

Paige bobbed her head to the side as she grabbed some alcohol from the fridge and took a swig straight from the bottle. "They fixed it again." Paige sighed as she sat on one of the four couches around the glass table.

"Dang it!" Julia sighed back into her computer chair and stood up, rubbing her hands through her hair in irritation. "Do you know how much coding I had to write to make those wires heat up internally? Do you realize how much effort that takes?"

Paige didn't respond. She would let her older sister vent out her frustrations with a monologue.

"Loads I tell you! I mean, I spent three days without sleep until last night! God, how the universe hates me!"

"Is that why you're still in your pajamas?"

"Huh?" Julia looked down and shrugged. "Oh, you wouldn't care if I was naked." Paige had to admit that she was right. They'd grown up together so there was nothing the two didn't share. "Or what about the system overload I completed last week to freeze the cameras from panning left and right? I mean, I'm dying here! Look at my skin! It's as pale as yours." Julia continued.

"Oh, you geek!" Paige giggled and laid back on the cushions. "Like you ever go outside except to flaunt your assets around?"

Julia smiled at her sister's retort and groaned, sitting down beside her. "Why won't they just hire a repair team? That's our way in. We're all prepped for that."

"I know why, Julia." Paige looked around and shrugged. "I got there just as they were changing the wires this morning. I was able to give the technician one of our special wires, so we can at least see what's going on in the room."

Julia nodded her head sleepily and laid down next to her while Paige turned to lay on her side to see Julia smiling at her. "I saw the feed come online. I suppose at least we have an eye on our main target then. That's our way forward after all. Did they hire that technician then? I didn't see a request pop up for one on their external server."

"Not exactly." Paige grimaced. "I found the guy who's been fixing the problems. The problem is that he already works there so he's on the inside too…."

"And?" Julia questioned.

Paige sighed, her cheeks reddening. "He's smart."

Julia smiled wider as she casually leaned away. "Well, you're good then. Smart guys are the easiest marks." Julia leaned in and nuzzled her nose with Paige's. "Maybe make him drool a bit, huh?"

Paige hummed for a minute in Julia's eyes as she watched her sister sigh and look away. "Maybe I could make him drool, but I like him. He's not like our usual marks. He's...unique…"

Julia raised herself to her elbows at her sister's softer than normal voice. She was only that way when she was distracted with something, or someone. It was when her sister was happiest, but….it could be deadly in their profession. And with a boy no less.

"Tess," Julia called over, using her sister's real name. "This is not the time to find your soulmate."

A face of confusion contorted on Tess's face. She had dyed her hair to become anonymous, and colored contacts to change herself as she had done for many years now. But what her sister was suggesting about Daniel was ridiculous.

"Soulmate?" Tess giggled and smiled over to her best friend. "That's not even close to what I was saying. I was just thinking he'd be a good lover, Tanya." Tess dropped her sister's fake name. "He's inexperienced, nervous, and such a sweetheart. Also...he's pretty good on the eyes." Tess smiled lustfully as she turned back around.

Tanya smiled playfully as she leaned forward and hugged her arms around Tess from behind, her generous chest pressed deeply into her back before she dragged her fingers alongside her neck seductively. "Geez, Tess! Wanting a man to satisfy your sexual needs." Tanya pouted playfully. "I thought I was enough to satisfy you."

'*Like we've done anything like that.*' Tess thought as she smiled back in jest. "Sorry to disappoint you, Tanya."

VI-JUST A DATE

The brightness of the screens hurt his eyes. They made his eyes water at times and sometimes he wished that there was a window in this room. Daniel smiled though. '*That would defeat the purpose of a security room, wouldn't it?*' With more technology came more time staring at screens and staying inside. Daniel whimsically thought of his friend Shawn and his job as a forest ranger. Days for him were filled with walking the trails, greeting visitors, and surprisingly for such a lazy man, building and updating new paths for the future.

Daniel leaned back in his chair and rubbed his tired eyes. Sometimes, Daniel wished he worked outside the museum building, checking the exterior of the building like the old days. But with cameras at every angle, there were less guards needed and less of a need to check those areas. Not all cameras recorded, but they allowed Daniel from this room to see everything on the premises, from the reception in the entryway, to his coworker leaning against the wall when he should have been standing up and watching the people. Daniel spotted a request signal light up and turned to the far-right monitor that showed his other coworker smiling at him from the other side of the security door. Daniel grinned and entered the command to unlock the door for five seconds.

The auditory buzz sounded and in came a burly old timer of their department, with frizzy white hair and though he wouldn't say it, a balding head in the back.

"Hey Daniel. Thanks for covering my shift." The man nodded as Daniel stretched and stood up.

"No problem, Sunny." Daniel replied, hiding a yawn from his coworker with the back of his hand, but all in vain as Sunny smiled towards him.

"Hey Daniel, I mean it, buddy. I couldn't put off seeing my grandkid in her play, but we're so short staffed here that no one else was willing to take over half my day."

"Don't I know it?" Daniel smiled cockily. "You can imagine me asking the other guys."

"What do you mean, Daniel? You haven't taken time off from work since you started here. I mean, I'm sorry, son. Maybe it's my old way of thinking, but Daniel, you need to find a girl to settle down with. "

"What? Sunny, I don't-"

"Kids these days, never settling down. Too picky, not putting in the work that comes with marriage."

"Sunny, I do have a life."

"I see that, Daniel, but are you open to that kind of relationship? You are practically the handyman for your apartment complex, and that's very neighborly of you, but how many girls live there that you think are attractive?"

"Well…. a few……"

"And you've just walked on?"

"Well……yeah." Daniel shrugged. "I guess…. I have been treading my feet a bit. I should be more open to new experiences and rejection."

"Trust me, Daniel. If I hadn't yelled at my wife that day, she spilled spaghetti on me at that dilapidated diner in college," Sunny smiled as Daniel saw the love still in his eyes after so long. "Man, I was a player; I yelled at her and then she yelled at me. And yet…. I went back to that diner every week after that, to complain to her about school, to talk about my regretting always dating the easy girls, and Daniel when she suggested I try a girl like her, it just clicked from then on. You have to sometimes take a leap of faith."

"Dang Sunny……Here I am, off a 12-hour shift, tired as hell, and you give me that deep advice?"

Sunny smiled, shrugging. "I have to practice for Sunday."

"Well, your sermon will surely reach someone." Daniel smiled as he unzipped his jacket and moved into the locker room. He quickly cleaned his face and loosened his tie. Dang that Sunny! Always giving him deep advice like that on life. It was a good thing he had decided to walk home today; he'd need the time to think about that.

"You have a great day, Daniel!" Sara called out as Daniel passed the receptionist area. Daniel would normally slip out the side exit past the gallery to cut across the parking lot, but he smiled wide when he looked ahead and saw a familiar young woman walking towards him, holding her child's hand in her own. As she spotted him, the girl slipped out and ran ahead, latching onto his leg tightly.

"Hi!"

"Hey there." Daniel smiled and rubbed the little girl's head. Daniel turned to look up and smiled at the young mother. "Welcome back. I think you like this museum a lot."

"My daughter would not stop talking and pleading to see you again. And this place was really exciting the last time, though I'm not sure I want to look at the paintings and galleries again."

"You know, the planetarium in the back is just about to start I believe."

"Oh! That's a great idea. Thank you."

"Have a great day!" Daniel smiled as for the second time this month, he waved goodbye to them. He may have a regular event in his life cropping up. He smiled as he turned back to head through the gallery. The woman was attractive, and her little girl was adorable. He'd love to have a family like that someday. Maybe next time he'd ask for her name and-

Daniel's tiredness left him at the heavenly sight that was before him. He was surely wearing blinders as he couldn't help but look at the young woman as if she was an angel. He couldn't believe she had come back so soon, and though her attire had changed, she still looked breathtaking.

Paige, if he remembered correctly, was sitting on the bench facing the wall where the Walter painting was located. His eyes zoomed into her face, her hair now in a braid around her head and down the back in a ponytail, before he scoped out her soft bare neck before they zeroed in on her pink lips. She was talking to someone apparently, as he saw her jaw moving a little as her hands reached along the bottom of the bench, as if memorizing the texture and the feel of the wood underneath her fingers.

He smiled as she was surely imagining touching the painting in her mind, the bench's wood a poor substitute for the frame around the painting. Daniel wondered if she had something with Bluetooth in her ear, but as she turned to look down at the wood, he saw that both her ears were empty. He smiled brighter. Paige talked to herself. That was adorable.

Before he could step forward, he got enraptured once again in the shine of her eyes; those deep blue eyes that he could drown in. With her hair framing her eyes nicely, it just helped to make her face shine. Damn, he had to ruin this vision to talk to her. Daniel smiled bitterly as if he was interrupting a major presentation to the world.

"Paige?"

At the sound of her name, the woman flinched and looked over only to gasp as she immediately stood up. She looked disheveled as she pulled her purse over her shoulder nervously and muttered to herself as she walked towards him. Daniel couldn't help noticing her change in attire to a short skirt that allowed him to see her upper thighs and her knees with soft leather boots just below them. On top was a nondescript black t-shirt covered with a light brown hunting jacket. She looked up, and Daniel sighed at the look of innocence on her face. Her creamy legs and neck were supple and scarless. And yet as she stopped next to him, she looked so vulnerable, opposite to how she'd been when he first met her.

"Hey Daniel…"

"…Hey. What are you doing here?"

Paige blushed before him as if she heard something dirty in her ear, and Daniel saw her hand smoothing back her hair over her ear in embarrassment. Had he said something wrong? He couldn't help but love the tinge of pink on her cheeks that formed as he greeted her. God, even if her hair was…. why, if her hair was colored strawberry blonde, she'd look lovely in this happy embarrassment. *'But she wouldn't think anything dirty, right? Look at her! So innocent.'* Daniel thought as he sighed at the sight.

Paige softly giggled guiltily, making Daniel wonder about the thoughts that went through her head. "You were right." Paige spoke aloud, turning around to point and admire the painting before her once again. "I just couldn't stop thinking about this painting. It is just so special and deep that I just had to see it again."

"Y-yeah." Daniel whispered as Paige bit her lip with another blush, looking as if she had just told an embarrassing secret. He turned to see that while she was looking at the painting, she looked nervous about something else. Immediate protective instincts flooded into his bloodstream. "Paige, is everything-"

"Listen Daniel!" Paige exclaimed, making the people in the room jump at the loud voice and looked annoyingly at the woman as Paige turned back to him. "Maybe I also came here to see you, okay? Maybe I…" Paige sighed in depression of her wording. "Maybe I came on too strong and, um I apologize, but um…would you have time to… dang it!" Paige cursed as she adjusted her purse again on her shoulder and looked down before breathing calmly. "Keep it up Paige!" Daniel smiled, hearing her whisper to encourage herself forward. "Look, do you-I-I-I should have called first!" Paige's eyes widened. "That's right, I had your number…. I-….."

"Paige?" Daniel spoke, Paige jumping out of her inner dialogue.

"Um, did you," Paige took a deep breath. "Want to get that coffee and movie this week?"

Daniel slowly smiled at this girl. So strong and yet….so indecisive. So that confidence and assuredness last week was all her pushing out of her bubble. She was really showing her vulnerabilities today, wasn't she? It made him really like her character. "You're asking me out again?"

"I-yes." Paige sighed tiredly. "I put myself out there last time to be forward, I guess. Oh!" Paige blushed at no doubt the memory of telling him that last time played in her head and Paige looked down to her shoes. "But you already knew that."

".... You know, now would be great."

Paige looked up in surprise and happy awe. "Now? Really? I mean, you don't have to if you don't-"

"I just got off."

"Oh!" Daniel smiled as he watched Paige glance at his tie.

"You thought I was on break?"

"Um," Her cheeks reddened. "I didn't think you were sloppy, so yeah."

"No offense. I stayed until late this morning. So that coffee? Can we make it a lunch date instead?"

Paige's smile grew bigger at his words. "That means yes, right?" She uttered, glee flowing out of her smile, showing her white teeth and dimples before she tried to put on a face of neutrality. "I mean, sure whatever sounds good."

Daniel smiled at the false front and Paige blushed back. He turned slowly and was glad when she looped her arm around his gingerly. Both adults smiled as they walked towards the exit, their steps matching the other's strides as if they were already accustomed to the other.

Paige smiled as Daniel opened the door for her as she stepped out into the sun. "Did you want to drive somewhere for lunch?"

Daniel sourly smiled back. "Actually, I walked here. I live close by, so I don't really have a car."

Some of his neighbors were always telling him to buy one anyways, but Paige just smiled at him, and turned them towards the parking lot down the main staircase. "I have my car."

"Alright then." Daniel followed before they stopped at a sleek black and red striped muscle car. He looked back at the girl as she shortly draped herself over the car and smiled back at him. *'Shy, forward woman, who was into muscle cars? Who was Paige?'* Daniel wondered as he opened the car door and slipped inside.

Paige meanwhile nodded as Daniel suggested a nice place and pulled her car to the exit of the lot. As she waited for the light to turn, she turned to smile at the sight of his fingers twitching on the glove box between them in nervousness. She blushed as she leaned over and intertwined her fingers with his as Daniel looked over in worry.

"Don't worry Daniel I don't bite," Paige smiled, before blushingly exposing her teeth "......unless you're into that kind of thing." The light turned green, and Paige sped down the road, all the while Daniel watched her confident posture at the wheel; now he could add adventurous to the list of things this girl was.

"So, Paige, what have you been up to?" Daniel asked as their waiter took their meals away. He'd prioritized eating more than talking since it had been nearly twenty hours since he last ate, but Paige hadn't seemed to mind one bit, eating her own meal while asking small questions between bites.

"Well as you recall last week that I'm new to town and so I've been looking for places to work. I haven't had any offers yet though, so I'm staying with a... friend."

"Are they close by?"

"Not really in the same neighborhood as your museum, but they told me about the gallery and how I should check it out." Paige mentioned before her fingers found Daniel's atop of her own and smiled at the comforting gesture.

"I'm glad they did." Daniel uttered and Paige bit her lip to smile back at the loving affection in his voice. "Why move though?"

Paige's smile froze in place and Daniel watched as her mood dampened for a bit. Paige looked out the window before sighing. She could at least tell him some of the truth. Just small fibs were part of a relationship, and the best lies held a truth in them.

"...My mom passed away...a few months ago. I just...couldn't stay there any longer. I had to move somewhere else..." Paige's voice simmed to a whisper as the pad of Daniel's thumb rubbed over her knuckles with a sense of similar situations.

"I'm sorry. My parents died too." Daniel whispered back and Paige looked deep into his eyes and widened her own. Here was someone who shared the same loss that she was going through. She could see the same emotions in his eyes; the anger that they were gone, the frustration of talking to them and realizing that you are talking to a memory, the love of their very memories of them.

"She was just...amazing, adopting my sisters and I." Paige sniffled a bit, as she slid the cup of water between her and him.

"Hey...Want to walk?"

Paige nodded happily as each paid for their portion of the meal before stepping back outside and just moving down the sidewalk into the small park next to the restaurant they'd stopped at. They didn't really talk, but Paige was grateful for that after the emotions she was feeling right now. This comfortable silence was not awkward at all, and she truly felt safe and comforted. *'Was this what mom meant by love?'* She wondered.

Daniel felt Paige slip closer into his shoulder and smiled as she looked up at him from the edge of his shoulder. "Can I ask you a serious question?"

"Shoot."

Paige didn't ask right away. She thought long and hard of how to phrase the question. She didn't have to ask him, but he was just so genuine and heart-warming that she wanted to know. "...Before my mom died, she told me that in the end she wished she'd found love over money. Do you think money is important?" Paige looked up cringing. *'Talking about money on a first date? Great job, Paige.'*

She watched Daniel's eyes widen at the question and exhaled exasperated out through his mouth. "Wow. That's a difficult question for a first date." But Daniel smiled. "You're lucky that I like a challenge." Paige smiled back and watched him shrug. "I mean, money rules the world and all, but not for me! I'd choose to love any day of the week. But it's still hard."

Paige had to admit that she was intrigued. Surely there was more to the answer than that. "Explain."

Daniel grinned at her as they passed by the lake and looked over it as they made their way to the movie theater across from the park. "Honestly, I don't care for money. I have a good job, I live in an okay apartment close to where I work, so I'm fortunate enough. My grocery store has nice people who talk to me every week about their days."

He shrugged. "After all that, I mean, I guess I just need a soulmate and-...no, that's not right." Daniel's eyes turned somber. "You remember your mom's laughter when you did something crazy and foolish?" Paige smiled brighter and nodded. "That's what I think love is; happy in any situation, trust that everything is going to be okay. When I think of love in a person; I'd like a girlfriend to spend time with, to be foolish with and just smile with. I don't have many friends; never made too many deep relationships that lasted through the years. But that girlfriend; she'd be strong and make my brain go dead to the world."

Paige's eyes shot up and looked at him in shock. "Dead? What do you mean?"

Daniel sighed as they stopped across the street from the theater. "Like...I can look into her eyes, I can feel her body's heartbeat, and I'm trying to listen to what they say.... but my brain isn't working right. I can't get over how lucky I am to be with her."

"Oh?" Paige smiled devilishly. "Then I suppose I should see what this does."

"What does?" Daniel asked, completely confused as Paige leaned up and planted her lips firmly upon his as her arms wrapped around his neck to pull him close.

Daniel was floored! This was how it felt to kiss a girl? This...feeling of completeness and yet agonizing yearning for more pressure. This pleasurable feeling was waning as he stared open eyed as Paige closed her eyes and began to back up. He didn't want this amazing feeling to end, so he leaned in and tried to pucker his lips and began to kiss back awkwardly.

He could feel it; Paige's smile growing into the kiss at his inexperience, but as his hands wrapped around her back and took the chance to hold her, his hand slipped, as he inadvertently stroked over her ass; Paige mewled as he deepened the kiss, and he smiled into the kiss himself as Paige leaned back, keeping her hands on the back of his neck, and leaning into his arms.

"How was that?" Paige asked confidently as she looked at Daniel's eyes, glazed over and smiling like an idiot. Paige was happily surprised by Daniel's daring side. Not many guys would chance a grab at her ass, but she could tell right away that he had been simply trying to hold her. It felt nice to be touched with such gentle, firm hands, and his kissing.... well....it was interesting to say the least.

As Daniel's eyes deglazed from the experience, Paige grinned in triumph. "So? Did I turn your brain into mush?" As he failed to respond, she smiled even larger. "Well then, I suppose I'm just the girl you're looking for."

Daniel blushed deeply and leaned forward as he brushed his nose lightly against Paige's. "It's just that I've never kissed a girl before."

"Well, you seemed like a good kisser to me." Paige whispered seductively, leaning in to kiss the edge of his lips. "Maybe you just need more practice?"

Daniel smiled at the comforting offer she gave and leaned in to practice kissing this girl that drove him crazy for just a little longer.

VII—CHANGE OF PLANS

Blood spurts out of his body, slashing out ten feet and sprays all over the glass, bathing the viewers in a classic sight of murder on scene. The man turned his eyes as he died to the room's window watching as inside, the two main characters made love on the hotel bed.

It was the passion of the movie that was stuck in Daniel's eyes as he tried in vain to watch it. He had to pay attention to the plot and the visuals so that he could talk about it after it was over. But how could he when a set of puckered lips suctioned on and off along his neck, making sweet noises that only an hour ago, he'd never heard so intently before.

Daniel held in a groan as Paige trailed up and down, her attention clearly not on the movie. They had missed the previews, honestly his favorite part of going to the movies, because they'd been sucking face outside the theater for a good thirty minutes. Just as Paige slowed her kissing and turned back to the screen, he couldn't help but try to catch his breath. Thirty minutes to practice kissing or watching previews. Any man who favored the latter was an idiot, and Paige knew how to kiss. He'd truly learned a lot from her since then.

Just as the lovers on screen parted and began to talk about the ordeal they were about to go through, Daniel finally felt his lower half begin to calm down. This girl was shy and adventurous. She was demure and crafty, and she drove him up the wall trying to figure her out. Just as Daniel finally caught his breath, he let out a gasp and looked down as a feminine hand deftly slid along his thigh, not on the inside, but not on the outside either. She continued to stroke the area across the line, a grey zone that he wasn't sure if she would cross or not.

As Paige laid her head on his shoulder and got comfortable, Daniel knew that he was slowly losing his mind. Before the kiss; they'd been stumbling, cute and nervous. That kiss had surged them forth into that intimate couple who couldn't take their hands off each other; the kind that Daniel had envied to be like so much in high school. It was like he was in that relationship of teenagers that got pregnant and were so full of love and didn't care who sees it; the kind of love that could produce a future.

For once in his life, he was wondering if this would lead to sex. Was Paige experienced in that? Where did she like to be touched? He'd better figure it out, so that he didn't look pathetic for his first time. By the way they were kissing, Paige was hopefully glad of his answer for this date and so had rewarded him with close intimacy from his neck to his thigh. Daniel looked down at her idle hand and then up to her face. He looked at her as his heartbeat increased tenfold. God...he was falling too fast, wasn't he?

Paige felt so comfortable on her date's shoulder. People didn't have comfy shoulders; they were bony and angled poorly and there was never enough softness. But for some reason, whatever the reason was, Paige was positioned just perfectly on Daniel's shoulder and neck. When she had decided to scope out the museum, she did not expect to run into him again. She was just supposed to place some things and take some measurements for their plan and maybe steal an employee list off the receptionist's computer. Not go on a date.

'But this is turning into such a nice date.' Paige sighed into the crook of his neck and thought of taking a pleasant nap. She had no doubt that Daniel wouldn't take advantage of her, and all the trust that he'd stay there watching over her. It was so pleasant around him; it was intoxicating. When he had admitted never kissing a girl, something obscene and powerful had filled her chest. In that knowledge, she had begun to teach him how to kiss and where to touch her, as if this would lead to sex. She didn't know, but she was edging into it. The idea of

being the dominant one with the experience teaching him to pleasure her; that was an intoxicating feeling indeed.

Paige's eyes fluttered open as careful masculine fingers lightly stroked her idle hand. She waited with bated breath as she watched his fingers nervously slide over her thumb and knuckles, before he tickled her, and she flinched. Daniel's hand slid off for a second, but after another ten seconds he surged forward with more confidence. His fingers stroked across the back of her palm and rested on top of her, his fingers just shy of resting along the spaces between her fingers.

Paige's breath caught in her throat. Why did he stop intertwining their fingers? She wanted them together as close as possible-.... Paige kept her eyes on the screen as she slid her hand around and intertwined their fingers together herself. She'd have to show this guy how she liked things. Why did she relish this feeling? She hadn't done so with previous marks before. Usually, it was hot and heavy or not interested at all. Too hot or too cold. This just felt…...nice.

Paige squeezed Daniel's thigh as he shivered with a gentle smile as she settled back into the crook of his neck. She'd have to be careful with this one. This guy was just a civilian; innocent and filled with honesty as if this personality of theirs was the only one they had. This feeling was too pleasant for her to drown herself in. If she didn't watch herself and these feelings, this persona could balloon out of control and this con could wither away. Paige smelled his cologne and whimpered. He smelled so nice. If she wasn't careful, this could turn…real…...

"That was nice." Paige mentioned as they walked down a block of small shops that were clearly aged and trying to stay in business. This road less traveled, and yet for the date these two were on, the chance to be alone on an empty street was a wonderful feeling.

"It was." Daniel nodded.

"You live close by, right?" Paige asked. "Since you don't have a car?"

"I could take public transportation." Daniel grinned widely but Paige smiled sourly and waited for him to confess. "No, I live only a block away actually."

"Want me to walk with you there?" Paige asked, and they waited for the other to answer yes or no. Paige smiled. "I don't plan on coming inside, if you're worried." She clarified.

'But something may happen when we end up there.' Both thought as they started to walk again.

"I'd like the company." Daniel smiled. Paige wrapped her arms around his bicep, and they continued their walk, though slower than before. Neither really wanted this date to end.

A thought reminded her of a question and Paige cocked her head to the side. "You know, Daniel. I don't know exactly what you do at the museum. I mean, you fix cameras."

"Well, I'm kind of a jack of all trades I suppose at my job. I took enough online classes to get a pretty good concept of technical stuff, so it's just easier for the museum to have me stay late and fix things up. Really, our system keeps shuddering in different areas recently, so I've been pulling a lot of hours." Daniel mentioned before blushing. "Sorry. Too much?"

"I like to hear about the details of your day." Paige cooed as Daniel smiled at the comforting gesture.

"Really, I'm just a security guard at a nice museum with wonderful visitors."

"Never want to run the place. Be the big boss?"

Daniel shrugged as they hit his apartment complex and came to a standstill. "Well, here I am."

"............ Here you are." The two of them edged closer with their heads, their lips begging for a repeat. "Which one?" Paige breathed as Daniel lifted his arm to point out the tallest floor and the corner at that.

"Wow. Top floor. Must be like a penthouse. You must be a good negotiator to get such a nice deal."

"Don't know….it was the one available…...Well um... "

"…………. Yeah……………..."

Neither had anything else to say. The date was over. He was here, and he respected her enough to not ask her inside for an evening of awful, first time, lovemaking. Daniel blushed. God, this was awkward. Why was he hesitating? He just needed to ask for another date.

Paige smiled up at him. "Well, Daniel……. I had a great time but-"

'Shoot! The blow off! What was wrong with me?' Daniel freaked inside his head at the 'But' word.

"Oh gosh. I'm sorry if I moved too fast!" Daniel blurted out, but Paige widened her own eyes at the outburst.

"No!" Paige giggled as she covered his lips with her finger, shutting him up as she stepped even closer to him and intertwined their hands together. "You were so nice and pleasant, Daniel."

"What I was saying was that I had a great time, but I do have somewhere to be tonight."

"Oh…."

"Also…. You're most definitely my type of boyfriend." Paige blushed as soon as she said boyfriend. *'I've never used this card before.'*

Daniel jumped at the…. confession. *'That was a confession, right?'*

"…. I was hoping we could go out again."

"You're asking me again?" Daniel uttered before his lizard brain caught up with her offer. "You'd want to do this again?"

Paige smiled and leaned up with her hands, using them to fix his tie for him that had been loose all night. "And this time, I promise I'll call." She whispered, their lips just an inch apart.

"I'd like that." Daniel whispered back. "Good night." He began to pull away, but Paige pouted as she pulled him closer, draping her arms around his neck, dipping his head down to within half an inch of her lips.

Paige quivered. *Does this guy really not understand how much I like kissing him?* It was taking all of her willpower to only go halfway towards him, her eyes screaming with want at him to complete the rest of the journey with her.

"If we are set on another date….and if we are going out on a more...deep connection, then the girl needs her goodbye kiss."

"Oh?" Daniel quirked his eye before Paige's pink tongue slid out of her lip and his eyes widened at the insinuation. "Oh!" He uttered and smiled wide as he finally closed the distance, kissing deeply as their bodies pressed tight together. Daniel tried out that move she'd shown him earlier today and was rewarded with a surprised, but content moan from his girlfriend.

'Girlfriend'...oh boy. He finally had a girlfriend. He couldn't wait for the next high school reunion and rub it in his bullies faces and- *'What the hell?!?' 'Daniel* widened his eyes as the trick he'd learned had only helped Paige as she slipped her tongue inside his mouth, twisting around his own tongue and stroking it, eliciting a moan from him as well.

Just as he tried to reciprocate, Paige slid down and away from him, her hair a mess compared to before, his hair matching hers, and their faces red with blushes as saliva broke upon his lips from her tongue in his.

"That's for the amazing date." Paige uttered softly, patting down his hair for him as she smiled devilishly. "Perhaps after the next one, I can show you some other things one can do with a trained tongue."

Paige turned after that, leaving quickly towards the end of the street around it. She took one last glance at her...boyfriend and saw him staying rooted to the spot, looking in a world of his own and looked down with a satisfied smile as she took the long way home.

She had taught him that move with his lips before they went into the theater, and he'd already mastered it. She'd never had someone kiss her back with her own weapon before, and she shuddered at what she could feel if she taught him more. Despite what Daniel lacked in his confidence, he was definitely a good kisser. *'Shame.'* Paige frowned. *'I feel like a tease……I should have uttered goodnight instead.'*

It took twenty minutes for her to make it back to her car and another ten minutes to get back to her home and workplace. She parked her car in the warehouse in the back and closed her door before edging around the concrete stairwell and entered the building's open core where Tanya stood there tapping her foot nervously.

"Finally!" Tanya sighed overdramatically and moved over to her partner in crime as Tess slid off her hunting jacket and moved over to a drawer next to one of the couches. "You took your earpiece out! I need to know when you plan to go in the black, Tess."

"Yeah, well I don't need you hearing every little thing I utter." Tess shivered, grabbing a comfy sweater, and slid it on. "Did you turn the AC up to the max again?"

"Yeah, I have my computers running through an encryption software for a client, and the heat would fry my board otherwise." Tanya shrugged as Tess looked at one of five worktables Tanya used where she had connected ten laptops together, using them as a homemade supercomputer. Tess smiled. Tanya had put all these computers together from scrap and a torch. Her sister did everything for her.

"You could have just installed another fan to the towers." Tess picked at while Tanya scowled.

"I don't need you nitpicking at my work. Speaking of work," Tanya grinned. "How'd it go?" She asked impishly. "Was he a gentleman, or did he fuck you silly?"

Tess held her tongue on her date, and bit back. "All those words you were whispering in my ear were the reason I took it out."

"Oh Daniel!" Tanya exclaimed playfully, making Tess blush. "Right there, Daniel!" Tanya recalled from her memory over the last week giggling. "You were dreaming about him in your sleep for days, Tess. And you're not easy to please either, so….? How did it go?" She drawled.

Tess looked at Tanya with a neutral face for all of two seconds before a silly, stupid smile appeared on her face. "He was an innocent, lovestruck puppy, and we didn't do it."

Tanya sighed with a depressed smile at the lack of dirty details. "Oh well. Anything else you have for me?"

"Yeah…. He's a Tech Guy." Tess simmered as the excited face on Tanya faded as black-eyed exhaustion flooded into her face, past her makeup.

"Well…. That's just great!" Tanya complained as she fell across the arm of the couch and sunk her whole body into the cushions and slung her slim arm over her eyes before cackling sadly. "There goes Plan Q!!"

"It's just another backup plan, Tanya."

"But we keep having to change them! If your boy toy is a tech, then that means that none of my computer skills will work then! All our plans include getting access to those cameras and the system. As it is, we can only see the painting with the single wire you got in for me as they found the malware, I was able to install, no doubt thanks to your Romeo."

Tanya wailed into a plush pillow. "I mean, I was supposed to go in as the repairmen and fix all the cameras so that we could go in undetected. They would erase our footprints as we moved in. I mean, Tess, it's been weeks, and this is our only clue to him! Now we have nothing but a good time!"

Tess blushed at Tanya's accusation, but she soon smiled herself as she sat down beside Tanya and rubbed through her hair, Tanya loving this when they grew up whenever she got depressed, but her smile was on the events of the last four hours. It was the best time she'd ever had for a first date.

As Tanya breathed out her exhaustion, Tess looked at the ceiling and smiled, almost lovingly. It was a great time she had this morning. In fact, she had loved the sole dedication Daniel had given to her. He was so enamored with her; she could have sworn that he didn't even give anything else his attention. It was…. a sobering thought for Tess, butterflies erupting every time he'd listen to her. It was nice to have a guy focus on her movements, on her words.

She paused in her memory at her question to Daniel on the question over love and money. Tess raised her left hand and looked at it; where he'd held it as she mentioned her mother. He was a steady rock to support her, to cling to in the worst of storms. She may just want to take that rock with her, to keep herself rooted a little bit more deeply.

'Wait a minute!' Tess froze and backtracked, her mind whirring. *'He never took his attention away from me.'*

Tess's white teeth shined brightly as she bent low to kiss her partner's forehead. "You know Tanya; maybe we're thinking about this the wrong way."

Tanya opened her eyes inquisitively. "What do you mean?"

Tess smiled. "Well, he likes me a lot. During the impromptu date, he never took his eyes off me. If I could distract him, then you can do the theft instead."

Tanya sputtered out incoherent words as she sat up, her eyes denying the content smile on Tess's face. "But you've always done the thieving for the heists, Tess! You've done tons of heists, and they've all been perfect!"

Tess shrugged as she stood up and slid around the couch. "Plans change, Tanya. You need to be flexible."

"Oh, I'm plenty flexible!" Tanya called out and Tess glanced back at her sister's slim, toned body, still only in a sports bra and underwear even with the AC on max, but a body that could fit in the smallest of spaces, and one that made men drool over.

"I can see that." Tess nodded as she went to a computer on one of the furthest tables Tanya had set up away from the rest, and began looking through designs, pulling up files that shot onto the wall in front of the screen, a small projector showing her the pictures in more detail, "but you still have to do it."

"Why are you going through my projects?" Tanya bemoaned as she turned on the couch to look over the top with just her murky eyes peeking over. "Those are all failures. I can't get any of those designs to work."

"You have access to the museum's schedule, right?"

"Well, yeah. That's a simple excel file. They didn't even put it behind the firewall."

"Then this will work."

"Tess, just do the thieving. Let me distract your boy."

"No." Tess refuted resolutely; Tanya heard a sense of possessiveness layered into her voice. "He's not the kind of guy who sees multiple girls. You'd just spook him. Besides, I've done your job before."

Tanya's thoughts derailed at that comment as she stood up to follow her sister to the table. "Okay! One; That so doesn't count!! I was in Prague being shot at, Tess! Two; that was an emergency because we were double-crossed. And Three; Those were real bullets, Tess!" Tanya yelled vehemently at her sister before her fingers stiffened. "Besides," Tanya whispered, "You know I freeze up being in the thick of it; I don't do well being on scene."

Just as she ended her argument, Tanya looked up at the wall as Tess stopped skimming and nodded at a particular design. "That could work."

Tanya widened her eyes as Tess began nodding her head. She knew what was coming. "Tess-No! I can't! - I can't possibly- "

"Make this work by Friday, okay?" Tess smiled as she stood up and moved away as Tanya bulged her eyes.

"Three days?!? Are you insane?!? I've been working on that thing for months and it's burned three sets of my lingerie! It won't work. Think of something else." Tanya closed her eyes, shuddering breaths edging out of her throat, but as she opened them again, her sister was there handing her pliers. ".... It'll never work."

"It will, Tanya. I trust your gadgets. They have never failed us before."

"And what if I can't?"

Tess shrugged and fell back against the couch, taking the spot where Tanya had laid previously. "Then we're screwed."

Tanya blubbered like a guppy for ten seconds before she harshly hissed towards her sister and moved towards another table. Tess watched her sister mutter about unfair expectations as she began to go through drawers and pull out the things she'd need to work on. It was unfair of her to demand so much…. but Tanya did best when under stress. Tess would know….as any team leader did.

VIII-THE HEIST

The moon was new tonight, casting darkness upon this section of the world. Most people preferred the full moon each month as it cast light upon the ground where people could take moonlit hikes and see far away. Daniel preferred a full moon as well, but what he preferred right now did not matter. Why? Because right now, he wanted to be anywhere but here at work.

The night shifts. Endless, standard, and completely boring. Daniel remembered when there were at least two guards on the shift, one in the guard booth, and one in the galleries checking for everything in place. He had loved that; going from gallery to gallery and just looking at the amazing works of art with no need to hurry. But now, he was the only one, staring at the images relaying their mechanical eyes back to his screens, four cameras to each screen on his displays.

Daniel sighed into his wheely chair. With technology came efficiency, but what also came were…...budget cuts. He couldn't count how many people every day he asked to obey the rules and not take photos of the paintings. They posted them online to be fun and show off, but over the years, people went less to museums as they could just look for them online. His museum was community focused and needed the money to support the staff. And with technology came less guards and more cameras.

Daniel shook his head at the thought going around that instead of guards, the board was going to hire retired people who were avid art lovers to sit in the galleries and watch the people. Like they could have any authority to tell a guest to please put away their phones. But oh well! The point was that Daniel was the only one in the entire building, and because he was the only one, he couldn't ask another guard to cover him to sneak off and be with his girlfriend!

That's right! Paige had called him the morning after their date, and they had talked for hours about more than a few sensitive topics, from governments to adopting puppies who came from bad homes. They spoke more on money, and Daniel wondered if his answer to love last Tuesday had enamored Paige into seeking another answer from him.

Paige had called twice after that, on Thursday and again this morning, and just hearing her voice was so relaxing and yet...so enticing. Paige on Thursday had stopped by his place, and the things he had imagined doing to her on his bed as she sat there was so hard to keep himself back from pulling Paige deeper into his chest.

She was intoxicating is what she was. He had yesterday off, and her interview had fallen through as they found someone better and cancelled her interview altogether, so time was not wasted at all. But the little things she had done to him drove his internal pressures to the max. She had shown up in a blazer at his door, her long skirt down to her feet but that slit in the side as she sat on his bed had looked so tantalizing, her bare thigh peeking out with every movement she made.

In all, they had talked for so long, only kissed a little, and she had left at eleven at night, having spent both lunch and dinner just talking about life and anything that came into their minds. They hadn't even turned on the tv or a laptop to watch videos. It was…. a great feeling to talk and not worry about what one said.

But that call this morning; he had forgotten that he had work tonight, the boss sending him a change in schedule Wednesday morning, and he was so annoyed that someone had decided to give him Saturday off and not Friday. But why care when Paige had called him this morning? Well, because she had mentioned how good he was respecting her body yesterday, but that…. she was hoping he would have read the signs better, reminding him that she was sitting on his bed.

Daniel groaned through his teeth at that chance to touch her body. He thought he was supposed to hold back, but he should have made his move! And then the worst part of the morning was offered to him. Paige had been quieter on the phone, and she sounded just a little nervous. But she had…asked if he wanted to come over and practice kissing some more, and… well be more physical. By come over, she meant asking him to her house. And now…. he had had to tell his week-old girlfriend no and reject her offer for physical affection! God, for the first time in nearly a year, he cursed his job and its random hours.

He sighed and rubbed at his eyes. Only a week he'd been dating her. Now, to be fair he'd known her for two, maybe three weeks, but he was falling hard. He saw Paige everywhere! He saw her in his dreams, he saw her on his phone from the few pictures he now had, he sometimes even saw her at---

"No way. "Daniel uttered. If he was a smoker like half his coworkers, the cigarette would have dropped from his mouth. She was not here. That was impossible. And yet as he clicked to enlarge the backside camera, he could only lean in and believe his eyes. There was his girlfriend edging down the back alleyway, almost as if hiding. She was wearing a nice knee length coat and hiding her body, but he'd recognize that brunette crown braid anywhere. Paige edged over the corner of the camera, but Daniel enlarged the next camera and… she was gone! Daniel shook his head. "Where did she-"

Oh God. There she was, standing at the back door itself. Daniel watched her eyes shift back and forth, looking at his bike locked next to it before she looked straight at the camera and shyly waved at it. No way. This was crazy! He knew that most guards here barely checked the external cameras. They didn't record because of the numerous complaints from the apartments around them and besides that, all the doors were armed. The walls had motion sensors installed. The hallways and galleries had lasers crisscrossing all over the place so even the guards couldn't get through without setting an alarm. They couldn't chance a call to the police for someone outside doing nothing wrong but waving at a camera.

Before she could wave a third time at him, Daniel was out of his seat and out of the security door, propping it open with a book, as was standard if the guards had to absolutely use the bathroom. He walked quickly down the hallway and halted at the exit door. "I…. really shouldn't do this." Daniel breathed and pressed his key card on the door. The beep sounded and Daniel edged the door open and took in the ethereal glow of Paige's embarrassed and hopeful face as she turned to face him, her hair spilling around her neck.

"Paige? What are you doing here?"

The look of a guilty lady was easy to see on her face, as Paige lowered her face into her scarf. "I um...I was in the neighborhood, just checking out the bar down the hill, and um...well, you said you'd be working." Tess mumbled. "I was wondering if you wanted to get a hot chocolate or something?"

Daniel held in butterflies that really wanted to come out. This girl was a hurricane; first she was forward and confident, telling him to come over tonight, but now that he had told her no, she was here in front of him, shy but hopeful to be with him. He could predict her path in a wide range of things, but it was the little things she did, like hoping to go for a drink, that made his heart melt. If he was honest, she was dangerous, and it was futile to deny her completely, and would he? Daniel was addicted; he was addicted to her every move.

"I really can't, Paige."

"Not for like, twenty minutes?"

"I'm the only one here."

If she had animal ears, they would have flopped down on her head. As it was, her eyes and body dropped down at the rejection of her offer. Daniel felt guilt surge through his system; She had obviously come all the way here, in the middle of the night, just hoping to have some time with him, and he really didn't want to turn her away.

"Oh.... I suppose I should have just waited for tomorrow. That's what we said we'd do. I just...I wanted to touch your hand is all." Paige whispered, reaching forward to skim her fingers lightly on his. "I'll just...talk to you tomorrow, I guess." Paige finished as she turned around.

"Wait!" A naughty thought crept into his mind as he surged over and grasped her hand, holding it tightly within his own. "I really shouldn't but...y-you want to see where I work?"

"Really? Is that allowed?"

"Definitely not."

"I don't want to get you in any trouble."

"I'm in trouble just by opening this door." Daniel grinned sourly. Paige bit her lower lip and smiled brightly as she reached up to her neck, flicking at the zipper of a choker collar on her neck that he had failed to notice. As Daniel turned around, he missed the reflective lens on the pendant on her neck and the small flesh colored wire taped to the underside of her choker.

Daniel leaned back to let her pass through the door, but as she passed, Paige's lips met his own in a flash, and immediately his body surged forward, pushing Paige back into the steel door frame, Paige hissing as the protruding metal slammed into her back.

"Sorry!" Daniel whispered as he pulled back, Paige shaking out her hands that had been behind her to ease the pain.

"No worries. I think it's obvious already how...addictive kissing the other is." Paige admitted with a soft whisper.

Daniel widened his eyes at the admittance. "You like kissing me?"

Paige shook her head giggling. "No... I happen to love kissing you. Hence why I couldn't resist. But maybe after we head inside? It's cold out here."

"R-Right." Daniel smiled and led her down the hall, hearing the lock click in place. His relief guard wasn't due for six hours. Honestly, he had all the time in the world to spend with his girlfriend, but he'd best keep a clock around; they seemed to have trouble keeping track of the time as a couple.

Daniel edged in front of her, and yes. He straightened his back to look taller; he wanted to look good for her. He edged her over to the security door, but her eyes looked confused as he followed her view to the door at the end of the hall.

"We can't go into the gallery? Maybe we could look at the painting again?"

"You really like it, huh?"

Paige smiled brightly. "I'm starting to wish I had a huge load of money right now so that I could buy it."

"Well, then you'd need five hundred thousand to start the negotiations."

"Hundred?" Paige looked over aghast. "That's...actually, I could imagine that."

Daniel chuckled. "Anyways, I already set the sensors for the night. The police are required to check on us even if they are turned off before 5am."

Paige smiled wistfully. "Shame. I thought we might kiss in front of that painting someday."

"Someday may come." Daniel uttered happily, nudging the book aside as he pushed the door open and walked into the room with Paige behind him.

"So, you're saying that you activated a whole laser grid and motion sensors so sensitive they activate at the movement of a fly?"

"No." Daniel chuckled. "That's too sensitive. Even this nice place still gets flies."

"Oh my god!" Paige exclaimed and hugged his arm, her breasts gobbling up his arm, making him blush as she surged forward into the room and stopped giddily at the numerous buttons and switches. You really do have some high-tech stuff in here! Is that a ball to angle the cameras? Oh, look at those monitors!"

Daniel watched her happily until she leaned forward and alarmed, he surged forward. "Paige, don't lean over them!"

"Huh?" Paige turned, just as she slipped on the desk and her hand pressed down on a button. Daniel quickly pulled her to the side and looked down for the button she'd pressed. "Sorry! What did I do?"

Daniel sighed as he entered his code and the button's code recycled back into standby. "Nothing. Just...it's important to not touch this stuff."

At the back door, nothing made a sound as the metal rectangle backed into the hallway, the door handle staying in place, but pushed open, nonetheless. A black clothed figure quickly slunk inside as Tanya rushed to pull silver sheets and silver poles inside the gap. She pressed a button on the poles as they expanded to form a pointed roof design seven feet long that covered the floor to halfway up the ceiling. Tanya smiled as the tablet she had prepped before she entered activated, it's camera taking constant pictures at the door and hallway.

She sighed as she waited a minute, looking through the thin material to see if the security door opened. It did not, and Tanya couldn't believe this thing worked as she reached back to the other side of the door and pulled out a modified skateboard built for the length of her body with larger wheels, freshly oiled. Tanya shut the door and bent down to lay across it. Tanya slowly, inch by inch angled the frame over herself, and touched her neck, activating the speaker on her neck.

"Inside. Making way to the atrium now." Tanya whispered as she edged down the wall, crawling at a turtle's pace.

"Shouldn't that have a safety button or something?" Paige questioned as Daniel looked relieved at her.

Daniel smiled at the question. "It normally has a case over it and everyone knows not to touch the red button, but then again, you shouldn't be in here."

Paige blushed and bit her lips seductively, causing Daniel to hold back his lust. "I'm sorry." She emphasized by wiggling her petite frame along his side, making him hot under his collar.

Daniel gulped. "Just don't... touch anything, okay?"

Daniel leaned in as he cupped her cheeks fondly, his focus deeply and solely on her. Paige's eyes seared deep into his own before she cast a glance at the hallway camera and giggled, before leaning forward and bit his lip playfully.

"You know, I've never…. made out in a museum before?"

Daniel gulped. Like he was going to say no to that. Daniel leaned in; his lips eager to practice.

At the sound of giggles in her ear, Tanya sighed happily and continued past the security door towards the main reception hall. That giggle told her that she wasn't seen on the cameras in the room, and she was proud that her device was working as she'd planned. But damn was she annoyed at Tess right now!

Sure, the device was working. Sure, she had finally developed a fabric that reflected to the cameras only the image that she wanted them to see, or in fact, to ignore the idea that anything had changed at all. But Tanya muttered to herself as she continued to push herself forward. Tess just had to rush this plan and hope that Tanya was smart enough to find a way.

She hated this plan! Her muscles yelled at her to stop after only five minutes. She only worked out when she had to, and when it called for her body to be maintained. This is why she wanted to fix the cameras to begin with! She had finally made this device work just this morning, and Tess had immediately called and set up the guilt with Daniel. Tanya had even concocted the pheromones that were on Tess's neck now, enticing the guard to pounce her friend in the secure booth.

So instead of the fit, expert, done it a million times Tess, here Tanya was, the usual kissing, sucking faced distraction, sliding no more than five feet every minute across the hallway floor, her muscles screaming at her for every second that she held herself and the poles up. After ten minutes, Tanya reached the staircase and flexed her arms out before sliding the wheels ever so slowly down the museum steps.

Tanya slid carefully from step to step, whimpering silently every time the board hit her chest. Her upper figure was sensitive damnit! And she was going to massage out the bruises when all this was over; that and a lot of alcohol. As Tanya reached the last step, a sudden drawn-out moan sounded loudly in her ear. '*Oh my god! Is she-*' "Tess, please tell me you're not-Ah!"

With Tanya's mind reeling from what her sister was doing, her hand slipped on the last perch and down she went the last ten inches to the floor, but her board banged on the ground, and flipped straight back...directly into Tanya's chin.

"MMMMmmmmm!!!" Tanya moaned and groaned into her throat, holding her chin with her hand as she hissed at the pain.

"You okay?" Tanya heard the guard ask in her earpiece.

"Yeah! Sorry but not…. not that way. Just…let me show you what I mean." She heard Tess assure him that nothing was wrong…and assuring her sister that she was Not having sex with the mark.

After just thirty seconds, Tanya blinked back tears and pain as she pushed on past the lobby towards the first gallery. Tanya cast a glance outside and breathed out her worries. Cameras she could sneak past, lasers she could reflect with the right material, but if anyone tried to look through those entrance doors right now, they'd see a crazy skater girl with a weird solar frame around her.

Finally, thirty minutes after she had entered the premises, she edged into the gallery where before her was the Walter painting. Now, she needed the right angles to hide herself while she did her work. "Tess, I need the angles…" Tanya whispered only for smacking and groans to fill her ears. "Now! She hissed, ending the lip lock sounds on the other end.

Paige heard her sister hiss at her and nodded her head as she backed up, and smiled at a sex crazed haired Daniel, who smiled at her like she was a euphoric angel. Oh, how devilish her mind could work.

"Daniel," Paige breathed, stealing another breath out of her mark's lips. "How about we take a picture to celebrate?"

"Here?" Daniel breathed, his eyes dilated and full of raging hormones. Paige felt bad about using the pheromones right now. She really didn't need to use them; Daniel already wanted to jump her and had been holding back since their date, but Tanya had insisted that this heist could take hours, and while Tess was sure she could keep Daniel's attention, she couldn't promise she could distract him for that long.

Daniel nodded excitedly as Paige turned around and aimed her camera between them and kissed his cheek. "Besides, this is kind of naughty, isn't it?" She whispered huskily as she lowered her hand between his thighs, Daniel's eyes bulging as he pulled her closer and began to kiss along her neck. "Ohhhhh…."

Meanwhile, Tanya smiled appreciatively as the pictures came to her. She couldn't have done it better herself if she tried. Tanya sighed as she inputted the angles into her device as the poles extended out to cover the camera angles. The hallways and front lobby had only one camera to block but this room had three, and as Tanya watched, the poles bent and hid the painting from view, showing the multiple cameras a picture of how it looked; how it had looked every night since it was installed here.

But back to thinking about her sister, Tess was always great at the art of the con. Take her on a real date back in high school and she steps on the guy's foot or insults him to his face but insert her in the hussle or a meeting with ulterior motives, and she walks out with money in her pockets. Tanya smiled as she glanced back down at the picture. She almost looked truly happy with that guard. It looked so real, like she… Tanya grinned impishly. Maybe her sister finally found a guy worth exposing herself to.

Tanya slinked forward to the wooden bench, before she slid the side paneling over until a gap appeared. A toothy grin appeared. It only took Tess three times to hide the equipment inside this wooden seat of the gallery. She didn't know of anyone else who could unglue the side panel so quickly and under the watchful eye of cameras. Tanya pulled out the bag of contents she needed from wires and glue to a box cutter. Once everything was set up, Tanya turned to the painting and edged her nose to an inch of the painting and smelled the canvas, shedding a single tear down her right cheek.

"I'm sorry Mom," Tanya whispered, and pierced the canvas edge with the box cutter. "Beginning to extract."

As Tanya worked, she listened to her partner in crime work, but for the guy being played on, he was thinking that he was the luckiest man in the world. Daniel couldn't believe that this was really happening.

"Oh Daniel~....Right there~...." He heard the amazing voice of his girl moan into his ear. How could he really be sitting here, happily trapped as Paige straddled his lap, her legs on either side of his own, and grinding heavily on his crotch. God! She was a beautiful Valkyrie who came to take his soul to Valhalla.

As Paige giggled into his ear, Daniel tried his best to kiss at the nape of her exposed neck. Gone was her trench coat upon the floor around his feet. Now she exposed her white blouse and black pencil skirt to his hungry eyes, and his eyes and hands could not remove his attention away from her body. He just hoped that he was learning to lavish Paige in kisses that were worthy of her.

Paige for her part listened in one ear as Tanya drilled away and in another ear as Daniel sucked lightly on her neck. Paige giggled softly as she backed up and undid her top button, exposing the top of her cleavage and the outline of her red lacy bra, as Daniel indeed learned quickly how to kiss her. "You mind trying something more...risqué?"

Paige didn't have to wait a single second before Daniel's mouth dipped lower to trail down towards her upper chest. Paige felt her toes curl as she felt Daniel's hands skim over her ass but denied her the pleasure of grabbing at them. Paige sighed sadly. She had worn a skirt hoping he'd touch there. It happened to be her best feature. Perhaps she just had to incentivize him otherwise.

Daniel gasped as Paige's hands slipped his uniform out of his pants and began to unbutton his shirt as well. Her hands seemed in a frenzy and Daniel only followed in kind. His hands shot forward to pull her body deeper into his, and Daniel awed as his palm turned rogue and slipped underneath the skirt and gripped the back flesh of his girlfriend's ass. How could a girl's bottom feel so amazing? It was... exhilarating.

And when Paige groaned again, her voice was...needy, and wanton lust shot through her; he could tell, as she grinded deeper into his hands and her lips delved deeply into his own. Daniel's eyes shot open in realization of her intentions. Was he seriously going to lose his virginity at work?!?

As Tanya worked diligently with the artwork, she smiled brightly. She swore that what she was hearing was like listening to softcore porn. All the moaning and groaning and soft whispers for where Tess liked to be touched were going to plague Tanya's mind for days to come, but Tanya grinned, nonetheless. This was the best blackmail ever!

Tanya breathed slowly as she refocused on the painting, her cutter slicing through the last of the fabric and separating it from the frame. The cut was done with an expert hand without a single piece out of line, and with the greatest of care. Tanya rolled up the canvas and slid it carefully into a tubed container before sealing it inside. Now came the fun part, Tanya thought as she smiled widely.

She worked quickly, pulling out of her bag all the things she needed; wet chalk, illuminated LED's and a large grouping of see-through wires. She attached each wire along the frame and measured carefully, cutting where she needed to and tying it all together. When she was done, she looked at the time and nodded. Not bad for an hour's work. Tanya wiped the sweat from her brow and turned on the device she had created.

"Please work. Please work. Please-Yes!" Tanya chanted as an image slowly projected into place, adjusting to the frame and darkness before settling in the place of the old painting; except when one looked at it, the wires were not there to hold it up, the slashed canvas hidden behind a projected screen of perfectly smeared chalk on the edges. The gloves on Tanya's hand would prevent any fingerprints and the only thing on the device was the code she'd programmed into it. It was just a dumb device that just did one job.

Tanya gripped the metal frame once more blocking the view of the cameras and dropped it over her as she began her arduous take of trailing her way back out the way she had come. "Heading for extract in fifteen minutes. Finish up in there," Tanya smiled smugly. "And try to clean up afterwards."

The warning was lost in the fog of lust and love making as Paige was only getting more and more into the art of making love for her soul-searching lover. Paige moaned as she delved further into Daniel's mouth, her tongue grazing against his own. Her own shirt was thrown completely open as her bare stomach pressed against Daniel's naked torso, his pecs pushing deeply against her covered chest.

She was utterly impressed at the virgin in front of her, and her heart soared higher as he rubbed at her legs with such affection and reverence. Paige groaned as he stroked his way up to her upper thighs, her skirt flipped up and covering nothing but a line of her waist. *'This…. This was too good!'* Paige thought as she panted inside Daniel's mouth. She had never felt so connected with someone before. Her breath was his breath; his heartbeat was her heartbeat; her soul…was his……*'God!'* Paige's heart skipped a beat. Maybe here was good enough to do the deed with him. Maybe she should just-

Tanya reached the door for the exit and slid it open, pulling out the folded piece of paper that had held the door from fully locking in place. Tess had slid it in when she let the guard push her against the wall, hiding her action from view. Tanya, now outside, separated her device and slipped it into her sack before she tapped her mic on her neck as her earpiece came back to life.

"Tess?" Tanya spoke, but only heard multiple chants and moans in her ear. "Oh Tess." Tanya sighed as she reached into her pocket and pulled out a simple red buttoned device. She was worried that this might happen, so she planned ahead. "I hope you're not biting anything."

Tess leaned in close, prepared to take off her entire persona and bare all for her soon to be lover, when a painful spark of electrical charge sparked out of her ear. "Oh God!" Tess spasmed, her entire body spazzing and shivering for a second before her rage of thought scowled at her sister. "GEEZ!!!"

"I'm sorry!" A voice cried out the apology right in front of her. Tess froze as she remembered where she was and looked to see Daniel looking guiltily at her. *'Why did he apologize? He didn't do anything wro-'*

"OH!" Tess hid herself under her persona and leaned over to the side of the desk.

"Huh?"

"Oh no! Daniel, it wasn't you!" Paige assured him with a kiss. "My phone's buzzing."

Paige flicked her screen and brought it to her ear. Paige heard her sister's far off voice talking to her as they'd practiced but looked over to rock her hips against his pelvis making him groan desperately and her smile victoriously.

"Hey Julia... Huh?" The practiced conversation led to her looking sad in front of her mark. "What is it? Where am I... At home of course... Alright...Thanks."

Daniel could feel the tension in her shoulders tighten as she hung up. "Paige?" Paige looked down to see him looking worried and nervous but also caring for her needs and mental health.

'He really just wants to see me happy, doesn't he?'

"Who was that, Paige?"

'Right.' Tess thought as her face turned somber for real. Their magical moment was officially shattered as their hormones moved to reset themselves. She had never had a time with a guy before with that amount of lust and.... love? Tess shook her head. No, she had to follow the plan, and it was time to finish this, and get out of here. Tess leaned back, put on her persona, and bent down to grab her coat, though her movements were slower than she should have been. She really didn't want this to end.

"...um my sister found a job for me but it's forty miles out of the city and I need to get there in two hours, or I lose it."

Daniel smiled happily as he stood to kiss her neck. "And?"

Paige sighed as she stepped back and sniffled. Time for the breakup. "Well Daniel, I'd never see you as much so there's really no point and... Daniel?" Paige stalled; stunned as he pulled her into a hug between their shirtless forms.

"I like you a lot."

"...Daniel?" Paige breathed; her breath suddenly shallow from the confession. "Daniel-what-" She tried to look at him, but Daniel hugged her deeper into his chest, preventing her from looking at his face.

"I want you to be my girlfriend even if we don't see each other too often, Paige. I know it's only been a week or so, but I want to see what this is between us, if this is real romance. Maybe it's just lust, but I want to know."

"Really? Y-You really want that?" Paige uttered. He had enjoyed spending all that time with her this much. Was this guy for real?

Daniel nodded into her shoulder as Paige's lips just barely graced his cheek. ".... I should go."

She felt Daniel shudder at her rejection. Silently, they buttoned the other's shirts in place, and as Paige readjusted her skirt, her real self couldn't help but tease him. " ...I'll think about it?"

To say Daniel's hopeful smile lit up a solar system was a bit much, but just a little. "I'll walk you out."

Neither dawdled to the door as Daniel pressed his card on the pad to unlock it, but as he opened the door to let her out, Paige leaned up on her toes to kiss his lips tenderly. She sighed as she retreated and stood in the doorway. "You're a good kisser." She sighed deeply.

Daniel was still stunned. "I really am?"

Paige grinned woefully. "Yeah...so call me tomorrow?"

"W-why"? Daniel asked, his hope freezing him in place.

"If...and I mean IF we don't see each other, and we're going out, which with that confession, I believe we are, we should still talk every other day to each other."

"...Alright then. I'll call tomorrow." Daniel voiced hoarsely; his voice suddenly gone.

She held his tie playfully in her hand and stroked his cheek fondly. "You do that." Paige turned around, her coat wrapped over her arm, and moved until she was around the corner and out of sight. Daniel stayed where he was rooted to the spot long after she had gone, his eyes having been glued to the top of her bare thighs which she had left her skirt tied up intentionally as the bottom of her ass peeked out at him, forever teasing his poor innocent mind.

At the next corner down the hill, Tess turned onto a street filled with bars and streams of drunks being let out for the night. She nodded to a blonde girl standing by a streetlamp across the avenue as Tanya began to walk up and smile. "You got it?"

Tanya smiled as she lightly jangled the artwork tube from her shoulders.

"And the decoy?"

Tanya smiled even brighter. "Don't worry. The battery will last three days, and it will slowly cannibalize itself so that when the techs eventually get to it, it will only show a battery for 4-5 hours. We're in the clear, Tess."

Tess smiled and started walking to the bar at the far end of the street.

"So…. you have a boyfriend, huh?"

"What?" Tess breathed, and then cursed as she flicked her microphone off on her neck. "…Fine. Let's talk about that at the next bar."

Tanya smiled brightly. "Indeed…. Let's celebrate!"

IX-GATES DOWN

"**M**omma!! Come on!" Came the shrill pleasure from a little girl that was becoming a regular to the museum. The little girl pulled with all her might to try to get towards the museum. Held within her tiny hand was her mother's hand as Yuki smiled down at her daughter Asuka.

'Here again, huh?' Yuki thought as she allowed her daughter to pull her up the stairs. They had been here three times already, but still after a month, her daughter loved the place. The section of the museum that Asuka had loved most was the planetarium that had filled her with such happiness and excitement that when they got home, she asked her mother when they could go again. Asuka just wouldn't go to sleep until she had promised her that they could go back.

Yuki had hoped her daughter had forgotten all about it, but after a week, her daughter remembered. Yuki smiled though. At least this was a good way to give her education while also getting out of the house.

"Momma look! It's the nice man!" Yuki turned as they walked inside the building where at the door, was the same guard that they had been welcomed by two times before. He was attractive in Yuki's eyes, but she preferred brown hair and a more confident man. This guy was nice and pleasant, and a good role model, just not her type.

Daniel nodded to the young mother and daughter pair as they entered the doors, and the little girl immediately rushed his leg and looked up at him excitedly. He smiled as he rubbed her head, the girl like an excited puppy as she rubbed her head back into his hand and smiled happily. Looking up at her mother, he smiled.

"Back so soon?"

"She really loves it here."

"Well, a great place to be on a Wednesday after all. Half off today." Daniel remarked, as Yuki smiled at the savings for her wallet.

"Really? Even better."

"Ma'am, if your daughter wants to come more, may I suggest you buy the child pass plan? It's free and after four visits, the fifth is free with a parent's ticket as well."

"Thanks. I may look into that."

"You two have a wonderful day." Daniel called out as he gently prodded her daughter back to her.

Daniel watched them walk off to the ticket booth until he saw two teens edging around the stairs. He smiled as he called into his radio and moved to the back wall. He turned and walked through a nondescript door and closed it. To normal people, it was just the middle of 3 doors on a wall. The one on the right was the men's bathroom, and the one of the left was the janitor's closet. But as Daniel turned back around, he had entered a secret staircase that led directly into the planetarium. The door at the top of the stairs led into a secret dark hallway, masking the light of the stairwell from view to keep the ambiance of the darker planetarium pleasing for the attending citizens of Kavala.

Daniel moved out of the stairwell and towards the entrance door, and just in time as the two teens entered hoping to sneak inside. As they approached, Daniel stepped forward, and both teens stalled. "Do you two have your tickets on hand?"

"Um...we...uh…"

"Yeah...Um…"

Daniel leaned over them and smiled. "Tell you what. Go back down and buy some tickets, and I won't take you boys into the back." He internally smiled as their eyes widened. He meant that they'd call their parents, but they didn't need to know that. "Come on, today's profits go to the Children's Fund of Kavala."

The boys nodded their heads and turned around, back down the circular staircase they'd just come up from. Daniel smiled. A nice way to start a shift.

An hour later, Daniel walked along his circuit into the gallery's second section and moved to the corner where he could stand and watch everyone in the room. It was actually a busy morning for a Wednesday, with around 20 people in this section. He noticed an elderly man and his wife taking a break from standing on their walkers to sit on the bench. And then there was a 28-year-old woman on her phone, not caring at all where she was as she texted in the middle of the walkway.

Daniel smiled at the absurdity as a few more people walked around her, muttering to themselves before looking to enjoy the local paintings. Daniel was happy that people came out to support the children today. But Daniel's eyes slipped to the Walter painting opposite him and couldn't help but reminisce on just how important it was to him now.

To think that he got a date with that painting, and after only two weeks, he had been frenching his girlfriend in the security room! After two weeks of dating, he had almost thought that they'd become one last Friday night. That's right. Laugh at him! Two become one! Boy, his high school friends made fun of him so much because he believed that he'd marry the first girl he had relations with back then.

Paige was...just amazing. She was gentle, compassionate, and provoked deep thoughts from him. If she offered it to him, he'd…. he'd go for it. Daniel looked down at the ground. He loved her….at least enough to want to spend his days and nights with her. Daniel slightly laughed at himself. But Paige was not ready for marriage. He could see that as clear as daylight. From the conversations and her thoughts on many subjects, he could see that she had plans to achieve, wants to strive for, a curious mind that still ached to run from place to place. As much as he'd like her to stay in place, he knew that she was a wanderer, a nomad who made friends and contacts everywhere she went. She never mentioned this to him, but he just...knew.

Last Friday night, she hadn't been ready to make this relationship more permanent; Daniel had fallen more than she had, he guessed. She wasn't ready to settle down; she wanted her life to be exciting and full of thrills, like Friday night. Daniel shivered with a smile. God what she had done with her hips, grinding along his-

"OH MY GOD!!!!!!" A scream echoed around the room from several people. Daniel's head surged out with many others turning to watch the horror coming to pass upon them. The Walter painting was dissolving!

'Well,' Daniel thought morbidly. *'Not dissolving.'* It was flickering on and off as if on a screen with bad reception. But then popping sounds made him surge towards the painting, as sparks flew out from the frame, and the painting fizzled away. Inside were small projectors and lenses, with many wires and circuits around the inside of the frame, and only the outside husk of the painting remained in place, the cut missing canvas perfectly rectangular in scope.

As people began to scurry away, Daniel's training went into action. He quickly reached for his radio and shooed people away from the doors. "Code 3!! Close all exits to Gallery 2!"

As Daniel turned away from the painting, a siren sounded as metal slats opened on the arches of the exits and grates of metal slid down between the opening of the walls, reaching the ground in less than three seconds, and locked into place, the bolts latching with locks that could not be undone except by police and the head of security and director of the museum.

"You almost killed me!" One guy yelled at Daniel as he had jumped back before the gates had come down. The quiet in the room after that exclamation was heavy as all eyes turned towards Daniel, in worry, in anger, but most of all, a hope for guidance.

Daniel looked back at the missing painting, and all the burnt wires and circuits professionally slid together within the old frame of the canvas. Nothing out of order and what he would expect from himself if he'd been asked to put up some kind of system. But it would take him days, maybe even a week to put this together. No way this had been done while they were open.

Daniel sighed as he turned around to face the angry masses. "Hello everyone. Everything is under control. I would like to ask everyone to calm down. The police are on their way and should be here soon. Please wait calmly and patiently and everyone will leave in an orderly fashion when this is taken care of." Daniel spoke as best he could.......it was not good enough.

"When will that be?!?"

"I have places to be!!!"

"I have no reception in here!!!"

"I have to go to the bathroom!!!"

Daniel gritted his teeth and tried to smile at the raging mob; annoyed, worried, and pressing into him, hoping that he could somehow show favoritism, and not wanting to stay in this single room with who they no doubt thought was a thief in their midst.

Outside the room, Daniel could just now hear police sirens of multiple cars sounding on the two approaches to the museum's front entrance and sighed. They were coming into the area, but they would not be letting people out of this room any time soon. No; lock down the other exits to the museum and wait for full containment.

An hour later, the museum was surrounded with caution tape and police at every exit, while just across the street on the manicured lawn, the green grass now bled brown as packs of dirt from over 15 news vans tore it up, as reporters stood in front of cameras, announcing the theft to the city and even more so, to the world.

While this happened, across the city, Tess groaned into the large open room, opening, and closing her bleary bloodshot eyes as she tried to raise herself from her makeshift bed, that being the couch. She stretched out her kinks, her black sleeveless shirt sliding off her shoulders as it was bigger than she was, showing off the black lace of her bra over her chest.

Tess clawed at the cushions, pulling herself out as her stomach moved above her knees, the shirt rising to show her lacy black panties along her porcelain white frame, the stark contrast in color standing out. Tess kept stretching out until a hammer went to work inside her brain and she whimpered as she curled back into herself, holding her head.

Tess looked over as a growl emanated from her throat to her best friend, sister, and co-conspirator who laid asleep on another couch. Curse Tanya for manipulating her into partying like she was 16 again for five nights in a row. That was crazy! Her only respite was calling Daniel while she was somewhat drunk to make her giddy and way too open as they flirted about Friday night and spoke to a possible future encounter of the situation.

Just as her arousal was making itself known, Tess watched her sister sleep and smiled. There was Tanya, her head crooked into the corner of the armrest and couch, with one leg draped over the top and another half on half off the couch after her knee. Her body was as twisted as could be. As Tess sat up fully, she sighed in reminiscence. The two of them had never really gotten used to beds during their childhoods, sleeping wherever they could, in any position and place that was comfortable enough. Even years after and now that they had money and places to stay, they rarely stayed in a bed. Tess's apartment upstairs was used more for her clothes and a shower for both of them than anything else.

Tess felt the headache return even stronger than before and hissed as she stood up and made her way to the fridge. With some mumbling, she managed to open the door and a nice cold bottle before bringing it to her lips for a quick swig. Hopefully this would assuage her wound. Tess leaned back, wanting comfort more than anything right now.

Tess brought the bottle back up for another swig but froze as her body quivered at the ghostly feeling of masculine hands grazing along her bare stomach, before slithering down to her upper thighs. Tess let out a rather sensual moan as those hands groped at her ass before slipping along her waistband and disappeared altogether.

"Yeah…...comfort." Tess smiled sourly. Like this bottle would take care of that. '*Oh well.*' She thought. At least it would dull the pain slightly.

X-FALLING IN LOVE

"And that's when I was alerted to the picture disappearing in front of me." Daniel recounted to the policeman, a tablet recording everything he said as the female officer also wrote down her notes on what she could infer from his tale.

"And how have the last few days been?"

"Pretty usual, I suppose."

"Any unauthorized personnel anywhere they shouldn't be?" She asked.

Daniel was about to say no when he stalled; his memory of his girlfriend humping his leg in the security booth popping up, but shook his head and breathed in. "No ma'am."

"Alright then," she nodded before she smiled over at him. "Anyways, I just spoke to your boss, and he informed me that you run the security system?"

Daniel smiled sourly. "Yes ma'am. Our tech guy doesn't work here full time, so I learned most of the stuff so that we don't have it down too often."

"That's actually great. Our own techs are on another case right now. Can you help out a bit?"

"Uh…is that proper in an investigation?"

"You would just be helping me get all the data and going through the records."

"Uh…sure, I guess."

Three hours later, Daniel groaned as he was finally released from the security room with a rather thankful detective. He got the impression that she'd been hitting on him more than the female officer who'd taken his statement, but that couldn't be. Geez, ever since he'd gotten a girlfriend, it was like all girls were hitting on him. He had a screw loose or something.

As he stepped outside, he began to make his way home slowly, his mind entirely out of his body. As he and the rest of the staff had been informed, the museum was closed entirely for the crime scene, until they went through everything that could be of use to them. All others had gone off duty while he had stayed to help.

He had left them just now, but after three hours of speeding up and freezing the camera footage, there was nothing to show from it. It was like no one had come in and stolen anything, and the last few days of footage showed the same as always, the painting never moving, but the water markings and time stamps hidden within the frames were still there. The footage hadn't been tampered with.

He overheard the police talking about the ingenious way of faking the painting there, how the lenses worked and how clean it was, with no fingerprints so far. More tests would be done, but so far nothing. As Daniel waited to cross the street, he remembered how the police tested the battery on the device and came up with 6-8 hours of available space. That would give them a good timeframe for when the robbery occurred.

He hoped they found the culprits, and he worried for Sunny, who was the only one on duty last night. But in crimes like this, the chances of finding the painting were slim, and a pang in his heart pinged his sadness. It wasn't his favorite painting in the museum's inventory, but recently it was his favorite because he had met his girlfriend with that painting. It was an emotional thing for him.

As Daniel turned onto his street, guilt rocked his body. He had omitted his girlfriend coming into the secure room last weekend. She shouldn't have been in there, and the repercussions for Daniel were immense. After all, that was the human factor, the weakness in security, people. He shouldn't have left it out; he should tell the police, shouldn't he?

'But if the battery was that short, just 6 hours, then she's innocent!' Daniel exclaimed inside his head. He felt guilty more so at even thinking Paige would do anything so cruel as stealing a painting. It was priceless, but so important to the people of Kavala. He imagined the two of them sneaking inside a no trespassing zone, and yes, sneaking her into his work to make out, but theft? She wasn't that kind of girl, and Daniel beat his inner demon up for even thinking so little of Paige.

What if he could have prevented this from happening? Maybe they should have added the rotating lock systems that other museums had, maybe he should have listened to that girl on the phone a month ago on updating their older cameras. Maybe they should have dropped the gates every night at closing time. The things they could have done would sadly have raised the museum's cost, and that just wasn't possible.

Maybe he was just harder on others, and on himself? Anger and guilt made him somber as Daniel opened the door to his home. He didn't even have the effort to take a shower as he just sat on his couch.

What a day…...he had seen that cute little girl, he had stopped those boys from sneaking inside; such a great start to a regular boring day in the name of security. And now…such a terrible day…..he wanted a hug.

'A hug….' Daniel's throat choked at that feeling. He wanted something physical, but no one around him to give it. His parents were long dead, leaving him to his own devices in terms of love and family. Maybe one of his neighbors would hug him? Daniel sighed. That was an awkward thing to ask of a neighbor, and besides, it was the middle of the day, no one was home. He just needed something tangible to keep him together, something…no. He wanted someone…...He needed someone special.

"…Paige?" Daniel's voice uttered within his apartment. She was a physical woman, and emotional, and… she was his girlfriend, but they were still new and hadn't set any defined boundaries. Wouldn't this kind of situation be too much too fast? As tears teamed in his eyes at the indecision, he looked down to sigh. His fingers were already dialing her number, deciding for him.

"How can you expect me to do that, Tess?!?" Tanya growled. "Stop Laughing!!!"

"I just trust you in a jam, Tanya." Tess giggled at her sister's growl. They had been laughing for a few minutes after Tanya had tried one of her crazy gadgets. It had worked perfectly!....for about five seconds before most of the parts ignited and Tanya had had to start all over.

Tess felt her stomach hurting from the nonstop laughter at her sister's expense, but it was time to stop teasing as Tanya was starting to get mad. She opened her arms mockingly and cocked her head cutely. "I'll hug you if it helps."

"I don't need a hug!!" Tanya exploded and walked off to the couch, but after a few seconds, Tanya sighed as Tess hugged her anyways. She gave in and pulled Tess into her as she hugged tightly, making Tess wince at the painful hug. "You're the worst sister."

"....I truly am." Tess shrugged as they continued to hug for a bit. "You are such a touchy person, Tanya."

"Don't get me started on you." Tanya snipped at her before they ended the hug and smiled. "Want some wine?"

"In the middle of the day? Geez Tanya, I have a project for Melissa to finish this week."

"Come on, Tess." Tanya smiled, "You know that Melissa won't move on the vault for what? Three weeks at the earliest? Besides, you're just helping her with the plan."

"I should still work on it."

"Come on. Where else do you have to be today?"

Tess sighed. "Alright. A few glasses, but no more all nighters."

"No promises." Tanya shrugged as she moved to the kitchen.

Tess sighed and held her head. *Please not another headache.* She'd spent the better part of the morning hungover, and she didn't want another repeat. As Tanya bumped the fridge door with her hip, Tess's phone rang. Well, one of her phones. Tess looked over to the small table where in a perfect line lay four phones and smiled as she grabbed the red one, taking the persona of her favorite character to date.

"This is Paige."

"Paige?" Came a voice that made her heart shudder.

"Hey, Daniel." Tess greeted; her voice softer than her usual voice in front of him. She expected him to start asking her what she was up to, tell her about his day, and just complain about the perfect weather of Kavala. Instead, there was just silence.

Tess recalled the way he'd said her name, his voice meek and depressed instead of happy. "Daniel? You okay?"

"...Can you come over?" Daniel's voice asked nervously, stalling over the last word a bit, and Tess stilled her response as her mind worked on what he was really asking, but a perverse smile soon appeared on her face.

"Why Daniel, this is so sudden. I mean to invite me over so soon is well..." Tess giggled out her excuse but stalled again when no rush to correct her came. "...Daniel?"

"...Please?" Her boyfriend's fragile voice sounded over the phone. She could hear the desperation in his voice, her heart for once in pain... wanting to make him feel better was her new prerogative.

"Tell me first what's wrong." Tess insisted as her sister handed her a glass of wine.

"The museum got robbed." Daniel whispered over the phone. Tess's eyes widened as she caught Tanya's eyes and mouth the word 'battery' to her. Tanya just gave her a half-frown. They had hoped the battery would last a little longer. As she turned her attention back to the phone, Daniel was finishing his confession. "...I'm off work for the next few days, but can you come over?"

"I don't know, Daniel. I really have some things I need-"

"I just need to see your face. I swear it will be fast...Please...Just... come over." Tess's rebuttal slipped from her lips, his words stopping her entire train of thought.

On Tanya's end, she had just sat down as her sister began to toy with her mark. Tanya's body shivered in delight and suspense as she imagined what her sister would do in a few seconds. She would say that she couldn't make it, delay, and say she's sorry, and then call back a few minutes later claiming that she'd changed her whole schedule around for him just so that he'd be grateful to her.

But instead, he must have said something interesting indeed as Tanya watched her sister freeze with her mouth caught open. Consider her interest peaked. Tanya leaned forward as whatever he had said must have been something sickly sweet, especially as her sister's eyes widened before they teamed with tears.

'...*Real tears.*' Tanya realized.

Her sister's lips turned into an affectionate smile as her opposing hand moved up to play with a loose strand of her brunette hair, twirling it around her finger as she bit her lower lip to lessen her smile. Tanya may spend more time around machines, but she knew the signs of love like the back of her hand. As she watched, Tess covered the phone closer to her ear as her body swayed side to side.

Tanya chewed at her lip. She liked this guy a lot, and the question was did she realize it? "...Say that again." She heard Tess whisper and visibly shivered at the way her heart leaped at the sound of his voice. She must have leaned on her phone too hard because the speaker turned on.

".... I need to see your face." Her mark's voice spoke, and Tess's eyes watered terribly, and she nodded her head.

"...I'll be right there."

Tess ended the call smiling wide and her heart pounding in her chest. She needed to get to Daniel's apartment and fast. She didn't like his voice all sad, and yet she knew that she would make it feel better. She knew that she was not leaving until he was smiling. Tess turned to grab a sweater and passed her sister grinning at her on the way.

"What's that look for?" Tess asked as she slipped the sweater on.

"Nothing really." Tanya smiled, but a smirk remained." It's just... Tess, normally you don't fall for the mark."

Tess took the comment in stride as she moved to the changing area, shrugging dismissively. "He's not the mark..." Tess stepped behind but paused at her dresser to realize what Tanya was implying, "and I'm not falling for him!" Tess refuted.

"Come on, Tess, you can tell me." Tanya smiled happily as she raised herself excitedly on the armrest of the couch. "Your body language doesn't lie. I've wanted to talk about boys with you for so long!"

Tess rolled her eyes as she leaned over to grab the tube placed there and leaned around the corner towards Tanya. "This painting!" Tess held it up high. "Alex paid for it with the blood money, and it's Amelia's painting! How dare he murder her and then display it!! He's the mark."

Tess heard Tanya giggle before she appeared around the corner to watch Tess change. She obviously didn't believe her as her smile remained smug on her lips.

"Whatever you say, sweetheart. All I'm saying is that you've never smiled like that when you are conning someone."

"And what would you know?" Tess refuted as she jumped into a fresh skirt, zipping it up a second later, her pants staying on the ground as she grazed through her hair to fluff it out.

Tanya simmered as she joined her in the mirror, looking at her from over her shoulder. "More than you think."

"Just say it, Tanya."

"Look Tess," Tanya lectured. "You know how to flirt, and you know how to seduce your way into the con, but the truth is that you've never fallen for anyone. Falling in love feels different; your partner looks better than anyone else you can think of. You feel different and will do things solely because they say something to you. It's not like a regular con."

"So what? It's the same thing with conning a loser, Tanya. This is to get back at Alex! Nothing else is implied in this, Tanya. I'm not doing anything to fall in love…"

"…...Except what she last said to you." Tanya muttered. And immediately Tess felt guilt erupt in her throat, choking her of her words at Tanya's comment. She had said it when Tess told her not to. A brief silence ensued as both girls stared at the other, not wanting to back out. Tess shook her head, whispering. "Don't do it, Tanya."

But her sister pressed on. "I'm sorry Tess, but you told me that Mom regretted not finding a soulmate."

"Tanya…" Tess choked as she teared up.

"She died alone, without that person that completed her life, who was the Yin to her Yang."

"Tanya, I don't-"

"But she settled for adopting us, Tess. You were her second chance at finding love. She loved us like her daughters, and I made her so happy when I found mine….and now you've found yours."

Tess looked at Tanya aghast with confusion. Tanya was crazy if Tess actually liked Daniel like that. He was just a mark….a romantic mark, but a mark, nonetheless. "Tanya, you're seeing things that simply aren't there. I don't love him. He's just a mark." Tess slipped on her shoes and moved to the door.

"…. Is it so wrong to fall in love with someone?" Tanya's voice countered as Tess stalled at the door and looked over. Tess gazed at her sister's body and then around the room. Maybe she wasn't looking at her as much as at everything she had that Tess did not. Quietly, Tess sighed.

"I suppose not…"

Tanya saw Tess leave out the door and rubbed her arms before smiling sadly. "Damn. She has a hard fall coming. Dang it, I guess I should call my guy...seeing her act like that just makes me miss him." Tanya spoke to the empty warehouse and checked the far clock. "I hope the kids are up by now." Maybe she should stop by today; no doubt she should drop off Aunt Tess's birthday presents.

Tess breathed hard as she pushed her body up the stairs to the fourth floor of the apartment building to pause and look back down the way she'd come. Why didn't she just take the elevator? Or better yet take her car from Tanya's to here?!? Tess groaned as she looked at her skin, glowing with a nice sheen of sweat from the ten blocks she had speed-walked over to get here fast.

She groaned as she reached the top floor, stopping to quickly massage her calf muscles. *At least I'll get good thigh muscles if I see my boyfriend every day.'* Tess stilled for the hundredth time in the past few weeks.

Boyfriend...for how much longer could she say that? Was Tanya, right? Was she laying roots down with him? She was his girlfriend because it made her cover story solid. She was his girlfriend because she got sensitive information about the museum in ways that seemed small, like the rotation schedule of the guards, when they took their breaks and who was late to work most days. But in another few weeks, the investigation may be over. Tess and her sister couldn't stay here in this city for long, moving around as they did. They were nomads; always moving.

Tess stopped in front of Daniel's door, her eyes glistening and her lips mad. She didn't want to stop seeing Daniel, but they could just continue this, right? She'd just do long distance. Stop by every few months, drag Daniel along for years. She frowned; Daniel deserved more time than that.

Tanya made it work for her lover, who now took care of two kids who Tess loved and adored as their aunt.... but... Tanya's lover knew her real name. He knew what she did for a living. Daniel knew her as Paige. Sweet, innocent, adventurous Paige.

These questions raced across her sweaty face as she knocked on the door to see it open immediately, showing that he'd been eagerly waiting for her. The way Daniel looked at her made her knees weak and her eyes shimmer. Her breath caught in her throat as she quietly spoke. "... Hey..."

Daniel said nothing back. Instead, he rushed his girlfriend and pulled her into a deep embrace and pressed his lips deep into her lips. Tess had a hard time falling into character as stunned as she was. Tess's eyes slid closed as she kissed back with a sudden surge of adrenaline. This Daniel who took the initiative; she very much liked this guy.

Before she could do anything else, Daniel pulled her inside as he caressed her hair and cheek, stroking her skin softly as he ever so slowly retreated, leaving a breathless girl before him. "Wow...That's a surprise." Paige assumed her role as girlfriend. She was still blinking rapidly trying to refocus when Daniel grinned sourly.

"Sorry." Daniel shuddered as he brought his lips up to her forehead, kissing it fondly as Paige's facade cracked a bit; she loved kisses to her forehead, just like her mother used to do when she was little. She even thought that someday, she would get a tattoo to match her mentor's. But that would never happen. Paige's mood dampened down to Daniel's own attitude.

"I'm sorry if that was forced, Paige. I just had to see you."

"Are you alright?" Paige asked as she edged closer into his grasp.

"Of course! I'm…" Daniel began before Paige's innocent hands reached up to stroke his cheek fondly, and he sighed, giving into the gesture as he let his walls disappear before this amazing angel before him. Angel or Devil, he was mesmerized by her openness and honesty. "No…. I'm a mess, Paige. I'm worried and stressing over nothing, and I just want to forget all of that for tonight."

Paige nodded her head. "Well, I'm here now. Anything I can do to help?" She asked innocently.

There was nothing innocent in Daniel's eyes as they swelled with red passion. No sooner had Paige cocked her head than Daniel had lifted her off the ground and pressed her harshly against the wall of his apartment. Paige's arms wrapped around his neck as her thighs tightened automatically around his waist. Daniel's tongue slipped inside Paige's mouth, where it twirled around Paige's own. To say that Paige was utterly astonished was fair. To say that her lust for Daniel soared; most definitely.

Paige pushed back with her tongue, slipping into his own as Daniel's newfound dominance wavered and morphed with her own as they settled for an equal pace as each member pulled the other tighter, Daniel by Paige's back as she pulled on his neck. Daniel slipped free of her assaulting attack and sucked on her open neck, as Paige leaned back and moaned in pleasure as he delved into her weak spot that he had found last Friday night.

Paige continued to moan over and over for him until finally they ran out of air and parted, breathing heavily as he continued to stroke her cheek. "You are so beautiful."

"Is that all you have to say?"

Daniel smiled before slowly nodding his head to the right. Paige's character broke for a second, as Tess smiled at what he was asking her to do with him and smiled with more passion than had seen before. She morphed back into Paige and nodded as they kissed once again. Daniel stepped back, Paige wrapped around him as they turned to the right and…. bumped straight into the open door.

"MMMMmmm…" Paige groaned as her back hurt, but the passion flowing through her system was sending more than enough signals to dull any pain she received. She leaned back with one hand and shoved the door closed before snogging commenced again as Daniel twirled his girlfriend around as she giggled and kissed all over his face as they moved into his small bedroom. As the bed came into sight, Daniel leaned over it as Paige half laid on the mattress and kept her legs around Daniel's hips, keeping him in place.

Daniel though was already working on Paige's sweater as she raised her hands and the material disappeared somewhere upon the floor. Her blouse was already halfway opened before he looked up at his handiwork; Paige's hands unzipping her skirt as his fingers deftly unhooked her bra behind her back, the straps flowing off her shoulders, the cups the only material keeping her hidden.

"You're all sweaty." Daniel uttered before he worried that the mood was broken, but Paige grinned sourly.

"I ran straight over. I thought you needed me."

"I do." Daniel whispered as he straddled her body and stroked her cheek. "I really do."

Paige's mind froze in place, for the last time, she watched him look at her with pure, unadulterated, genuine affection that Paige's heart, mind, and soul, skipped a beat. Such a single beat made her breathless, it made her lightheaded, it made her stomach queasy; it made her say what she'd been scared to ask ever since they had first locked eyes.

"You are falling in love with me, aren't you?"

It had been growing steadily since that day and now, eighteen days later, she had asked it. She was always the one who led these activities; asked for his number, showed up at his place of work, taught him how to kiss, and now, would teach him something that she was scared to admit, but Daniel said it for her.

"I am." Daniel admitted freely before he gulped, his eyes turning back to a cerulean blue. "I want...to make love to you, Paige."

Paige widened her eyes at him even asking. She was clearly in agreement; he need not ask. But Daniel taking charge put a stir in her stomach; one that she knew that Daniel could sate. So instead, she smiled fondly and played with the back of his head, twirling a stray lock of hair around her fingers.

"Then make love to me, Daniel, and fall deeper as you do."

Daniel moved to undo his pants before leaning up and sighed morosely. "I'm sorry if you don't feel good the first time."

Paige awed and pulled him closer playfully kissing his lips. "You're just nervous. It's your first time, I get that." Tess smiled sarcastically. "But don't worry. I won't judge. Just do you."

Daniel saw the smile and for some reason, it irked him. Was she saying that she thought her first time with him would be bad? No, he realized, as he looked at her Cheshire smile. She was baiting him, daring him further into her abyss of desire and lust.

"...I'll do you." Daniel growled into Paige's face and delved into her loving embrace as they moved onto more...sensual activities.

Thirty minutes later, both young adults breathed heavily as they finished their first love making, Daniel's arms shaking wildly as he struggled to keep his full weight off her girl- no, off of his lover. As Daniel slid sideways, Paige moaned pleasantly as he joined her on the mattress, both under the sheets as sweat poured out of their skin, their bodies emptying of the adrenaline that had rushed them into action.

As they continued to breathe erratically, Paige stared up at the ceiling, her eyes dilated and still adjusting as she for the first time swore that she saw stars near the end of her vision. "...Wow...That was really good Daniel."

Daniel's ears heard the labored breathing, as he slowly turned his head to see Paige looking at him with different eyes. For some reason, she looked different to him now. More...regal. "Really?" He croaked before taking a huge gulp of air. "I thought it was short."

"Not too short," Paige's hands lightly shook from the jitters, turning her head and body as she slid her body over his right side until her body was flushed with his. She smiled as she cuddled into his side and giggled when his eyes openly ogled her nude body on his. "I didn't last half the time that you did with me."

Paige knew he wasn't truly listening when he leaned forward and kissed her straight on the lips. Her lips fizzled and popped like fireworks as they shared a passionate kiss between the two of them. Time was not a factor as they lazily swapped breath between the couple. After some time, again they didn't care what time it was, Paige leaned back and Daniel held her cheek in his hand, rubbing it fondly as Paige smiled.

"You are amazing Paige." Daniel breathed as he pulled her in for another round as he kissed her forehead and tucked her head under his as she heard him sniffle and tighten his hold on her. Paige readjusted only slightly into the crook of his neck, feeling Daniel's arms drape over the back of her waist as her legs intertwined with his. "I'm so lucky to have you."

Paige felt his arms start to slacken around her as he was no doubt about to pass out. "It's me who's lucky to have found you." Paige uttered back. Daniel didn't respond, and when Paige looked up, he was fast asleep.

Tess smiled sadly. It was his first time after all, so she really shouldn't have expected him to be able to go another round. Tess smiled contentedly as she stared out the window at the last rays of the setting sun. Tess paused in her musing to think about what her sister claimed she saw in Tess's latest actions.

'Maybe Tanya was right. Maybe I am falling in love with him just a little bit.' She smiled, snuggling deeper into Daniel's sleeping embrace, herself trapped in his arms. Not trapped...loved. Tess closed her eyes and yawned as she let her thoughts and eyes drift off to happy dreams. Daniel's part of the con was over, and they'd never need to use him again, so she could enjoy him and he her for however long these feelings lasted. These feelings were just too good to pass up. Besides, what could go wrong when you were falling in love?

XI-BEYOND THE MISSION

The sky began to lighten with pale pink and orange glows on the horizon. It was a lazy sunrise for a day that seemed to transcend time. It hovered for a while below the deep blue night sky, as it lightened the darkness until a light replaced the dark, and as the sun crested over the horizon, it soon shot forth on a straight course into the sky, bringing its warm rays into the room of a fourth-floor apartment.

The warmth only served to annoy the two sets of naked bodies inside the bed by the window, and they seeked one another, tightening their embrace upon the other, as masculine hands slid along a toned arm and slid down to squeeze a perfect rear. Feminine hands soon joined in the motions, lazily grazing the nails along the muscular back of her lover. But then the rest of her body slid along the masculine's pelvis, long, slender porcelain legs sliding and entangling themselves around the man's opposing body as both occupants of the bed began to stir and awaken.

Paige opened her eyes long before her lover and used the time to lightly stroke her fingers through her boyfriend's gravity defying hair. Daniel began to turn around, and as he did, she dropped her fingers down to his back, tracing along the scars that lay there in near porcelain invisibility yet for the tanness of his skin, that only served to highlight them instead. As Daniel sat up and stretched his arms out, Paige looked up at him.

She wanted to ask him about that someday, but not right now. They must have hurt for him to receive so many scars out of it, and it was probably emotional to talk about; hence she would wait to ask. She had somewhere to be for the next few days and didn't want a fight in case it was more than just emotional. Daniel finished stretching out and turned to receive a kiss from Paige which made him smile at her eagerness to always kiss him whenever he wanted it. It was their signal; the sign that they were two people falling in love, and the one in front of them was their soul's ultimate desire, forever pulling them closer. Paige herself felt it growing every day since she'd entered his apartment and he confessed...that was five weeks ago.

"Morning." Daniel breathed, his lips hovering just an inch from her own, refusing to separate more than this.

Paige giggled right into his face as she sneaked in a chaste kiss to the edge of his lips. "More like afternoon. Did you sleep well?"

"Best when I have you beside me." Daniel whispered huskily, making Paige moan as he groped her ass openly, pulling her higher to nip at her collarbone.

"But you have the night shift tonight, don't you?" Paige frowned, as Daniel nodded and got up before heading to the bathroom. Paige watched him walk away and as the door closed, she sat up in his bed as the blanket pooled into her lap, exposing her upper chest to the room. Paige let her persona drop and knees were soon brought up to her neck and arms wrapped around them as Tess looked up at the window and out to the city of Kavala.

Tess smiled; they'd had sex five weeks ago and Tess hadn't ever gone back to Tanya's place. Sure, she spoke over the phone and met with her, but she basically lived here with her lover and even when she was left alone on the nights he had to work, she felt safe, like she could make a home here; like she could be happy forever.

Tess shook her hair out and looked around the room. Tanya had stopped by to check out the place and bring her stuff over after the first three days she hadn't come back. Tess smirked; three days in a row sounded small, but it wasn't like Tanya or she were staying where they were consecutive days, even with the warehouse where she kept all of their stuff. They were trained to never be that predictable. Habitual yes, but never for sure.

Tess slid out to the edge of the bed herself and stretched out, her backside to the bathroom door to entice her lover as she did so. She had told Daniel after her first week here that she had gotten a good paying job, and it was more of a consultant kind of job. Suffice to say that Daniel was jealous that her talents were in such high demand. Tess had hinted that she made quite a bit more than he did, and with less hours too. But Daniel had taken those feelings and showed her just how much he could take care of her sexual tensions. Suffice to say that while Tess made the money of the couple, he was improving hand over fist in learning all of her weak points.

Tess shivered as she stood up, phantom hands gripping every point of her body that would make her weak in the knees. Daniel had gone slow and sensual with Tess, and she knew it; it was lovemaking, which was the prelude to full on wild and crazy intercourse. And now Tess's only problem in this relationship were the day trips that she left this safe space, her character of Paige staying here in Daniel's arms as Tess did her dirty work, insistent on making sure that her mother's life was avenged. She was an avenger; she had no other goals beyond that.

As Tess slipped on Daniel's black shirt over her torso, it dipped to her waist, not hiding her lower half at all.

'No other goals, huh?' Tess paused to think. Sex had gotten good, even great a few times, and she liked the guy a bunch. Could that count as a goal after all of this was done? Tanya still said she was in love, but only two months had passed between them. Tess knew that she was still falling into this ideal of love with Daniel, but she couldn't say it aloud, lest her heart forever lock itself on this man before her.

Tess shook her head as she continued to slide her panties on as she shook out the idea. It wasn't a goal that she could have after what she was going to do with Alex; the things she imagined doing to him made this romance a sure failure. After all, this could be a long-term fling for her; adding blood to this romance would not hold this relationship together.

As Tess bent over to put on her skirt, Daniel took that time to step out of the bathroom in a towel, his hair still drying out from the shower. But Daniel stalled in the entryway to the room as he looked to her body's angle and sighed. "You looking like that makes me think you want a repeat of this morning, Paige."

Tess smiled as she pulled her character up in place as she stayed where she was a second longer, letting him look at what he was dating before standing up, zipping the skirt in place. "Maybe I do want another round, Daniel, but you will have to wait until I get back in a few days."

He responded by hugging her tightly and growled into her neck before kissing her lightly. "I'll be ever so eager when you come back." Daniel uttered before leaving the room to get changed for the day. Tess watched him leave, his shirtless back shining as if she was seeing heaven open up before her. She shivered away the lust growing inside her and moved to grab her shoes for the day.

Yep, nothing bad about falling in love.

XII-THE BANK

Regal. Majestic. Powerful. The building that she was standing in was all those things and in that order. As one came in through the gold leafed doors, they came upon an atrium of quartz walls and rouge furniture spread out among the room, each on a Persian rug of the finest threads. Gold-gilded bars separated the room by a third, with desks and computers locked behind the gates that allowed the safe flow of money and valuables. To the left of the room, the chairs and couches were arranged into a lobby while past that, a number of desks and computers stood most empty, awaiting clients to help them. This place was a bank; one of the most secure and hidden banks in the world.

On the outside, they were indeed listed as a bank and normal people did bank here, but rarely did they have problems that justified them coming inside; rather, their clientele was from a richer, more anonymous group of individuals that wanted privacy above all, hence their need for only the best of service. For that, the employees were overseen by a strict, polished woman who was always watching over them from the second-floor archways, where the top officials and safety deposit boxes were located. If one looked closely, they would see a fair skinned woman in a business suit, checking off a list of requirements in her head.

Her name was Marya Campbell. That was Marya with a 'Y.' Not an 'I' but it was pronounced like 'Maria.' It was something done on purpose by her parents, and that was what she was raised to be. A woman filled with poise, purpose, and perfection. As Marya stood above the archway on the second floor, looking down on her employees, she knew each one of them and what they were worth, just as she knew her own.

What was perfection, but in the eyes of the beholder? Marya was half and half in her ancestry, half Scottish, and half Persian. Her husband was half Indian and half English. Both of their parents had been half and half too, their mixing of origins interlacing to keep that 50% ratio. Purpose: Their parents wanted children with their background and origin so that they would lead similar lives.

For being 46 years of age, she had married her husband at the age of 26 for simple reasons; he had married her for the same reasons. That being financial; they could afford a bigger house and pay less taxes if they were joined together in an official marriage; they could afford more together than alone. Money came first; love second on their conjoined list of a happy life.

That wasn't to say that they were not compatible. She fulfilled her wifely duties, and he his. Neither had complained once to the other about their time in the bedroom, and they were sated by their sexual desires. That wasn't also to say that they did not plan for the next generation. Their children were 25% of four different regions of the world, and they expected their children to pass that 25% to the next generation to not be seen as racial at all. They had one girl and one boy, in that order, and just enough for the two adults. Two children per household to hold a steady population with some families having three in case of childhood deaths along the way. Immigration would help to hold their country steady as their cities currently blossomed from wealth and industry.

Marya of course had not taken any maternity leave off to have her children and had used her vacation days to care for her children before nannies were hired to provide for them. More than some of her employees, Marya noted as she spotted a younger female trying to make her way to her window quietly. Alas, as she looked up, Marya's eyes aligned with hers and the young woman, Emily Bounder was the name on her nametag, bowed her head in respect before turning to ready herself for the day. Her first week back from maternity leave, and she no doubt had a rough morning, but that was no excuse in this place of business. This was a bank, and the customers would only see the best of service from any of them.

Just then, the main door was opened by the doorman and in walked a young woman in a sundress of purple and pink, the bottom of the skirt billowing up behind her as she moved. Her white skin was very much blinding, emphasizing her lack of time outside. Her hair however was a dark brown, showing that she spent time in her life outside, her hair was straight down her face, down to her ample chest, but her chest was covered, and most would look back to her sky-blue eyes and her eager smile.

All eyes secretly watched her move to the section of the lobby and carefully sit down, placing a picnic basket down into her lap and looked ahead, her body obviously strained to be still while one foot jiggled excitedly every few seconds.

"May I assist you, ma'am?" Emily walked forward, helping the customer right away as was trained by them.

"Yes. I'm hoping to get a business loan today."

"Of course. I'll just ask you to fill out this form on the tablet, and I'll let the loan officer know you're here in a few minutes."

"Thank you," the woman nodded her head politely as she placed her basket on the floor next to her chair and took the offered tablet before biting her lip lightly. "Can you walk me through it?"

"Of course. It would be my pleasure."

The bank had opened not forty-five minutes ago, and this was their first customer. At the sound of another bell, all eyes but Emily's turned to welcome the next customer. Emily would not shame the customer before her by looking at another; this was the commanding respect of their bank that their customers expected.

As it happened, it was not a customer who was being let in. Down the three steps from the entrance came another woman in a plain grey jumpsuit, black boots on her feet and rubber gloves on her hands. She had on a ballcap that had her company's logo on it and her brunette hair was in a ponytail out the back of it, with sunglasses over her eyes.

She trudged around a red mechanic's bag of no doubt many tools needed for their profession and moved past Emily's shoulder as the young employee did not give her even an acknowledgement, but instead leaned forward to correct an error in her customer's application. As they stopped just past the teller cages and in front of the main staircase where an assistant manager stood, she blew up a piece of bubble gum and popped it, the pink stretching over her mouth as she took off her sunglasses, revealing a sea blue set of eyes.

"I'm here to fix that problem you called about two hours ago." The manager nodded his head and moved up the stairs, while the technician stayed in place, waiting for him to give his approval to follow.

"Right this way, ma'am." The loan officer spoke up a few minutes later as he stepped up to the woman in the lobby chair. He noticed her ease of getting up, noting her young body, and internally wondered how much credit she was hoping to get. She seemed in her mid-twenties to early thirties, but the application was a business loan, so perhaps an entrepreneur.

The young woman stood up and followed him as they moved only some feet away to his desk. The woman smiled gratefully as the officer pulled out the chair for her. The officer took his own seat on the other side where the computer faced him and smiled gently. "Now then, what was your name, ma'am?"

"Amelia, sir."

"And what kind of a loan were you looking to start today?"

Amelia's eyes widened in glee and the officer gulped back a sigh. *'Another one of these girls then.'*

"Oh! You'll love this!!!!" Amelia leaned over the desk, the vendor pulling out the basket which she set on the table. Immediately, a tasty smell wafted into the officer's nose, and it was so as she pulled the basket's top off to pull out muffins and a piping liquid of coffee and set them before him. "I want to open a cafe! I have all sorts of my own family's creations, blended over 20 years in the business! Taste!"

As she leaned forward eagerly, shaking the man's hand with a firm, hopeful affection, the man sourly grinned back. "I'm not too sure about this loan, Amelia. Do you have any references or things to be leveraged?"

Amelia leaned back, saddened at the man's crass words, and shook her head. "No… this is my first time trying to get a business loan. I have outstanding credit, and I was the top of my class at culinary school. I just…didn't have any extra after I paid off all the loans for school. But I have the experience and the perseverance to get it done."

The loan officer smiled at the young girl's spunk. "Tell you what. Why don't I get the head manager for you?"

Amelia's eyes brimmed with tears. "Oh! You could do that for me?" At the officer's assuring nod, tears fell down her cheeks, showing her emotional side. "That would be splendid!" The girl smiled kindly. "Such great service you have here." The officer smiled back and picked up his phone.

The tech meanwhile waited at the bottom of the steps before looking up to the top to see the assistant manager motion with his head. She moved up the marble steps, mentally counting thirty steps as the manager pointed to her ear.

"Do you need that earpiece, ma'am?"

"It's set up for my tablet to find things while I have my hands full. That allows me to work faster and with more accuracy."

"My apologies. I was just curious." The man backed down as they continued down the employee's entrance door. He pressed his key fob against the door which blinked green and buzzed as he moved inside, keeping the door open for the technician who passed the clear glass door.

"I can see it's very secure here."

"Indeed. We are the most secure in all the region. Our boss is very proud of that fact."

The technician smiled at the boasting of the 2nd in command and continued to follow him until they reached the manager's office. It was as they reached the office that the loan officer called up to Marya's phone as she picked up.

"Yes?......Of course I can assist you, Marcus.…...Yes, I'll be right down."

"Marya?"

The woman looked up and saw her assistant and the female technician. "Who is this?"

"Ma'am?" The technician spoke up, her voice ruff and unrefined. Marya would imagine this person was used to a more hands on approach to life, which was a shame as her face was pretty enough for even fashion. But if they were easily raised by a hands-on approach, then she respected that. "You had problems with your computer?"

"Oh!" Marya smiled gratefully. "You're here early. When I called this morning, they said that you wouldn't be able to come until tomorrow."

"Well, I was in the neighborhood this morning and the job was rather simple in hindsight, so I looked at the job in the area and figured that you would like the speedy repair. Harsh and Wake company doesn't like to make our customers' lives any more difficult than they already are." The technician's voice changed a little, more feminine and with poise and eloquence. "We try our utmost best for our customers."

Marya smiled. "You must say that to all your customers."

The woman smiled back guiltily. "Yes ma'am. Practiced in the mirror so that I can sound nicer. Now then," The tech paused to pull out a tablet from their bag. "Here are my credentials-"

"-Oh, you're good, I'm sure." Marya rushed out as she noticed the minute she had spent talking and therefore leaving a potential customer in need. "I actually need to head downstairs for a bit. You don't need me to log in, I presume, otherwise, you'll need to wait for me to return."

"I should be able to see if that's needed after an initial scan. But if I do, then of course, I will take a seat and wait. Hopefully it's just a simple fix."

"I hope so." Marya smiled and left the room, her compatriot following her back down to his post. The technician opened her case and rearranged some things around before sliding a device into the computer's port and sat down before the computer. She sighed out through her nose and touched the device on her ear.

"...In position."

Downstairs in the lobby, Amelia paused in her explanation of her finances to nod slightly, her own earpiece hidden underneath her straight locks of hair. "What I mean is, I'm sure that I can raise the capital, but having a set amount I can use as collateral in the initial cost would be ideal."

"That sounds rather reasonable, young lady." Marya spoke up as Amelia turned and saw the bank manager exit down the staircase and made a beeline straight for her. "And how can we help you today?"

"Oh! First let me-Ah!!" Amelia screamed as she had jumped up from her seat and leaned too far to extend her hand in greeting. Her sleeve slid around the edge of the lid, and as it pulled over the cup, the contents spilled out along the desk, like a tidal wave upon fresh sand.

"Oh my god! I'm so sorry." Amelia blurted out her apologies as all three rushed to grab papers and devices away as the hot liquid seeped off the desk and began to dribble on the ground. "I am such a klutz. I greatly apologize! I really don't-"

"It's alright ma'am." Marya rushed out to turn to her employee. "Marcus, please rush to grab some towels and disinfectants."

"Yes, Ma'am." Marcus the loan officer rushed out of the area to find the supplies. As they looked away, Amelia rushed to hold the computer at an angle, keeping it dry from the liquid, as from between her fingers, a small device snapped in place on the port of the computer.

Marcus quickly rushed back, wiping away the coffee as Marya looked at the ashamed client, and rubbed her back comfortingly. "I assure you ma'am. Don't fret over this."

Amelia sniffled, and reached into her purse, pulling out a handkerchief to dab at her cheeks. "Thank you."

"So then," Marya took a seat down before the computer as the officer finished up the cleaning. "I'm told that you were hoping to get a loan. How about we check some things. Sound good?"

"Oh Yes, please."

"Alright, just let me sign in and see what we can do for you today." Marya smiled, typing in her credentials, as Amelia cast a fleeting glance at the plastic end of the computer, noting the small blinking red light inside the now filled in port.

At the manager's computer, the log in page was open, and without touching the keyboard, the password inserted itself into the necessary areas before opening to a pristine desktop with only shortcuts for folders and on hand copies were located. The password entered from the keyboard below on the floor of the bank and the technician smiled.

After the desktop appeared, the technician quickly went to work, swiftly typing away and going through backdoors to access the files she was looking for. After just two minutes, she was into the customer list and zeroed in, her eyes skimming quickly down the other files checking for the second list she needed.

Soon after, she smiled as she opened the accounts list and entered her own account number, pressing search as the computer started checking the entire database for her. As she leaned back waiting for results, she smiled as their goals began to come true. Four weeks to trace the money for the stolen painting back from the insurance company who had secured the Walter painting at the museum. Another week and sneaking inside the company to find out which account the money had been placed in. And finally, the technician smiled at the glowing name on the screen.

"We found you Alex....or shall I say Tommy Smith." The technician whispered proudly as she printed out all the details and logged out before standing up. As she moved everything in place and disconnected the wires, she tapped her earpiece and spoke. "All set. Extract in two."

Amelia heard the time and leaned forward with a frown. "I'm sorry. Can you repeat that?"

"Basically Amelia, you just don't have the right references to start this loan."

"Oh! I feel so ashamed." Amelia had the decency to blush. "My mother assured me that she was the right reference. She is a business owner."

"It's not that, dear. You need established, local companies who acknowledge your work. Surely your culinary degree was local?"

"...I did take some internships with some Michelin restaurants in Kavala."

"Oh! That would be perfect. Simply get their recommendations and send them to me personally."

"You would do that for me? Really?"

"Of course, dear. Here is my personal number. We make sure that all our customers get the best of service."

"Oh! There must be something I can do to repay you-"

"There's really no need, Ma'am." Marya shook her head, the manager's eyes spotting the tech waving her over from the bottom of the stairs. "If you will excuse me for a moment."

Amelia waited for her to turn away before leaning back and grabbing the basket off the desk, taking the hidden chance to grab the key logger out of the computer.

Marya walked forward and smiled hopefully at the technician. "Do I need to go back up?" Marya internally sighed. She needed to get their accounts updated as soon as possible.

"Actually, I just need you to sign this ma'am. I was able to find the problem."

"Really?" Marya smiled intrigued. "What was it?"

"A trojan, ma'am. From an email most likely."

"Oh, I feel so foolish."

"Happens all the time, ma'am."

"Thanks again for coming so fast. I really do need to access the sensitive information from that terminal."

"Of course." The technician nodded her head before turning around and moving to the door. But she was stalled as Amelia tripped over her heels on the carpet and skipped in front of her before the technician steadied her with a hand on her waist.

"Thank you." Amelia blushed as she glanced over as the two women made eye contact.

"Shall I walk you out, Miss?"

Amelia smiled brightly, her eyes glowing with happiness. "I'd like that."

Marya watched as they walked out together, approaching the door, talking like complete strangers as she overheard the standard questions asked of any newcomer. So different the two were, but perfect in their own way. Marya cleared her head and hurried to her desk. She had much to do and must do it perfectly.

As soon as they cleared two blocks, the two women smiled brightly.

"You got it?" Amelia asked.

"Oh yeah." The technician nodded happily, pulling off the baseball cap to let her own brown hair flow.

"I was really worried, Tess." Amelia ended the farce, running hands through her luscious brown locks and groaning. "I hate switching roles with you. It's hard to fake an entirely new persona that I'm not used to."

Tess smiled back at her. "Oh, come now, Tanya. That orchestrated trip at the end. Perfectly executed. And you look great as a brunette."

Tanya grinned sarcastically at her sister. "Of course, I do. I look good in any color, even your unique strawberry blonde hair would only serve to highlight my own beauty." Tanya sighed relieved. "It's over though. Let's just get to the apartment and wash this out."

As Tanya complained in groans and muttering, skimming her fingers through her hair, she failed to see that her sister had stopped and turned to face her. "Tess?" Tanya asked, but then saw Tess smile apologetically.

"About that…" Tess let her words hang in the hair as Tanya's eyes widened and her fingers froze mid-graze through her hair. Her mind ceased to work as she shook her head negatively.

"You didn't, right?"

"Sorry…..."

"No! You did not actually dye my hair brown, Tess!!"

"Just for a few weeks!" Tess insisted, her hands trying to placate her.

"Tess!" Tanya seethed.

"Hey! You wanted to meet Daniel, right? Well; he thinks you're my sister." Tess replied with her own hands trailing through her own brunette hair.

"I am your sister. We could have just said that I was adopted, you dolt!" Tanya growled, stomping off a few feet further as Tess walked after her.

"Come on, Tanya. Please understand; you were right; he's special to me…I need this from you." Tanya turned her face away in anger and Tess huffed at her.

"Fine! Just go home then and you can talk to me when you realize how right I am."

Tanya sighed through her teeth and muttered. "Just go back and fuck your boyfriend, you sex addict."

"Tanya…Tanya…..."

"What?" Tanya shot back as Tess sighed and nudged her head to the side.

"I'm your ride back." Tanya heard her sister's soft voice and followed her eyes to the van beside them. She scowled as they each got in from either door and Tess bent down, sparking some wires as the stolen maintenance van roared to life and they began their trek home.

That night in the predawn of the next day, the door to the apartment slipped open silently as Tess snuck inside the apartment, she currently stayed rent free with her boyfriend. She edged inside with shoes in hand to keep her feet silent on the floor as she kept the lights off to not wake him up. Tess smiled as she turned to silently close the door, having oiled it up only a few days prior.

Tess smiled as she edged to the bedroom door and would have congratulated herself if not for the corner of the table. Tess gasped and stifled a scream of pain as her knee slammed into the table, trying to keep quiet, but bolts and screws from her spare projects rolled off the table and clanged on the wooden floor, booming like jets in Tess's ears. Tess made her bruised way to the bedroom door and slipped inside; obviously she hadn't memorized her boyfriend's place just yet.

She looked inside to see Daniel sleeping on his side facing the inside of the room, but he was still asleep. She hadn't woken him. Tess smiled as she opened the bedroom door wider and closed it before moving to the bed itself and began to quietly strip out of her clothes. She let her blouse fall to the floor, followed by her skirt, and then undid her bra until she had stripped to just her panties and stockings. Tess lazily slipped under the covers and faced away from Daniel, her breasts free with the rest of her upper body and slowly closed her eyes, ready to be lulled to sleep by listening to her lover's breathing. But...there was none to be heard.

"...Morning." Daniel suddenly breathed into her ear and Paige shivered as his hands slid under her body and pulled her flush against his shirtless chest, cupping her breasts as he began to lewdly tease her.

"I was trying not to wake you up." Paige pouted playfully, her hormones already succumbing to the mind addling mixture of pleasure that Daniel elicited by her mouth as she moaned lightly.

"It's time I usually get up." Daniel whispered as he pulled on Paige's hip as she turned over onto her back as Daniel moved over her and began to assault her neck with butterfly kisses, Paige clinging to his body as she lightly humped his chest and hips with her own.

"Did you miss me while you were gone?" Daniel gruffly asked, making Paige shiver at the huskiness in his voice.

"So much it hurt." Paige giggled as she rolled them over again in a battle for control, but once again he emerged on top of her and continued to kiss her neck longingly.

"I missed this feeling." He uttered.

"Daniel, don't you have to go?" Paige simmered down. She knew his schedule like the back of her hand. She realized that he'd been delaying his time so that he might just see her.

"You know……..I think I'm sick. I need to stay in bed with my sick girlfriend who infected me when she slept beside me."

Paige smiled lustfully. "We slept all night?"

"………Maybe….…"

"Don't take too long." Paige whispered, but both heard it in their minds. *'Come back and let's fuck.'*

"I won't." Daniel stepped out of the room to grab some things and call his boss. As soon as he did, Tess ditched her panties, but kept her stockings on, knowing that he loved dirty things like that; her wearing clothes that covered nothing. She shivered. If he was calling in sick and not just late, then he'd be pleasuring her for a while before he took his time fucking her.

This was what she had wanted to celebrate with after getting Alex's pseudonym he now hid under. And Smith? What a dumbass to use such a common last name. She almost felt sad she even spent time looking.

Daniel sneaked back in through the door and saw his girlfriend there laying spread out on the bed, looking at him as she bit her finger between her teeth, looking naughtily. "Damn, you drive me crazy." Daniel smiled as he quickly moved to the end of the bed, sliding his palms along her smooth legs only to spread them further, opening her wider as he pulled her closer to the edge and dipped his head down as Tess looked at him with unbridled love in her eyes. As the pleasure began to crescendo up her spine, she looked up at the ceiling and wondered for hours, thinking that there really was nothing better than these feelings she was experiencing with him…...Not even the thrill of the heist she had just pulled.

XIII-THE TEAM

Even in a secret hideout, one had to move furniture. As such, Tess and Tanya bent down with their legs, dropping the couch between them in place. Both girls sighed and stretched up before moving away to other parts of the room. The couches in the room were now placed perpendicular to another, three of them creating a 'U' shape on the center of the room, all in front of a glass board that Tess was moving into place in front of them.

"Did you add everything to the H Drive, Tanya?" Tess asked across the room as she locked the board in place.

"What do you take me for, Sis? Of course, I did." Tanya rolled her eyes, picking up her tablet and sliding her finger over it, the device unlocking from her fingerprint and movement. Tanya pranced over to Tess's side before activating the glass screen as it came to life, the glass shimmering as electricity danced along the large see-through panel.

"Just wanting to be sure is all." Tess smiled. Tanya gave her a playful shove before she began sliding designs and schematics from her tablet and up to the glass screen before the two daughters of Amelia Walter. As Tanya spaced out the diagrams and readied the presentation, Tess moved back to the glass table in between the couches and grabbed a glass of lemonade, taking a quick sip to calm herself.

"Don't worry, Tess." Tanya assured her without turning around. "They'll come on board with the plan."

"I'm sure, Tanya. Everyone has a stake in this, but will they be okay with the plan? I don't know."

Tanya smiled as she turned back towards her sister. "Well, if all else fails, we can always bomb his house. I can get my hands on some dynamite from the mining city close by." Both girls giggled, knowing that neither would kill Alex; at least, not that way.

"Did you start the fireworks without me?" A voice called out as the girls turned their heads excitedly. Before them was an Asian girl walking into the room from the main entrance. Tess quickly placed her drink on the table and ran over to hug the bun haired girl, hugging the shorter girl who embraced back with a tight hug of her own.

"Megan! I'm so happy to see you. I'm so happy you're here!" Tess screamed happily and embraced her tighter as she dipped her face into Megan's shoulder. Megan herself smiled as Tess's body shook with great restraint, trying not to cry. The last she had seen Tess was her crying over their mentor's corpse as she fled the scene of the heist.

"Well, I'm happy to be back in the area." Megan shrugged out of Tess's grasp, but Tess smiled back and readjusted her blouse, hiding a string of tears out of the corner of her eye.

"Where were you hiding?"

Megan shrugged. "I was in Japan with one of my boys."

Tanya walked over and hugged their Asian counterpart. "Hope it wasn't Abby's cousin. She'll kill you otherwise."

But Megan smiled devilishly back at Tanya. "If you don't tell her then I'm in the clear. Maybe I could...convince you to not tell?" She smiled as Tanya crossed her arms and listened on as Megan told her of her recent exploits.

While the two talked, Tess smiled and watched the two reunite after months apart. Megan Higurishi. A Chinese girl whose arms were strong and who always showed it off with sleeveless qui-paos and traditional outfits. But even without her clothes and strength, just who was Megan? Well, for the team, she was their explosives expert. She had the steadiest hand that anyone knew of and could thread a cable through the eye of a needle and with only one second to look at it. Anything chemical that blew up was her specialty.

As Megan ragged at Tanya's new color of hair, Tess remembered when Amelia had found her after a rather badly planned jewelry heist when Megan was sixteen and newer to the field. She had mixed the wrong concentration of explosives and so when the blast had gone off, a huge part of it blew back on her, burning her chest and arms into third degree burns. Amelia had paid for everything, and fourteen surgeries later had her looking normal once again. But that horrible event didn't seem to discourage her in her profession at all; instead, she became ready for more lucrative and fun challenges, and if there was one thing about Megan, it was that she loved a challenge.

The sound of the elevator dinged as the wooden bars slid up from the garage in the back of the building. This time Tanya turned to smile wide as she pranced along to the other side of the room and ran at the girl who was just entering with luggage on her arms. Tanya jumped into the air hoping to hug the older woman before her.

"Oh no you don't, Tanya!" The woman exclaimed as she slipped out of Tanya's hugging embrace as if Tanya was covered in oil. The woman's hair was as dry as corn and frizzy when she let it go, so she always had it styled in four ponytails behind her head. As Tanya tried to hug her again, the girl eeped and stepped back. "Come on! I just had a shower!!"

"I'm not that dirty!" Tanya laughed as she finally wrapped her arms around her prey as the girl sighed dramatically and dropped her bags to the floor and hugged back.

"I'm so charging you double for this." The girl muttered, but Tanya just giggled and hugged back.

"Melissa always forgets just how much Tanya idolized her as if she was a big sister growing up, doesn't she?" Megan smiled, shaking her head as she leaned back on an armrest. Tess nodded her head in agreement as she watched Tanya happily annoy the woman who was six years their senior.

Melissa Saria; Hardware specialist and team supplier. Tanya was great with software and hardware as well, but Melissa could run circles around Tanya on operating the equipment in the field and adapting on sight unlike her. As the supplier, there was nothing Melissa could not get her hands on. She could con her way into vehicles, goods, and products that no one should be able to get but she procured it like no tomorrow.

Tess smiled as she listened back in on their conversation, sitting beside Megan as she did so.

"What do you mean you're not dirty?!? You little minx you are! Always the tease, like a pinup model! You're the one laying in old warehouses in your underwear, Tanya!"

Tanya scoffed. "Oh yeah, 'I'm the model.' Says the bikini girl getting a tan in the desert! How you don't die of heatstroke is beyond me."

Tess and Megan chuckled at the annoying atmosphere these two gave off whenever together. Melissa was like an older sister to them all, telling them off and what was right whenever she could, but Tanya just happened to be her favorite to do so to. Melissa hadn't been saved by Amelia like the others. Instead, Amelia had saved her younger brother from a serial killer in a dark alley, and Melissa, in kind, had helped her in a job at the time. Over the course of years of help, Melissa had turned from working as a blue-collar worker into their life of crime.

'Crime?' Tess thought to herself and smiled. Such a grey area of crime they took part in. These girls didn't use guns or threats. They did not rob the weak. They were professionals. Ones who used their bodies, their skills, and their minds to get their tasks completed with great efficiency. They knew what they were doing, and they were some of the best in their line of work, the next generation of high-class band of thieves.

Tanya looked around herself and smiled at the sight of Megan. "You two got here alright."

Megan shrugged as she put her feet over the back of the couch and hung upside down at her. "Yeah, my passport seemed to do okay, but those aliases you got us Tanya were cruel!"

Tanya shrugged. "I needed to make sure you weren't recognized." Tanya smiled slyly over her shoulder at her older friend. "After all, Melissa; you are wanted for arson in Kavala."

Melissa puffed her cheeks out and sighed angrily. "Hey! That company was testing on animals."

"Still can't do that and give your name." A soft-spoken voice called out from around the corner of the hallway before a crash sounded with a squeaked voice accompanying it. Tess and Tanya both sighed with a smile at the sound. This sort of thing always happened with their newest member of the team.

The door around the corner finally closed and around it appeared a black haired bombshell who backed into the room. Her arms stretched in front of her as she turned to the group and smiled. "Hey girls."

'One... Two... Three... ' They all thought before the light fixture that she had run into that hallway appeared behind her and fell, crashing onto the floor and making more noise than before. The girl turned her head back wincing and looked back at them ashamed.

"You asked the rookie to come?" Megan gawked as the girl frowned back with a glare. Before a fight erupted, Tess rushed between them and held them off.

"Hey!" Tess called out, silencing everyone as they turned to their leader. "Everyone here was there that day and saw what Alex did. This assignment; it's personal for all of us. Abby has a right on this too, Megan, and it doesn't matter if she is perfect or not. She's in on this."

Megan smiled in resignation and shrugged before Tess turned around. "It's really good to see you, Abby." Tess spoke as she embraced her friend and Abby hugged her back in gratitude.

"Thanks for letting me in on this." Abby mumbled quietly and sniffled as she backed away. "It was my fault that it happened. I was supposed to frisk everyone there, but he slipped by me before I even saw him arrive. I need this; I can't move on until I clear my reputation." Tess smiled gratefully and kissed her cheek affectionately.

In came Abby. The most recent addition to their crew after Alex. Her skills- mediocre at best, a complete failure at worst. Her stealth- terrible; a child could murder the president of a major company before she could sneak into a room. Her crux was confidence and once she achieved that, Amelia had said that she would be as legendary as the rest of them, but what made her valuable on the team was actually her agility and flexibility in many areas. She didn't have a specialized skill in one but could fill in the gaps of a missing member well enough until they got there.

Tess had spent a year living with Abby before their big con last year teaching what she knew, and now Tanya had taken her under her wing to show her the tech stuff. She was their youngest member at nineteen, while going to one of the best colleges around and a very high IQ to boot; she was on her way to a very prosperous life in crime and led a future company to greatness...unless she got caught as they all worried about her lack of subtlety.

Abby ended the hug with Tess and glared back at Megan. "Good to see you too, Megan. I appreciate the lack of confidence in my skills...... Oh! And next time you take Jake out of the country, let me know!"

Megan had the decency to blush just a bit before her cocky attitude returned. "Oh! I'm sorry if I want to take my boyfriend on a couple's only trip away from his helicopter family and little cousin."

"He was supposed to be taking his LSAT's."

"He was distracted." Megan smiled lovingly as half the girls shivered and the other half smiled. Megan was definitely banging Abby's cousin; it was a fact that Abby resented after having introduced them when he surprised them at the wrong moment. Suffice to say that Megan and he had hit it off soon after.

"Alright girls. Now that everyone is here, Let's get started."

"Just the five of us, huh?" Melissa questioned.

"You did always like odd numbers, Melissa."

As everyone sat down on a couch, Tess stayed standing up, and tapped the glass as the screen woke from sleep and came to life, showing all the information that Tanya and she had collected since making this plan.

"Four months ago, Tanya found this painting hanging in a museum here in Kavala. It's one of Amelia's masterpieces as an artist before her life with all of us. She never really sold them and as such, she had given them to her friends and charitable establishments. We almost passed this off since Amelia was after all born here in Kavala; that was until Tanya found that someone had bought this painting for twice its worth and put it in the museum to bypass needing insurance, wanting to own something of hers to prove that they killed someone great. We believe this to be Alex."

"Insurance companies do that?" Abby asked, cocking her head to the side.

Tess nodded to her younger teammate. "Museums have guards and securities on par with most banks, so they are seen as good places to store paintings. And because they are so secure, people donate their works to museums who in return show them to the people of the nation and the world. It gives the museums money to operate, good for a nice feel to the local community, and allows people to see the history of art."

"Okay Tess. We know you love art and if we let you, you'll go on and on forever. So, paint the picture for us, Tess." Megan smiled with a knowing smirk. "Tell us first; How'd you get the painting? I heard it disappeared 6 weeks ago, so it had to have been you two."

Tess looked around the room of the girls and noticed their Cheshire grins and their shoulders leaning in. She smiled in defeat as she sighed and nodded her head. Thirty minutes later, Tess had explained Tanya's failed attempts at getting into the museum's security and then how Tess charmed a guard out of position and distracted him while they did the actual heist.

"Wow, Tanya. You actually did the real heist?" Melissa whistled. "Way to step up! You didn't flinch in the heat of it."

Tanya rubbed her chin nervously, remembering the pain the board had inflicted to her jaw going down the stairs. "I know how to be professional, Melissa."

"And you deleted the footage while making out, Tess?"

"Didn't need to, Megan. Tanya's device kept her from appearing on the cameras. I just had to distract the guard from actually looking at the cameras in case Tanya's frame peeked out, but she did a fine job, so I didn't need to do anything special."

"Oh no, Tess. You pulled some extra tricks all on your own." Tanya quipped, making Tess blush at just how close she came to fucking in that room.

"So, in total, Tanya and I conned one of the guards there and took the painting."

"So, you were with the guard on multiple occasions then, Tess? That could become a hamper if he mentions you in the police inquiries. I mean, does the guard know you?"

Tess smiled sarcastically at Melissa. "He still knows nothing, and he told me everything he told the cops just last week when we had lunch."

Melissa blushed bashfully. "Sorry. I just meant your face and your real hair and name. Love the brown hair by the way Tess, and Tanya too. So... normal for once, it's refreshing."

Tess smiled. "It's always nice to walk down a street without everyone looking at you."

"I'm sure your figure still turns heads and-Wait! You said still seeing him? Are you still in contact with the guard?"

"Yes. Tess is currently dating him to keep us in the loop with the police investigation just to stay on top of things." Tanya butt in, cutting her sister off. Tess herself held a sour face for a second as dating Daniel was more than just an info backup, but she nodded anyway before continuing.

"A-anyways, we've tracked the buyer's account to this bank," Tess spoke as she highlighted the image on screen, "the bank of Kavala and we hope to have something soon on where he lives. Alex is here, girls. I know it."

"We're with you, Tess." Megan stood up and pumped her fist.

"Yeah, let's kill that bastard." Melissa scowled as she agreed to the plan.

Abby meanwhile remained where she was, nervous as the group split up around the room. Abby's eyes shivered around the room before she walked over to Tess and pulled her aside to the entryway where Abby herself had entered.

"You don't need to worry about the plan, Abby. Just relax." Tess smiled, hoping to comfort the newer girl.

Abby meanwhile looked up at her mentor, and the one she'd spent the most time with so far on the team. "...Are you really going to kill him, Tess? I don't want to see blood on your hands." Abby looked up as she finished talking.

Tess's eyes bore into Abby's eyes making the younger girl gulp in submission. "It's too late for that, Abby. When I'm done with him, he'll ask me to end his suffering, to end his life painlessly….and I'll say no."

Tess walked off and Abby shivered as a dark aura surrounded Tess's eyes. Abby may be the newest on the team, but her eyes saw what others did not, and right now, Tess's murderous intent was black as night. She didn't like scary Tess. She wanted her friend and mentor back. Where was the girl who was always eager to laugh on the job? Where was the compassionate, strong willed woman that Abby strived to become? Abby sighed. She could only hope that after Alex was killed, that she could help restore Tess to who she really was.

As Abby watched Tess head over to Melissa, Tanya was with Megan working on some metal tubes for launching stuff, torches and wrenches sprawled out all around them as the engineers of the team worked on their equipment, prepping, and maintaining it for if and when they would use them. As Tess left the room via the staircase to grab something from the loft, Megan turned to her partner in crime.

"So then, just how real is the relationship between Tess and the guard?"

Tanya sighed with a smile as she wrenched a nut into place before handing the same wrench over to Megan for her side. "You noticed that did you?"

Megan smiled back as she tightened her own side and meekly shrugged back. "I know a deep yearning when I see one."

Tanya nodded her head. Megan knew because she herself got that way whenever Jake was mentioned. "Honestly, I think it's serious."

"Danger to us?" She voiced back.

Tanya shook her head. "Done his background. He's an honest citizen of Kavala with nothing hidden in his past." Tanya reached down and started the sedaline torch, as the white-hot gas settled into blue. "The danger is from our side of the fence."

XIV-MY SISTER TANYA-I MEAN JULIA

Tess waited patiently as she sat on her boyfriend's bed, twirling her thumbs as she lightly bounced her knee up and down to hide the nervousness that coursed through her body. She paused for a second at her choice of words. *'Boyfriend.'* Tess silently chuckled to herself and gazed out the window to the lush garden on the ground floor. She had really fallen deeply in love with him, hadn't she? So why didn't she ever say such a thing to him?

As Tess looked at the greenery, she couldn't help but wonder how she was lucky enough to have him in her life now. Tess turned her head to look at the mirror on the wall above the dresser and made a sexy pose while grazing her fingers through her brunette hair, her blue eyes reflecting back at her. Tess paused again while she looked at herself; she had a boyfriend, but for how long exactly?

She was bringing him into danger now, wasn't she? What exactly was she pulling Daniel into? A life of crime, moving from place to place, changing yourself every few months so that people know you as someone else, but never the same person as another. Tess felt a deep pang of guilt wrap and twirl around her stomach at all the lies she continued to live with while she dated Daniel.

He...He didn't even know her real name. Here she was, thinking as Tess, her real name and main persona, but in front of Daniel, she was Paige, innocent, intelligent, adventurous Paige, who had a submissive, embarrassed side to herself when starting up a romantic situation with someone new. No; Tess looked down and sighed. She knew that her own self was bleeding into Paige's persona with an increasing fervor.

Her more than forward sexual openness, her dominant personality to be in charge.

Tess smiled nostalgically. But also, the nice things; the lanquidity of being a homebody, laying on the couch and watching romance comedies as she liked to do between jobs. Just a nice little hike through the forest or a swim through the lake and just lying there in nature was her form of relaxation. She...she was letting her outer personality crack as time went on.

She looked down in shame. Daniel didn't even know what she really did for a living. Even after these past few months, she still hadn't told him exactly what she did. He didn't ask, saying that he didn't care as long as it made her happy. He respected her, and she felt her confidence buoyed by that respect, and she felt terrible at keeping it secret, even if she didn't mind stealing from those who could afford it.

Tess sighed and shook back her meager thoughts. It was too late now. She was falling and digging her hole deeper with Daniel than ever before. Now she had forced Tanya to be Julia in real life and meet Daniel as her sister visiting family tonight. It was one thing to lie about herself, but now she was adding in a family. Tanya was her actual sister, adopted just like Tess by Amelia, but she was already married to a husband who loved her and had the cutest daughters ever born to this world, and Tess loved Ami and Yuki like the nieces they were, but they'd never get to meet Daniel.

Just one wrong word, and Julia would be Tanya, their mother. They knew nothing of what Tanya did in her life either, but her family was so content, and happy. Tanya took time off from their missions if Yuki or Ami needed her at school or home, and Tess wondered if that was what her life could be like. Would it be enough? Living as a housewife with little rug rats running around, stealing artworks and wealth from rich men while her husband lived beside her believing that money wasn't essential to a happy life. Could she live her life in all the lies? Maybe not.........but she would at least be happy.

"Paige? How do I look?"

Paige turned around, her dress whipping around her frame and smiled at Daniel's attire. His pants were nice black slacks and pressed to perfection, his shoes freshly polished and shining, but…. his red dress shirt was a little wrinkly even though he'd ironed it and everything just before his shower. Paige giggled at the appearance as she stepped over to her lover and readjusted his tie before pulling it and him down to her lips for a slow, passionate lip-locked embrace.

"You look amazing. My sister will love you. I just know it."

Daniel smiled gratefully and Paige felt butterflies flow through her stomach. "I hope so. I want to hear all those childhood stories after all."

Paige slowly looked down, her nerves getting to her, but Daniel was quick to hold her hands and swung them between the small gap separating them to get her attention. "Hey. I don't need to meet her if you want to see her by yourself."

Paige shook her head ruefully. "No…no, I do want you two to meet. I'm just nervous I suppose. I've never had someone so close before that I'm willing to introduce."

Daniel smiled and kissed her cheek affectionately. "Come on. I checked our reservation and it's almost time."

"Right."

The two of them spent the time walking towards the restaurant that Daniel had thought would be a good upper-class restaurant for his meeting with his girlfriend's sister. Paige knew just how much he wanted to make a good impression. She had offered to use her car, but where they were walking, they'd have to park it anyway and it was only eight or nine blocks away. As it was, Paige's car now stayed in Daniel's allotted space for the apartment complex. While Daniel didn't have a car, he'd usually let others park there as a good neighbor, but now his girlfriend had a monopoly on the spot, further cementing the idea in many of his neighbors' minds that they were steadily falling in love.

With some small conversations and a comfortable silence to distract them, they reached their destination a few minutes before their meeting time and were content to wait outside the restaurant. The restaurant in question was the Sliced Duck, a high-class restaurant that did not seat anyone who was not dressed up for such a rich and classy event, but not too big that only the super-rich could afford it. They wanted people to make a night out of coming to their establishment, and not just a small family outing.

"Daniel, I'm excited for you to meet her." Paige whispered hopefully after a minute.

"...I'm nervous too, Paige." Daniel read her inner thoughts, making Paige giggle and hug his arm further into her chest, the action more normal than special now. It was where she liked to hold him close and intimate. They were both touchy people and always stayed close beside the other, feeling awkward to stand apart.

Just as the giggles ceased, a nice car pulled off the road and into the car lot, before it slid up to park directly in front of the restaurant in the green colored twenty minute parking spot, making Tess cringe. That was definitely her sister. The door opened and Tess felt Daniel stiffen at the sight of her.

Out appeared Tanya, in a stunning silver dress shirt, with small flickering pieces of fabric that reflected the lights of the restaurant everywhere around her, shimmering around her slim body while also accentuating the decent gap of cleavage spilling out the middle. Flowing down her frame followed a slim ruby skirt that ended well above her knees. Her bare arms almost showed clearly if not for the matching ruby jacket that stopped halfway to her waist. All in all, it looked risky and very provocative as her long legs pretty much showed all skin, only strips of her heels hiding parts of her feet as she made her way towards them.

Daniel couldn't help but compare the two girls as they moved to hug the other, their brunette hair matching lengths and color as their bodies looked very similar. As they whispered and giggled together, the only true difference he could see were their faces with similar smiles and eyes being different shades of blue.

"You are such a tease, Tanya." Tess jeered as they hugged the other tightly, hiding a jealous blush. Who knew that faking the reunion of a sister would pull at Tess's real emotions so much?

Tanya giggled playfully and lightly bit her ear to egg her on. "Don't be a hater, Tess." Tanya whispered. "When I introduced my fiance, you came out to introduce yourself in nothing but a towel and bent over so many times." Tanya glanced to the side and saw Daniel's eyes skimming over the both of them and shivered at the attention. "Besides, your boy toy over there is totally checking us out."

Tess blushed as she glanced back and indeed, Daniel was comparing both of their bodies. But Tess didn't mind too much at all. Boys looked at many women every day, but after thirty seconds, forgot most. Now, looking at her sister may be more of a long-term worry in some circles, but Tess only smiled wider. All her life, she compared her own body to Tanya's, wishing she had some parts of her in body and personality. One could call that an idol in a way. And besides that, it didn't matter where Daniel got his sexual appetite from as long as she was his only lover.

"Now then," Tanya smiled as she backed up from the tight embrace. Tanya turned her eyes to the man next to them and openly glanced over his frame, clearly checking him out as he had done to her, making him gulp nervously. "Paige, who is this delectable man standing next to you?"

"I'm Daniel." Daniel reached out, taking the opportunity to shake his girlfriend's sister's offered hand, noticing the rather tough blistered palm, despite looking soft and manicured in front of him. It was obvious to a detail-oriented guy like Daniel that while she had a pretty face, she did not mind getting dirty with her hands. "Her boyfriend."

"I'm Julia, Paige's older sister." Julia boasted, and Daniel could see from the way that the two interacted that Paige respected Julia like the older sister she was. Eager to please and wanting her approval over her own.

"Shall we head inside?" Daniel suggested, and not five minutes later, they were shown to their table near the edge of the room, the waiter ogling Paige's sister as she shook off her jacket to show off her bare shoulders and arms.

The three sat together at a four top, one to each side with the silverware and wine glasses before them. As the waiter left, Tanya only had to watch as she looked between them, her lips turning upwards more and more as her sister literally slid, inch by inch, closer to her boyfriend and held his hand in hers above the table. Not that Tess could see the romance right in front of her face; it only made Tanya believe it was stronger than ever. Tess had it bad, and it was serious; Tanya could see the glow of the two surrounding them, the romance that intertwined the both of them together permeated the air with quite some potency to boot.

"So, Daniel," Julia began, letting her menu drop to the table to glance at the two lovers, but mainly at Daniel who could become a possible newcomer to the family. "Let me get down to it. You've dated my sister for how long?"

"3 months or so." Daniel shrugged as he tried his best to look at Julia, but his eyes still slid sideways, his gaze not bearing to stay away from Paige's own as she rubbed his thigh affectionately and dipped closer towards her face, his brain short-circuiting for a few seconds.

"And I assume having sex for just as long?" Julia asked nonchalantly as she sipped her wine.

"Yes ...I mean-" Daniel affirmed offhandedly, his mind far away as he stared into Paige's eyes deeply swooning but realized the question too late and looked over and blushed deep as Julia grinned wide in triumph at his and Paige's matching blush.

Julia leaned back and smiled. "So, you must be great in bed." She spoke as a statement, as she glanced her eyes up and down his frame again.

"W-Why would you think that?" Daniel blushed. It wasn't like he had any experience before Paige had entered his life.

Julia shrugged happily. "My sister was never too active growing up in school or otherwise, but she knows what she's doing, I assume." Paige blushed and pleaded with her eyes for Julia to quit it, but Julia continued, her need for revenge from years ago bursting forth. "She's never asked me for advice on the matter, but you're the only one she's ever brought before me. You must be very special to her."

Daniel looked over at his girlfriend and smiled, squeezing her hand affectionately as Paige flinched in her seat, before she glanced down, her mind frosting over as she stared at their fingers interlocked together. "She means a lot to me as well." Daniel spoke low, as if whispering to a lover their heart's desire.

Paige leaned in closer and looked up as they shared a kiss briefly, their lips slipping alongside the other in a sluggish manner, neither lip minding if it took eternity to find out everything about the opposing muscle.

Julia sighed sweetly at the sight; it made her miss her own lover, and her little girls too. "Well, the love and adoration is there, but I must move onto more logical questions, Daniel, if you don't mind?"

"Go ahead."

"Well-..." Julia paused as they all ordered and asked for wine. They waited patiently as the sommelier poured the drinks, while internally, Daniel hoped that he's doing well. Julia smiled as the guy left and continued where she left off. "So then Daniel, what is it that you do?"

"Well…" Daniel blushed a bit. He didn't mind the work he did, but he did know what others thought about his choice of work. "I work security at a small museum."

"Oh?" Julia cocked her head inquisitively. "But Kavala used to be the capital city of an old kingdom 400 years ago. Surely you protect some nice works."

"There are many fine works there." Daniel affirmed. "We even added a nice park around it as well as a planetarium in the last 4 years, so it looks modern and fresh."

"Does it pay well?"

Daniel shrugged. "Enough. I never cared for too many things growing up."

"How so?"

"Well. I grew up in an orphanage until I was 7 when I was adopted. My parents, when they were alive, never stopped working, and they tended to spoil my sisters more. I just...always wanted a nice family and just enough to get by to be happy."

Julia turned her gaze upon Paige to see her smile and squeeze her lover's hand in response. It was obvious to her that this was the first time talking about this topic between them, the micro expressions on

Tess's face telling her so, and it was completely genuine. "Would your wife work?"

"Maybe." Daniel spoke thoughtfully. "I'd honestly like working enough so that if she didn't have to work, she could volunteer and stuff for the community, but girls like to have jobs, right?"

"Indeed." Julia agreed before leaning over closer to him, intently on continuing the conversation. "You know my sister is a consultant, right?"

"Sort of. Never really explained it in too much detail." Daniel frowned.

"Well," Julia began. "The thing is...she mainly works for me." At Daniel's confused face, Julia smiled. "You see, my friends and I grew up and we were working hours and hours on hard projects, and we were getting nothing from it! So! I decided we could find special jobs for us to be billed as external, a consulting company of sorts. It pays much better than a regular job and the hours, while awkward and random, are nice."

Julia saw her sister blush as Daniel muttered. "So, you're the one who's always interrupting us."

But Julia still heard it. "Oh! I may be interrupting some of your um...romantic encounters. Paige likes working for her older sister, right?" Julia teased.

Paige smiled robotically and nodded her head slowly as Julia scoffed playfully. "I know you love it, Paige. But Paige here is my multi-talented sister. Versatile in tech, a good leader, good communicator. A number of companies go directly to her which I allow because it builds the business, and because...well, she is my sister."

"Well, I guess that's alright." Daniel accepted as he turned and kissed Paige's cheek.

After that, the conversations continued between the arrival of the food and eating. Paige herself was pleasantly surprised by how well Daniel was eating, cutting his food in small parts, and eating them one at a time and never with a full mouth. She found it so cute, how he was really trying to impress her sister. But after tonight, she'd make sure to tell him that it didn't matter if she liked him or not; she liked him, and that's all that mattered.

"Paige, come with me." Julia spoke up as she wiped her mouth with a napkin before standing up. After a chaste kiss, Paige followed her away from the table, as Julia turned to see Daniel gazing and comparing both of them once again. The girls headed to the bathroom and stood in front of the mirrors and as another girl left the bathroom empty besides the two of them, began to reapply their makeup.

"So... he's a keeper for sure." Tanya broke character and smiled more genuinely for her sister. "He respects you so much, Tess and is clearly in love with you." Tanya paused in reapplying her lipstick and smiled even more. "...and I think you feel the same way." She looked over as Tess held a pensive expression and her hands gripped the sink hard, the blood in her veins rushing towards her knuckles. Did she have something important to say to her? It sure seemed like it. "Tess?"

"I know." Tess looked down and breathed in deeply before exhaling slowly. "Tanya, I should have confided in you sooner, I mean, I wanted to tell you the second we reunited but...but the thing is that I've been thinking about what Amelia said to me before she died. To make memories-"

"-With someone you love more than money." Tanya finished as Tess looked up startled at her sister's mirrored reflection. Tanya smiled tearfully. "She told me those words just before I met Matthew. Tess, he's a great guy and I'm happy for you. Truly I am. It's just...you can't tell him what you do."

Tess shook her head in agreement. "I can't...ever."

Tanya saw the sadness and worry oozing out of her sister's body and rubbed her shoulder to console her. "He's just too good, Tess. He's a knight, and you can't corrupt a knight, even for love..."

"That's what I wanted to talk to you about, Tanya." Tess gulped nervously. She hadn't spoken to Tanya or anyone about this for weeks, the topic bottling up inside her mind until it began to break out, but now it had to be said. "You see...I think... that this will be my last job..."

"What?" Now it was Tanya who was aghast as she turned her sister's frame to look at her in the face. "Y-you can't possibly believe that. And Tess, you run the crew!"

There was silence between the two sisters, as Tanya watched her sister look back at her with a questioning look doubting her statement. "Do I?"

"What do you mean?" Tanya retorted, confusing eyes bearing into Tess.

But her sister just smiled at her. "You're the one getting everything ready before the cons. You're the one ensuring our safety during and after them. Even when I became your sister, you took care of me as much as anyone else."

Tanya blushed at that. "Well, you were my baby sister, so of course I'd take care of you. Tess, why do you think Amelia had such a young crew?"

Tess smiled wider. "For us."

"Exactly…" Tanya paused. Their mother had made this crew for them, and her sister, who adored their mother more than anyone else, was willing to give that up for one man. But there was a big thorn in her idea. "...Do you really think you can stop?"

"I... don't know." Tess's unsure voice whispered in response.

Tanya sniffled a bit as she leaned forward and embraced Tess in a deep hug, sniffling into her shoulder. "I feel like I just lost Mom and now I'm losing you."

Tess looked into Tanya's dyed hair and smiled hopefully. "Come on, Tanya. I'll still be around. Maybe I can just help you plan things out-"

"-Deal!" Tanya rushed out, hugging her even tighter. "No take backs." As they stepped back from each other, Tanya smiled sourly. "I'll miss having you with me all the time."

"Hey! We still have a job to do. I'm not going anywhere just yet, so we can talk about it later."

"Right." Tanya nodded, before seeing Tess's lipstick still undone. "I'll let you finish redoing your makeup." Tess nodded gratefully and turned back the mirror, and as she turned to the door, Tanya smiled with a suspicious smirk. Now for some questions without her sister around to distract him.

Tess's shoulders sagged in relief as her sister left her alone. She liked him; she really liked Daniel! So happy was she to finally confess to Tanya her choice in the matter of Daniel. She just…Tess sighed as she looked straight in the mirror, her reapplied lipstick covering half of her face. She couldn't keep this up much longer; this hiding her sudden escapes from his loving embrace, her constant lies she told to let her leave his side. With Tanya's cover as a consultant, she was covered for now to get Alex, but also, this way, she could…build something real…something solid and sturdy with her lover, her boyfriend, her… soulmate? Tess smiled. That sounded really nice.

"Welcome back Julia." Tess's ear buzzed, making Tess roll her eyes. Oh right, she still had her earpiece on. *'Weird though,'* Tess thought. Tanya hadn't had it on when she arrived. Maybe she hit something. She was always touching her newly colored hair, never preferring to dye it like Tess.

"Thank you, Daniel. While my sister is still in the bathroom, I was hoping to ask you something serious."

"Of course! I was wondering when the big sister was going to give me the speech."

"Oh! I wouldn't worry about that. I think you're a good match for my little sister. Daniel, what I wanted to ask is…if you think Paige is marrying material?"

Blood flooded into Tess's ears. *'Tanya, you Idiot!'* Tess screamed to herself in the mirror and dragged her fingers through her hair. What was she thinking? She was scaring him away! It was too early! She wouldn't be able to handle it if he took it badly and left-

"Honestly Julia, I'd ask her now…" Tess's mind froze. Did he have a ring on him? Was he going to propose? "…But she's not ready for that kind of commitment."

Tess looked down as he completed his sentence. She gazed down at her fingers where one of her rings lay. She always changed them out, but never more than one. She looked at her empty ring finger. Was she not ready for marriage? Wasn't it just a piece of paper? Just a way to tell the government that you were together? Or…no, it was more than that. So, what was she not ready for?

"What if she was ready?" She heard Julia ask back.

She knew by the pause that Daniel was rubbing the back of his head nervously. He always did that when there was an awkward pause. "I feel like I know her so well…but you know her better." She heard Daniel sigh into the air. "I feel like…maybe it's just me, but there are times…. not many but…times when she thinks I'm not looking and I see her as someone else, someone…I don't yet know. Like she's hiding some form of herself. Maybe once I know her as well as you Julia, once I can see every side to her, I'll ask her. Mind you," she listened to Daniel's sad chuckle, "I don't plan to end things anytime soon; I mean I feel lonely just at the thought of being without her. My memories before her…I thought I was content back then, but now I'd just feel sad and depressed. I was just a fraction of what I was before she came into my life. She's in my future, your sister and I."

"That's sweet, Daniel. I'm sure Paige will love that." Julia spoke with a Cheshire grin as on the end of her earpiece, she heard her baby sister's choked up tears that were surely falling down her cheeks.

Paige sat down in her seat, but before Daniel could turn back to his meal, Paige rubbed her face deeply into his shoulder, resting there.

"Paige?" Daniel chuckled. "You, okay?"

Paige looked up with a deep blush and smiled just a little, her teeth shining over at him. "Better than ever." Daniel wondered for a second why her eyes were already showing her after-sex blissful sheen in them but shrugged it off. Maybe he was meeting her expectations for the evening.

"SO!!! Daniel, are you thinking about the long term of this relationship?"

"Are you implying something?"

"Well…" Julia smiled a bit into her wine. "How many rascals did you expect to have? "

Paige's arms tightened around Daniel's for the single second he thought of his answer. "As many as she'd be willing to have."

"Oh Daniel." Paige cooed and pulled him in for a deep kiss. She was going to give him something special when they got back home.

"Hello there." A voice emanated next to the table, interrupting their kiss and while Daniel turned to the voice, the girls tensed, as each sister's hand slid down their legs where tiny knives lay hidden. It couldn't be him. It couldn't. It was too soon. But as they turned their heads, there he was, his stylish, rich boy clothes permeating the room with his smell.

"Tommy!" Tanya sputtered out, surprise etched over her face, as she called out the name they'd found as Alex turned to her. "Paige, did you know Tommy would be here?"

"No Julia. I would never have guessed."

"Hello girls." The black-haired savant smiled, lecherously looking them up and down. "Miss me?"

"No." They said together, but Alex leaned over the table and smiled at Daniel, and Daniel stared back, unabashed but protective as he felt Paige's fingernails dig deep into his thigh.

"And you are?"

"Daniel Thompson."

Alex smiled and even more so as Tess edged in front of him, almost on top of his lap. "Tommy Smith. Nice to meet you, Daniel. So! How about I sit down and-"

"Actually, we were just about done."

"I see. Well then-"

"I'll walk you out, Tommy." Julia offered and all was tense before he smiled in resignation.

"Very well." Tommy smiled as Julia's fingers gripped his bicep and began pulling him away. "Daniel, you beware these two. They're very interesting, I assure you."

"...Paige?" Tess followed them out with her eyes before looking back at Daniel. She had to maintain her cover, but she needed to make sure Tanya was safe as well. Tess sighed regretfully.

"You'll have to forgive us, Daniel. Julia is not on good terms with Tommy and-"

"-Neither are you." Daniel interrupted as Paige looked at him before nodding.

"He and I don't see eye to eye at all."

"Anything I need to worry about?"

Paige kissed his cheek. "Nothing I can't handle. I'll see you at home. You got the bill?"

Daniel smiled assuredly. "Yeah. Check on your sister."

By the time Tess made it outside, the two were having a deadly stare off. Alex looked as pompous as ever, cocky out in the night air, while Tanya's sexual look had slid into a caged hawk about to surge down to claw at her prey. Tess easily cornered Alex on the other side and trapped his back against the brick wall of the restaurant.

"What are you doing here, Alex?"

Alex chuckled even when he was faced off against two females on the hunt for him, their prey. "I was already here in Kavala. The real question is why are you?"

"What?"

"You two are still chasing me?" Alex laughed aloud, further enraging the two brunettes. "Seriously?"

"You killed our mother!" Tess hissed.

"It was just business, girls." Alex retorted calmly, shrugging as he did so.

"We are thieves! We don't deal in death-"

"And I do." Alex smirked, his hand pulling his suit jacket open, showing his gun holster and gun above his stomach. He smiled brightly as he turned his gaze upon Tess. "I got a nice call today, Tess. You are pathetic, you know that? A rookie mistake at that. What's the matter? Couldn't let Tanya do what she does best?" Alex chuckled. "You probably just had to do it yourself. You always have to have it your way after all."

"What do you mean?" Tess seethed. He was mocking her. Seriously? But as Alex smirked deeper, a chill ran down her spine. What had she missed?

"A con at my bank? How quaint. You really should have left Tanya to do it, but your pride demanded you get it." Alex continued to mock. "Still don't understand?"

"Well, when you saw my account, you left the manager's history of the account lookup in the logs. I chose that bank for a reason...the reason being that they check their records every day." Alex spoke as he watched her eyes widen. "The bank manager called and asked if my account looked fine. It was, but I knew better."

Alex continued to gloat. "And also, really.....Paige? Julia?" Alex chuckled darkly, holding in his laughter. "I mean come on! Using your civilian names? And are you sure you want that, Paige? With that time in a psych ward in your bio?"

Tess sneered and prepared to pounce, imagining at least seven ways of choking him without anyone hearing them, if Tanya's steady hand hadn't stretched out and gripped her wrist, holding her back. Alex smirked as he took the opening to escape the corner of the building and walked to the edge of the sidewalk.

"Look, I came in good faith. What I'm telling you girls is to back off. Last chance." Alex paused and thought back a few minutes ago before smirking "...Or else, Tess, your little boy toy may meet a similar fate as your mother."

Tess twisted around and leaned forward, but Tanya held her back, just barely. "You touch him and-"

"Oh! Tut-tut, Tess. Emotional, are you?" Tess bit her tongue, but he continued to smirk. "You know, it's rare for you, Tess, to lose your composure. Very...Interesting. Have a nice night. And a good life." Alex laughed as he began to walk away, and Tanya held Tess's shaking hands.

"Don't worry, Tess. The girls are already here. The viruses and the equipment are well hidden. As soon as we locate all the money, we'll pounce and drag him through a woodchipper."

Tess frowned darkly. "Not enough pain for him."

Thirty minutes later, the sound of the garage door opened, and the sisters walked in silence into their hideout. Neither spoke as Tanya changed out of her clothes and Tess grabbed the bottle of wine and sat at the couch before her sister joined her. Tess began to fill the glasses, her hand jittering between the glasses until she passed one to Tanya, keeping one for herself. Both girls raised the glasses, and then with a surging rage, Tess slammed her glass down, the glass shattering against the concrete floor as the wine seeped in all directions.

"Real cool, Tess." Tanya muttered. "Now we'll need to clean that up."

"Dammit! How'd he find us so fast?!?" Tess raged, before tears bubbled up and spewed out of her eyes. "I'm such an idiot! I can't believe I left his profile up on the computer or something, so they gave him a call."

"Tess...I think it's over."

"What?!?" Tess was shocked. "Tanya, you can't mean that."

Tanya looked over sadly. "It's done. He knows we're after him."

"So what?!? We find his stash; we make him pay...and we kill him." Tess pleaded, but Tanya looked back at her tiredly, shaking her head.

"Tess, Mom wouldn't want that-"

"I want that!" Tess screeched. "He needs to die for what he did to her!" Tess surged forward and hugged her sister in a tight embrace, as Tanya felt tears falling onto her neck. "He got so greedy that if the police hadn't shown up, he'd have killed us too!"

Tanya accepted the embrace but leaned into her ear. "But Tess, you can't ask me to call the others and get their help. You'd be putting their lives in danger as well. We operate on surprise and stealth, not straight up fighting." Tanya kissed her sister's cheek, sniffling as emotions ran high between them. "How could we ask them to do that?"

"They'd do it... for her."

Tanya sighed, breathing out her hopeless attempt to end this. "You're too emotional to think straight."

"And proud of it!" Tess gasped back, her tears fully immobilizing her voice as it cracked, her voice begging more than trying to produce a clear argument. But it was enough for her sister to give up and nod back.

"...I'll call them over here. We'll let them decide on their own, but Tess, he knows we're here. He'll have guards now and dogs and more than enough money for a private army. He will be crafty and might try something to get you to ignore your plans. Don't let him sway you from the team."

"Good." Tess growled darkly. "He'll need them to keep them from me." Tanya gulped at Tess's expression. It was not one she had seen before, and one she hoped to never see again.

That evening, Daniel heard the keys jingle and ran out of the room to see Paige just putting up her jacket by the door. He just stood there and watched her silently and slowly put her stuff away into slots that had been set aside for her for weeks now. He waited for her to notice him, but after she started to rub at her eyes, he rushed to her aid, hugging her close as she quickly latched on and refused to let go. Daniel waited for her to calm down before rubbing her back to soothe her.

"You alright?"

His answer was a young woman shoving him into a wall and kissing him deeply before sighing into him once more. "I just miss my mom right now." Paige whispered, and Daniel nodded, knowing that his girlfriend had a hard time dealing with her mother's recent passing.

"Alright." Daniel finished, kissing her cheek as she kissed back. He must have done well to take care of her sadness, because not ten minutes later, Paige's hands dipped down to his pants belt loops, pulling his pelvis over her own, making his attention focus solely on her.

"Now then, back to this evening with you meeting my sister and talking about marrying me someday."

"Y-You heard that?"

Paige smiled brightly and brought him in even closer. "She may have hinted at your words a little. You were so zealous for me, and my heart soared for it. ...**Daniel....I love you.**" Paige voiced into the warm rooms that she now called home, ignoring the wedding bells in her ears as she waited for him to say it back.

"I love you." Daniel spoke in a loving whisper, as they leaned forward to kiss. Daniel quickly picked his beloved girlfriend up bridal style and moved to the bed to make love as they both repeated those very strong and emotionally binding words throughout the nights to come.

XV-COULD SHE LEAVE

Where Alex was living could have been a fortress. A few million well invested had given him a beautiful chateau in the rich side of Kavala, out of the way from the riffraff of the small town that used to be the small regional capital. He had spared no expense at upgrading the brickwork and brought it to the modern era, with only the best of the entire continent. The marble from Italy, a beautiful waterscape wall made from Malaysia in the outdoor garden where the water lightly graced down to the pool on the floor before irrigating the flowers from Japan around itself as if an amphitheater of an Eden surrounding it. Anyone who knew Alex would laugh at this posh residence. He was just trying to live the high life. What a bastard.

But as stated, he had made many upgrades to the place. He had broken into the Kavala housing archives and stolen his own home's plans, ensuring that no one would know what was in store for them should they try to learn how to get in the easy way. Top of the line surveillance cameras and motion sensors littered the premises and tall stone walls surrounded two sides of the residence, the remaining sides dipping down into a three-hundred-foot ravine below. It was very much a secure fortress of a home, though to a real criminal, it was just more of a chore.

On top of one of the far hills partially hidden by the trees, an electrical van sat below a service poll, where two females watched the place from above with high end binoculars and laptops between them.

"So then…"

"Go on, Melissa." Tanya spoke back, allowing Melissa to speak her mind.

"I know what Alex did, making your sister feel like a fool last week and all, but I have to ask, why were you with her and her cover? It's protocol to keep our lives separate."

"She uh…" Tanya stalled as she leaned back and looked over and slowly shrugged, smiling as she did so. "She wanted me to meet her boyfriend face to face."

"So then…getting a pretty deep cover then?"

"Something like that. One camera facing 90 degrees east on red wall, and white wall has a camera looking right at it."

"So, they cover each other? Logged it." Melissa clicked on the areas indicated and inputted her own coordinates. "Besides that, though, Tess seems…. I don't know exactly how to put it. She seems…happier since Amelia's death. More open and approachable."

"She was always approachable, Melissa."

"Yeah, but there was always a shade over her smiles. She always held something back. Now though, that shade seems to have been dropped. Is that because of this Daniel fellow?"

"Pretty much." Tanya nodded before she groaned. "Damn it. Sumara alarm system. That's not going to be easy to hack into. Maybe I'll have Abby talk her way into the local office to get the codes. She's been itching to do something on her own rather than assisting us with our own projects." Tanya leaned back and exhaled. But something was bugging her and after a minute she turned to see Melissa biting her cheek. "What?"

"…Maybe she should get out while she can. She'd be happier if she grabbed her boyfriend and ran for it."

"If Tess was here, she'd slap you for accusing her of leaving the team." Tanya spoke back concisely; the team didn't need to know about Tess's plan to leave them after all of this. Tanya herself was still working through the pain that would come when she was alone and by herself. But Melissa's viewpoint was different from the rest of theirs and was one of the reasons why she was a valued older sister to the team.

The difference was that Melissa had killed before. It wasn't something she liked to talk about; something about avenging the ones that had tried to hurt her brothers. She had killed them in cold blood with them begging for mercy, and she had given them none. She had told Amelia her secret in the days after she'd done it, and after a few years, had told Tess and Tanya during a night of heavy drinking and many tears.

So, Tanya nodded her head. "You know that Tess doesn't look at you differently because of that, right?"

Melancholy filled the smile of Melissa's face as she faced Tanya. "I know that." She sniffled and looked down at her fingers. "This isn't for everyone. I've spent so many nights lying awake, too scared to fall asleep and see their eyes and bloody faces scowling back at me. Trust me; there is something you lose when you kill someone. Something you can't get back. I fake it, you know. Always trying to smile. It's easier when I'm with you girls. But if Tess goes through with this, she won't be able to stay with such a nice guy, someone who I'm sure thinks the world of her. She'll crack one day; she'll tell him everything, and he'll leave her, and then she won't forgive herself."

"What are you saying?"

Melissa looked over and grimaced. "Just that someone has to kill Alex, but maybe that person isn't Tess…maybe it's someone older, who can take it and survive."

"Tess would never ask you to do that."

"She wouldn't need to ask. Maybe I find Alex first before her endgame. Maybe he and I struggle, and maybe she is spared."

"…I'll take it under advisement." Tanya spoke back, her eyes looking back at the house. "Guard back on patrol of the outer grounds at 15:37."

"Marked. What next?"

XVI-STATE TROOPER SIMON BECKETT

aniel awoke to a nice peaceful morning, the breeze sliding through the open window in his room wafting nicely above his bare chest. His eyes scanned the room tiredly, his body begging him not to wake up after a long workweek, but he had to go. Slowly, he edged out of bed, careful to not wake the sleeping beauty lying next to him, exchanging his arm with a pillow as Paige wrapped around it tighter and continued to slumber away.

"Ouch!" Daniel cursed as he stepped off the bed, and right onto his girlfriend's tall heels. He stifled a groan as he rubbed the sore spot and looked down at the clothes strewn on the floor from last night. Daniel sighed; getting ready for work was a struggle today. He continued around the bed to his dresser, pulling open a drawer as he rubbed at his eyes. Opening them, his throat rumbled again.

He closed the drawer that contained his girlfriend's panties, bras, and nightgowns. He should know by now which drawers were his and which were hers but cut him a break! He had already worked a full week already and was now going in for a surprise meeting. He silently put on his uniform, tying the laces of his boots tightly and clipped his shirt together. With everything in his pockets, he did his favorite thing of the morning; he leaned over and kissed Paige's forehead, and even though asleep, a content smile formed on her face as he exited the apartment and began his walk to the museum.

Daniel closed his eyes and let the rays of sunshine warm his body. It really was a nice day out, and that made him even more grumpy since it was such a wonderful day. Bitterness and anger boiled inside his chest for the first time in a long while towards his workplace. The notifying text had arrived just as he had gotten his girlfriend's top off last night and completely ruined his plans of spending time with her this weekend.

For some reason, his boss had requested all of the guards to come in today but had not said why. Of course, Paige took it in great stride and said that they could always go out the next day he had off, but he was mad now that it was such a nice day. He shouldn't hope that his girlfriend would do something sexy with him later tonight when he got home, but he really, really hoped she would.

Daniel made it to the back of the museum with little time to spare and saluted the camera above the door and opened it as it buzzed him inside. Daniel quickly joined his coworkers in the main lobby, since there really wasn't a conference room in their small museum, and the break room was laughable for all of them to squeeze into. But he joined the eight guards in a semi-circle as everyone talked amongst themselves as they waited. It wasn't long that they needed to wait as after a few minutes, their boss appeared coming down the staircase and as he stood before his team, he frowned at his men.

"Alright you guys. Thanks for coming in on such short notice. I know that it's not ideal; yes, I know Nathan, you had a vacation day planned for today. The police still have some questions that they'd like to ask you all." The guys groaned in displeasure as two men appeared behind their boss.

"Sir, we answered their questions." Daniel voiced, complaining. His boss and fellow coworkers knew how annoyed he was since he mostly covered everyone else's vacations and sick days. But he had a sexy, hot girlfriend now, and his buddies at work knew just why he wanted to be anywhere but here since he had let slip last week just how often she 'spent the night.'

"You did, Mr. Thompson." An older gentleman stepped around their boss and stood before the men. Daniel only had to take one look to know that this guy was in charge. He seemed to try to convey that he was rather lazy, but to speak on behalf of another to answer a retort from a complaining employee gave it away. And to know who he was with no introduction...this guy had a good eye. "However, that was with the local police; I am Detective Simon Beckett; this is Detective Orion." The man gestured to his partner. "We are from the State Troopers. One at a time, we'll ask each of you in to refresh ourselves if you'd please."

"Alright, everyone!" Their boss clapped his hands to grab their attention. "That means that you are all getting overtime and get to double up in your patrols! Go ahead and relax more today, just not in front of the guests. Dismissed."

"Daniel! You're up!" Nathan called out over the radio to the five-year veteran. Daniel looked over the railing of the planetarium and made a final check as the lights began to glow darker and made his way out and down past the reception desk.

He saw detective Orion talking to the receptionist team who for once were using all the chairs available, but continued, moving into the interior hallway and then to the security booth to stand at the door.

When the buzz sounded, he opened the door and saw the other detective paying him no mind, his trench coat pulled back to his gun and holster on his belt, his badge clipped next to it. Like his own hair, this man's hair defied gravity, but unlike his own, this man's hair was sleek and shined against the white light in the room.

The man was so focused on the many rows of cameras on the four monitors, one of them showing him the copies of the night of the robbery sticking out to him. But Daniel smirked for a little, seeing Nathan on a call smoking a cigarette while no doubt being yelled at by his wife. He had ruined their anniversary today and if she found out he was smoking again well...the guys would see him with a black eye the next day. His wife was a scary woman for five feet tall, a semi pro wrestler in the minor circuit.

"Ah Daniel, right?" Simon finally turned to him, acknowledging his entrance even though he himself had been the one to let him enter.

"Yes, sir." Daniel nodded his head.

Simon frowned apologetically. "Forgive me, Daniel, can I call you by your first name? I know how much everyone hates coming in on their off days, so I really appreciate your cooperation. I just have some questions that came up in the reports that I'd really like some clarifications on."

"Why is robbery with the state cops?" Daniel questioned before the officer's own questions began.

Simon smiled a little and nodded his head. "You boys keep asking that. The police did their investigation but no clues at all popped up. Sometimes, they just don't have the expertise and manpower to dedicate so much time to these kinds of investigations. It gets bumped up, and my partner and I specialize in this kind of stuff..."

Daniel's mind wandered, imagining his girlfriend sliding down his neck, suckling lightly, adding one hickie after another before beginning to unbutton her blouse.

"...Also, we recently got an anonymous tip to check some things out."

His daydream broken, Daniel shook his head to clear it and smiled. "I see. That's a relief." Daniel smiled. "Hopefully the painting is returned without hassle then."

"What about the thief?" Simon asked after the nonchalant statement. "Wouldn't a guard such as yourself want the perpetrator arrested?" He asked, assessing the man before his eyes.

Daniel shrugged. "My priority at this museum is the restoration and protection of the artworks. People really liked that painting; it called out to the locals of Kavala for some reason that no one could explain. And I uh...met my girlfriend with it." Daniel coughed away his blush at admitting that; it was still awkward telling a stranger.

The detective smiled. "Oh, how nice to meet a girl at your work. That's how I met my wife, but she was delivering a lawsuit to my table. But I digress. Look at this technology though." Simon swiveled the camera to face away from him, showing a small battery or something in front of him on the table.

"So fascinating, isn't it? They make things so small nowadays, and the innovations that go into this just astound me. It's truly amazing. I'm getting too old for this kind of thing."

Daniel cocked his head confused. He seemed maybe ten years older than him. "Surely not."

Simon looked over to smile at his mistake. "I just mean tech wise. I need someone younger, someone who knows the ins and outs of these kinds of things. Luckily my wife has a large family, so I went to my nephew at the local electronics store. Do you know what this is?"

"That's the device that did all this, isn't it?"

"Part of it." Simon admitted as he put it into the palm of his hand, the device looking like a rectangle of microchips and wires. "You see, it's extremely interesting. My nephew called it a "booby trap" battery."

Daniel edged away from the device. "Then I'd avoid it."

Simon smiled at his aversion to being near it after that. "All of the energy is gone from it now, so don't worry too much. But you are quite right, one may assume that this is just a thin computer that can be made to do anything the creator wanted it to. It truly is a wonderful design, and already I have some bigwig politician trying to close the case so that he can use this design for 'research'."

"But I digress. Now you see this part is interesting. He told me that only a few people can make a workable one; machines can't go near it as it screws with their charges. One's hands must be so slender and deft that my nephew was certain that only the concept could be made before he looked at it for me. And besides all that work and dedication, there was only sabotage in mind with this kind of device, let alone attach it to anything useful besides to drain another device."

"But again, I digress. In the end, my nephew explained that this battery cannibalized itself over time. About seventy-two hours' worth of it."

Daniel widened his eyes. If it wasn't done on that night, then it wasn't Sunny's fault when it happened. "So Sunny wasn't the one on duty."

"Quite right. It has 6 compartments you see and every few hours, the circuits tap the compartments together, frying up the circuits and making them useless. And so, when the local techs looked at the battery, they assumed it had six hours on it. That's the work of a serious professional. But this seventy-two hour changes a lot of things."

Simon reached to the desk to pull out the work chart that they kept there, as he turned to the log. "I love it when companies write everything down. They can't be changed without redoing the entire page. It holds everything needed, very specific things in fact. It seems you were on duty that night, Daniel. I was disturbed when I read this log though at the empty slots. No one else?"

"No sir. I locked up at 9, and the last guard left at 10."

Simon blew out a breath of surprise. "My, I would never have thought such high tech can reduce guards. They must trust you a lot to leave you guys around millions of dollars of precious artifacts. But I-"

"Digress?"

Simon smiled happily. "Yes...So! 10 you say? Well then, what is this keyed access for the back door at 10:45?"

Simon watched as for the first time, Daniel paled and looked at his body rather than in the eyes and stuttered a bit. "Um...I thought I heard something."

Simon nodded in understanding. "That's right. I was informed that you don't have exterior cameras."

"Only on the roof sir. We had residents complaining about being spied on, and since we have guards actually watching them…" Daniel insinuated.

"I see...well then what is this other opening at 11:56pm? Just before Midnight? Did you hear something else?"

Now, Daniel was silent, but Simon moved on. "Oh, look at me. I'm not trying to accuse you, son. I apologize if I gave off that feeling. Now then, the only person in the entire building was in here, correct?"

"Yes sir."

"This button here." Simon tapped the plastic safety box on the guard's desk and watched Daniel gulp back some saliva. "It was pressed at 10:51pm."

"Yes sir." Daniel breathed heavier. "But I turned it back on right away."

"I did spot that on the time log." Simon nodded his head, spotting the report in which the guard had written all of this down...exactly word for word. "Only five seconds was it on, but the question I have is why was it off in the first place?" Simon tapped the box again. "You have this box covering it. Why, you need a key just to open it! I hope you didn't unlock it as a test."

Daniel's demeanor turned into a smile at that. "That's new sir. The old safety cover had become broken over the years, but we had taken it off to replace it, but the replacement took a while to arrive but it's close to where we have to work, so it was an accident just waiting to happen."

"Of course." Simon nodded before taking a seat next to him. "Daniel, can I ask you something?"

"A-Anything you want."

Simon looked at him directly in the eye and Daniel shivered. "You should get it off your chest, Son. It is never a healthy thing to keep the truth bottled inside. I'm not an idiot, but I expect honesty. They say the guilt rots the soul quicker than it builds up again, you know?"

Daniel breathed out and sighed in defeat. His voice whispered into the room. "...I let my girlfriend inside that night."

Beckett's intent stare turned into an amused smile. "Is that all? Tell me about her. Since she was in here and all that night."

A huge smile of sunlight made itself known on Daniel's face. "Her name is Paige. She's amazing; smart and confident. I never thought I'd ever be with a girl like her. I get all nervous around girls, I yell suddenly or clamp silent, but not Paige. She coaxes the part of me out that I like about myself. She's someone I can say anything to. No secrets or anything like that. She actually asked me out here at the museum."

"Young love is a wonderful thing to be struck by. Is she a local girl?"

"She moved here recently, actually." Daniel boasted, as his buddies were always telling him that foreign girls were more exotic, though they were all a part of the same continent.

"She was new to town?" Beckett's eyebrows twitch up.

"Yes, and we...we hit it off really well." Daniel looked down and let out a happy laugh of wonder. "She's so...forward, you know? Always doing things to egg me on, to do something… crazy every other day or two." Daniel blushed, realizing that he already said that to the detective, but the officer smiled and nodded again.

"So did she just show up that night or did you two plan for that time?"

"Yes, she did surprise me. You see, I was trying to be romantic, and I had planned a special night to try to woo her. It was still early in our relationship, and I was also nervous-...sorry." Daniel blushed madly and breathed out to calm down. "Anyways, I was supposed to go on a date with her that night, but my schedule changed all of a sudden."

"I saw that. Very sudden indeed." Simon agreed, looking at his notes for the schedule. "What happened exactly? When you let her in?"

"Well, I let her in and showed her in here. I couldn't really turn off the grid and such as it was already activated."

"Of course. She saw the cameras?"

"Well, yes." Daniel stuttered and blushed, "but we were um, occupied."

"I see…"

"And so, when I let her in, she saw all the cameras and she leaned on the button. I checked everything though! Nothing was out of the ordinary."

Simon looked at him and saw his honest face. "I can understand that, Daniel. Most unfortunate. My colleague doesn't agree with me, but I think that the thief somehow followed you inside in that very moment."

Daniel's teeth cracked at that comment. He was angry at himself suddenly. Could he have let the thief in?!? "But don't worry." Simon patted him on the back. "We'll get the painting back. The state troopers always get the job done. Can you send the next guard in?"

"Of course."

Finally, his day was over, and Daniel was so excited to finally head back to his fantastic girlfriend. She had just texted him a picture of her bare leg with the question. *'You wanna?'* underneath it. Of course, he did!

His adrenaline was pumping and so he quickly unbuttoned his uniform and put his things in his locker. He paused for a bit, staring at the metal, admiring the cute local girl setup picture she'd taken for him last month that now decorated his locker. They had gone so deep so fast. Never would he have thought to fall so far after only three months. But it was just that she made him feel so powerful. He was willing to break his rules for her and-

"Daniel!" A sudden call from the door had Daniel turn to see his boss looking towards him with some papers in his hand.

"What is it, chief?"

"...I'm sorry, Son." The boss sighed and passed the papers over. Daniel looked down in confusion until he read the top words. His boss had just handed him a pink slip.

XVII-TOMMY SMITH

"What?" Daniel looked up, stunned at his boss's choice. "B-But sir, I... what?"

"The detective told me you let someone in. That was your girlfriend I know, but I have to make an example."

Daniel was stuck staring at the paper in front of him again. "How could he- but I- Sir, please." Daniel looked up pleading. "I've given 5 years to this place-"

"-And that's why I'm not firing you here on the spot." His boss sighed dejectedly. "It's a shame to me too. I thought you could take my job in a few years. Now I don't honestly know who I could leave it to." His boss left the room, Daniel left standing there, before he grit his teeth and slammed his hand on the locker, making a small dent in the cheap metal.

'Dammit! I made one mistake! What the heck?!? Just one little mistake and I'm gone?!? I lost everything I care for?!? I've given years to this place! The security system was a joke before I came here and spent countless unpaid hours updating it all! I've never even asked to be compensated! Why I-...'

Daniel breathed all this out before pulling the picture of Paige out of his locker and smiling bitterly. His anger left him there as he stared at her smiling face. His first dangerous thing in his life was because of Paige. He broke down his walls when he was with her. He let her into his workplace because he trusted her. She was a slingshot that spun him around in crazy directions. He even shoplifted a scented candle on one of their dates, though he went back and paid for it later that week.

Daniel stepped to the back door and stilled just before grasping the handle. He glanced back at the security hallway, and through the frosted glass was the museum and people who he'd come to think of as a family. He held his breath and held in his pain, and breathed out, letting it all go.

His life wasn't here anymore. It was with Paige. She was an honest girl and he-he loved her. He dug his hand into the pocket of his jacket and fingered the ring that lay hidden there. She'd definitely say no. No way she'd agree so early in their relationship. He could tell that she wasn't the kind of girl to easily settle down. She was always on the move. It was way too soon, but he didn't care. He just wanted her to know how deeply he cared about her. Daniel opened the door and stepped out into the fresh air.

"Hello Daniel." A deep voice called out to him. Daniel's reflexes shot up instantly as he twisted his body to the right, where a black-haired individual leaned on the back wall of the museum, his rich attire and scarf around his neck made to attract attention that his eyes told him that he wanted as much as he could grab.

"You're...Tommy, right?" Daniel freaked a little, hiding a shudder in his throat. Tommy was stationed near the camera for the door, but just outside it so no doubt if detective Beckett was still in the security booth, he'd only see Daniel.

"Yeah. Good to see you again, Daniel." Tommy grinned confidently, but Daniel was not sure this was at all a coincidence. Tommy was behind the museum and the houses around here knew everyone and held a strong aversion to any newcomers. No, Tommy was here with a purpose.

"How'd you know where I worked?" Daniel asked skeptically.

Tommy smiled wider. "Not too many people with your name."

"Not that common." He muttered to himself. Best get done with him and get back to his girlfriend. "Why are you here?"

"I came to give you advice."

Daniel let out a puff of air in a short chortle. "You give...Me advice?"

Tommy slowly nodded his head. "Yeah...stay away from Paige."

It was now that Daniel smiled wide. A silent chuckle made its way to his lips at the new realization. Never would he have thought this would happen to a guy like him. Plenty of fights in high school he had seen with this scene, but to happen to him? Never would have thought that it would happen to him. Daniel began to walk out of the alley, smiling back at Tommy. "Wow. Is this really going down? You the jealous ex warning me off?"

"Not like that." Tommy insisted, casually looking at him up and down before frowning. "You're going to get hurt."

"I doubt that." Daniel's voice rumbled. He turned his body away and began to walk around the corner. He was done with this clown. "Look I have to be somewhere so-"

"-She's pretty flirtatious, isn't she?" Tommy finally spoke up, starting his piece of advice as Daniel froze and cast a glance back over his shoulder.

"I mean, she really does look like a damsel; so innocent, and so nice you think she'd never do anything bad. You have sex, yes?" Tommy smirked in victory as Daniel couldn't help the blush that formed on his face. Tommy took the silence as a yes.

"She makes it seem like she's so dominant in the relationship, right? Always telling you where as a couple you go, always getting to pick your activities and always, always deciding when sex is allowed, and yet you love that because when you enter that room and you're in that bed, she lets you take charge, showing her supposed weak side, tell you that you're so powerful in the bedroom activities that you are an amazing lover. Three, maybe four months, yeah?"

Tommy finally pushed off the wall and moved to stand before him, the same height as Daniel as both looked at the other in the eyes.

"Maybe tonight, maybe next week, it'll happen. She'll ask, while you're distracted by her womanly ways, to take charge that night in the bedroom, and you'll allow it because it's her that's asking. It is at that moment that you need to stop. It is at that moment that she will hurt you."

Daniel watched as Tommy reached into his jacket pocket and pulled out some photos and turned them to Daniel, whose eyes widened at the sight of the pictures; of Tommy's stomach and sides bruised and purple. "What are-"

"-She's a Sadist, Daniel." Tommy grabbed at Daniel's shoulder, holding him still as desperation voiced through his mouth. "She steals from people, literally is a thief of the heart! She loves breaking people down. That's what she did to me. She turned me into a bad guy; I did things! Things I can never get back, and it was all for her pleasure and she is a sadist who loves to pull your strings in every way until you break."

"But she broke up-"

"-Did she say that?" Tommy looked at him like he was sad he didn't believe him. Tommy sighed in defeat and bit his lip in shame. "No, I ended it after she got me arrested, suggesting things I didn't even do because I told her we should break up, and even changed my name! Don't you find it interesting that she chose the very city that I escaped to?"

"I-I…" Daniel stalled.

"Do you know where she is right now?"

"At work." Daniel replied quietly, but his words held no conviction.

"Really?"

"Um…it moves a lot."

Tommy nodded his head and looked deep into his eyes. "So, she tells you she's flexible, but you're at work and she can surprise you?" Daniel's own eyes widened. The detective's words came back to him. *"I think the thief came in at the same time as you let her in."* Daniel quickly shook his head. He had to get these stupid thoughts out of his head!

"She is always around you, isn't she?"

"That's a good relationship." Daniel bristled, but even he knew his back was against the wall.

"Fine… I'll leave." Tommy frowned in defeat and began to walk out of the alley himself. But as he turned towards where the alley connected with the cobbled street, he looked back. "...Did you know that Paige isn't her real name?"

"W-what-...?" Daniel's world turned upside down. Of course, it was. She was Paige. Who would lie about their name?

"I'm telling you Daniel; she is a liar and will throw you under just to see you beat and battered. Ask her that with her being sadistic and pulling you closer one of these days. You should get out while you still can."

Daniel watched Tommy disappear into the neighborhood and leaned back on the wall of the museum. Why had he come here? Just to warn him. And just who was his girlfriend? Daniel gulped. Damnit. It was now stuck in his head.

As Daniel walked home, the thoughts plagued him, and he was stuck thinking that Tommy may be right. Did he really know his girlfriend? Just who was Paige? The thoughts would not leave him!! As he waited for the crosswalk to change, his inner thoughts started to accept what Tommy said.

Paige did control every part of his life. She was in every part of it, from snuggling in bed, to simple walks around the town. Daniel blushed. If he could admit it to himself, then she probably knew his password to his bank account. She'd asked about his finances, and he showed her. They were only dating for three months, and he had no secrets from her.

But there were good parts too! Because he was so honest, he always saw Paige's shoulders sag and relax, opening to him her innermost thoughts and adventurous side. Because she took care of the outside world, he did feel emboldened to take charge in sexual relations because she let him, but she was so caring that she listened to what he said in everything and changed her mind if his side was right.

"She followed me here." Tommy lived here, and Paige moved here? Was she a stalker? Daniel groaned into his hand as he started walking again. The start to their relationship felt that way. Love didn't happen like a movie. She got his attention and asked for a date. They forgot

and she came back to ask again? A perfect date with a first kiss to second base. After that, he'd opened his whole life to her.

Wasn't his life just perfect before her? His neighbors loved him.? He had a secure job he enjoyed? No. Daniel shook his head. He had been lonely, helping those around him in a desperate search for a connection, but with her, he had just been happy to have someone look at him like she did. Like...someone who loved him.

She was his longest relationship, longer than two dates and a kiss to the cheek before her entrance into his life. He loved her and enjoyed showing her just how much.

So, what to say about Tommy's words? Daniel finally stepped into his apartment building and stood at his door, the door where Paige and he were beginning to settle down together. No! He must be lying about the whole thing. He was the stalker and he'd followed her here. That could be the case too! Besides, she was an angel to him.

Daniel nodded his head at the finishing thought as he reached for the door to open it only to gasp at the devil before him.

"Hey Daniel~" Paige purred towards her lover with her long leg up on the couch, her body covered in black latex and mesh bands with black boots parting for the succulent, revealing skin of her thighs, a one piece suit that barely covered her up, leaving bare her stomach, arms and cleavage for her breasts to protrude from and her rear to stand out with a collar of latex at her neck to hold it all up. She was a vision of everything lewd and tempting in what every guy wished their girlfriend was willing to try and blood surged in a panic through Daniel's body.

"P-Paige?" Daniel uttered, stunned in awe. She'd never looked like this in front of him before. In his mind maybe, but not like this.

Paige looked up at him through her eyelashes, looking demure as could be. "I went to the specialty shop around the corner and thought I could try it out."

"T-that shop?" Daniel gulped deeply. He could never go in that shop on his own, too much blushing and of an obvious coward to go in. After Paige had shown interest and their activities began edging into the bedroom, he had hoped to ask if she was interested, but...dang.

"Uh huh." Paige uttered the two syllables with her teeth lightly biting her tongue. She smirked as she slinked off the couch and moved closer to the door before she pulled him inside to begin kissing him with a passion that he had not felt before. It was dark and powerful and... lustful. Daniel's eyes opened wide at the realization that this was pure unadulterated lust. He'd always wanted to feel this with someone he loved.

Daniel quickly dropped his stuff and kicked the door closed as he eagerly kissed back, wanting to explore everything that Paige had to offer.

"I thought," Paige voiced aloud as they parted between every kiss to breathe, "with it being the weekend and all...oh yeah...that we could have an all-nighter. You know?"

"I'd like that." Daniel smiled brightly as he eagerly gripped her body flush against his. As he kissed her back, he looked deeply into Paige's honest happy smile, and his grip on her uncovered love handles tightened as he pulled her ever closer to his body and kissed her deeply. Screw what Tommy said. His girl was amazing and thoughtful.

For Tess, she moaned lustfully as she felt Daniel grip her harder than ever before. *What brought this on? Was it the outfit?* Tess blushed madly as he dipped her a bit to kiss her harder. She'd seen it last week in the shop's window and hope had bubbled up that Daniel would be willing to try some roleplay and such, but this eagerness made her weak in the knees. No... she had to keep it up. She'd been slow and let him take the lead to build his confidence, and he did a fine job on her, alright, but in heated moments like this, she liked switching roles back and forth the most. With the experiences between them, maybe he'd let her lead for once?

"Hey...Daniel? I was thinking." Tess spoke up as her deft fingers undid his last button, before she pulled off his shirt, and they stripped and began backtracking into the bedroom. "...I was thinking that maybe I could be the dominant one tonight.... Daniel?"

Tess blushed as she looked down at his bare chest. Maybe he didn't like a girl in charge? Maybe he always needed to lead in the private moments. Tess cast a hopeful glance up and saw a stunned look on her boyfriend's face and smiled. Oh! So, he was just surprised she wanted to lead. Tess giggled as she pulled at his belt loops to tease him closer. No doubt with what she was wearing, he wanted her to be more submissive. They could try that too, but she wanted first dibs.

"Don't worry...I'll be gentle." Tess whispered seductively into his ear before she lightly bit the lobe playfully and began to scrape her fingers over his body. She wanted him so bad tonight, "...Daniel?" Tess's eyes stayed closed as she frowned a bit. Usually, he'd be marking up her throat with kisses right now...." Daniel?" And his hand would explore her skin and along the outfit she tried on.

Tess pulled back a bit, cocking her head in worry. "Daniel?" His eyes were shaking. Did he get off already? Didn't he know that she loved that shy side to him as much as the other sides of his inner self? "What's wrong, Baby?" She paused; her body held up by his arms as she leaned back with a frown.

"Huh?!? Nothing!!!" Daniel madly shook his head and swung his arms out to his sides.

"Ow!!!" Tess yipped as she slipped between his fingers and slammed into the edge of her dresser before sliding to the floor. Tess hissed at the feeling of a bruise along her back and rear, the fabric not blocking any of that area.

"Oh god! Paige! I'm sorry!" Daniel rushed to his knees and rubbed her back soothingly, helping the pain edge away.

Tess felt the pain recede and sighed a little sad but still content. "It's okay Daniel. I should have talked to you first. You can lead tonight. I was just wanting to try some things and-"

"-Actually, I can't do it tonight."

"Of course, you can." Tess purred as she reached over and hugged him caringly, smirking playfully. "You're always eager to please and enjoy our times together. Because you worked over today, I mean..." Tess licked her lips sensuously. She'd finished all her own work back at the warehouse early so as to have this time together "...We have all night." Tess edged in to seal the kiss of approval of a lustful and adventurous night.

"Paige no!"

Tess froze. *'D-Daniel said no?'* Tess huffed in shock and looked down. This was a first, but she could still see that her boyfriend was in pain and feeling guilty for saying no. She could admit that they were doing it a lot, so she could hold off a day or two more.

"It's alright, Daniel. We don't have to do it, I guess. I just thought we both enjoyed it whenever we could. Can I… can you at least tell me why?" Daniel looked away, shame on his face as Tess scooted closer. "Daniel what's wrong? You can tell me."

Daniel looked over into her eyes, and finally caved with his deep secret "…Tommy came to see me at work."

Immediately Tess's body went stiff as a rod of metal. She tried to play it off by stretching her body out a bit, but Daniel's eyes were much too observant of her action. She was an expert con woman and she found it really hard to hide even the smallest of things from his ever-watchful eyes. Only his trust in her words kept him oblivious to what she was, but what she showed him was who she was on the inside.

"Oh?" Tess played into her character more. "What did he want?" She asked, playing with her hair nervously.

Daniel looked down at his hands. "He told me to leave you."

Tess's worry lifted and she smiled, reassured and calm. "You wouldn't do that to me."

Silence. It was the worst thing you could hear as a con woman. Silence gave the subject time to think things through. Silence meant that they didn't believe you. Silence meant that they were sure about your character being a front and false. The silence gnawed at her mind as a full minute passed between them.

For the first time since she began this path to loving Daniel, she felt scared and unsure, and goosebumps shot up along her spine. The silence shook her trust right out from under her. "You wouldn't… Right?"

"Well…" Daniel held back hot water edging out of his eyes. "He showed me pictures of how you beat him up when you were intimate. It's just got my mind thinking that-"

"Daniel, you can't trust what he says!" Tess exclaimed suddenly, the anger at Alex even talking to her boyfriend was a low blow and was a violation on her own body. Now, he was saying they did it? "H-he and I never had sex, Daniel! He's lying to you."

"He said that you lie about your job all the time."

Tess had to deflect the answer from herself. She had to control the situation. She had to maintain her place. This was what Alex wanted. For Daniel to have doubts, to hurt her as much as possible so that she'd have to risk Daniel versus killing Alex. She wanted both and damnit! She'd have both.

"I have been vague with the jobs. I admit that." Tess shrugged, "But I don't know if I'll end up with the contracts, Daniel. It's all very last minute and word of mouth and with all the needed travel, it's hard to tell you exactly what I do because I do a lot of different things and it's confidential too so I'm not supposed to discuss my professional life. You understand that, right?" Daniel weakly nodded his head and Tess smiled in relief and victory. She could handle any curveballs Alex sent her way. Their relationship was solid; no cracks at all in their foundation.

"See?" Tess leaned in and snuggled up close. "We just have to be honest with each other and nothing could ever-"

"-Is Paige your real name?"

A crack formed in the foundation. A major tremor began to make it grow and expand...

Tess froze in her tracks, her body refusing to escape the storm that was suddenly approaching her at breakneck speed. Her safe refuge with her lover was suddenly as rock hard as the day her heart broke when she lost her mother. Her plan to wait until the heist was over shattered as liquid surged up from her ducts. Tears threatened to escape, but she held them back with all her might and leaned back and looked away, where it was safe to let them flow out.

"It's not." She whispered as she cradled her legs between her arms to hide the jitters as her lover looked at her under a new light, a light of disbelief and suspicion. She couldn't believe it. He'd seen her one weakness in that single encounter. Alex had found the single crack to hurt her, and no matter what she did now, Daniel would always feel betrayed, lied to, deceived. This would foster hate and anger that would spout through many arguments to come, and she couldn't hide it completely.

Tess began to think of a lie. She was injured as a child- she was accused of- no. Tess casted a small glance at her lover's face and sighed sadly. She couldn't keep lying, but she couldn't say the whole truth. So, she settled for something sort of murky and grey.

"I changed it after my mother was murdered." Tess admitted, which was true. "I didn't want that part of my life anymore." Why would she? Her previous character was a good student and a caring daughter, but she was only skin deep, and not as fully fledged as Paige was after four months that had felt like years. A bitter smile made it upon her face.

"I just wanted to be myself, someone smart and yet willing to be forward and gentle at the same time and I am that person...with you."

"Paige." Daniel's voice strained, as a shuddering breath whispered out of lips, but Tess shook her head with a few tears flying off her cheeks.

"I'm not ready to tell you my real name, Daniel. Every time I hear it, I'm reminded of her, of my dead mother, and I can't help that," Tess breathed in a large breath of air and turned to hold his hand. "...but I love you. Surely that counts for something, right?"

Tess pulled on his hand, pulling herself over and began to kiss Daniel to show him how much she loved him. The worry and heartache felt like a knot on her heart, but then it lifted!

Daniel's lips began to slowly kiss back, and the knot began to untie itself. Why did she have to worry at all? Her boyfriend was so innocent and caring and he'd never leave her. Tess pushed in more, her hand touching his neck and began to slide down the front of his chest.

But then Tess felt him pull back. She tried to follow but his hands held her shoulders back as he separated from her and shook his head sadly.

"I'm sorry. I can't do this."

"No…" Tess sniffled, her tears spilling full force out of her eyes as the knot slipped lower and tightened. Tess reached up to her heart and gripped her chest as it throbbed as if being suffocated and choked. He didn't accept her for what she was? He didn't love her? Surely, he did!

"Danie.-"

But Daniel touched her lips with his finger. tracing her cheeks and she sat there, stunned as he swept over her face, clearing away the tears that he had caused, but he still looked at her with dejection. "I need the truth in everything in my life. I thought you were that girl for me…" Daniel's eyes turned a bitter red as tears flowed out his eyes too, as he rushed to stand up and paced madly along the length of the room, using his arms to try to cover his tears. He turned to look at her and then whispered. "And you're not even real. I can't do this anymore."

"Are- are you breaking up with me?" Tess breathed, her throat constricting and choking her whole world into tiny pieces, her life with him shattering before her very eyes. But Daniel's eyes widened at his words and rushed to pull her up to his level, before he held her hands, rubbing them slowly.

"No! I'm not…I mean… it sounds like that but…you are still so amazing. But Pai-…" Daniel paused at her name and Tess felt the strain to say a name that he felt had played him like a puppet on a string. "… Paige. I just…." He looked deep into her eyes in finality. "I need some time to take this in. Can you leave?"

Tess's mouth opened like a fish in a trap. She looked down at her attire and back at him. "L-Like this? But I… I don't want to leave you alone." Tess tried to coax him into letting her stay, but he stepped further away. her touch a searing blaze now on his skin instead of a cool, welcoming embrace.

"I'll be fine. Just…give me the weekend. I'll know by then."

It was over. No more discussion. No more time for her to change his mind. Quietly, she moved around the room in her sexual attire, filled with not lust but utter shame as she grabbed her purse and moved to the closet by the door. She found her black trench coat to cover her and got her things in order before she was suddenly standing at the door.

Everything had been slow, nothing fast like their whole relationship. This was...different, and Tess hated this feeling. A pathetic reminder bubbled out of her throat. "Don't forget you're fixing Ms. Bazir's faucet tomorrow."

"...I won't."

"And-..." Tess held back her tears. "Don't forget that we're....that you're out of bread and milk."

"...I'll stop by the store."

"...Daniel?" Tess turned her head to see her lover slowly walk over to her, his eyes in a longing gaze as he looked deep into her own. No words needed to be said as she nudged forward to kiss his lips with quick passion, with whatever love she had left to give him she did.

She let herself fall back to the door. "I do love you, Daniel. I haven't lied to you about that for a single second that I've known you." As she closed the door, she stayed where she was, and couldn't even hear his footsteps retreat to his room.

After a minute, she began to move down the stairs, tying the coat tighter. This was a walk of shame, of utter rejection. This wasn't her fault. This wasn't Daniel's fault...the knot on her heart snapped as she reached the last step above the ground floor.

Tess turned to the wall and threw a hard punch, her body hissing as she made contact with the wood. But still she punched it, over and over with everything she had.

'This is all his fault! That damn traitor, that murderer! Just when I'm happy with my life, he steals my mother! And just when I'm happy and have fulfilled my mother's dying request to find someone I love, he stole him away too!'

"Thief!"

(Crack)

Tess opened her bleary eyes and started bawling. There was her hand, wrist deep in the wall, with the wood bent in four or five directions, but as she pulled it out, blood on her knuckles dropped on her bare thighs, showing the bloody shame of her life.

She dropped to the floor and bawled, the neighbors in the homes around her no doubt not willing to open and see the disgraced woman crying her heart out. She was all alone, with no one to love her as... Tess's thoughts disappeared as she looked at her jittering pale hands. She was nothing. She had nothing. Sure, she had money and a good crew...but she was hollow inside.

Tess stayed in that hallway for over an hour, not moving, not thinking, just staring at her bruised knuckles. But when she finally staggered to the lobby doors to the outside world, she could only think of how Alex was ruining her life, and she had to get him back for this... payback's a bitch, isn't she?

XVIII-CLIFFSIDE BREAKUP

Inside the warehouse, the team of thieves were hard at work. Megan was working on some contraption on a table, a sedaline torch in her hand as she welded parts of it together. Melissa had grabbed Abby and together, they were working to get needed supplies for their plan. Abby was working on ordering parts from multiple shell companies, while Melissa was yelling at manufacturers over the phone.

They were all trying their best to ignore the moping girl on the center couch. It had taken three days just to get her to come out of the loft above them, and Tanya had kept them out of the rooms up there to give her space. There was no longer any use hiding it now. Their leader had fallen in love with the man she had tried to con. It was an inevitable event that happened to grifters, who went into a high euphoric state when they were twisting emotions and becoming someone new, and Tess was one of them.

She was laying around on the couch as the other girls on her team discussed and did the things to prepare for the trials of the upcoming heist, but her eyes were glossed over, not registering anything that they were doing. Once everyone else had been taken care of, Tanya tapped the spoon on the edge of the cup that she'd been preparing and set it down on the marble island before grabbing the cup of hot chocolate with marshmallows and took it over to the couch before sitting by her sister.

"Here." Tanya leaned over, as Tess's eyes looked not at her, but at the cup, her frail looking fingers slipping out from the sleeves to grab the offering from her hands. But she did not drink it, just watched the hot contents melt the bobbing marshmallows.

"Thanks."

Tanya stayed where she was, watching the worry etch its way all throughout Tess's eyes. She may be with them now, out of her safety cocoon of a room upstairs, but inside, Tanya could only see her sister's inner mind as void and hollow. She had been working hard to assure her of the eventual outcome, but it was slow work. She only spoke to Tanya so far, and that had taken the better part of the night for her to open. Tanya, Melissa, and Abby, back from her college courses, had been home at the time, and when Tess had come back in a rather sensual attire and crying her eyes out, they had surged forward, hoping to help her out. Now, Tanya just had to help her mental state. "Tess... he'll call."

"...Tanya, it's been seven days." Tess whispered, her throat tightening as tears threatened to spill out her morning's intake of water. She didn't want to cry in front of her team again, but she gave in and clutched her hand over her heart. "I can't stand this, Tanya. I can't take it anymore. It hurts...my heart hurts so much. I...I shouldn't have conned him in the beginning. I should have gone in bare, with my real name and everything...I should have been honest with him."

"He'd have turned you in, Tess." Tanya urged the facts at her, but Tess shook her head.

"It wouldn't have mattered...surely not." Tess muttered incessantly. "He loves me, doesn't he?" She sniffled more and looked morbidly back at Tanya. "I'm living a lie, Tanya. He doesn't even know what I do in real life! I didn't think it mattered, but ever since we stopped needing his part of the plan, I've fallen into my character too much Tanya. I am Paige. I can't stop lying to him at every turn. I don't want to lie anymore, Tanya. I'm one push away from telling him everything because I'm afraid to lose him, Tanya."

Tess shivered uncontrollably, the sobbing in her throat ready to burst out as a full pained banshee. "I mean, he's never even pushed me for it. He's so caring; he just believes me like an idiot, but I love that idiot."

Tanya coaxed the cup up to her lips, making Tess calm down as she rubbed her back soothingly. "I bet he does know what you do in a way. It's mysterious what you do, and he finds that mystery part of the reason he loves you." Tanya spoke from the heart, before her own skipped a beat. She may love her sister, but she bit her lip, thinking of her own family and her own life back at home. "He probably just doesn't ask out of respect for you."

"You know, maybe this won't be so bad, you know? Daniel may have lost his job, but you can tell him that you can financially support the two of you. He'd become even more conjoined to you than ever before, and I'm certain you two would fall even further in love. I bet Daniel can still-"

"-No!" Tess screamed suddenly, before Tanya rushed to cover her mouth.

"-Shh!" Tanya whispered as she hugged her sister deep into her chest, keeping her raging sobs quiet as the girls looked over in concern. Tanya knew how much Tess hated showing weakness, so holding her this close to hide it was the best she could do. "Tess, don't spiral out." She whispered urgently into her ear,

"He's probably lost his job thanks to me." She sobbed incessantly into her chest. "He's broken because of me!" Tess's breath slowly evened out, as if she was separating from reality.

"Tess?" Tanya questions after a few seconds. Had she fallen asleep? Tanya backed up just a smidge and saw the darkened eyes of her sister. It was dark; ominous and a painful wrath came as words to her mind.

"...And it's all because of HIM." Tess seethed through her teeth. Suddenly she stood up, shrugging her sister's arms off and moved off to the desk that held Tanya's laptop.

Tanya stood back up, her sister's sudden standing pushing her down, and looked perplexed over at her sister as she began to make her way over to her. "What are you doing?"

As Tess pulled out different programs quickly onto the screen, Tanya's eyes failed to follow most of it. "Alex's on the move." She muttered.

"We know where he is since Abby clipped the trackers onto his car."

Tess turned to Tanya's rack of clothes, her fingers deftly sliding along the material, looking for something specific. When she found it, she stopped and began to change before all of them, making them all look back at Tanya confused. "Tess?" Tanya tried to question her, but she grabbed the outfit and changed quickly and moved to leave.

"Tess, where are you going?" Megan asked finally.

Tess cast a glance over and slipped some keys into her pocket as she looked at the girls for what seemed like the first time in forever. "To get even."

"Tess! Don't!" Tanya yelled to try to get her back, but she was gone. After a few seconds, the back door closed loudly and she looked guiltily at the girls, who frowned at Tanya.

"Tanya, you called us in to reclaim our score." Abby spoke up, usually the shyest of the group.

"Yeah, this is personal Tanya." Megan agreed, the bite in her voice clear as day that she felt lied to. "We're losing our chance for a surprise attack. It'll be ten times more difficult."

"I know." Tanya sighed, looking back at the ghostly image of where Tess had stayed all morning on the couch and leaned on the cushions where her head would have been. "Tess, what are you doing?"

Up along the coast, wind ripped across the open waves, the roar of the crashing water against the cliffs a mighty blast as they shot fifty feet up into the air before falling back into the heavy surf. The heavy mist upon the rocks surged up the bluff, wetting and slowly eroding it over the course of its thousand-year battle to carve a scar into the land.

Meanwhile, along the side of the cliff, a small two-lane road wound around the cliffside, zigzagging along the exterior as it moved up and down along the coast, with a huge precipice hovering over the road and a straight drop to the churning waters below without any barrier between them, and yet despite the danger, many cars chanced the route for the picturesque view. Cars sped along, slowing down only for the tight turns at every end. But one car in particular was the outlier of the rest.

Indeed, this car was expensive, with the body sitting low to the ground, the outer shell of it piercing through the heavy winds as it zipped in and out of the two lanes, passing through gaps with mere inches between two cars. Honks sounded with every passing, but it was music to the driver's ears. With the windup sound purring out of his electric engine, Alex pulled the muscle out of his million dollar car, pushing it even faster into the tight turn, nearly colliding with a family's buggy, before speeding down the coastal highway.

He loved his car. There were almost none like it, only twenty-six of them were made as a prototype and it was expensive as hell, but he shrugged it off. Maybe if he'd only taken his share, then he may have struggled, but it wasn't the first wet work he'd done in his life, and it wouldn't be his last, his first being that of his own brother.

Alex had thought himself an avenger when he was younger, people pitying him and his rich upbringing after his parents and younger brother's untimely demise, but he hadn't felt anything but a call to something deeper. He'd taken their pity and molded it into a world of favors and bribes, and to avenge his family.

But when he'd been standing above his brother's dead body, he felt no relief, his family was dead for four years by then. No; he'd felt exhilarated! The power of life is so strong in one's own hands and even a young adult like Alex loved to be the smartest in the room. He'd joined that hag's crew because he was the best planner in the world, and she was old enough to be a grandmother. But when he saw young Tess, he'd seen a competitor.

He thought he liked Tess; she was as beautiful as himself and carried herself with a faux shyness that brought people into her cage of influence, getting what she wanted with the pull of an invisible string. As Alex swerved around a small freight truck, he chuckled to himself. What a nostalgic morning he was having.

The way she was a chameleon was simply amazing, but she was never a leader in his eyes. She relied entirely on her attractive sister too much to split the load, on the other girls who she trusted blindly. Keeping the excess fat around like that college girl with the milky white eyes, the one that Alex was forced to help out because she couldn't do anything right.

Alex cast a glance forward and spotted his destination for the day and sped up even more. He was growing bored in his grandiose home of his. He would get a new crew together for a robbery or something, anything to get his blood pumping. Maybe some wet work was involved while he was at it.

Alex turned into the parking lot of the cliffside restaurant, a Michelin star that specialized on seafood which he gave to himself every two weeks to the date, his table always on reserve now that the workers knew who and what he was, revving his engine loudly for his own amusement and yet smiled brightly as he thought of his conversation with that idiot who Tess had conned so easily.

Was she really trying to get him back for stealing the money? He knew from a single glance that she'd fallen for her own mark. Pity because she had so much potential, but to fall so readily into a simpleton made her weak. She'd never beat him. He swirled his car around the lot and pulled to the valet under the overhang.

As he stepped out, a young woman in the restaurant's valet approached him from the booth, and Alex licked his lips as he casually eyed her body. He was feeling peckish for a warm body, and girls like this one were so eager to get with one of their rich patrons. Her blonde hair pulled into a ponytail in the back, accentuating her soft neck and unbuttoned gap of cleavage of a vest. She'd do nicely for the night.

"Like it?" He gloated as the girl looked down and away, swaying her feet. He smirked and threw his key fob over and the girl eeped as it hit her chest and fell to the ground. Alex smirked as she bent at her waist to pick it up, exposing her backside to him. Definitely posing for his attention, yes?

"No joyriding, you hear me?"

"Of course, sir. The car will drive itself." The girl's sultry voice whispered submissively towards him as she slid into the driver's seat and closed the door.

"And maybe," Alex leaned on his car, marking eye contact with the young girl through the open window, "I could let you take a spin tonight? In more than just a car."

The girl blushed. "I... I have a boyfriend…. but," as she fingered the wheel fondly. "…He and I aren't seeing each other in the same eyes right now…"

"Just a spin." Alex smiled darkly. He just wanted a night after all.

"All right," the girl winked and drove up to the private spots located at the top of the hill. Alex watched for a second before turning to walk into the restaurant. Perfect. A meal now…and a meal later tonight.

Damn her ass was fine, so supple and sublime and he'd have fun with her, twisting her innocent eyes until she practically loved him. Her blonde hair was somewhat unique, and her eyes were stunning and- Alex gripped the wall in a panic, his position frozen in place, before he twisted around with wide eyes. Her eyes…they were emerald.

The valet had just closed the door and began to walk back towards her post, doing nothing but her job as the car was parked at the top of the parking lot, in clear sight of the windows of the restaurant for everyone to watch over in safety and solitude.

The girl's eyes found his and he began to doubt himself as she smiled flirtatiously in his direction, her long legs gliding gracefully towards him across the pavement. And it was in that lifting of his doubt that the car began to move.

The back wheels slid backwards from the space it had been assigned by the valet, the front wheels spinning along as the car picked up speed quickly from gravity pushing it down the ever-increasing slope of the cliffside. Down it streamed, speeding past a few couples hanging around the outdoor fountain and slipping past the entrance as Alex ran to the edge of the lot.

With a sleek design built for speed, the dynamics of the car only helped it surged back towards the small stone wall that stood proud and strong on the edge of the cliff, but from the second the bumper touched the wall, it crumpled like paper and his coveted, limited edition, million-dollar prize shot like a bullet down to the sea below.

Five seconds passed as patrons screamed before a shockwave exploded from the bottom of the cliff, and Alex stood stock still as black fumes began to waft up from the hell below. People already outside rushed to the edge to look at the amazing wreckage as customers inside sprinted to the windows looking at the scene of his car split in three major pieces and many smaller ones to break it down.

As all these people focused on the wreck, another fancy car slid into the valet spot beside him. The open window faced him, and Alex jerkily cast a glance down to the driver only in murderous intent to glare at the valet who was shaking her brunette hair out of the blonde wig.

"That's for talking to my boyfriend." Tess quipped before revving her exotic engine and floored it, the car zooming out of the lot and down the road.

Blood boiled out of his mouth as Alex reacted to her taunt. "I know you're coming for me, Tess! You little bitch! You won't get away with this!!!"

It was just after noon when Daniel looked up from his coffee table, his eyes black and bleating from his lack of sleep. He'd turned in his keys just yesterday to the museum and Sunny and the boys had thrown him a going away party, the boss had only told them that he was leaving the museum, the nice guy that he was.

It had been fine until they had started ragging and pestering him, saying that he must have had to get a higher paying job because he knocked his girlfriend up, right? And had to marry the girl? The jokes hadn't stopped, calling him a future trophy husband since she made more than him, and maybe he was moving in with her and it was too far away to commute.

Daniel had smiled the best he could while he was there, but once he had gotten home, he just sat on the edge of the bed and spent the entire night dreading the thought that blew up in his head. No doubt Paige was mad at him for being a coward. He knew that once she was in the mood, it was hard to get her out of it, and to make it worse, he had asked for three days, not seven! God, he was a coward, too scared to even call her. He should have at least sent her a text telling her how beautiful she was and that he was sorry that he was taking so long to decide.

Daniel cast a glance outside to the playground in one corner of his apartment complex and smiled bitterly as he spent a few minutes watching a six-year-old sister playing with her little brother. Tears pricked at his eyes, as he heaved a great sigh and covered his eyes in his hands again. He had thought of marrying her, of starting a family together.

Their whole relationship was built so quickly, in just four months, probably on rocky and unsuitable ground to begin with, but in his heart, he loved her. He didn't want to break up with her, but he had to, right?

Wasn't it all built on a lie? She wasn't honest with him, calling herself by another name and lying about everything she was and- wait... Daniel cocked his head slightly as he thought about that. Not everything.

What was in a name? Just the identity of the person you were talking to. When he was official, he was his father's last name of Mr. Thompson. But he remembered growing up wanting the name Madic because it was his mother's maiden name, and he liked the sound of it better. He was Daniel, but as he found out just months ago, his heart surged and rushed with content feelings of love when his lover would call him Danny instead.

But still, she didn't trust him, and an even darker thought appeared in his head. Something that detective Simon had pointed out. The thief came in when he was there and with Paige. With her. All those little actions and situations- could she have been a part of the robbery?

His mind changed Paige's innocent self into a false front and thought deeply. A thief would lie about their name. Heck! They could change their appearance and dye their hair, right?!? But stealing from people...before Tommy pointed out her name, he wouldn't have believed it, but she was stealing months from him. Couldn't she have done it?

(Knock)(knock)

Daniel stood from the table and slowly moved to the door. His neighbors had stopped by to check on him the last few days, seeing his pain clearly on his face, but he didn't want the company right now. He'd answer to be polite and send them away. Sometimes, a person just wanted to wallow in their shame.

Daniel opened the door and swallowed his leaping heart back down his throat. There was his girlfriend...in a uniform? Was she trying to seduce him again? Not to say it wasn't helping her, but...he saw the black circles around her eyes and for some reason he was glad that they were both suffering from this.

"Hey…" Paige's voice whispered over to him, as she looked slightly to the side in guilt. He hadn't called her yet after all, and yet here she was, without warning and unannounced.

"Hey…what's with the uniform?" Daniel cast a small smirk at the question. She was trying to seduce him, right?

But the guilty smile she sent him tiredly made his heart skip a beat. "I drove Tommy's car off a cliff."

His eyes widened, but Daniel said nothing. What could someone say to that? So, he uttered, "Oh…"

Tears formed in Paige's eyes as she finally looked him in the eyes, the sadness and lack of sleep as obvious now as night and day. "Daniel, look! I'm sorry, I-"

"-Come in." Daniel gestured with his hand, while his mind stirred. He didn't mean to interrupt, but his body moved on its own, ignorant of what he thought or wanted to let his girlfriend say first.

It was the happiest thing to do however as Paige took the sign as him forgiving her. Her over eagerness erupted with fresh happy tears as she launched herself forward, her body quickly joining her boyfriend's frame as she latched around his neck with her arms encircling him, his own hands already resting on the small of her back. Damn, she felt perfect this close to him. But he could feel it still; as she pressed her body close, the way her entire figure shivered and positively dripped in need and want to be at his side, like a puppy wanting to be pet by her owner.

"I love you." Paige whimpered, kissing along his jawline, and kissing that perfect spot that made him growl. "I'm so sorry, Daniel. I'm sorry I lied to you! Please Daniel, I need you in my life! I'll never lie to you again! I-I'll tell you everything you want to know! Please." Paige sniffled into his neck, moistening the area as tears slipped down her cheeks. "I...I don't want to lose you."

Both slowly leaned back and looked at the other. Paige began to lean in, but she paused, giving him a second to join her. He did not, so she leaned even further, and Daniel and she joined together as their lips kissed slowly, their fingers deftly stroking the other's face, tracing the small curves and ridges that was their image. As the sound of kissing sounded louder, the hands slipped lower, Daniel's hands rested on the small of her back as Paige's hands skimmed over the front of his chest, pulling him ever closer. Daniel was in nirvana, feeling ecstatic and content to have her in front of him. Then as Paige began to undo his buttons, all those feelings left him. He pulled back from her and pressed his forehead against hers.

Paige sighed in sadness. "We're...we're good, right?"

A huge thought pried open at his mind, one so big and stupid, that he almost couldn't even fathom why he was willing to do it. If his younger self had thought this, he'd call himself an idiot. Inside his body, his heart felt like it was cracking. His personality...because of her, he wasn't who he was anymore. He was someone different and He.... Tears pricked at his eyes again. "Paige...I can't do this anymore...."

Her hair moved so slowly, as if frame by frame, starting bunched up against him, and slowly cascading to frame her own tear-stained face, as she looked up and stared into his eyes hoping to see something else; fresh tears fell down her face as she no doubt saw the change in his eyes, in the way he looked at her. It was different, more powerful, his feelings set now forever in his opinion of anything that was her.

"...Y-you can't." Paige sniffled and shuddered as they parted, the realization dawning on her as fresh tears formed in her eyes. Daniel grabbed her hand and rubbed her knuckle with the pad of his thumb.

"I can't do it. I'm sorry..."

XIX-CONSEQUENCES

The door to Daniel's apartment shut with Tess's face towards the solid wood. She casually turned her head and made it two steps before her palm flattened against the wall and she froze in place. Slowly, her other hand gripped at the space above her heart, and she let out a low whimper as she struggled to breathe.

So, this was how it felt when one pulled one's very existence out from under them. This is what she did to her marks every time she disappeared to never reemerge. A bitter smile graced her face. It was just her luck that she had that very experience happen right in her face.

After another minute or two, she finally shuddered less and took a small gasp of air. This was just how it had to be from now on. His very being was now imprinted on her heart, and she knew that she would never love another. He was the only one she could love this much that her heart broke for him.

Tess moved forward, down the stairs and out to her car that was in their….no, his spot. As she slid inside, her finger hovered over the push button for the ignition. She wondered if this was how Amelia must have felt her whole life. To have had the love of someone who had changed you into who you wanted to be, to give up everything that you were in the past and be made anew.

To have it like this, Tess knew that she was about to do things that her coworkers wouldn't agree with, much less her sister, but she couldn't become anything but what she had decided in the moments after Daniel said he was sorry.

A shiver crept into her skin as she rubbed her arm nervously, backing out of the spot and towards her crew's place and her now reaffirmed residence. She was really going to miss this persona of hers. She had gone much deeper being Paige than any other persona before, and if she were honest, Paige would never truly leave her; she'd be with her on those cold dark nights, and in the dreamy memories of good peaceful days. But she was Tess Miles, world class thief, and out for murder, and she had a job to do.

An hour later, Tess breathed in her courage and stepped out of her car and moved to the door to her home and team headquarters. It was only a ten-minute drive, but she'd been thinking in the dark garage for the better part of a half hour, thinking through all the reactions her team was going to direct right at her.

They were smart women, and no doubt had heard her come in, and she had let them stew in their anger and feelings of betrayal long enough. Tess looked down at herself and laughed miserably. Who was she to put on costumes and outfits? This was totally Tanya's field of expertise, outside of tech.

She placed her hand on the door handle and breathed in deeply. "Please don't hate me too much." She whispered as she turned the handle. No one was directly behind the door, so she pressed on down the concrete hallway, her shoes echoing along the hard floor. She made two quick turns around the jutting U shaped wall down the hallway and emerged directly in front of her entire team, glaring at her.

"What do you have to say for herself, Tess?" Melissa asked lowly, her voice barely audible to the group. Tess looked down at herself and shrugged.

"I was stupid; I wanted him to feel the pain I felt when he ripped Daniel away fr-"

"You bitch!!" Tanya screamed into her face as she rushed forward and sliced her flat palm through the air, making contact with her left cheek, slamming her down to the ground as Tess crumbled to the floor. Abby pulled her arm away and held her back.

"Tanya, calm down!"

"No, I will not calm down!" Tanya yelled back, before spitting her words violently at her adopted sister. "Do you realize what you've done, Tess?!? Because of you, he found our bugs!"

Tess looked up in shame towards Megan, who nodded her head. "He called for another check of his house and the grounds too. And a deep check too. He got them all."

"And he found the trackers for his cars as well." Melissa piped in. "Poor Abby spent weeks following him around and putting those in place already. All for nothing now."

Tess rubbed her swelling cheek, opening and closing her jaw as she stumbled like a newborn deer to try to stand up. "I'm sorry girls. Anything good happen?" She asked morbidly, but Tanya threw her hands away, pushing Abby away as she growled at her sister.

"It's all gone Tess! He went straight to the banks and pulled out all the cash! It's no longer anywhere! Closed all of his accounts- all our work was wasted because of you!"

Tanya continued to lash out, her fingers jabbing through the air at her, painfully telling her everything that went wrong, and yet…. Tess began to smile.

"And another thing! When you go out without telling us anything, then we- what the hell are you smiling at?" Tanya breathed tiredly.

"……….He moved it….."

"…So what?" Tanya held in another exasperated scream. "I can't track it if it's physical, Tess!"

"Tanya…" Her sister spoke for the first time in front of the group as she began to smile with hope on her face. In fact, it looked like she was hatching an insane plan in her mind.

"What?" Tanya quipped, her anger abating.

"…It's tangible……."

"What?" Tanya repeated, but beside her, Abby gasped as she edged forward to embrace Tess's shoulders as both girls began to grin broadly at the other.

"It's physical." Abby spoke up to the others as they slowly smiled together as a group. Only Tanya turned skeptically to look at each of them, like they were insane before she sighed and grinned sourly in defeat.

Tanya walked up to her shivering sister and hugged her tightly, as Tess sighed into her embrace, her hand still holding her cheek with the red handprint clear as day on her porcelain face.

"You always were one for the classics, Tess. So an old school heist, huh?" Tanya nudged her to follow as Tess grinned brightly only to wince at the pain. "Let's do it. But first...let's get you some ice."

"Where did you learn to slap like that?"

"Oh! I've practiced all my life." Tanya smirked. "After all, you and I were Not close when Mother first adopted you."

XX - TOUGH NUT TO CRACK

A day later, Abby and the girls were all standing around their central room, watching as Tess and she went over the various obstacles that they would face when assaulting the heavy fortress that was Alex's mansion.

"Alright girls," Abby spoke as she rubbed her neck nervously. "So, this isn't going to be easy, but I-I… We think!" Abby looked at Tess who smiled and nodded her head. "We can do this thing."

"Hell, yeah we can." Megan smiled as she leaned over a couch towards the screen.

"So then, the security on the mansion is insane and was the primary reason as to why we weren't going to attack Alex there." Tess pointed out.

"The security system is quite top-notch." Abby repeated.

"You can say that again." Tanya bristled. "Sumara tech has been offering hackers five million dollars if they can hack inside. Four years, no payouts."

"Anyways, the cameras run on a closed alpha system, with recurring loops every ten minutes, meaning that we can't just hack the cameras and be invisible."

"Can you get me the angles?" Megan piped up.

"Way ahead of you." Tanya motioned to Melissa who brought up the camera locations that they had mapped out weeks ago. "There are three or four cameras that offer some form or another of a small blind spot for us. Not enough for a real technician to plan for, but we're just coasting by them, so we can work with that. Abby. Just make sure that any calls to Sumara come to me so that they don't undo my changes to them."

"So, then we just need to hack the network then?" Melissa asked.

"Wouldn't work." Tanya shook her head as she sipped her lemonade and got closer. "All of those wires are linked together, barely bigger than three threads of hair, which is why it's hard to notice. Besides that, they only emit maybe five millimeters off the wire, so I would need to be practically- no I would need to be attached to them to have access. The good thing is that they are all connected, so while expensive as hell to install, a physical attack is much easier. Bad part is that they covered all the areas of the grounds pretty well."

Tanya pointed at a small part of the diagram on the screen, nodding to herself before grimacing. "Pretty disgusting design if you ask me. Since his mansion is so old fashioned, it looks wonderful, but he no doubt busted the old school architecture for security. Get me in there girls, and I'll get us in."

"Okay," Melissa sighed in defeat. "I get that we can't touch them remotely, so you're saying we hack the wires that support the security itself?"

Tanya hummed before shrugging. "It'd be really tricky. All the main wires run through a pipe underground. What are the dimensions, Tess?"

Tess frowned. "Barely big enough for a teenager to squeeze through, and that's with a lot of bends and twists." Tanya nodded her approval as Megan wrote down and circled the pipes on the screen.

"You know," Megan piped in, scratching her head in annoyance, "Alex's going to run out of money if he keeps spending it everywhere as he is."

"I noticed that too." Abby agreed. "He doesn't care about making it last at all."

"Amelia always did mention how he was always looking for the next score."

"Does he have another heist coming up?"

"Seems like it." Tess nodded to Abby who loaded up the garage of his mansion. "When Abby and I went to recon yesterday, he had four new SUV's, all built for suspension and reinforcements around the doors. It may just be for a security gig, but maybe a warlord or politician in the future."

"That's going to be a pain if we get caught while inside. They can have a car for each of us."

"Or some of us give them a clear target. Either way, we'll need some fast wheels to get away from them if the guards chase after us."

"Maybe they don't see anything on the cameras at all. What about cutting the electricity entirely? We have a stolen maintenance van after all." Tanya chimed in. It would be easier on her side to not even go through the security system.

"No good." Melissa cut her idea down. "They have three backup generators, each in separate locations along the grounds and they are specifically designed to cover each other's sections in overlapping districts of the house."

"How long until they activate?" Tess asked.

Melissa hums. "Maybe 20 seconds."

"That's doable."

Melissa shot a questioning look over to Tess. "For what?"

Tess grinned and shrugged nonchalantly. "If it gives us time, it's worth it. I'll think of something."

"So, besides the virtual security, all we have left are the physical obstacles." Abby released a nervous breath.

"Abby, each and every one of us can surely scale the outer wall easily enough."

"That's not what I was referring to. The real thing is that there are ten guards for this mansion that could be watched over by three. That's more than the art gallery that Tess and Tanya hit, and these guys are a rung below mafia in what they're willing to do. They're just dressed nice, but I've followed them to some bars, and they are not nice guys. Cocky, paid well, and strong do not make them good company."

"And anything not on the patios is set to be squeezed to death." Tess sighed as she sipped her drink. The silence that followed her statement had her look up to see them question her. "Show them Abby."

"They freak me out, Tess."

"Me too, but the other girls need to see them."

Abby gulped and pressed the video button before a camera's view appeared facing the wall. Slowly, it rose to show the green grass of the lawn, the oak trees far off in the distance with a patio and large pool and jacuzzi in the back by the glass doors further into the home. And most of it was showing no cameras at all, which would be great if the entire field of grass was not slithering back and forth in the video.

"What are those?" Tanya asked, narrowing her eyes until sleek pieces of steel and joints appeared and disappeared over and over again as machine parts slithered place to place. "Are t-those snakes?"

"AI-enabled snakes. They are as fast as a cobra's bite and as strong as a boa constrictor squeezing around you. You get one of these on your legs girls, and it's not letting go without the leg."

The girls shivered as they watched the footage continue to show at least ten of them slithering through this area near the back side of the mansion, a weak point of some places, but these snakes held it up to the name of a deadly fortress.

"What about birds and such?"

"No animals are on the property except dogs, and they are within an interior courtyard as well."

"Motion sensitive I suppose."

Tess simmered as she leaned across the map and diagram that the girls had made for the mansion, at all the angles and obstacles that they would have to go through to achieve their goals. "Alright girls, we are going in one week from today."

Most of them just widened their eyes, but Megan looked at her perplexed and spoke up. "Why so soon?"

Tess cast a perceptive look her way, her face already knowing the answer to her question. "You are telling me you can't do it?"

Megan pouted back but pressed her chest out defiantly. "Oh no! I can be ready in three days. I'm just being cautious here. I just want to know why we would rush this?"

Tess nodded her head and spent a few seconds looking over each of the girls around her, her thoughts assessing each one of their strengths and weaknesses, knowing where and how to push them to their peak efficiency and where to leave them be.

"Alex knows we're coming; he'll want to move his money out fast. We need to get to it before he has a chance to make this place impregnable."

Tess paused as she spotted a bulletin pop up on their screen, of the electronic traffic that they could gleam off his internet connection through his provider and smiled with a knowledgeable smirk.

"Tanya, are they still hiring a guard?"

Tanya looked over at her sister and smiled. "Yeah. Came in this morning that Alex wants two more guards."

"Put in your application. You'll be our way inside." Tess waved her hand as everyone dispersed to begin their tasks that had to get done in one hundred and sixty-eight hours from now. As Tess looked back down at the spread-out map of the mansion's layout, Tanya stared at her back, perplexed by her sister's choice of Tanya's position for the operation.

"Hey Tess? I really should be the one doing the tech side of things on this. I have the most experience there. Besides, surely Abby is better. Alex doesn't like seeing any of his security guards around, so she won't make contact with him. And besides, she's still just a rookie, so she'll be able to act innocent better than-"

"Tanya, a word." Tess glanced over and made quick eye contact before walking away from the center of the room. Tanya immediately followed her; the other girls looked down at their work. They knew better than to argue with a mastermind of Tess's caliber.

However, Tanya knew that she hadn't offended Tess. No, whatever she wanted to tell her, she didn't want the others overhearing. That thought cemented it in her head when Tess moved around the corner of the room, towards their staircase for the rooms and the hallway for the garage. No, the glint in her sister's eyes told her enough to know what to expect. Tess had looked at her as if hiding a secret mission from the rest of the team, and Tanya knew that it was for their mother. There was no other reason other than avenging their mother.

Tanya noted her suspicions to be true once she turned the corner to see Tess leaning against the adjacent wall, staring right at her. This was the one area that didn't echo in the entire building as she joined her, leaning against the concrete wall opposite her.

"You don't usually argue with me in front of the team." Tess noted.

"You don't usually make mistakes like that."

"...It needs to be you."

"Why?"

"It... just does…"

"That's not a reason. Don't treat me like part of the crew. I'm your sister."

Tess breathed in worriedly, and sagged back into the wall, letting her arms and her guard drop down. Tess breathed out and gazed back into Tanya's vision.

"If I tell you, you can't tell the others, no matter what. I... I need you to do something for me. Something that I would never ask from anyone else. Something that I can only entrust to you, my sister."

Tanya felt the chill that flowed slowly down her spine and shivered. It may be dangerous, but this whole mission was. Besides, she'd do anything for her little sister. So after a second, Tanya smiled back at Tess's guilty eyes.

"Alright. What is it?"

XXI-DIRT, HEIGHTS, & RATS

Watching cameras is not an exciting job. Ninety percent of it is watching the screens repeat the same thing over and over again. At least when you work in a museum, you have young moms showing their kids around, and a school trip with some teenagers trying to sneak off and touch a painting. Guarding a mansion, watching the grass outside slowly grow, was not for everyone, but when your employer paid you three times the normal rate to do this, you did not complain. In fact, you relish the chance to do so, to have an easy job where you can score a high earning.

From the wall of the mansion, the row of cameras watched as a figure approached in a large sun hat with baggy garb around their body, pushing forward a large machine that scraped at the grass below. It was just the hired help being given minimum wage to cut the grass, and in return for the quick work, they would not be deported. Simple as that.

The machine continued its very slow advance, the clunky behemoth making angry growls and snarls in the gardener's ears as they pushed it inwards. But right around the halfway point of the mansion, the machine revved harder and black smoke engulfed out of the pipes and billowed up into the air. The guard no doubt laughed as this was the most exciting thing to happen all week, and therefore, he missed everything.

The gardener began to throw rakes around the machine, screaming at it as they dug their deft hands through the bags attached to it. After another minute though, they calmed down and bent down to look

191

under the engine. Off came the sunhat, showing the Chinese buns of the woman who could make everything explode, Megan.

She reached under the hallowed husk of the machine that was blackening her face more and more by the second and pulled out two long cylindrical tubes as well as the pedestals to hold them in place and slid back with them in hand. Mobile mortars, specially engineered with her own hands.

She placed them three feet behind the tractor, the thickened smoke blocking the cameras' angles as she slid each piece into place. Megan turned back to grab her tools under the machine as well as two bags of wet red substances that were her part of the plan. Without her, they weren't getting in.

Megan clicked her tongue in her cheek, activating the microphone along her neck and cleared her throat. She never liked wearing these things. They itched and rubbed her skin raw. "Knight at the castle gates."

Below that soft grass lawn, dirty water, filled sewage and garbage flowed through pipes that were more than a little weathered and rusting. The water filled only a third of the tube, due to the recent lack of rain in Kavala, but still the pipe filled with water to the top as the pressure built around the blackened form that was making its way up the pipe.

Abby cursed into her mike, her eyes prickling in annoyance, feeling like she would throw up every time something in the water touched her dry suit. She groaned madly as her wide college hips hit a snag in the tube and she moaned as she wiggled her butt through the perpendicular turn.

"Why did I get stuck with this?" Abby muttered to her team on the other end. It was the first sentence she had spoken since she entered the pipe an hour ago that wasn't a string of curses like a sailor.

"Because you're the rookie, Abby."

"Yeah, yeah. I hate this team." Abby groaned as one of her devices beeped out how close she was to her target. As she wiggled forward though, her bare fingers graced something wet and furry.

"EWWW! A rat! Get it off, get it off!" Abby squealed, her loud voice echoing in the cramped space. The rat in question was already long gone, but still she spammed and breathed heavily.

"Abby, get a hold of yourself. You got this."

"I swear, if I come across rats again, I'm going to-"

"Cut the chatter."

Abby silently pushed onto her back, her entire lower body now dunking into the dirty water, and adjusted her fogging goggles, murmuring to herself about rookies getting the dirty jobs. She understood completely where her strengths lied and being the youngest and thinnest meant that she was a prime candidate for, you guessed it, spelunking in a pipe.

Abby slid her hand along the top of the pipe, as she held a device in her hand as a laser projected outwards from the other side, red lines flowing through its sight until she came to a cross section where many wires met on the other side.

"How far am I?" Abby whispered out.

"About three hundred and sixteen feet in the pipe."

Abby nodded as that was the correct distance. Abby soon shivered as she slid her other hand down her packed like a sardine body to slide a razor-sharp straight cutting saw about five inches long. She lined it up with the image she had seen and turned on the device as it began to chip away at the pipe.

"Nightingale arriving at construction site."

Up and above from where the mansion lay, a maintenance van bumped along a dirt road along a hilly outcropping, before the tires stuck in place, digging into the gravel as the van came to a stop next to a hundred-yard beam of wood with lines near the top.

The door to the van opened as a uniformed woman stepped out, decked out in her grey and blue outfit, with the sigil of the company she was representing laying on both the breast of her shirt and on the cap she wore.

But as she stared at the base of the wood, her fingers jittered. She slowly moved her eyes up the length of the pole, trying in vain to ignore the freezing chatter of her teeth as her heartbeat increased rapidly.

"You in position yet?" Abby called out suddenly.

"Give me a minute!" The woman whipped towards her earpiece, even though her teammates wouldn't see the action. Her eyes pooled a little in tears as she stared at the top. This wasn't her cup of tea at all. She grew up in a flat desert! No tall places to worry about falling off to your death. Did she trust Megan's equipment? Of course! She herself knew that the material she'd ordered was top quality, but still! That was so tall!

"...Melissa?" Tess's voice came over the waves of fear.

"...Y-yeah?"

"...You got this Melissa. I know you do."

"I don't know. I mean-"

"-Melissa...be the wind."

That little joke made her giggle aloud as she shook off the fear that kept her rooted in place and turned back to the van door, bending over to the equipment that lay across the bed of the vehicle.

A minute later, she looked back up with determination in her eyes, and a set of equipment attached to her belt and over her shoulder. "Wind rider, starting the climb."

Abby let her hand slip back, the saw in her hand sliding out of the lines that it had created. She slid it back into her pocket and pulled out the square that she had cut through and threw it further down the pipe as she shined a light into the gap, showing colors of white, grey, and black wires all bundled together before her.

As one hand began to slip the wires down towards her, her other hand pulled clamps and electronics from her inlaid pockets. But alas, she had to really squeeze herself with every little movement she made. She could hear Melissa's shuddering breaths from climbing the pole and held in her own breath, as her body began to swell up the entirety of the pipe. She didn't like tight spaces either, but she'd be damned if she let her team down just because of a little panic attack!

Finally, she grabbed a small tablet and attached it to the cables before sighing and relaxing her body. Her fingers held the wires and began to count out the ones she'd have to attach to.

"Nightingale in position."

Megan sighed, snapping the last of the pegs down with her mallet, holding the cylindrical pipe in the correct position. The sun had been such a killer and it was nearly the end of the day already. She sighed loudly in victory as she untied her sunhat, pushing it to the back where it held around her neck.

Dusting off her costume, she stood up and began to walk away from the scene, leaving the lawn mower hissing and sputtering its grayish white fumes to cover the mortars that she had finished setting up. She finally grabbed her cell phone and turned on the wireless network and smiled as the mortar's cameras showed up on her screen, with angles and trajectories hovering ghostly in the pictures.

"Knight in position. Ready to charge on your count."

Melissa edged up to the next metal rung, her rubber sole fitting just right into the slot as she snapped her elastic belt around the other side of the beam with her hands. The belt looped ever higher, helping her move closer and closer until she finally reached the box at the top of the tower, just below the lines above.

She looked back down, and her eyes narrowed at the many feet she'd fall if she made one wrong move now. She carefully took an extra carabiner and clipped it around a second belt and attached it to the other side of herself. Finally, she let go of the beam with her feet.

Her body slacked in the belts and hung her just over the box itself. She breathed easier and inserted the stolen key that they'd gotten last night from an easily fooled employee and looked at the machine inside with a bar for the power.

"Wind rider in position."

"Vixen, on your go."

"Alright." Tess called out from behind a tree on the opposing wall that Knight was at. Her hand reached up to her ear and tapped twice, as she spoke to the other side. After getting a response, she tapped the side again and switched back to her first channel. She breathed in and released a heavy breath, as her eyes opened wide and filled to the brim for the mission at hand.

"Let's begin."

XXII-BREAKING ENTRY

"Let's begin. Nightingale, prepare the splint."

"Roger. 10 seconds."

"Wind rider, on my count." Tess called out as she looked at her watch on her wrist. "10, 9, 8…."

Melissa listened to her leader count down and steadied her hand on the lever.

"3, 2, 1…Now!"

Windrider pulled down on the lever, as sparks flashed before her, and the transformer above her began to whir down, as down the line, electricity began to shut off one by one.

"1…2…3!"

Wind rider flipped the switch back in an upward position, and the entire area reset and powered back on.

"Your unit is now live."

"Attach the splint." Nightingale heard from her cramped location and breathed in as she clipped on the last wire and quickly began typing on her hand sized tablet, starting up ten different programs, each with their own purpose and area to attack, like viruses infecting the body.

"Nightingale, do you, have it?"

◄■ ■ ■ ■ ■ ■ ■ ■ ■ ■ ■ ■ ■ ■ ■ ►

Meanwhile, inside the guardhouse of the mansion, the power flickered off and two muscular guards looked at the other.

"Do you think-"

"Power outage?"

"Probably. But the generator should-"

Their conversation was interrupted as their monitors and the lights flickered back on. "Ah! Just a power surge."

"That's what you get for living way out here away from the main grid I tell you."

"Um, sir, wouldn't that be the best time to take down the cameras?" A young voice called out from the back of the room.

The two men turned back to smirk at the new recruit's comment. Their eyes appraised the blonde bombshell that was just finishing up, changing into her uniform of black and red, her hand frozen on the belt where her walkie talkie, keys, and a pistol resided.

The men gazed at her lewdly and smirked harder as the girl's throat bobbed up and down as she nervously looked back down, cowering a bit at her superiors.

"Sorry. I've been watching too many movies."

The first guard smiled and swiveled back to the monitors and began typing commands into the system. "You're not wrong exactly. I mean maybe if they wanted to attack right away, but they'd have to get our generator first, not last."

"And the power came back on." The second guard called back. "They should at least hit the right areas to hinder us. Besides, they'd need some serious skill to maintain our rotating systems even if they took down our cameras, since each system covers them, and will reset them again."

"Enough dawdling." The first guard called back again. "Now head out on patrol. Show us you memorized your hallways you were given yesterday. You said you could handle that, right?"

"Yes sirs. I can handle the rotating paths. Where do you want me to start?" The rookie called out from the door.

"Hallway C to corridor G and then wait at room 11."

"Of course." The new girl rushed out, before sliding out the door.

"That newbie has such a nice body." The second guard chuckled as he turned back to the monitors.

"Hey, man, you already have a wife who's quite the looker."

"What are you saying?"

"I'm saying that I get first dibs on the new girl." The two laughed.

The female guard slid out of the room and turned towards the direction they had mentioned, the door clicking shut as her hand moved to her radio, as she deftly powered it on, and switched to channel 3, when her fellow guards were on channel two.

"Are we a go, girls?"

"......"

"......"

"......"

"Girls?"

"We're here now."

Tanya nodded her head; her secured code for the radios was now their strength, with ears on all the guards.

"So, you heard all that, Nightingale?"

"Of course, I did...Teacup." A mocking voice came across the airwaves.

A deep blush erupted on the guard's face, and she sniffed annoyed at the little group of gaggling girls on the other end.

"It's not funny!" She hissed. "Please give me a real codename, girls!"

"Well anyways," Abby chimed in, her fingers sliding across the keyboard on her stomach in the pipes under the house. "They don't see anything I don't want them to."

"Sonar scan is up." Tanya spoke as she turned a corner, pressing the badge on her uniform as it blinked blue and began to hum lightly, whirring up as it began its function. For thirty seconds, no one spoke as Tanya continued to walk along her assigned corridor until a click sounded and the device stopped emitting sounds. "Well?" Tanya whispered.

A hum answered her on the other end. "Just layering the scan over the official blueprints now." Abby called out as she typed commands into the computer.

As she waited, Tanya turned to the next hallway and looked down in either direction, noticing the expensive mahogany walls and floor. She never thought she'd be the one going in for infiltration. A short con yes, a disguise for an hour perhaps, but looking like her real self? Wow! Her sister's plan had worked perfectly.

Yesterday when she got the job, Tanya had been strip searched, the men of the entire security detail watching her, all appraising her body and looking for weapons at the same time. Alex had obviously warned them about cosmetics and false hair, as the guards had scraped at her hair and along her sides, so to go natural was indeed the way to go.

She had to give it to Tess; during the interview, leaning over and some flirting with the head guard had paid off. And yesterday at meeting the rest of the boys, Tanya had acted the part perfectly with Tess's suggestions; performing as a tomboy who wanted to play with the boys, but shy and more submissive to a dominant male. The men took her in right away, and lowered their walls for who could be like a little sister or a bedmate. If she'd had more time, she would have liked to flirt with the other new guard too to cement the con, but their time was short.

"Okay girls, so not as different as we were expecting. A few sections not in the blueprints. I have the cameras and I've erased your frames, so stay in the sight of them, alright? If you leave the sight, then wait for me to reinsert you."

"So, we're a go?"

Abby smiled as she tapped one final button on her device and spoke. "You have fifteen minutes everyone."

"…. Eagle," Abby relented over the radio to Tanya, who finally breathed happily and smiled at the camera in front of her. "Start searching in the east room."

"Vixen, you're up."

"Roger that."

Tess stepped out from behind a tree in all black, her outfit completely suspicious and complete with a black beanie, but her brunette hair formed a ponytail behind her, and she smirked as she charged forward.

With no need to worry about the cameras, she ran straight at the wall, a long rifle bag slung over her shoulder. She pushed off the ground at the last second, her other foot pushing upwards from the wall itself, launching her up near the top. Her deft fingers grazed the lip of the top border and pulled herself up over the lip as she laid flat against the two-foot-thick wall. She lay prone for a count of ten, waiting for any hidden sensors to go off, but soon sighed and clicked her tongue in triumph.

"Alright Knight; time to joust."

Megan smiled as she came back to the lawn mower and smacked it with a wrench as it coughed and sputtered loudly on the other side of the mansion, masking the sounds as she tapped the launch button on her phone.

Near invisible smoke shot off from the pipes, ejecting from the mortars as five feet of meat soared over the entirety of the mansion, over the roof itself and arched downwards until the metal rods from within the meat sunk into the grass on the courtyard where Tess overlooked.

Megan smirked at her triumph. The local high school had been all too eager to test her "experiment" for the last two days. That high school test worked perfectly as she hit right on target, each ten yards apart.

Tess watched the courtyard, looking through a small scope in her hands as the metallic snakes completely ignored the meat and kept going on their predicted paths. Inside her head, she held down her annoyance. That should have worked!

"Knight, they didn't go for it-"

"Wait for it." Megan smiled as she ducked below the mower and flipped the screen to another button and activated a second set of Bluetooth enabled devices. Small pumps hidden inside the meat began to activate, simulating a heartbeat.

For Abby and Tess who could see, they couldn't stop the shivers of dread from erupting down their spines as instantly, the snakes struck the piles of meat, squeezing and coiling around them, each snake overlapping another as they squeezed all over the meat roughly, until one could not even see the meat at all, just a mass of silver and grey slithery metal on a metallic rod.

"Here goes nothing." Tess shrugged before she quickly launched herself off the wall, quick to slide down the other side and raced for the gaps between the metal rods. She sprinted as fast as she could, past the edge, past the center, and then past the grass of the snake lair.

Her feet landed on the paver stones of the pool and slid along the wall until she stood at the poolside door, and just in time as the door handle dipped down and opened outwards, as a loud beep sounded in the vicinity.

"R3, is the pool door open?" A radio called out from the door as the guard's eyes stared right at Tess's face and reached for their radio.

"No sir," Tanya replied, "I can see from here that it's closed. It must be a bad wire." Tanya spoke as she smiled brightly at her sister. Tess smirked back as she slipped through the opening as they shut the door, and the beep sounded again.

"How's that?" Tanya pressed down on her radio, "Is it still going off?"

"No. Carry on."

"Copy. Will do." Tanya finished before both women looked at the other, one in a guard's costume and the other as that of the classic thief. But in their hearts, they were the same, thieves to the core, in search of their hidden treasure.

"Anything?" Tess questioned hopefully. The sooner they found it, the sooner they would be done.

But Tanya shook her head, frowning as she did so. "Not really. The boys in the camera room let their guard down just as you expected, but we can narrow it down. They were all too eager to show me the east wing."

Tess shrugged. "It's a start. I figured they wouldn't be forthcoming about it anyways, and not for a newbie even more. You continue to check here in the west wing, and I'll check out the back with the bedrooms."

"Tess," Abby chimed in, her voice agitated. "I know that's the likely place to have it, but Alex wouldn't be so generic. And besides, that's all the way across our planned routes. Do we really need to-"?

"Just show me the way." Tess spoke with a neutral tone, and immediately, the decision was made for them.

"Alright." Abby gave in. "Next left down to the basement level, full across it until you hit the middle of the house, then you'll need to head up two floors past two guards who are circling the area and it should be the third on the right."

After a second of mouthing the directions, Tess answered curtly. "Alright." Tess moved to walk away but paused in the doorway. She looked back at Tanya, who was preening her outfit like a bird about to fly and turned back.

"Hey." Tess whispered before she hugged her sister tightly. Tanya eagerly embraced her back as the two stayed close to the other before leaning back. "No one dies today."

Tanya smiled back, a sad smirk on her face, the morbid tone not amusing her at all. "None." She watched as Tess snuck away with her equipment on her back and breathed out what nerves she had left.

"What should I check next?" She spoke quietly into her mike.

"Head to the right and check the library." Melissa responded on the other side of the line.

Meanwhile, towards the far side of the mansion, an exterior door opened and closed.

"Outside is clear."

"F1, head to hallway 4."

"Roger that."

XXIII-THE HOUSE

Tess lightly jumped across the twenty-foot drop, her body as graceful as a gazelle as she moved up in the wooden rafters above the hallway down below. Her eyes stalked the guard below her as he slowly walked away, his eyes gazing in either direction as he moved.

She didn't have the luxury of waiting, so she urged herself forward, over wooden beams she pranced, her bag still slung tight on her back, the strap digging in between her chest and at her right shoulder, but soon she reached the end of the hallway and began to descend the walls back towards the soft padding of the carpet.

At the last ten feet, she dropped silently just as the guard turned the corner and sprinted straight across the intersection into a small alcove and threw herself at the curved wall, pressing her body into the hidden corner, as another guard appeared at the end of the new corridor.

Tess counted to twenty before her eye slipped out from behind the rim of the alcove and spotted the guard directly in front of her, his back to her as he turned towards the hallway she'd just run from.

With a silent step, she appeared within inches of the guard's back and spirited away, down the corridor and into the door at the center of the wall, and closed it, all before the guard had a chance to look back.

Tess let a soft smile grace her face at the soft click of the door. She was here in Alex's bedroom, and yet as she turned to look at it, only a frown could appear on her lips.

Alex's bedroom was structured like a hotel suite, with a bedroom hidden in the back and right here before it was a lounging room with some dressers, and couches if he felt like lounging around in the comfort of this more private part of his home.

It may look nice, but to her, it looked gaudy and held no character at all. You could look in any number of designed home journals and get better than this. This room simply looked like he had no character inside his soul.

Tess immediately set to work, checking everywhere around the room for her team's treasure. At a simple glance or two, she could see the numerous forgeries of amazing paintings littered over the left wall of the room and quickly lifted each of them a little to check for anything hidden before resuming her search.

If Alex had indeed emptied his accounts, it was either in hard cash or substitutes, something that would hold its value. True that he could buy paintings and try to move them, but he'd never do that in front of their watchful gaze. It was too easy to swap a suitcase or piece of luggage with another with a simple change of travelling tag. No, he would not make it art.

Tess sighed as she finally closed the top drawer of the dresser near the entry door. It wasn't here. It was a long shot, but she'd still had to check. Abby would be reloading the cameras again in five minutes, so she had to get hidden soon and-

"How much are we talking about?" A voice asked as the door to the bedroom opened. Tess had no option but to run at the opening door and as she did, she slid into the small triangular space between the door and the wall and sucked in her stomach as the handle pressed into her abdomen. Just in time as the man entered the room.

"Yes, I can agree to that."

Tess's eyes narrowed darkly as the voice spoke again. Alex. The man who took her mother right in front of her eyes. The man who purged her idea of ever wanting to live a double life with her criminal family and that of one with her...beloved. Tess shivered with a pang of her heart; it ached and pleaded with her to kill him right here and now. She really wished Tanya had given her a baton.

"Yes. I can pay for my own protection...it is not a problem. I'm a pretty good shot myself." Alex's voice rumbled whimsically.

Tess slid just her head sideways, until half of her face could see the man, and frowned as he laughed lightly into the phone. "Don't worry too much. I'm always protected." He spoke to the phone in his right hand, as his other hand dug into his inside jacket and pulled out the symbol of Tess's nightmares.

Alex's gun. It was an old nine shot, made for stopping a man in their tracks, but did not splatter their blood all around like larger calibers did. She'd only seen it once before when he'd shot Amelia, but it had been ingrained in her nightmares since that day.

She watched as Alex's body tensed a little and Tess smirked as the person on the other end must have said something against his perfect notion of himself. He placed the gun on the dresser and began to move away.

"Look, I am not going to spill my guts out on how I made my fortune. I was told that you were discreet. Was I wrong?"

There it was ten inches away from her arms. It was so tempting; Tess's arms itched to take it and shoot him. But could she grab it before he noticed? She'd have to expose herself and their whole operation. The girls would be scattered for years or dead if he caught them now when they were together. Should she go for it?

"No Mr. U. There is no need for you to tell me what you've done to gain your wealth. I simply like to know how much time we will need to scrub away your old identity. Any big enemies that could chase you here is all I meant to imply." The mysterious man spoke on the other side of the line.

"They can't chase me that far. I made an error in trying to stay in their backyard and that has come to be a... displeasure."

"That is most fortunate then. I have no other questions, and we will receive your funds shortly I assume?"

"Yes. I'm glad we reached an agreement. I'll be there in three days. Everything is to be transferred in its entirety. I will-!"

Alex spun around, the hairs on his neck sticking up as if telling him that he was to be attacked. His eyes fluttered across the room, from the entry door, along the backside of the couch. His eyes turned to the dresser, and he relaxed his guard. He saw nothing.

"...Sir?"

"Yes, I'm still here." Alex shook his head. "I will transfer the entirety when I am safely on the boat, not before."

His hand slid over the rich mahogany and picked up his gun and placed it back in his holster. He did love to admire it so. It was a family heirloom and he'd never get rid of it.

"Back to the lodgings I will be staying at. I am used to a certain level of...comfort..."

Tess sighed silently as Alex grabbed the door handle and closed it behind him. That was close; he'd been practically looking right at her! Her arms were still jittery from the enticing thrill she could have had, but she'd had a different kind of thrill instead.

"Vixen?" her sister's voice whispered into her ear.

"Yes, Eagle?" Tess echoed back as she moved to the entry door and scoped out the hallway to make sure it was clear.

"I found it. In the 2nd lounge on the 1st floor."

"On my way." Tess called out as the door shut quietly...as if she was never there.

"One minute everyone. Get in the view of a camera." Nightingale called out the warning time to her team.

'Easier said than done.' Tanya thought silently as she held her breath, her body flat as a board as she looked up at the ceiling from her laid out position on the couch in the lounging room. She watched the shadow of a figure enter the hallway in front of the open doorway to the room and held still.

The couch was right next to the door, and if the figure stepped even a little into the room, he'd be able to just see over the top of the couch and see the new security guard laying down on the job. But when he called it in, he'd find out that she was supposed to be over ten corridors away and then there'd be questions. Questions on how she was on screen over there and yet here, and if that happened, then she was done for.

Tanya had spoken lightly with these men and their backgrounds were not shrouded by white light in the slightest. They were in this for the money. So, there was a price tag on her body if it came to that. But today was not the day she would be dying it seemed as the guard soon continued to their next corridor, without batting an eye.

"Eagle, in position?"

"Don't rush me." Tanya whispered into her mike as she flipped over the back of the couch and sprinted towards the hall, freezing just outside it.

She breathed in her adrenaline and calmly walked down the hallway, as practiced with Abby the day before. Her gait was perfectly copied and rendered on the camera across the mansion from her real position, and then erased from the current footage. Tanya continued back and forth until Abby's calm voice spoke into her ear.

"All clear."

Tanya clicked her teeth, sagging as she leaned on the doorframe of the room and waited. "Tess, where are you?"

"Watching your lazy ass." Tess's muffled voice sounded in her ear.

Tanya knew her sister's expressions too well and simply gazed to the right down the hallway to see a black clad Tess sliding down the corridor from the ceiling, using the thin hallways to her advantage.

Tanya made a motion with her hand as she looked the other way and her sister edged over to her, her body ready to spring into another room at the sound or sight of another guard.

"You found it?"

"Over here." Tanya confirmed as they headed inside the lounge that also served as an old-fashioned study. Tess shook her head at the uninventive look of the room, with red couches and brown bookcases against the walls. *'How unoriginal.'* She thought. There was even a baby piano next to the wall on the far side of the room. *'Alex doesn't even play!'*

"It's worse." Tanya read her thoughts aloud as she pointed forward. Tess's gaze turned to the wall across from the entrance and immediately, the painting set her teeth on edge. *'How dare he.'* It was a modernist impression, but the subject was clear as day, showing an older woman lying on a warehouse floor, with rivers of blood spreading out from around her body.

"Hey. Come on." Tanya encouraged Tess forward, keeping a hold of her jittering hand as they moved to either side of the painting. With practiced ease, they lifted the frame silently and edged it slowly off the wall, checking for any alarms but finding none.

"Damn." Tess cursed as she turned to look at the safe behind the painting.

"What?" Tanya questioned.

"That bastard had to pick the Kornora 7XV5." Tess groaned just a little as she looked at the 3 by 3 feet, steel covered front of the safe.

"Problem?" Tanya asked, looking at her sister, but Tess smiled back, confidence brimming in her eyes.

"No, just longer. It doesn't change the plan with my equipment." Tess studied the door and began to plan out what she needed to do. "Check in at your time Tanya, and make sure no one is coming here. Our next loop is coming up in thirty minutes."

Tanya nodded her head as she backed up to the doorway and looked both ways. Her radio hadn't told any of the guards to go down this way in the next ten minutes, so she really had no need to worry, so she leaned on the doorframe again and waited as lookout. Casually she took glances back at her sister at work, smiling as she did so. Tanya smiled as well. Unlike her, Tess was an expert in more than just one field of thieving.

As her sister watched, Tess set herself to work, taking off the bag from her shoulder and laying it on the ground, unzipping it and rolling it out as all the contents flipped over and showed themselves to her enticingly.

Tess glanced back at the safe and frowned. "No need for the locks for now. No, just get the electronics." She muttered as she unclipped a tripod and moved it to the front of the safe. She expertly raised the top until it was directly in front of the lower lefthand side. If she remembered correctly, this company's latest model had their electronics located there. Since all their previous versions were in other parts of the safe, this was the best place to start. Alex would have wanted the best, so the newest model for him.

She leaned back on her knees to pull a drill over to her and snapped it on top of the tripod. The drill had a long thin nose but no sharp end to it, but Tess flipped on the drill's power and a thin stream of heat shot out three inches in front of the drill, and immediately the metal directly in front of the head began to buckle just a little.

With a steady hand on the tripod, Tess held onto the rotator, edging it centimeter by centimeter, as she drilled the slide forward at a slug's pace, until it finally touched the metal and began to slide inside, as if the metal was like churned butter.

It was only two minutes later when she felt the drill slip past the resistance and slowly reversed her course, sliding the drill back out whence it came. All that one could see was a hole the size of a pill bug in the otherwise perfect safe. Tess pulled the tripod over and turned back to her equipment, but simply grabbed a rubbery tube, a water bottle, and a thin wire.

Tess slid the wire into the water bottle, getting it wet. In the meantime, she moved the rubbery tube flush with the hole, and squeezed the end of it, shooting colder air into the hole to cool it down. After that, she grabbed the wet wire and slid it into the hole, leaving only a small piece outside. Now for the fun part.

She grabbed the water bottle and began to slowly slide water droplets down the tube. The water attached itself to the wet wire and easily slid along its surface, ejecting itself on the inside of the safe and on everything in its reach.

With her ear to the safe, Tess smiled wide as a soft whirring sound sped up rapidly and hissing sounds made the sputtering sound of death. It was finally as she leaned back that the indicator near the top of the safe and the fingerprint scanner both glowed low and then shut off, useless now.

Tess turned back and pulled the drill to another side and began again. "Now for the locks."

Meanwhile, four minutes to the second, Tanya reached for her radio mike. They had twenty minutes before the next camera rotations, and they'd found the safe. As long as a guard didn't head this way, they were safe.

"This is R3. Route complete, no sign of changes. Next directives."

"R3, check in with F1 for rendezvous at corridor D3."

"Roger." Tanya let go of her mike's button. "Damn." She cursed as she clicked her tongue, activating her other mike to speak to her team. "Nightingale? Is it as bad as I think it is?"

"Not going to be easy." Abby sighed over the line. "The rendezvous is over two complete hallways away and down to the right. You'll need to avoid another guard and the two dogs in the central atrium if you're going to have a chance."

Tanya turned to glance back to take a last look at her sister. Tess was finally done with the drill and was now flush with the safe, her body pressed into the metal like a lover, with an ear in place over the second hole she'd made for the rotating gears.

Tanya saw her right hand turn the manual dial digit by digit until she stopped, her left hand writing down the number in neon directly on the safe. One number down, and seven to go. But when she was this focused, Tess wouldn't even know she'd gone until she got back.

"On my way." Tanya confirmed before she lunged forward, sprinting down the corridor as fast as she could, her hand holding down her jangling keys to keep silent on the move. Tanya knew that after this corridor, it was a ninety-degree corridor to the left and she was good with dogs.

'Damn it.' Tanya froze at the edge of her hallway, staring aghast at her fellow guard down in the middle of the corridor, lounging on the wall. She nervously tapped her leg, waiting for him to move.

"Damn." She cursed as he just stood there. He wasn't going anywhere either as he moved to take off his radio. If he were closer, maybe she could knock him out. No, Abby couldn't fake another person's gait at the same time as hers. Tanya sighed and looked up at the rafters, her mind working feverishly. She didn't like to copy another, but her sister had used them, so why couldn't she?

"Nightingale, how big are the corridors?"

Five minutes later, Tanya dropped back towards the ground, edging down either side of the wall with her arms and legs spread out to either wall. Having used the rafters, she'd been able to bypass the guard and dogs altogether, and now she was in position. She sighed and breathed in her adrenaline, settling for a small smile for her accomplishment.

Not out of the woods yet. In the last minute, Tess had called out that she had six numbers down. They didn't need to hide any more. The plan here was obvious to the team, and they'd discussed their plan of action for this. If Tanya was paired with a guard when the safe was opened, she would simply have to knock out her fellow guard. Abby could hide a prone body for a while. Yep, that was the original plan, made on the table back in their warehouse.

"Julia?" A voice called out across the hallway. Tanya's body froze in place as she turned her body to face this guard that knew her name.

A young face unaccustomed to the dirty jobs that the other guards were used to, an honest face that couldn't stop to help protect people's property from harm. Eyes that showed hurt from lies and deception, and that of a broken heart.

A new uniform lay on his attractive frame, but his blonde hair just made him look the same anyways.

"Daniel?" Tanya whispered aloud, her mike's receiver picking it up.

Daniel smiled sourly, reached for his holster, and pulled out his gun.

XXIV - GAME'S UP

lick, click, click. The repetitive sound echoed quietly through the hole of the safe, telling her that these numbers of the dial were not what she was looking for.

Click, click, clack. The pin slid a small portion into the hole before stopping. A false tumbler meant to trip her up, but she had caught this number twice before and would not be fooled.

Tess didn't know why, but for some reason, she loved this part of the job. The quiet stillness of the room, the small gaps of the watered electronics fizzling on and off with positive charges of energy, the finality of facts. It was in the knowledge that perhaps no matter the chaos of plans ebbing away, promises of futures dissolving like the sands of time, safes always remained just as they'd always been; a soft delicate beast that with a lot of care and precision, any could be tamed.

Click, Snap! Tess paused as she leaned back on her knees, noting the number that had more than told her that it was important. But the question was how much. Tess was close; she could practically pull down on the handle and open the safe to see the glory of a job well done hidden inside.

But instead, she leaned over and placed another number on the board before her, scratching one number out for another in its place. She wanted to make sure all her numbers were correct for when that handle was pulled.

"Six numbers down." She spoke into her mike, telling them to move into the next stage in their plan of operations. She had looked back when she spoke out the number for three locks and had seen

Tanya sprint away down the hall. She'd be back here soon enough and then they'd be off, living new lives of different values and morals, unrecognizable to the way they looked right now. It was all going to plan.

"Daniel?" Tanya's voice permeated through the sound waves, and Tess's fingers stopped moving. Tess closed her eyes and breathed calmly, a large lump trying to jump out of her throat. Okay...so he was here... and-

"What is he doing here?" Wind rider yelled out to the team.

"Tanya, you need to lose him. He knows your face." Megan whispered urgently.

"Eagle, say again." Tess breathed out slowly and leaned back to the safe. "Who do you see?" She needed confirmation on who Tanya had said was in front of her. If indeed it was Daniel in front of her, then the next course of action was to-

(Creek)

Tess sighed in defeat as a loose floorboard sounded behind her. It appeared that it wasn't just Tanya who had been joined. The game was up for her as well, but she could at least still speak.

"I'm done for now." She calmly spoke into her mike before pushing up from her knees to stand up. She swirled her head to turn and glare at Alex himself, leaning casually in the doorway, a smirk on his face as dark as a bird who ate the scraps of flesh off their prey. There was a reason after all why he always went by Raven when on heists.

"Hello Alex." Tess turned her body to face him. Best to not let him get behind her again.

"Daniel?" She heard her sister repeat on her mike again, and prepared to whisper something back to Tanya, before a sudden gunshot echoed into all ears of those listening in.

(Boom)

Tess craned her head, the sound booming and echoing into her head and as she reached to cover her offended ear, she froze halfway to her ear, her eyes opened wide as before her, Alex had stood up with a shudder, his own hand reaching up to cradle his offended eardrum.

"No." Tess let a strangled whisper escape her. "What-"

"Channel 3A, right?" Tess shivered as Alex smiled through the pain, rubbing at his ear as he shook out his eardrum and only grinned wider once Tess's eyes widened. "I must say, Tess. I am most impressed with how well played you did with the heist. But it seems like you lost a partner again."

Tess shivered, her entire body jittery from adrenaline and emotions. Her sister...gunshot...Tess breathed through the fear but could only gulp as Alex spoke to the whole team with his own mike turning on. "Hello girls. Such a long time passes without seeing your lovely faces. I don't get to see you all? That's not very nice. We should see each other soon…" Alex paused as an amused smile graced his face. "How are you doing Tanya? Still breathing?"

The jitters ceased at that. The sound of rushing blood drowning her senses quieted and Tess stilled as she listened closely. Indeed, there was shuttered breathing on one of the mikes. Tess composed herself. She hadn't lost another, and she wouldn't lose anymore.

"Girls, abort."

Down in the pipes, nobody remained squeezed inside, only a broken tablet wiped clean and a broken section of pipe with cable sticking out haphazardly. A few miles away, no one stood on the wooden electrical pole, as white smoke began to billow out of the stolen maintenance van, as inside, a small orange glow began to spread through the vehicle. And just outside the wall of the mansion, the white smoke continued to cough out its noxious breath, hiding only metal picks in the ground; no tubes to remain where they had been placed.

"Oh well. I suppose I do have you." Alex smiled at Tess and edged deeper into the room, as Tess slowly gave ground. As he approached her, she moved off to the side, opposite to the window near the piano, and he strode to the safe, lightly caressing his hand along the smooth surface and checking the numbers that faintly glowed on top.

"I suppose I am quite the lucky man. If I didn't have your radio signal, then you may have made it into this safe." Alex smiled over to his old teammate. "Tut-tut, Tess. Just two numbers away as well." Looking away from his security system, Alex turned to smile connivingly at her. "But then again, I chose this safe specifically because you've never practiced on one before."

Tess simply glared at him. There was no need to argue against him. He held all the power now. Her team was gone. She had told them to abandon her and save themselves. She was now all alone. She had to leave now, before the situation changed further; two sets of feet walking towards them caught her attention, making her body jolt in place.

"Tess, don't even think of escaping." Alex called out as he moved to stand between her and the safe, only ten feet away. "The guards I've hired spent most of their time working with companies and countries preventing escape exactly in mind, even if you were an expert in evading others."

Tess could feel Alex's eyes raking over her body as shivers ran down her spine, her eyes seeing the whimsical and predatory look in his eyes. "But don't worry. I won't kill you. I know you don't have too much experience, but maybe you'd do well in the human sex trade, eh?"

Tess glared darkly at the man. Like hell she'd ever let that happen, and Alex would know that once out of his sight, she'd disappear like a ghost in a dream. A vile retort began to crawl up her throat to verbally assault him, but the footsteps were turning the corner, and her eyes soon broke at the sight in front of her.

Alex smiled brightly as his compatriot's wounded eyes looked to her right, whereas his own jubilant aura lay hidden inside, his day only getting better at the change of fortune.

Tanya stumbled into the room, her uniform still pristine except for the bleeding wound of burgundy pooling just underneath the crumpled edge of her shirt, the love handle of her waist cupped over with a bloody hand to vainly stem the flow. She took a few shuddering steps forward, her teeth clenching as she moved, but her other hand was encircled by a muscular arm forward, as a gun continued to aim at her back. Tanya made eye contact with Tess and both pairs of eyes teamed with stemmed tears. No words had to be conveyed as they spoke volumes without speech.

"Ah! Daniel, how nice of you to join us." Alex called the pair over with a wave of his gun and the new couple stopped just between them, breaking the reunion abruptly as Alex's smirk deepened. "And he even brought your sister, Tess. How quaint, isn't it?"

But she didn't respond to his jibe. She didn't even hear it as her whole body buzzed with a surge of desire and despair that swept through her body at the man who had just entered.

"D-Daniel?" Tess uttered the single name, having not seen him since their last night together. *'He...he looks sick.'* She noted as her ex-loved one looked back at her. Her gaze saw his eyes darker than what she'd ever seen them as, and his skin was flaky and unhealthy. A bitter thought simmered that at least she hadn't been the only one to suffer the breakup. Daniel watched her for a second before he nodded his head in response, making her shiver at the action, her entire body lighting a second flare that made her heart ache.

Her heart's ache told her everything she needed to know. He had not nodded his head to acknowledge her recognition of him. There was no need to ask him the question that had been on her tongue; her lover had shot her teammate, her comrade, the first friend she'd made for life; he had shot her sister. There was no need to ask that question, yet another popped into her mind, one more serious than the last.

" W-What are you doing here?" She uttered a second time.

"...Stopping you, Tess." Came Daniel's defeated response. It sounded strangled and weak to her curious ears, but only because she could see in his expression that he perhaps had not truly expected her to be here, to not have run away when she should have. But here she was.

"Exactly." Alex smiled in triumph, loving to rub salt into the wound on her heart. "You truly know how to pick them, Tess. This man of yours came to me and offered his expertise in security. Naturally I looked into his background, and with a stellar work history and all that, I took him in." There was silence for a few seconds as he began to twist the corkscrew deeper into her mind "...After all, you did get him fired from his last job."

Alex smiled wider as Tess shivered at that. "I told him I was expecting a thief and said that it was you. He was reluctant a bit in denying it, and defended your honor in fact, proudly stating that there was no way that you would come here, that you would not do this, but here you are, proving that I was right all this time."

Alex's eyes gleamed as he reveled in his speech of the victory he had accomplished. "He was still such an asset though as soon as I hired him. I put him to work, and boy am I glad he came; he helped me out so much! You wouldn't believe how many blind spots I had before I decided to add in a few more cameras on a second hidden network, and on a different set of wires too. One that only sends the signals to my phone that is."

Tess's breath shuddered. Their plan had been ruined by her lover's expertise. He had given Alex the vision to see them. He had seen things that they could have gotten away with if that second network wasn't there, but it was, and here they were. But then…

"So, you saw us coming." Tess spit out with clench teeth. "I swear Alex, I will never-"

"Never what?" Alex cackled. "Bend the knee? Of course not. I'll pack you off to Calagra in chains, knowing you're miserable and your spirit broken will give me peace."

"Now as for Tanya…" Tess's eyes looked up in horror as the gun trained on her swiveled. It turned away from her and stopped on death's door in front of her sister, the edge of her vision shimmering as realization dawned on her.

For an injured Tanya, blood sliding past her fingers to the plush carpet below, her mind cleared before her. This was the part that she was meant to play, it seemed, and she only had one thing she could say. "…. I love you little sister-"

(Crack!)

Tanya let out a sharp gasp, coughing as her body jerked for a single second. More blood slipped out, the edge of her lip tasting of iron as her knees buckled and she crumbled to the ground. Her vision swayed and distorted as her breathing ceased its functions. *It's funny though.'* Tanya thought grimly. All she could smell was gunpowder, and she wished she had time to smile; her husband always smelled of gunpowder.

"I'll kill you!" Tess's war cry pierced the room as she lunged at Alex, her fingers ready to pierce his face and cripple the eyes that he loved so much. Tess leaped through the air, her fingers skimming the air just before him before an arm encircled her waist and pulled her away. "No!"

Daniel pulled on her body, holding her back as she struggled to free herself. Not even his embrace could cool her raging emotions. "Tess! You can't." He whispered into her ear and tilted her until she froze, her vision impaired as she looked at her sister on the ground, crumbled on the floor with her beautiful blond hair now covering her face as underneath her stomach, blood began to slowly pool over the carpet, staining the fabric forever.

Alex breathed a little heavier, adrenaline pulsing through his body as a wave of power and authority over life overcame his sensations. This was the feeling that got his body going, this was such a rush!

He smoothed out his hair, his fingers shaking as he looked back over at his captive, as Tess continued to flail in vain to get out of Daniel's hold on her, his own eyes looking lost and confused about the situation. He should be confused; he hadn't seen death before in front of his eyes.

"I'll … kill you...mother...son of a…"

"Now, don't be overdramatic." Alex sighed with an annoyed roll of his eyes. "So, I killed her. She wasn't going to make it to a hospital anyways. And you know what? If you fail to obey, then I will track down every member of your team and kill them too."

Alex moved forward to stand in front of her, as she struggled less and less, trapped in Daniel's hold, her adrenaline leaving her as he grinned at her smugly. "How does that sound? Hmm?"

Tess's jaded eyes softened, and she looked down and away from him, giving up the fight. Alex smiled whimsically as he brought his hand forward to graze along her soft hair.

"Man...to think I had a crush on you when I first saw you all those years ago. Turned out to just be lust really, but you'll fetch a nice price either way." Alex lowered his palm to cup her chin and tilted her face up, and like a viper, Tess took her revenge.

Her mouth opened wide, her teeth gleamed as she shot forward, and bit down as hard as she could upon his hand.

"Ah!!!" Alex screamed bloody murder as he ripped his body away from her, but his hand wouldn't budge. Alex quickly slid his other hand towards her face to pry her teeth away, but Tess acted appropriately.

She brought her foot down hard upon the shin of her ex-lover, as Daniel grunted and fell back, rendering her arms free. Tess let her teeth ease off on Alex's hand, as her own digits slid down to the side of her thigh, where she had hidden a combat knife from within a secret pocket and slashed it forward, as Alex's unbalanced self flew backwards towards the wall.

She made quick work as she turned around, slicing through the air just as Daniel made to grab her again and was met by a mangled grunt as Daniel's jacket ripped open as a small slip of blood appeared along his arm.

With enough space to herself, Tess ran straight to the piano and jumped over it, a feat like that of parkour as she popped her hip just over the side and continued to the window. In her adrenaline filled haze, she did the only choice available and lunged straight at it, the glass shattering from the impact as her body pierced right through it. With her body hitting the grass on the other side and the bloody knife held to her chest in her right hand, Tess sped off, running as fast as she could to escape another death.

XXV-THE CHASE

"Sir, we heard the window shatter! Are you-"

"Get HER!!! You flipping idiots!!!" Tess heard her own radio buzz wildly as she sprinted across the yard, switching channels as she went. She turned the corner, moving through the hedges, when a guard appeared in front of her. He moved to grab her, but she was quick to slide under his arm before she grabbed at the back of his shirt and flipped him into the air. She was gone by the time he fell to the ground, coughing in pain from a broken rib.

Another guard was exiting the courtyard door she'd used to enter, and without a second thought, she braced her arm outwards, clotheslining the guard as he too, joined his partner on the ground. But they were sturdy enough as they recovered and ran after her in pursuit. A wall that jutted out at her waist blocked her way, but she kicked off the ground a foot before and brought her body horizontal for a second, sailing above it, parkour and adrenaline fueling her system as the guards stopped and began to run around for another way through.

She cast a glance at the black SUV's, their imposing frames silent as the grave as they waited for a moment such as this. As Tess dipped between the robotic snakes still slithering across the pulsating meat sticks, she spotted a guard slide into the van. Seconds later, the engine roared to life.

"Damnit!" Tess cursed as she ran faster towards the high wall. Megan said she and Abby had disabled them. Apparently, Alex had had them checked a second time. Tess bit her lip nervously at the thought of her ex-lover telling him to check them again. If he did, then surely the next thing he would do would be to-

Tess's thought left her as she ran up the brick wall, her feet slapping silently as she reached for the top, pulling herself up and over until she looked back and saw the body's silhouette in the house. Her sister, just through the broken and shattered window, deep in that room, lying on the floor, unmoving. A lump of sadness and grief filled her heart, as reddened eyes closed to hold back tears.

"I'll see you around, Tanya." Tess whispered.

"You girls get out safe?" A voice sniffled back tears over the radio.

"Same line, Tess." Alex's voice sneered from the other side as he ran behind his guards, each of them jumping into one of the four SUV's that lay on the driveway. "Get in you idiots!" He screamed as the two guards who Tess had eluded jogged into their cars, holding their sides to ease the pain. His own side door opened, and Daniel moved into the seat, a laptop set up in front of him to help track where the thief was escaping to.

Alex hit the switch for the gate's bolts to unlock themselves and put the vehicle in drive. And no sooner had he done so than a red and black motorcycle, made more for off-road than on, appeared from the bushes and shot off down the black asphalt, picking up speed as they went.

"After her!"

The SUVs roared to life and followed her down the hill that overlooked the small city below it, their heavy engines working well to catch up to the woman on the bike. Through nimble curves and edges, they followed her down, having traveled this road for months as rare mansions appeared on each side infrequently, before being swallowed up by trees and open fields of brown grass and prairie.

As they closed the distance, the first split in the road appeared, as the biker turned left, leaving the city altogether. Each SUV turned accordingly, like a team of precision drivers as each wheel followed the other. Alex nodded to Daniel who typed into the laptop; the formation of the vehicles changed from single file to 2 X 2, blocking both sides of the two-lane road. Alex smiled. They'd catch her in no time.

The SUV's curved around the bend of the hill and Alex's eyes widened as suddenly, grey smoke sprayed out from the biker's back tire, but the tire was no longer sending her away from them. No; instead, Tess was now wheeling directly towards them, her speed topping out as she brought her wheel up menacingly as her helmet glared sunbeams into their eyes.

"What is she-"

"Look out!" Daniel yelled as Alex jerked to the left, missing her by inches. But then it dawned on him that he shouldn't have dodged her at all. Tess's motorbike zoomed by each of the four SUV's, sending them careening off the road and onto the dirt of the ground off to the side.

"Turn them around!" Daniel ordered into the mike by his neck, and Alex smirked in approval as he backed his SUV up and then began to chase their ex-teammate back down the hill. His other three vehicles joined and caught up quickly, the men a little shaken from the near collision, but that's what Alex assumed Tess had been trying to cause. His men would need a real collision to shake their loyalty to him if she hoped to escape them.

Now, she was heading for the commercial side of the city, with more people and less room to maneuver to catch her. If he lost her, then she would disappear into the crowds, being the chameleon that she was, and he was not about to let that happen.

"B4, head east on Rose."

"Roger." The guard affirmed as his vehicle peeled off down the road, keeping its distance and waiting for further orders.

"B2 get past her and box her in with B3."

"On it." A second guard affirmed as the other two SUV's shot forward, following the bike as they began to weave through the light traffic, as honks began to sound along the way. After another minute, B4 zipped across on Rose Avenue, but the bike was nimble and dipped down and curved around the bumper at the last second. As Tess continued to zip away from them, Alex looked to his fellow occupant beside him.

Daniel was typing intently at the laptop, turning the satellite data he was seeing to use as he typed suggestions to the other vehicles on possible roads to flank and pursue their target. A small dribble of blood still dripped down from his arm, his work shirt pulled up to his elbows, but the fabric was still bloody from where his ex had sliced at him, leaving what was sure to be a thin scar on his skin forever.

Alex, however, could see it on his face that he was facing another scar on his heart. He looked so conflicted with the current situation; stuck between his job and the girl who had betrayed him; caught between what he saw as the justice of the law, and the woman who broke it every day. Alex saw the widening eyes of this man next to him and knew the reason he was spacing out: he was still in the room they had rushed out of, back with that body that would need to be gotten rid of once they were clear. Alex needed him here though, helping him catch the girl. For that, he had few options.

"You know why I had to kill the other girl, right?" Alex's deep voice sounded inside the SUV.

Daniel cast a look down to his lap for a second, biting his cheek for a second before he nodded his head, his mind skimming over the data he had received the day he signed on with the man beside him. "I read the file you gave me, so I know what and who she truly was...but it's just that...she looked so helpless. I mean, I wounded her already. Surely we didn't have to-"

"That's exactly her poison, Daniel. I've told you what she did, and you've read exactly what she was capable of."

Alex hid a smile from his face as he watched Daniel's mind think back on the profile he'd given to him. The girl known as Julia was really Tanya Solovski, with an expertise in technology and surprisingly an expert in unarmed combat.

A black belt in jujitsu, taekwondo, and five other art forms that he couldn't even pronounce. Alex thought back to when he told Daniel from his briefing a few days ago. Her strength had always been in looking like a damsel to everyone's eyes and then overpowering with death holds and strikes, a bodyguard hidden in the shadows for their team that Alex himself hadn't been privy to until he had been with them for a full year.

"Daniel, I told you that night that I've seen her kill guys before without a weapon, so you must agree that I couldn't let her live, right?"

Alex smirked openly as Daniel nodded in agreement, buying his well-crafted lie. Tanya had never killed anyone. She was just the hidden muscle to get out of bad situations, but using this guy was just too great an asset; upgrading his surveillance, directing his men as if he was a master tactician, a good honest innocent man doing his best to get the job done. He was very much satisfied to have gained his assistance.

"Watch out!" Daniel exclaimed as he looked up at the road. Alex looked forward as well and pulled the wheel erratically to the right, narrowly scraping by a pedestrian in the crosswalk. Alex spun his wheels back to the left as the SUV slid around the corner, cutting off two cars in the process, as metal carved into metal: the two cars conjoining together in a debauchery of two becoming one.

Alex pressed on his gas again, and the SUV righted itself and continued forward, avoiding what could easily have been the end of their pursuit for good. But they were still on her tail as the bike sped down the sloping road, towards a valley the locals called 'The End.'

"Catch up to her." Alex spoke calmly into his mike, as B3 in the SUV up ahead shot up behind her and prepared to ram her. Alex's eyes gleamed as he watched her look back briefly, imagining her looking back in hopelessness, but instead, the helmeted figure faced back ahead and pressed down on the center of the console of their bike.

Immediately, black smoke shot out of the tailpipe, bursting backwards at the leading vehicle. The SUV disappeared for only a second, but as Alex passed the smoke, the vehicle looked fine. And there the bike was, just ahead of them-

A series of bursts of air erupted from B3's vehicle, as each of the four tires burst out and broke the seams of the rubber, the steel rims skidding along the ground, sending flaming sparks all around as the engine itself sparked along the asphalt. The SUV came to a standstill, put out of action as small spikes lay upon the road, their tiny pins aimed at the sky as if proudly in triumph.

Alex's vehicle zoomed past the disabled car and let an annoyed smirk rest upon his face. "So, she's armed."

The roar of the motorbike sounded ever louder as they sped down the rest of the hill before the valley marched up again towards another slope. B1, Alex's call sign, and B4 followed from behind, more wary than before to get directly behind her, but she was running out of room, as more traffic appeared around him as the minutes-long chase passed them by.

"There is a bridge up ahead."

"Perfect. B2, cut her off."

The said vehicle had been following from a parallel street all this time, and at the order sped ahead to get to the bridge first. They passed the bike as the road the others were on bended with the hill and reached the other side, before sliding into position across both lanes of the road, effectively boxing her in.

Alex smiled as she entered the steel guard rails of the bridge, the roar of the highway below drowning out the constant screaming of the bike. He watched as his men of B2 rushed out of the SUV and drew their weapons, aiming at the driver. The wheel of the bike jumped upwards, the tail of it nearly scraping the asphalt as three shots echoed through the air, one hitting the tire of the bike but not the intended driver.

The wheel fell again as the helmeted figure revved the engine even higher and sped at the vehicle blocking their way. *'No way.'* Alex thought she was crazy, before the back tire suddenly screeched wildly and she turned ninety degrees, directly into the guard rail. The wheels of the bike jumped into the air with precision, before landing on the rail itself, bending the steel under the weight of the bike before they jumped off again.

Alex slammed on his brakes, his and the other vehicle who were supposed to prevent her reversal, frozen in shock and anger as the bike fell perfectly onto the highway down below, fitting with precision beside two cars before speeding off to the north and edging out of sight.

"Let's go!" Alex yelled at his men, as the three remaining vehicles skidded backwards and crossed the short brown grass to merge onto the highway, honks and curses following in their wake. "Daniel, find her. We…. can't let her escape."

Daniel nodded as he moved back to the computer in his lap, clicking and scanning furiously with another guard from inside B2, each pulling up satellite footage of the area, overlaying it with expensive software, erasing cars and trucks and freight as they tried to narrow down to the motor bike in question.

Meanwhile, Alex tried to speed up his engine as much as he could, the SUV groaning now after the number of bad maneuvers it had done so far. He had to find her, he had to kill her; if she died, then it was done. If she died, then he was scot free!

"I got her!"

"Where?"

"She got off the highway and is heading down an old road that takes her out of town."

"Let's follow her then." A guard spoke up from B4.

"Okay, we'll-" Alex began.

"Alex if I may?" Daniel cut in and Alex nodded. "I know this town. If we go down two more exits, we'll be able to cut her off if we take these turns." Daniel suggested as he pointed to the turns in question on his screen.

"You're sure?"

"Yeah. Let's do it."

Ten minutes later, Alex was smiling madly as he spotted Tess taking off her helmet and swishing out her hair as he raced towards her. But it was easy to see them on the road, and he finally knew why she chose a dirt bike for her escape as she quickly slid the helmet back on and dipped off the asphalt, and onto the sloping hills and grassland next to it.

"This could get bumpy." Daniel muttered as the three vehicles surged at her, boxing her in on three sides as she tried to swerve in between them, the engines of the SUVs purring as they crisscrossed between each other, trying to knock her off the bike itself.

Tess surged into a group of earthen holes off to the left, and B4 followed her from behind as the other two raced around a hill to cut her off again. Tess dove into a rather deep hole, gunning her engine to give her a boost of speed as she surged up the other side and jumped into the air, over the space where Alex approached and continued.

B4 however, wasn't so lucky, its wheels sliding along the dirt of the earthen crater, wet from a few days of rain that hadn't yet evaporated. Still, they revved their engine, riding up the wall of the crater as the bike had done, but they did not jump. And because they did not, the SUV slammed into a huge tree trunk, laying menacingly on its side. The SUV hit the trunk with all its might, but the trunk was not the one that moved.

Instead, B4 flipped over the top, metal bits and sharp ends flying everywhere as it spun in the air above the hill, parts flying everywhere as it cartwheeled directly in the line of the others. "Move!" Daniel yelled as Alex swerved as well as B2, as their compatriot's vehicle in B4 rested on its side, its occupants dazed and unconscious with shattered glass and metal spiking in every direction.

Alex looked to the right as the bike skidded along the small mound, shredding dirt down the small slope, as Tess no doubt counted how many of them were left. With a fearsome gaze, he wheeled his SUV expertly around and charged for the bike, as the dirt spun once again and they were off, with only two vehicles on their tail.

Alex crested the ridge, shooting down the mound repeatedly as he drove up and down the bumps here and there as the bike jumped over ditches and caverns hidden in the rogue grass. Tess on her bike swiveled back and forth, the sputtering of her engine waning as Alex smiled. An off-road bike only had so much it could handle, unlike his vehicles which had been upgraded for any occasion. B2 joined from the other side, and together they began to close the distance side by side, leaving the bike rider with less and less space to maneuver.

When she leaned right, B2 turned right, and when they turned left, Alex petered away. She was not tricking them into getting behind her again. A grayish smoke bubbled out of the bike's engine and Alex smiled widely at the dying engine. It was over.

"Cliff!!!"

"What?" Alex faced forward before slamming as hard as he could on his brakes. The vehicle swayed side to side, wheels seizing along the gravel as their momentum failed to slow fast enough. Alex spun the wheel to the side erratically as his SUV slid sideways, the wheels finally finding traction as the vehicle came to a stop on the edge, a quarter of the driver's side wheels out in the air.

Through all of this, Alex had seen Tess lightly brake on her vehicle, the weight of the bike much easier to stop than his four-ton counterpart, but also unlike his lucky save, B2 didn't see the cliff at all and so, at full speed, it jumped into the air, careening downwards the thirty or so feet to the ground below it. It landed with its suspension snapping, the wheels punching into the wheelhouse of the vehicle, and the lower half crunching as it met the ground, but the momentum of the vehicle carried it forward until it hit the outcrop of rocks ahead of it. The SUV rested at a sixty-degree angle, edging up towards the rock face on the other side, with one wheel atop athe jagged earth, the others on the ground, and heavy smoke hiding the people from view.

Alex breathed angrily through his teeth as he saw his last members out of commission. "Dammit!" He glared past Daniel to the top of the hill as Tess crested the ridge of the next hill and slid out of view.

He pressed to choke the engine, but instead of bursting to life, a deft whine erupted. "Oh, don't do this! You bloody piece of- stupid machine!! Work dammit!" Alex cursed as he jabbed the accelerator and pressed the engine repetitively.

"Alex, she's gone-"

"Don't tell me that!" Alex roared hotly. "Get this thing moving!"

"It's stalled, Alex. You have to give it a few minutes."

"Then follow her on satellite, Daniel! Don't lose her!"

"Okay. Breathe."

Alex breathed heavily as he continued to curse. "She planned all of this!!"

"What?" Daniel looked back hesitantly. "You had her. She-"

"Oh Daniel, you don't know her like I do. She had plans for everything when I was around her. You can bet that she had a plan for every contingency."

"So, she planned to escape all along?"

"No. She made a plan to escape without being seen; another in which a member is captured; or like just now, running away, leading us on a goddamn goose chase as she whittles us down. She looked for locations and planned those jumps and stalls."

Alex looked back at Daniel who looked back at him unconvinced. "Come on. Daniel. There were times you came home, and she convinced you to do things, right? And if you found a way out, she slid something else in?"

At Daniel's lowering eyes, Alex frowned. "Damnit! We need to find her. She can't win!"

"Alex...it's over."

"What do you mean?"

Daniel sighed, sagging in his seat. "She's off the grid. I can't find her on the satellite."

"But how? She couldn't have-" Alex froze mid-sentence. He slowly looked around himself, turning in his seat, at the grassland, thinking about where they were. "Daniel, show me where she was last."

Daniel turned the laptop towards him and pointed. "Right there. Heading straight out of town by the look of it."

"Zoom out a bit."

"O-okay." Daniel shrugged slowly, doing as he was told. But as he did, Alex's smile only grew.

"Wider......one more...there!" Alex leaned over, checking the streets that Tess had last been spotted. After three seconds, he leaned back, his body relaxed, and his arrogant smirk returned. "I know where she's heading. and if she does follow her plan of trying to lose us, then we should just beat her there."

"Are you sure she went there?"

"Positive." Alex smiled as he turned the ignition, the SUV roaring back to life, and as he turned the vehicle around, a massive grin spread across his face. "Back to the beginning, eh Tess?"

XXVI-END OF THE LINE

Thirty minutes later, Alex pulled in stealthily towards the large building in front of him, the dirt crunching quietly under the wheels. As he stopped at the corner, he could barely contain a sudden urge to yell in excitement as before him, about three hundred feet away was the blasted bike that had crippled his fleet of vehicles, leaning up against the wall of the building.

As he looked to the doorway, he finally spotted Tess with her brown hair down to her shoulders, sneaking along the wall, before ducking inside. "There she is." He spoke as he slowly moved the SUV forward until it stopped right in front of the opened dark doorway, next to the bike.

"What is this place?" Daniel breathed as both stepped out of the vehicle, leaving the doors open to not alert anyone inside.

"This, Daniel, is the warehouse where her mother passed away in an accident."

"How did you know she'd come here?"

"Wasn't too certain really." Alex shrugged as they began to walk forward, towards the warehouse overhang. "I just placed my bet on the fact that Tess is sentimental that way. She loved her mother, and anything she loves, she just can't leave alone for too long." Daniel looked over to confirm what he thought, and Alex nodded. "Yeah, Daniel. Tess eventually would have come back for you and tried to twist up your life so that you might take her back. She really does have a tragic past though."

"What do you mean?"

"I mean that I didn't write everything down for you. She spent some time in a psych ward after her mother's death if you didn't know." Alex fibbed.

"…. I didn't." Daniel shook his head and began to enter the building. "Let's get this over with." A hand pulled on his shoulder however and he turned to look questionably at Alex. "What?"

"Daniel, you go around to the back and start from there. I don't want her escaping when she thinks that she's safe. I want her alive for the authorities, you hear me?" Alex watched Daniel nod in agreement and ran off to the edge of the warehouse and disappeared.

"Good guy…. bad judge of character." Alex cackled as he moved into the dark and creepy warehouse, reaching into his holster and brought his gun out into the open. Tess wasn't leaving here alive. All of this was ending today.

Alex looked at the open area where all this had started, imagining the ghostly circle of the team that had led him to the biggest score of his life. If he imagined it hard enough, he could probably see the blood on Amelia's body and a broken Tess stretched over her.

As he turned the corner to check out the various rooms over the warehouse, it took all he had to hold back a mad laugh, settling for an evil smirk instead. He had to give it up to Daniel. That man's sense of justice was easily skewed so much that it wasn't even funny unless you were the one lying to him. So easily tricked into betraying a girl like Tess, who Alex knew was a hopeless romantic at heart. He always knew that underneath that professional attitude was an obviously subservient, shy girl who just wanted to be loved.

Obviously, she hadn't been admitted to a psych ward for her mother's death. No; two years ago, they had needed her inside to sell the con for a doctor who worked there. But Paige was the name she'd turned to using as her cover story, so she should only have expected him to jab the facts in even deeper than the lies.

Clearing the first room, he could only think that no doubt he had helped to break Daniel's trust in her even more when he told Daniel what she did for a living. His eyes had widened in shock at that revelation, almost too big for any human, but it was quite the stunning information after all.

Daniel wanted fairness and respect in all his life, but even his eyes were seeing through Tanya as Alex killed her, as if Daniel was already holding something darker inside, something that was just under the skin, just waiting for the chance to bubble up to the surface. It no doubt intrigued him and as Alex stepped into the second room, tightening the grip on his gun, he thought it almost a shame to have to kill him as well when this was all over.

His good heart was just too much for his own good. He still believed Alex's story about Tess's multiple attempts to rob him of wealth and stalking him. He was tearing apart his ex-girlfriend's life as he himself second guessed everything that he was asked to perform. How much more could he say before Daniel himself suspected that he was just as rotten as Tess? Just as greedy and vain and seeking an ever-alluring thrill of the score. They were the same, Tess and he; Tess just lacked the truth that was life; and that truth was that everyone dies, everyone can and should be stolen from, and if they can't do it, then they should disappear and not bother living. The world was a cruel place, filled with terrors, and only the rich and privileged had the currency to acquire happiness.

"Not here…" Alex muttered aloud as he continued his search, the sun sliding through the open slats in the roof. *'Was it really already around sunset?'* As soon as he was done here, he'd have to start packing for his trip.

Now, how to deal with Daniel after he killed Tess? Alex was no fool; he saw it when they met each other after a week of separation, the love and affection that brightened through their eyes at just the glimpse of the other. Daniel's hand had tightened as he readjusted himself to act tough and distant for the job at hand, and Tess had tried and failed to act like she hadn't had her heart skip a beat. But given enough time, he'd give in and accept her back.

Alex paused with a cruel smirk in the doorway to a third room. Maybe he'd show the body to Daniel and kill him when he was in tears and heartache? Make it look like revenge or betrayal? Like Tess was attacking him and he defended himself? Alex shook his head. No.

Daniel was a good guy; he had friends and people who would all state that they were happy, and he'd never hurt her if he tried. He'd make it sudden and from behind without a sound. More merciful, right? He could join beside her as if two lovers reunited in the afterlife. That sounded grand.

Alex paused in this open room, with a single old table, dust covering the entirety of it, the old hinges of the four doors nearly broken as all of them bent inwards instead of tall and straight; the old and broken furniture to his right all piled up and beginning to rot.

He casually looked between the objects; a broken light still plugged in, the energy waning as it cast a pathetic glow near the back wall behind him; at the glass above him shedding the last real light into half of the room, leaving the other in near darkness; at the ripped tarp haphazardly covering an old chair in the corner, and some old crates between the light and the door he had just entered from. Once in the middle, his feet stood still; he heard the small drip drip pattern of the water sliding down the soaked walls.

"...You really want to hide here?" Alex voiced aloud. "...Such a bad spot Tess...too open for someone like us."

Within a flash, Alex had spun around. His feet slid in a half circle as he raised his hand confidently and fired his gun, the boom that followed erupting in a cacophony of sounds and revelations through the entirety of the warehouse. And out of the shadows beside the glowing lamp, on the flickering side of a lit wall, blood splattered lightly upon it as Alex clicked his tongue in disappointment.

"I guess you'll die slowly then."

A wheezed breath escaped the black void as Tess stumbled out of the hidden corner of the room and scrapped at the wall beside her. Within a second, her legs buckled as she fell to her knees onto the cold cement, holding her stomach as blood pooled and began to soak into her black jacket, shaking with the chills and rogue energy as adrenaline surged into her system as blood left it, draining away down her sides. Blood began to edge out of her mouth as she tried in vain to rise, and she finally collapsed back against the wall, her breathing fast and shallow, but still her eyes showed only vengeance and a deadly determination.

Alex though just smiled and shrugged innocently, as if in apology. "Oh Tess, don't give me that look. You deserved it. You shouldn't have been hiding like that. You know that I could have given you some mercy. Your sister died quickly, remember that?"

"I-I'm going….to…to Kill you." Tess struggled to pull herself forward, her arms quaking as she leaned heavily on the wall between the crates, trying to move away from him as her eyes began to glaze over with a grey sheen.

But as she finally grasped at the wood of the crates on either side of her, her gasp for air erupted in a coughing fit, and by the time she recovered, she was trapped in a corner again, Alex moving forward to stand on the other side of the path, blocking her in with nowhere left to go.

"Y-You're a d-dead man." Tess stuttered out, her lips shivering from the lack of blood in her body. However, Alex was like a cat playing with his food. As long as she didn't leave this room, then she would die, and he could do whatever he wanted in the minute that she had left.

"Tess, come on." He chided. "We've been through so much together. Can't you reminisce with me for a bit? I mean I know you so well after all."

"This is where we met for the first time all those years ago. All those heists you and I pulled…claiming to be lovers, newlyweds, and close friends, remember?" Tess said nothing, and Alex frowned as he did find a certain pleasure in gloating. "None of that matters to you anymore? I mean, how many objects were you and I able to steal? We were such a good team, Tess."

"…You're a thief?" A voice sounded out from the far doorway as Alex whipped his head around to see Daniel walk out, dazed, and confused from the sudden influx of changing realizations. "Then…. then you're just like her!" He accused angrily, before his eyes widened at the sight of the gun in Alex's hand, pointed right at his ex who was leaning on a crate, her extended arm beginning to spasm from the strain of the weight.

Alex grimaced as he mentally cursed Daniel's timing. He'd gloated for too long and Daniel had come in too soon that now Alex could not afford to let him leave. *'Such a shame.'* He thought as he closed his eyes and breathed out slowly. He'd been leaning towards being merciful in his death. So much for facades.

"Yes, Daniel." Alex admitted as he added a slight tremor to his extended arm that was holding the gun, tweaking his voice to be scratchy and hoarse as if he were on the edge of breaking down and crying. "I can be honest and say that years ago I was a thief, but I got out." Alex took a step forward and pressed the gun against Tess's jacket, pushing her back against the wall with a whine from her lips. "Tess here never let me forget it. Always demanding another score, another hit of that addiction that is thieving."

'Yeah right.' Alex thought on the inside. He craved the rush of adrenaline when he could watch his victims cry and become like children from what he'd done to them. They were just pawns for him to play with.

"I'll n-never let you go." Tess strained her voice before she coughed again, a string of blood flowing down her cheek to dribble down her chin and struggled to stand straight against the wall as Daniel moved to stand beside Alex on the other side of crates, looking between the two of them.

This was what he craved. Alex watched in hidden glee as he watched Daniel struggle to decipher the truth from the lies, the deceit preventing him from choosing a side any longer. This was it; his breaking point as Alex watched Daniel's tangled web of honor and justice suffocate under a girl who he still loved, even as she died in front of him. His inability to harm her face to face. Alex's eyes seemed to spin madly as he leaned forward; he craved to see this turmoil in those cerulean orbs; the innate desire to protect and touch her, and the tight exterior holding him back; holding him away from an enemy to his ideals, to his entire being. He was shaking! His good guy facade was cracking and soon he'd be broken and weeping. He was-

"Don't try to sell yourself short, Alex." Tess finally wheezed, her knees quaking as she slid down the wall, her skin pale and filled with goosebumps. "I was there for it all, Alex. The sun stone of Aria. The teardrop diamond of Erudite. The necklace from the museum of the Forgotten Kings. You and I had a lot of adventures together."

Alex looked up astonished at her, before a soft laugh filled his lungs and he smiled wide. "Oh? Now you're feeling nostalgic? Of course, you're too mad after I shoot you to talk, but now in the last moments…" Alex's laugh died down after a few seconds and he sighed contently. "…Yes. I will admit that stealing those items were the best thefts of my life. I mean coning that little girl into taking the package through airport security in Aria, that was all me, but I can admit that I couldn't have done it if you hadn't acted so distressed on the phone when you spoke to her."

"With my way of gathering intel and your masterful feats of thievery and conning the marks, we did so much together, didn't we?" Alex sighed, nodding his head, the gun for the first time lowering a fraction down towards her feet.

"You ended it-"

"You and your mother ended it!" Alex snapped, seething through his entire body as he sneered and walked straight to her frail form. "Your mother is what caused all of this!" He yelled down at her, as he brought up his foot and kicked straight at her stomach, stomping right at her wound.

"Ah!" Tess whimpered as he kicked at her two more times before she fell to the cement, holding herself in a semi-ball with her arm covering herself from further harm as Alex raged in front of her.

"Do you think I was stupid?!? I was already planning three more jobs when Amelia announced she was retiring to me in that condescending tone of hers." Alex rolled his eyes, remembering her authoritative eyes, demanding they listen and hang on her every word as if she were the true leader of the group.

"Now, alright, she was slowing down the rest of us; that I'll admit to. Practically in pain for as many days as she was healthy. Getting really old; That I could live with, just let her fall off the wayside and we continue on-but no! To add insult to me, she went and named you the next leader?!? No way! I gave years to our team and then she goes and gives it to her bastard daughter?!? I wasn't going to stay for you! You who hung on her every word, who worshipped the ground she walked on. You who can only think of the old ways and how to make her proud of you. I wasn't going to stand for that."

"You could never...never see the big picture, Alex." Tess wheezed out, smirking at him condescendingly.

Just like...what Amelia used to do! Alex bent down beside her, gripping her shirt within his fists as he brought her struggling form up to face him. "I see everything." He emphasized by staring straight into her eyes, but it was irksome as her smirk widened even further, more blood slipping further out and dropping to the floor.

"I never told you this as a courtesy, Alex, but you praise your eyes too much. That precious intel you brought in? Half of the time it was garbage, and the other half you had gotten without any thought to the mental state of the marks you were getting it from. There were too many times where mom had me to compensate for your errors, but I never liked your plans. They were childish and cruel-"

A sudden tug on her neck jolted her from speech. "Maybe I take a razor blade to your mouth first, huh? I'll slice you up instead. I mean, my eyes are bad. How about I take your eyes to compensate for my own? Huh?!? How does that sound?!?"

Alex breathed heavily as Tess simply smiled back. "Childish. Unlike you who always cuts corners, I do the legwork. I'll never stop hunting you, Alex. You will never be rid of me. You killed Amelia. You killed my mother; you killed my sister-Ah!"

Tess coughed as Alex surged forward, slamming her back into the wall as she gasped for relief. "So what?!? I killed Amelia because she was ready to die. The only way out is death; A thief never retires; everyone knows that." Alex snickered back at her. "And Tanya died because of you. Don't try to plant that death on me, sister. You came after me in the end. Face it, Tess. You will just keep losing those closest to you if you keep chasing me."

The gun raised with his hand to Tess's temple, his grip on her shirt keeping her in place. "Think of me killing you now as an act of mercy to all that pain." Alex brought his finger to the trigger, his digit closing the distance on the trigger as it shuttered and began to back up, the mechanism beginning to move, beginning to slide the hammer back as the sound of black ravens filled his ears.

Suddenly, a pair of hands launched at his side, shoving him away from his kill and as he stumbled to a stop, back in the center of the room, he could only look in stunned amazement back at Daniel who was glaring at him, his body directly in the line of fire where Tess lay prone on the floor, hidden by his frame.

"You were really going to kill her?" Daniel uttered, his voice full of astonishment and rage, his eyes narrowing at his own accusing gaze. "You really killed her mother?"

Alex saw that the ruse was up. Daniel had chosen the girl that had brought him into their world. He smiled darkly with a wicked gleam in his eye. "I shot her with the same gun I killed my brother with. My father's gun to be precise...and now I use it on you." Alex spoke as he raised the gun and fired. The gun went off and Daniel grunted in pain as he fell to the ground.

But as Alex turned to finish off his nemesis, there she suddenly was, standing right next to him. Before he could react, Tess struck out with her leg, kicking him right to the center of the gut. Air escaped him at terminal velocity as he stumbled backwards, hitting the far wall away from them. As he tried to rush forward, Tess was in front of him again, and her fist was buried deep into his stomach, choking the air from his lungs once more.

Alex fell to the ground, limp as a board and Tess pounced on top of him, her fists doing work as she slugged at his face repeatedly, trying with all her might to cave his face in. It took all his wheezing strength to hold his hands above his face, but when they blocked her, she aimed at his arms and chest, turning his body from red into a blackish purple mess for later.

His eyes turned black and blue as he saw dizzy stars swirling on the ceilings, his face bloody from his broken nose and gaping through his teeth. And the surge only stopped as Tess breathed heavily from the rush of adrenaline leaving her body.

"T-Tess…"

"Daniel!" Tess turned back and with his dizzying gaze watching her, Tess jumped up and ran over to his side…. easily too and eased him up as Daniel groaned and sat up...with no blood on him whatsoever.

"...What?"

Alex jumped to his feet as Tess turned back and grinned victoriously. "It's over, Alex."

In a matter of seconds, a cylinder flew into the room, and bright light engulfed the three of them. "Police!! Stay where you are!!" Shouts came from all of the doors as multiple men in black cloth and armor raced inside, converging on the center of the room.

Groaning erupted from Alex's mouth as he grabbed madly at his face and curled into himself. His eyes saw the gun on the ground next to Daniel's feet and he internally smiled.

"Thank you for saving me officers! That's the thief! Right there! My guys called you, right? She tried to rob me at my house! I tried to run, but she dragged me here!"

The police rushed towards him and reached for his arms to pull him up. "And her boyfriend shoved a gun in my face! They're crazy! Please you have to-" Alex stalled as the arms pulled at him roughly before he was spun around and shoved against the wall face first. "-What are you doing?!?" He screamed as they grabbed at his hands and brought them behind his back, taking out cuffs as they went. "Unhand me, you pig!!"

As he struggled, two men entered the room from the center entrance and with long casual strides, moved to stand before him as the officers brought him back to face them.

"I must say that it is nice to meet you, Alex." The first man spoke lazily, his entire posture laid back and his hair spiked up crazily, as his black outfit laid pristine and proper on his frame. "I am Detective Beckett of the State troopers, and this is Detective Orion. He was most interested when you mentioned that you used your father's gun on your own brother."

"Y-you couldn't have-..." Alex denied before he widened his eyes and turned to the right in shock as he watched Tess accusingly as she unbuttoned her shirt in front of two female officers, to show a bullet proof vest and-

"Wires!?!?" Alex roared as he jumped at her, only to be pulled back as two officers struggled to hold him still. "You bitch Tess! I'll kill you!"

"Take him downtown."

Alex continued to scream profanities as he was escorted out of the room, and Simon stood in the center of the room, idly looking around before he reached down, drawing out a pen from his pocket to slide through the trigger of the gun on the ground, before picking it up and sliding it into a waiting evidence bag as an officer took it away to be filed and cataloged.

Simon now turned to the couple now sitting on the crate, as Tess looked up at the ceiling and a medic dabbed at her bloody lip, checking her over for any serious injuries she might have incurred, Daniel leaning over from the other crate, his fingers intertwined with her own.

As the medic finished up, Simon took their place in front of Tess, and she looked up bashfully at him. "Hello again, Simon." She greeted him softly.

"You are truly a strange one, Tess. Can I assume that you had that all planned out then?"

(Flashback)

Tess looked back as she slid into the doorway, spotting the SUV where her boyfriend sat in the passenger seat, as she jogged down a few doorways until she stopped at the room beyond the one she would be using to capture Alex. In front of her was a plugged-in refrigerator, stocked inside with the equipment she would need.

Opening the door, she pulled out the bags of pseudo blood packs before attaching them to the vest on her body just above her stomach.

Shutting the door, she ran to the other room as she listened to Alex whisper from the entrance for Daniel to go around the back. Just as she knew that he would do; separating them up and preventing them from speaking, just as she had told Daniel what would happen.

Stepping into the darkened room, Tess turned the light on and slid into the darkness by the metal door, where a party cannon was attached to the backside. Tess took two of the packs and shoved them into the barrel of the cannon, before she grabbed the remote beside it.

She breathed out silently, listening to Alex's quiet footfalls as he entered the room just before this one. Zipping up her jacket to hide the vest, she dug through her pocket and grabbed a small capsule and popped it into her mouth between her teeth.

Her finger on the trigger, she waited with bated breath as Alex entered the room and looked around before she saw him smile and readied herself.

"You want to hide here? Such a bad spot...too open for someone like us." Alex turned quickly and fired his gun into the darkness where she stood, and in that moment, she bit the pill full of fake blood and clicked the button as the party cannon splatted the blood packs against the wall and the blood in the packs on her vest began to escape to her jacket, pooling a circle of blood. But Tess stepped out into the light, completely unscathed.

"You could say that." Tess shrugged as she leaned forward, her hand extending to meet his own as she handed a flash drive over to Simon. He took it into his possession and moved his palm up and down, as if weighing the contents on it with the case at hand.

Simon finally sighed as he looked at the couple in front of him, their eyes apprehensive at his coming words. "You know what I still need to do, correct?"

Tess gulped at his insinuation. Of course, he still needed that, but at the steady hand that tightened its grip on her own, her shuddering ceased and she nodded her head in defeat. "Can I have a minute?" She pleaded quietly.

"Of course." Simon nodded and moved away to give them some space.

"Tess?" Daniel voiced to comfort her, but instead, Tess turned quickly to her lover and kissed him deeper than she ever had before. Her body and his pressed together as if they were one, their snogging passionate and full of unspoken feelings that both knew but neither had to convey with words. Their intertwined fingers stayed locked with the other, but their other hands reached around to pull them ever closer, as close as possible.

Finally, after a full minute of lip lock, their lips parted with a heavy heart to the attraction to stay together. With labored breaths, they only managed ten or so inches between their lips, hot breath tickling their faces as their arms refused to let go, the both knowing that this may be for the last time. Daniel's fingers reached forward to caress Tess's wetted cheeks as she draped her hands together behind his neck, his remaining hand holding the handle of her waist lovingly.

"You were bloody brilliant today." Tess sniffled as she leaned into his palm. "You led Alex to all the red herrings just as I told you, and that chase was perfect. You would have been a perfect member of my team." She blubbered lovingly.

"Hey, I'm an innocent bystander here." He cajoled as Tess giggled and leaned in again, not being able to maintain the facade she'd kept up since the night they had parted for what felt like forever ago, kissing him once more. Daniel smiled as she backed up, but grimaced playfully as he licked at his lips. "Though I don't like the taste of your blood."

"It's vinegar with tomato paste, idiot." Tess smiled and cooed lovingly as the pad of his thumb stroked her side.

"Still, I can't believe this worked."

Tess smiled tearily at his melancholy. "I had you, didn't I?" Daniel held her close, feeling her begin to shiver again in his arms. "Daniel?"

"Yeah?"

"...I want to run so bad."

"I know." Daniel nodded, stoking her cheek again. "But Tess, you promised."

Tess nodded back, tears now freely falling down her face in rivers as she silently cried. A few minutes later, Simon returned, carrying his own set of cuffs in his left hand. Tess broke their embrace and held her wrists out to the detective in surrender.

"You'll wait for me, right?" Tess turned her head to look back as the metal shackles slid onto her wrists.

"I'm going with you." Daniel confirmed.

Simon watched the two and sighed at having to break the reunion. "Tess, I take you in as a protected witness to reduce your years in prison. Daniel can follow in the rear car, but let's head to the station. We'll get you something to drink and then you can tell us everything...leaving nothing out."

"Yes sir."

XXVII—TO TELL THE TRUTH

The beeping sound of the machine echoed in the small breakroom, and Simon stood up and turned off the coffee maker. He added just a single pack of sugar and added some cream to cut down on the bitterness that he had perfected over the years for his specific preference in taste.

Taking the cup to his lips, he took a sip and smiled bitterly. '*Yep. Still bad coffee.*' Compared to his wife, he really couldn't cook or even heat something up to save his life, so he treasured her and her career as a creative artisan of sweets, and their daughter, well, they needed to keep her out of the candy jar at times. It was a long day for him, and he was definitely not done with it, but when he was, he was going to go home, hug his daughter, kiss his wife, and maybe take a nap before taking his daughter to preschool in the morning.

Simon, with cup still in hand, made his way past his office and down the hallway to the interrogation rooms. Stopping at the last two, he nodded to the officer standing outside the door and walked inside, spotting the young man standing at the glass, intently focused on the girl inside.

"Daniel, right?"

"Yes sir. We met before."

"We did at the museum."

"I didn't expect you to show up."

"Well...Tess and I have been chasing each other for quite some time now." Simon smiled bitterly before turning to him. "Now then,

I'm going to go in there. I am allowing you to watch with my officer present, but you may not come in. Understood?"

"Yes sir."

"Good man." Simon nodded and walked back out, turning into the room next door, and walked straight in. It was his third time in the room today, but this time, he wasn't leaving until he had everything. "Hello Tess."

"Evening Simon." Tess greeted quietly, her eyes looking at the back corner as the last rays of the sun shined into the room. Her fingers lightly scraped at the edges of the skin before her fingernails, the cuffs only allowing her five or six inches of separation before they linked around a steel bar in the middle of the table, ensuring that she couldn't leave of her own cognition.

As Simon sat opposite her, he smirked. If she wanted to, he was certain that she could get out of them, but to stay calm and collected proved to him that she wanted to be here. With that in mind, he reached for his phone.

"Alright Tess…" Simon began as he tried looking for the app hidden in the phone. "…. we are going…to…. there it is." He smiled as he opened it, and then frowned tightly at the greyed-out screen.

"Trouble?"

"A bit." Simon admitted. "I was never very good at technology."

"How you ever caught me is a mystery." Tess rolled her eyes dramatically.

"Well, you turned yourself in."

"True…. mind if I look?"

"Hmm…eh? Why not?" Simon shrugged as he passed it over. Tess's fingers surged across the phone, bringing up icons and numbers that Simon had only seen in his IT department when they were geeking out. But after only thirty seconds, Tess handed it back, and it opened like it was brand new. "Thanks."

"My pleasure."

"Well then…" Simon activated the app again, and a visual microphone appeared, the red-light flashing green. "This is Detective Beckett; 7th district State trooper on the 5th of October. Beginning interview and confession of subject. State your full name, your real name for the record, and leave nothing out."

Tess's posture relaxed as she closed her eyes, mentally preparing herself before she gazed forward and began her life story.

"…. My name is Tess Maria Miles-Walter….and I am a thief…….."

(One Week Ago)

Tess felt Daniel's lips touch hers and darted forward, pressing her body against the length of his, trying with all her might to press the love she felt for her lover down his throat and hopefully reaching into the deep depths of his heart to his very soul. Daniel's lips pressed against hers harder and she took it as a sign as she relaxed a little, her arms encircling his neck as she pulled him atop her on the bed, his hands sliding along her body to caress every inch of her.

"Paige-" Daniel murmured into her ear and Tess cooed at her name on his lips. Just as she was assured that he loved her, his hands suddenly left her sides and pushed on the mattress, pulling him up and away, breaking the kiss before a satisfied conclusion could be made. Tess moved to groan and complain when she saw it.

Daniel's face, his lips pulled into a tight line, his eyes watery and saddened, his resolve…set in stone.

"Paige I can't do this anymore."

Tess tried not to cry; she bit her lip, crushing it between her teeth, she held down the shakes and shivers as her whole body pleaded and begged to be let loose. Tess fell to the bed, her eyes broken as her steady stream of tears bled down her cheeks with the passion of love from her very soul.

"You can't…Daniel, please." Paige begged, shaking her head. "I can't …. I can't lose you-"

"Paige," Daniel interrupted once more, this time leaning even further away as time began to separate them into two differing realities of life. He was a real person with nothing but truth on his shoulders; she was a thief in the night. "Paige," he started again, drawing her attention. "I don't actually know that much about you. I've told you so many of my secrets, but I can only recall a spare few of yours, if they're even secrets at all."

"Dan-"

"I don't know what you do. I know you've told me it's consulting with technology and other things, but I never hear about your day with a customer, your outrage that they didn't take your advice, your happiness that your plan worked out. How can I even begin to trust you again?" Daniel whispered before he grabbed her shoulder hard. "I don't even know your real name!" He angrily spat out, frustrated with her.

Paige began to tear up from his grip and his words, her eyes closing as she began to let her body react. Tears bubbled at her eyes while her throat began to constrict. Yet suddenly, Daniel's lips were pressed tightly on hers, kissing her harshly in unbridled passion.

Paige only cried harder as she wrapped around him again to hold him in place. She didn't care that they were seconds away from breaking up forever; she didn't care that he couldn't live a life with her not knowing everything that she was. All she wanted to know was that he felt something for her; anything! So she kissed back deeply, kissing him until no more breath was in her lungs.

As they parted and Paige let go, her hands moved to cover her eyes which were clawing at her face, stinging her with what felt like vinegar.

"...I love you..."

Paige's eyes shot open, her tears froze, and her entire body lay frozen in place. She didn't say anything back as Daniel manhandled her, dropping her arms down to her sides, before caressing her brown hair as he scraped her scalp and made her resist a coo.

"I love you...This version of you." Daniel sniffled as he continued to caress her head in his hand. "This version is smart, a forward girl who is shy after being so, who gets embarrassed by her ideas, yet always goes through with it. This version of you is kind, playful, and always happy when I'm around."

His caressing stopped. "But this is only a piece of you. I'm not willing to live my life with a piece. I want all of you, every dark secret, every romantic thought, every pointless fight when we disagree. I want all of you; not just the part that you allow me to see."

Daniel looked down and saw her glistening eyes and her stunned face, embarrassed that he had said those words to her. They were deep in his core, and yet they flowed out so easily for him. But she still didn't respond, and his whole body shuddered.

"Please." Daniel looked away from above her on the bed, his eyes not able to look upon her prone form any longer as his heart ached more and more with every passing second. He loved her damnit! "...I can't lose you Paige, but I can't keep you either. If there's anything I can do, I'll do it, just-"

"-My name's Tess." A shy, insecure voice finally uttered.

Daniel froze as he slowly titled his head back to hers. Angry tears lined down her porcelain face, red swelling at her eyes, her throat crackly and hoarse. There she lay, down on the bed underneath him and straight into his eyes. She was completely defenseless and at his mercy. "W-what?"

Paige shivered, as if breaking right in front of him, and he didn't know how but another girl suddenly appeared in her place, a girl who looked the same, but...different.

"My name's Tess Miles. My profession....I'm a thief."

Tess began to lean back up, nervous as hell, but it was pointless now. She had nothing left in this world more important to her than Daniel. He loved her, and no matter what, she wanted to stay by his side.

Daniel leaned to the side as this girl, Tess, sat up beside him. Just when he was about to ask what she stole, she backed up further and brought her fingers up to her face as she turned around. After a second, Daniel curiously watched as two small plastic bubbles lay in her hand. Had they come from her eyes?

"God those always hurt after a bad cry." Tess sniffled and looked back, making Daniel's breath leave him. Gone was the brilliant blue water that dragged him into the depths, to be replaced by a brilliant emerald, as lush as an old growth forest.

"Your eyes are green...."

Tess sniffled. "Yes, they are...I used you, Daniel." Tess confessed. "I stole that painting from the museum, and I conned you so deeply. It was no coincidence that I showed up when I did. I didn't mean to drag you into my world...not initially. You were just so.... normal! I distracted you that night in the camera room as my team snuck in and grabbed it. I-I have no good reason to give as an excuse, just that I stole it so that I could find the man who killed my mother."

Daniel's voice must not have been working as Tess looked back at him. But then she breathed in and began to tell him everything about her; her early life growing up, Amelia raising her, Tanya her sister in crime, everything. Through it all, Daniel said nothing. He just listened to her whole story without a single interruption.

The sun was on the horizon when she was done with her life story. Possibly for six hours now, she had told him about every con she had ever done, every crime she had ever committed that she could think of that was relevant. All her secrets flooded over the edge, trying to release the weight tied to her legs so that she might float to the surface and to him.

Tess breathed quietly as he sat there, gulping back her nervousness as his eyes crinkled and thought about her confessions. She did feel better though; light and open. She had no major secrets with him anymore, and hopefully he'd be okay learning all the smaller ones if he stayed with her, small chance that it might be.

"So... nothing violent?" Daniel finally asked.

Tess shook her head. "Never. I target wealthy people, but...some cons involve regular people too, so it may not be violent physically, but mentally?" Tess sighed through her mouth. It was a weak answer, but it was the best she could think of with her love life on the line.

Slowly, her eyes widened as Daniel's hand slowly moved to her thigh and stroked her skin there. Tears began to prick at her cheeks again, but Daniel edged closer and began to dab at them with the pad of his thumb.

"So… your hair is usually blonde?"

At that, Tess smiled brightly. He wasn't freaking out. He accepted her. "Brightly so. It shines so much brighter when I'm not wearing dye, but it's the real me so I've only worn some wig or dye otherwise."

"…So, he killed her. Alex killed your mother."

Tess's eyes glazed over with a murky fog. "Yes…but I'll kill him."

She could imagine it now; a dark basement, Alex locked away and beaten within an inch of his mortal life as a knife lay in Tess's hand. But that thumb on her cheek turned to grip at her chin and forcefully grabbed her attention to look at Daniel's eyes piercing right through her.

"Tess, have you killed before?

"Well…" Tess squirmed her face in his grip, not wanting to look right at him, but couldn't look away in the position he had her in. "No, but-"

"-I can't take you if you have blood on your hands." Daniel stated.

Breath almost left her lungs at that. He had wanted her to stop with the facades; Paige was dead and gone for him. He demanded no more secrets and half-truths; she just told him everything. And now; give up her revenge?

"You mean…You won't still take me after?"

"Tess," she shivered at her name on his tongue. "I want to be with you, but… No more thieving, no more trouble. Just you and I, with the world around us to love each other in."

"I… but I need him." Tess whispered desperately. "I need to kill him. He killed my mother…" Tess's voice turned desperate. Daniel saw her shivering like an addict going through withdrawal and pulled her into a hug, which she greedily accepted, pulling her arms desperately around his neck and shoulder as she sniffled into his neck.

Daniel stroked her bare back comfortingly for a few minutes as Tess herself continued to shiver. But slowly his hand slid lower over her hip and squeezed, earning a groan of approval and her attention as he dipped down to kiss her neck below her ear.

"Then take this deal."

"Deal? What do you mean?"

"...I help you-"

"No!" Tess struggled suddenly, her body thrashing as she broke contact and stared at him madly. "No way! I could never ask that of you, Daniel!"

"Tess-"

"You're good and innocent and-"

"Tess-"

"You're like a knight! Noble and-"

"Tess!" Daniel chuckled into her ear as he pulled her back in. "Let me finish. I'll help you get Alex. Anything goes, except two things; you can't kill him, and after this...you're done, with all of this."

Tess looked down, and bit at her lip, the hardest choice of all. "You realize what you're asking of me?"

"I do." Daniel nodded. "I'm asking you to give up your livelihood, to give up your revenge, to leave the sister who has been your spine and support all these years. I'm asking so much from you; I know what I'm making you choose between."

Daniel graced her cheek again, as Tess swooned under his touch. "You're a smart girl, Tess. You managed to steal that painting without anyone seeing you."

"You saw me."

"Fine. So that your sister wasn't seen. Point is, you're resourceful. Just find a way to not kill him."

Tess growled as she hugged her lover again, grating her teeth at the thought of not digging a hole for that murderer. And yet? *'...I suppose I could let him live...'* Gears started turning in her mind, *'...I could ask them...they'd have the power to do it...but then they'd know where I am...'*

"Okay..." Tess whispered, and the confused smile on Daniel's face was like a beacon of ethereal light.

"Okay?"

Tess's grip on his waist tightened as she circled her thighs around them and squeezed. Daniel blushed back lovingly as Tess nodded. "If this is going to be my final theft, then I'm going to make it my piece de resistance."

With a surge of confidence, Tess kissed his lips and held him close. "You know," Tess voiced whimsically, "I used to think that it was all about the con. All about getting a score. To prove that I was superior, that…I just wanted to make my mother proud of me. But mom told me about love, and I found you…I love you, Daniel….I'll do it. I'll do it for you. I'll do it for us."

"Now then," Tess began as they broke apart, their limbs extending out towards the other. Daniel looked over at his girlfriend and his eyes widened. His girl radiated with a different glow around her. It was powerful, and attractive and- "Focus!" Tess giggled as she swatted at his hand on her thigh, Daniel blushing in guilt.

"Daniel, Alex can't know we're still together. For this to work, you need to badmouth me, look broken in front of him. That's his weakness. He feels superior around weaker minds, but if you hide yourself in that facade, you'll be able to lead him around to what you want to show him."

Daniel's grip tightened on the small of her waist. "I can do that… But how will I talk to you?" I mean, if I can't see you, I at least need to hear your voice." Daniel leaned in to place another peck to her cheek. "These last few days killed me, Tess. I don't want to do that again."

But Tess shook her head, denying him. "God, Daniel, I want that too, but it's too risky. Alex watches everyone, double checks everything." With a stroke of her hand along his face, Tess smiled, consoling him. "But we'll be okay, because unlike last time, we'll only be playing the part of breaking up."

"Think more old school than that. My old email should be alright. I've never shown it to anyone, and Alex for sure doesn't know about it. I'll give you the password. Leave it on the table for you before I leave tonight."

Daniel nodded as he began to leave the room to give Tess some privacy. But as he reached the bathroom door, he paused and looked back. "Tess?"

"Hmm?"

"Is there...anything suspicious there?"

At that, Tess's cheeks turned a shade of pink. "Yeah...backups of certain things I've done..." Tess gulped nervously. "You can delete them if you want, just don't read them."

Daniel slowly nodded as he moved to close the door. He didn't need to know everything in her past. But he...he was her future.

"He's my future, you see." Tess admitted to the detective.

"So, all of this is for your lover." Simon confirmed as he wrote notes and opinions down for himself, watching and listening to her breath, her tone, and the way she spoke. Tess smiled in pure love and with an abandoned exterior facade, leaving the interior of a romantic to show herself in front of him.

"So, you plan to be with him in marriage or long term?"

Tess smiled brightly. "When I get out, y-yeah..." Ten seconds of silence passed before her statement was completed. "If I get out...then I hope that he'll still want me after all of this. The only way I got some sense of justice was if Alex went away forever, and I needed... some kind of deal to lower my time in prison..." Tess glanced from the glass mirror back at Simon with a sad smirk. "That's why I called you, Simon."

Simon leaned back in his office chair, stacks of folders on either side of his desk, and a laptop turned on just off center to his right. He was just about done with his day, having put Pete Bosco, a man wanted for killing three people across two counties, in jail.

Now three hours later, his fingers ached with a vengeance, silently screaming at him for typing up his report of the entirety of the case. Luckily, he had been working on the report since the beginning so it wasn't too bad, so now he was just holding down the fort for a few hours until he could return home.

A homesick feeling made him look to the sole picture frame on his desk, to look upon his wife Katy, who was holding her lookalike daughter between Simon and herself for cute spring photos with bright colors and a spring thaw.

He couldn't help but smile at the stupid yellow tie that she had insisted he wear, and that he bring this photo of them to work to remember them. The whole squad room had poked fun at him, or praised him for being such a dad, but he loved them so much. He'd do anything for his wife, in love with her since they were kids.

Shaking his head to get back to his work, he looked to his left and sighed at the small microchip that he'd found at the scene of another murder just yesterday. He knew that it had to be important, but when it came to technology and better thieves, he was truly at a loss.

He was not tech savvy; his phone shut itself off or his laptop battery died, and he couldn't put complex tasks into a command key or whatever it was called. He kept having a partner help him with that stuff, but they were always shorthanded, and he knew that he was going to have to study harder than ever to learn this stuff and keep the bad guys away.

"Detective, call for you. Line 4." A guy called out from the open door to his office. Simon nodded his head and reached for his phone. As the officer in charge, he just hoped it wasn't another retaliatory complaint call about his guys.

"This is Detective Beckett."

"Simon…" A feminine voice spoke. "This is Tess Miles…Do you remember me?"

Simon grinned wide in defeat as he leaned back in his chair and put his boots up on his desk. "So now you're the kind of criminal to call and gloat about our lack of evidence? No, you're the girl who slipped right past us in the open cemetery without anyone realizing it. Of course, I remember you. You're the only cold case I have on my record." Simon spoke aloud before he simmered down, remembering the words she had last spoken to him. "Did you kill your mother's murderer yet?"

The line filled with a heavy silence, of debate and choice of words to say; Simon figured she'd be coy with him. "...My boyfriend suggested I call you..."

"Boyfriend?" Beckett's eyes raised up. Was she pulling something on him? Just to pull a fast one on a detective that was handed her file six months ago. No, she didn't fit the profile, but also, Simon heard something different in her voice, a more gentle smoothness in it, and he was curious. "...This is new..."

"He truly knows me, Simon..."

Simon smiled hopefully. "So, you told him everything..."

"...Yes, everything..."

Simon smiled on his end of the line. She sounded...different for sure. Still prideful about her skills and talent, and confident in what she could accomplish but...balanced, settled....in love. She had matured in life.

"So then?" Simon pressed forward. He didn't bother tracing the call. She wouldn't be that stupid, and he didn't have the manpower or authority to search for her. "What did you call me for?"

"...He says I can't kill the man..."

Simon smiled at that. A criminal the girl may be, but she was still young and quite intelligent. He didn't want her to cross that line between white collar and red, and if this boy of hers was pulling her back, then he would want to support him. "Smart man. He's right, you know. I'd hate to see you again with blood on your hands. But why call me?"

"...I want him to be put in a dark place where the light doesn't shine. I want him to stay there the rest of his life."

"If he truly killed someone, then he won't get away."

"I have a plan, Simon..."

When she finally stopped talking on her side, Simon slowly sat up in his chair and smiled. "So, you're saying that you can get him to admit to theft and murder? Multiple crimes that you also committed with him? That's damning, and I'm sure my bosses would approve of working with you."

"However," Simon leaned forward at his desk. She may as well know all the facts. Even if he was sure she knew them already. "Tess, I can't give you immunity. You've done too much in your life. I can offer to speak to the DA…….Tess?"

"…That's okay Simon. I'll accept that."

"Tess, I shouldn't really advise you against this, but …if you do this; your boyfriend may never see you again."

In the bedroom with an eye on the door to the bathroom, Tess sat on the edge of the bed, listening to the sound of running water from the shower. A glimpse at the dresser next to her showed her a picture of Daniel and Tess together, her hugging him from behind with her tongue playfully sticking out as he struggled to reverse their roles for the photo. It was innocent and lovely…and normal. It was what she wanted her life to become.

"If I ever get out, I'll see him again. But I can't lose him now. If this is the price I have to pay, then I'll take it."

"Very well, Tess." Simon voiced over the phone. "Just tell me the time and the place."

"I didn't really need to know my own part, Tess." Simon smiled as he looked up from his notes, but Tess was in a trance of her own life now and as she moved on, Simon heard the heavy emotions beginning to affect her speech, her throat parched and beginning to lace with tears. And unlike before in a room similar to this one, she was not faking them.

"And then, Tess? What happened then?"

"I uh…" Tess heaved a shuddering sigh. "I spoke to my sister."

XXVIII-FOR THE LOVE OF ANOTHER

The workshop was busy with machines slicing apart at steel and girls hard at work. Megan was beating out the tubes for the launchers while Melissa worked with Abby on uploading the software that she would use in the sewer line.

"And you're sure that there's no alligators in there? "

"Abby, for the thousandth time, there are no alligators in sewers." Melissa sighed.

"Hey!" Abby sputtered. "If Alex has robotic snakes, then he could have alligators too!"

"Don't worry, Abby." Tanya called back. "I've checked the line. There's no electrical currents strong enough down there for those kinds of things."

Melissa sighed gratefully and looked back at Abby. "Happy?"

Abby nodded her head.

"Scaredy cat." A whispered chuckle escaped out of Megan's lips and Abby slid a glare her way.

"Why you-"

"Enough." Tanya interjected, as the two girls sighed and got back to work. Tanya sighed resigned to the fate of the two forever fighting. This was why you didn't date another member's family, but Megan loved Abby's cousin. It came with the territory sometimes, and Tanya was no better, having her own sister in the crew. Tanya shook her head smiling. If they could complain about each other, then they had confidence that this plan would work. True, they still had four days to get everything ready, but it would work in the end.

'The end, huh?' Tanya's demeanor saddened at that. Tess was running out on them to be with the guard, and some of the team didn't like adding him into their plan to begin with. To do all this work so that he could tell Alex where to look was a great distraction, but if he didn't act the right way or say the right things, well, there was a reason that Abby got a nasty scar on her first mission with them in the desert.

But in the actual heist, he wasn't doing anything. Tess had assured them of that. Just false information. Speaking of her sister, Tanya looked back to the hallway that led up to the loft, and there her sister stood at the balcony watching over them, before giving her a nod.

Tanya nodded back and began to set her equipment down and power it off. Her sister wanted to talk to her. Taking a relaxed pace, she walked over to the hallway, spotting her sister leaning against the rail halfway up the staircase looking at her nervously.

Tanya quirked her eyes at the expression and leaned against the opposing rail from her, as their knees almost touched in the small space. "So, Tess, what did you need me for?"

Silence greeted her, and yet Tanya didn't pester her to talk. Tess was always thinking and spoke exactly what she wanted to say, but after her last rendezvous with her ex-lover, she'd been dominant in their team, yet aloof; quietly debating something that Tanya figured she'd decide when she was ready.

"How's the uniform fitting?"

Tanya smiled confidently, her posture slinking into a sensual pose as she mocked. "The guards will be all over me tomorrow."

As Tanya giggled, she held in a ticklish eep as her sister's hand reached forward and caressed at the gap between her sports bra and her leggings, right where her stomach met her hip.

"Tess?"

"...So...I need Daniel to do a part of the heist."

Tanya slowly nodded her head. Getting him to get his hands dirty would solidify his relationship with Tess, and she was all for it.

"How can I help?"

"...You are so beautiful." Tess spoke aloud again, not answering her question as she caressed at the skin some more. "There's not a scar on you, is there?"

Tanya smirked. "I've been lucky to not make any mistakes like that...Tess, tell me what's going on in that head of yours."

Shame flooded her sister's cheeks. "I need you to do something for me, and you're not going to enjoy it one bit, but I need this from you. You're the only one I can trust...it's a request, not an order, so you can-" Tess began to rush out.

A delicate white hand, that was manicured to perfection, graced her cheek, stopping her blubbering in its tracks.

"You don't need to ask for anything, Tess. You're my sister. Now... what do you need from me?"

"I... I need you to...."

Tanya moved down the hallway and stopped as another guard rounded the corner, his blonde hair matching hers, and his blue eyes a lighter shade than her own.

"Daniel?" Tanya voiced aloud with a surprised question in her throat. All along the airwaves, the other girls sputtered and asked why he was here, while Daniel continued to walk towards her.

Tanya wanted to cry. This man was stealing her sister away; not just taking a part of the con like the other girls knew. Tess was giving all of this up for him; all the lucrative scores, all the rush of conning someone that you had spent so much time on, all the attention that moved to seek you out.

She was sad, because this truly was her best plan ever with this crew; their peers would recall it as her piece de resistance. The final con of Tess Maria Miles-Walter.

As Daniel reached her, Tanya dug out a small envelope from inside her guard's jacket. They couldn't speak since Daniel had given Alex their frequency and was even now talking to Tess on the other line. As he read it, she smiled sourly.

To leave this life required a great sacrifice, a queen's gambit, and for Tess, Tanya was her queen, her strongest connection to this life of thievery and the con. As Daniel looked back at her, he smiled sourly and nodded to her. She could only shrug in faux apology. If he didn't love her with all his heart as the letter she'd given him stated, she'd take Tess back from him. A little warning to keep him on his toes.

As Tess asked into her mike to confirm who it was, she breathed in as Daniel pulled out his gun and pressed it into the side of her stomach. A scar for the loss of her sister from this life.

'But I'll see her more than enough.' Tanya resigned in her mind. Miles was a criminal, but Tess Thompson would be a civilian. She could see her nieces more often and babysit them more. She'd just be a regular aunt now, so Tanya would see her plenty.

"Daniel?" Tanya voiced again over the mike, giving the signal to Daniel and Tess that the plan was in motion. Daniel's finger pulled the trigger and Tanya's eyes bulged out as the bullet shot into her body and gasped for air.

With legs and lungs shaking haphazardly, Daniel pulled her into a tight hug, which she happily accepted. *'Damn.'* she thought. For a knight, Daniel was willing to get his hands dirty for his princess.

As Alex spoke and cajoled her sister on the other line, Daniel grabbed a large bandage from his pocket as Tanya worked to scuff up her uniform and bring it up over the wound. As Tess had explained to her, Daniel's gun would pierce her skin, but in this location, would not hit any vital organs, and with a packet of blood strapped to the outside of the bandages, Alex would only see her wound still bleeding when in reality, it was already patched up.

With Tanya's weakened state, Daniel took his place under her arm and helped her back towards the safe where their goal was located.

This wound would cement everything in place; Alex would see her wound and forget about her martial prowess, Tess would escape, and the guards would follow on a goose chase, and Tanya, though weakened, would be able to take down a guard and then they were home free.

Alex would go away forever, and her sister would be happy. Tanya hissed and breathed heavily as they neared the entryway, both for the benefit of the radio waves and as an outlet for her own pain. She never expected in life to get shot by her sister's lover.

Daniel dipped back off her arm and pulled her into a deep hug as Tanya shivered and hugged back. "Don't worry." He whispered. "I'll take good care of her."

Tanya nodded into his shoulder, unable to speak. She knew that was the plan. She just hoped it turned out that way.

"But that's not what happened, was it, Tess?" Simon stopped her, reaching over to hand her a tissue as tears streamed down her face, her voice cracking as snot choked at her nose and throat.

"No...it didn't go to plan." Tess fingered the glass before her, but it still took a few minutes to get her tears under control.

"I... she was...my sister was injured. I made sure that it would look that way. Alex always had a sick pleasure in seeing someone hurt and he didn't kill those who were...I mean I didn't think...do I have to talk about this?"

"I'm afraid you do. You admitted that you had her shot on purpose? Why?"

Tess frowned woefully. "Tanya is one of-w-was a favorite among my kind of people, Simon. Many teams want her in their crews-w-wanted..." Tess took another minute as she tried to get over the change of present to past.

"They wanted her badly. She always refused on my behalf but kept them in the loop. She had great communication with them and helped when she could. She was well liked. I had planned on making Alex believe that I could say that he ordered her shot and then there'd be blood in the water for the rest of his life. He's not the best liked."

"There is blood in the water."

".... Yes...my plan didn't work out like I planned." Tess replied solemnly. "We...we were supposed to direct him towards me, and he was talking to me. I thought his sole focus was on me."

"But?"

"I was distracted…by the heist, by my boyfriend…by the fact that I had my sister shot. I got her shot, and it's my fault she's dead. I gambled too much. I had a chance to grab his gun earlier to prevent this and I didn't take it. He had that gun, and I couldn't guarantee her safety."

"We both knew the risks, but she was willing to take that step further, knowing that I couldn't do it. I had to rely on her. I just…. wish she was still here. I miss her so much." Tess dropped her head to her arms and sobbed into the stained steel table, as Simon wrote down his observations into his notes for the case and confession.

Simon looked up and clearly watched her body sag at the end of her tale, now three hours later. It was a lot of information that would prove critical in understanding the criminal psyche. There was a level of respect for one's craft and deep bonds as different crews supported others. He'd have his work cut out for him over the following months. This was only the subject's first debriefing and multiple more would follow, but he could give her a few minutes to grieve.

To think that just months ago, she had lost her adoptive mother beyond her control, and delved into a deep rage and went to the edge to kill her mother's murderer. Then for that same murderer to have also killed her adopted sister because her plan was just a tad too risky…he knew how she must be feeling on the inside.

He supposed that she would be broken if not for the boyfriend in the room behind him, one who she wouldn't be able to hold onto for much longer.

"…I see; I'm sorry for your loss." Simon bowed his head as Tess peeked her eyes up and sniffled as she straightened herself back up. "So, the whole chase to the warehouse then... Was it all so that your sister could escape with less guards? Why couldn't you have staged it in his home?"

Tess smiled sadly in response. "I may be a criminal and you could have entered on that basis, but you couldn't have swarmed him at home with his guards present. They would have stopped you, even if for a few minutes, and by then, he would have escaped. I... I couldn't give up control like that."

"Interesting. We already know about the vest with the blood. So, I believe that ends your testimony." Simon summed up as he reached forward and grabbed his phone. The room's recording would stay on, as per regulations; the recording of her confession, however, was direct evidence.

"That was quite the story, Tess. With the evidence we've gathered and with your testimony, I am certain that Alex will go away forever. This is Detective Beckett. Interview and confession ended at 7:16pm." Simon finished and stopped the recording, saving it to his files.

"Why don't we get your boyfriend in here, hmm?" Simon asked as Tess's spine straightened up in hope. Her eyes shined as she smiled, nodding her head. Simon smiled as well and moved away, pulling the door open to see Daniel standing there impatiently.

"Five minutes."

Whether or not he heard him, Daniel rushed for his girlfriend, who giggled and tried to hug him back. His arms encircled her slim waist as his lips delved as deep as they could into her own as the rattle of chains flooded the room.

Tess's knees jumped off the ground, trying to ensnare her lover's waist as her arms tried to do the same with his neck, but both sets of limbs fell short and kept snapping her body back. Tess groaned ruefully as she kissed Daniel with all her heart and as he dipped down to suck lightly on her chin and neck, she wanted to scream at the shackles chaining her to the chair and desk respectively. She wanted to be more than intimate after today's events even if it was in a police interrogation room.

"Danny~," Tess cooed, as his hands settled on her sides, playing with her bare skin there. "I'm going to miss you so much."

"I'll visit every week until you're out." Daniel insisted, seeing the immaculate gleam in the back of his girlfriend's eyes light up at that.

Meanwhile, Tess blushed at the thought that had emerged from his promise. Maybe she could work in conjugal visits into her deal? She knew that Daniel wanted a family, but she was going away for at least ten years. If she got pregnant, then he could raise their children while she was away. She still had some accounts hidden that he could access.

A deep blush filled her cheeks though as Daniel caught the way her eyes glowed at his offer. If she was inside, she wouldn't be a part of their lives. She'd never get to hold them in her arms until it was too late. She didn't want her children to grow up seeing her behind bars, and certainly not born inside a prison.

Fresh tears erupted down her cheeks as she finally managed to grasp the collar of his shirt and pulled him in. Surely the five minutes were up, because if she didn't let him go, then this moment would never end. She wasn't ready to give it up.

"Ms. Miles-Walter." Tess's eyes twitched at that last name; her mother had hyphenated their names to ease their transition into her children, but she'd never truly gotten used to it. "…Tess." Her eyes opened as she and Daniel parted an inch of their lips and turned towards Simon who stayed on the doorway.

"Yes?" Tess breathed out, her hand not letting go of her boyfriend's collar as he bent down to her level of the chair, hugging her closer as she fell back into his embrace.

"…I have a proposal for you." Simon mentioned but said nothing else.

"…And that is?"

"Do you know what the white-collar program is?"

"Traitors. Thieves that work with the government to catch their fellow thieves."

"That's right. After you plead guilty, I'd like to see if you'd want to work for the government."

"…I don't know, Simon. I'm pretty irritable if the person doesn't get me."

"…well, then what if I wanted to hire you?"

"You?"

"You know a lot of Tess, and with today's growing technology and large complex heists, I feel like I'm a step behind nowadays. I could use your expertise."

"So, what, then? I plead guilty and you come to the prison, and I help you out."

"Well," Simon smiled. "I was thinking more of a work release."

Tess's eyes widened in hopeful glee. "You mean...outside?"

"I mean instead of prison, in the direct sense. There are some caveats mind you. You'd have to always wear a tracker. You can't contact known criminals unless I approve the visits or for the work involved. And of course, a rule that you must stay and live in the same residence as a trusted citizen to oversee you."

"And…" Tess breathed out shakily. "That could be someone close to me?"

"Not normally, but if I trust them, then I'm sure we could work something out."

Tess took one look back at Daniel and smiled brightly. "Where do I sign?"

Simon smiled contently. "I'll go get the papers. In the meantime, why don't I get you out of those cuffs?" At Tess's eyes gleaming, he smiled. "Just so you know, there are twenty state troopers outside this door, and they all know your face."

"I won't leave, Simon." Tess affirmed as her wrist came free, "I have everything I need right here."

As Simon stepped back, Daniel enveloped a jubilant girlfriend who hugged him back with full range of motion, contently sighing into his chest as he hugged her deep.

"I can't believe I don't have to go to prison." Tess shivered with relief.

"It's better than that." Daniel gripped tighter as Tess looked up and smiled. It was. She had her man, and those thoughts in her head… they could be a reality.

"Daniel…I want to marry you someday." Tess uttered.

"Next week sound good?" Daniel cheekily offered, but Tess just shook her head and kissed his cheek.

"That was a proposal, right?"

"Of course." Daniel affirmed.

"And Daniel...I want a family too. I've never really said it but-"

"Don't worry, Tess." Daniel grinned widely as his hands dropped to rest on the small of her back, just above her ass. Tess let an aroused whimper sound out. "As soon as we get home, we'll have plenty of time to try for a family." The amazed grin on Tess's face was all the answer he needed.

Meanwhile, Simon smiled at the lovey dovey couple from the doorway. She truly had evolved from a calculated mystery into an innocent romantic who would do anything for those she loved. And if she was as good as he thought she was, then that caseload on his desk was going to drop considerably. Simon turned to walk out the door when his phone buzzed. He looked down and hummed to himself before he looked back at the snogging couple, who were lost to anything else but the other's loving embrace.

"Oh Tess; one more question."

Tess continued to suck on the lips of her soon to be husband, pulling back only to playfully bite at his thumb as he ghosted over her lips and cheek. "Go ahead, Simon." She whispered, not even glancing in his direction.

'Best to ask now while she's distracted.' Simon thought to himself. "My team made it to the mansion and just now opened the safe, but there was nothing inside. Do you know if Alex saw you coming? Any idea where he hid it?"

Tess leaned in again to kiss Daniel's lips, her eyes positivity aglow with a rush of adrenaline for a job well done and her future life with the man she would spend it with before her. She shuddered as she pulled back to groan softly at the briefest gap in their lip lock, her eyes not leaving Daniel's gaze as she answered.

"I don't know, Simon. I never managed to open the safe."

With shattered glass upon the floor, a rogue wind lightly blew into the study of Alex's mansion and the curtains billowed further into the room. Bookshelves full of rare stories in hardcover bindings lay hidden behind both red sofas and a plethora of bags and equipment next to a steel safe that lay unopened.

The setting sun arched what little rays it had across the piano with a shined polish and upon the body on the floor. Blood still pulsed out of the wound and pooled out around the thief, ruining the carpet beneath them; their body as pale as a ghost and hair flowing in strands across their unmoving face. The blood seeped through the carpet, and finally slid underneath the clenched hands that had laid prone there since the body had fallen and the window had shattered.

"Police! We have a warrant!" came the muffled cry from the front door of the mansion as it was bashed in, the sound barely reaching the room, the mansion being too big for anyone to yell to reach everywhere.

The hand unclenched and flattened against the carpet.

"Oh god." Tanya groaned as she flexed her fingers out and stretched upon the carpet, her legs and arms splayed out to the furthest they could go before she pushed herself to her knees and stared around the room in a foggy haze.

The room was still blurry, and her eyes begged to shut again, but Tanya rubbed at her eyes before wincing at the jabbing sensation at her neck. With wobbly legs, she stood up to a shivering throat as she held in a scream. Her stomach wound began to drip with blood again as the bandage had moved when she had fallen.

Tanya's eyes teamed with tears as she gingerly prodded at the wound before reaching behind the wound to the needle mark that was just at her hip where Daniel had stabbed her before they had entered the room, the action quick and with precision. The effects had been swift and timed perfectly with Alex's rant before he had shot her in the head and she went down, the venom in the syringe lowering her vitals and breathing to barely keep her alive.

She staggered a few steps, the venom still clearly affecting her paralyzed limbs as she steadied herself against the piano. With a sudden bout of nausea, Tanya pressed her hand to her neck and felt the blackening bruise that was now forming along it. It would be on her for weeks after this, but Tanya smiled as a bubbling fit of giggles escaped her lips. It had worked...the whole plan had worked!

Inside Alex's room, Tess stared at the gap between Alex and the dresser. Could she grab it in time? She had to try. So, with a snake's speed, Tess reached forward and snatched the gun on the dresser and brought it behind the door where she lay hidden.

As Alex talked on the phone with his upcoming departure, Tess slipped the magazine of the gun out of the handle and reached towards her jacket pocket. Her gloved hand slipped inside with the magazine and pulled out another one, identical to the first. With eyes trained on Alex's back, she clicked it into the gun and carefully placed it back on the dresser.

Alex's head suddenly turned her way, but she kept herself hidden, frozen in place as Alex grabbed his gun again and slid it into the holster at his side. And with a wide smile on her face, Tess clicked her radio once, the short tap on the airwaves telling Tanya that all the preparations were now complete.

Tanya's fit of giggles ended as she straightened herself and glanced at the shattered glass. Tess had escaped out the one area of weakness in the guards' routes; Daniel's route to be precise, and with gloved hands on the magazine, only Alex's prints lay on the gun that had killed her. Or at least would have, had they not switched the clip to hold rubber bullets. It had hurt, and would hurt for quite a while, but it was a willing sacrifice on her part.

As her legs became more stable, she walked forward towards the safe surrounded by the equipment Tess had tried to use before she had to flee. She reached out and traced over the steel cover and hummed as her fingers ran over the numbers that lay written on it. Two numbers remained to be written on the safe to tell everyone the combination and Tanya was out of time.

Keys and heavy boots clomped in the hallway and surged into the room. "Hands up!" Came a command and Tanya did so. She turned around slowly, as a Cheshire grin encompassed her lips.

Before her were three policewomen, decked out in midnight black uniforms and touting guns pointed directly at her…. but she wasn't afraid. The uniform's top buttons were undone for breathability, showing the cleavage of the women in uniform before her, and the fact that before her was a brunette in a bun, a blonde with a mocking glare, and a ebony haired girl with a soft smile made her feel right at home.

"Glad you could make it, officers." Tanya nodded curtly as she backed up to the safe. Before her, the policewomen took off their caps and became what they truly were; conwomen ready to finish the score of their lives.

Tanya chuckled at the girls before her as she bent down to spin the tumbler around. Tess and her plans never led them astray before and never would again lead them. What was she, the older sister, to do being the one in charge now?

'Maybe just retire.' Tanya smiled at her little joke as she pulled on the handle of the safe and the door swung open, already unlocked by their former teammate before Alex had even entered the room.

Inside were a few bars worth of gold, a number of bonds and some stacks of money, but in the center was a simple usb port and as Tanya slid her connector inside it, numbers began to whir in front of her tablet as the electronic currency added to her account.

As the machine continued to add to their score, Tanya turned to the girls, to her team, with blood dripping down her skin out of a still deadly wound that would kill her within a day if left untreated. The score of their lifetime was now theirs for the taking, and even with her hair matted with stolen donor's blood, Tanya smiled unapologetically with her co-conspirators, with their eyes full of the euphoria of a job well done and giggled darkly.

"The classics are the worst, aren't they?"